Kaelen

A MAFIA OMEGAVERSE

BOSTON SINNERS: BOOK 1

MICHELLE LOVE

Dedication

For all you deviant little gremlins out there who want your men to knot
you in a nest of plush blankets while covered in blood.
This one's for you.

Content Notes

POTENTIAL SPOILERS

Kaelen is a dark romance story with themes that may be triggering to some readers. Below may include potential spoilers.

Included in this story:
- Graphic violence
- Torture
- Verbal & physical abuse (not between MMCs)
- Abusive parent
- Sick parent
- Animal abuse (implied/ off screen. Not by MMCs)
- Kidnapping
- Attempted assault/forced mate bond
- Dubious consent (in the context of an omega's heat)

Omegaverse

WHAT IS IT

This book is an MF omegaverse.

It can be read as a complete standalone story with a HEA (happily ever after).

Omegaverse is a subgenre of romance where characters possess a secondary biological designation that appears once they enter adulthood.

The population is categorized into three main roles:

Alphas (dominant), Betas (neutral), and Omegas (submissive).

These are not shifters, but they possess some of the same animal-like tendencies.

Alphas are larger and stronger than the other designations and inherently dominant and more aggressive. They have a knot at the base of their penis that swells and locks them together with an omega for thirty minutes to an hour after orgasming. They also can bark, which is a dominate tone omegas are susceptible to. Honorable alphas only use their bark to protect an omega during their heat to ensure they eat, bathe, and drink water. Or they may use it in other life-threatening scenarios. During intense moments of desire, alphas can go into a rut. During a rut, alphas lose sense of self and can only be calmed by knotting an omega.

Betas are normal humans. They cannot bond, but they are key in pack life. Both alphas and omegas can bite and bond betas to them and the pack.

Omegas are the smallest of the designations. Their scent is strongest to alphas and when pleased, they perfume, making their scent stronger and letting alphas know they are attracted to them. Omegas go into heat three or four times a year once they have their first one. Heats last anywhere from three to seven days. During that time, they need an alpha to knot them multiple times to satiate the pain that comes with heats.

Prologue

WILLOW

My mom was a shell of the beautiful omega I had grown up with. Hollow, tired eyes stared at me. I kneeled on the bench beside her bed, dabbing a cool cloth along her forehead. Her chest rose with shallow, uneven breaths, the faint, reedy sound making my face fall.

I forced the same tight expression I always wore around her. My omega fussed, my instincts pushing me to nurture and heal. But nothing worked. After seeing doctor after doctor, none of them knew what was causing my mom's health issues. The sickness was a slow, relentless tide, pulling her further and further away from me.

"Willow," she rasped, her nails weakly scraping over my forearm. "Go. Your father is waiting."

A breath whistled through my nostrils as I stifled my groan. The last thing I wanted was to find Dad. Sadness crept into my mom's features, forcing me to plaster on another fake smile. I didn't want to upset her. She needed to rest.

And not to worry about me.

If I didn't find him soon, she would spend the entire evening upset. Worried that Dad would lose his temper with me... again. It didn't matter. I'd rather he took it out on me than her. Subconsciously, my fingers grazed over the spot below my collarbone. The place where my skin puckered and the raised burns marred me.

That had been the night I realized the man I once loved was gone. The night I knew my dad no longer cared for me. When a potential donor grabbed my ass, I shoved him, telling him to fuck off. After the event, I assumed he was going to check on me, but no.

Instead, he punished me.

Greed, corruption, and fear twisted the alpha in our home, making him unrecognizable. Despite knowing what he was capable of, I still pushed him, unwilling to always cower in his presence.

Now was not one of those times. I needed to keep my mom relaxed.

"You're right." I sat up, pressing a kiss to her temple. "If you're up when we get home, we can play Scrabble and watch a movie."

"I'd like that, my sunflower," she said, patting my hand. "Love you."

"Love you too, Momma. Get some rest."

With a heavy heart, I left her, holding up the hem of my silk gown as I padded out into the hall. My hand slid along the wooden banister. I floated along the stairs like the perfect porcelain doll he expected on a night like tonight.

All eyes would be on him, meaning his omega daughter must be flawless at all times.

I carefully moved down the stairs, unsteady in my heels. By the front door, my father paced, staring at his watch and grumbling.

When he looked at me, I stuttered, taken aback by the fury swirling in his storm-ridden gray eyes.

"Willow," he hissed, closing his fingers around my upper arm and squeezing. I winced, already feeling the bruises form beneath the crescent marks from his nails. "We're going to be late. You will be exquisite tonight. Do you understand?"

"Of course," I said, the sweet words laced with defiance.

I knew better than to antagonize him. My mom regularly begged me not to, her colorless eyes glistening anytime she saw a new bruise on my tanned skin. Sometimes, for her, I nodded politely and submitted to my dad's whims, but other times, I needed to fight back.

If only to remind myself that I wasn't completely powerless.

Even if I was.

I was no better than a trapped bird in a gilded cage. My pretty feathers sparkled in the light, but every night, I returned to the home that felt more and more like a prison.

He released me with a shove, and I stumbled back a step.

Glaring, he straightened his tuxedo jacket, an icy indifference masking his features. I rubbed the sore spot on my arm, sliding into the back of the limo with him. My arm throbbed, but I did my best to ignore it, not wanting to give him the satisfaction.

Downtown Boston glittered with bright lights as we drove through the city.

My father hadn't always been like this. He had been kind once.

A good alpha to my mom and a wonderful dad.

He became a senator to be the change he wanted to see in the world. To make things better for everyone. Except power and greed corroded all the good things about him. That, combined with the threats against me and Mom after he sponsored an omega wellness bill. He changed. His need for possession was no longer about safety, but control.

The door to the limo opened, and I gracefully took his offered arm. Cameras flashed, all trying to get a photo of Senator William Sterling and his daughter attending the charity event for Boston Children's Hospital. Now that he was running for governor, the spotlight had never been brighter.

Inside, chandeliers dripped with crystals, twinkling with golden light. Women in designer gowns and men in crisp tuxedos milled about, their laughter a brittle, unnerving sound. Dad guided us through the room with practiced ease, introducing me to alphas with more money than sense.

They leered at me, making inappropriate comments that I shrugged off.

Suddenly, the air was too thick and the walls were too close. I needed a minute. Short, hurried breaths stung behind my sternum, panic building in my belly. I excused myself, promising to be back in a moment as I wound through the crowds, making my way to a balcony. The light breeze hit my face, uncoiling the tension in my body.

A waiter appeared, and I took the offered flute of champagne even though I didn't drink. My nails clinked along the glass stem. The din of voices quieted as I stilled, frozen in place by a piercing stare from across the room.

Bright green eyes—the color of a summer forest—held my stare. My heart thudded, hammering against my ribs in an untamed staccato. A mountain of an alpha stood behind those captivating eyes, dark ink peeking out from the collar of his shirt.

A well-manicured, rust-colored beard framed his sharp features, his matching locks tied in a bun at the back of his head. I licked my lips, my feet moving of their own accord as I made to move closer to the mysterious alpha.

I tended to keep away from alphas. But my chest ached, a warmth blooming in my stomach when his eyes met mine. I couldn't deny the pull dragging me in. Perhaps I would meet a fate like Odysseus when he heard the sirens' call.

Unlucky for me, I didn't have a group of men at my call to restrain me to a ship post.

I made it halfway across the room. He followed my movements, unblinking. His brow rose in a challenging way that made my thighs press together. Fingers snared my wrist, yanking me back.

An omega whine caught in my throat, the alpha's nostrils flaring when the sound reached him.

"Come, Willow," my dad hissed, summoning me like a dog, snapping me out of my trance.

For a long time, I had hated my father, but at that moment I wanted to slap him, consequences be damned.

I didn't see the green-eyed alpha the rest of the night. I was disappointed, my omega whimpering at the loss. Part of me thought he had been a figment of my imagination.

Chapter 1

WILLOW

After a night of exaggeratingly fluttering my lashes, I spent the next day disappearing to one of the few places I felt at peace. Snowfield. The horse rescue I volunteered at. If I wasn't there, then I went to one of the local shelters, enjoying cuddling up with the dogs.

And right now, all I wanted was to forget the previous night and focus on the skittish stallion.

I always had a talent for dealing with broken things, having an intense understanding and bond with them. When April first brought him to the stables, he kicked and bit at the handlers. I almost preferred that to how withdrawn he had become. The gorgeous black stallion curled up in his stall, his back to everyone.

Most days, I sat with him while he ate, getting him comfortable with my scent. He had been hostile toward the alphas on the farm, indifferent to the betas, but with me, I was the only omega, and he tolerated me.

Barely.

Today, he grazed in the back pasture for the first time, even letting me put a halter on him. I smiled when he didn't retreat from my touch. It was progress. Slow but steady. Someday, maybe, he would let me ride him. A lustrous shine glimmered on his coat, twinkling in the sunlight now that he was eating more.

He remained nameless.

Like most of the horses the owner rescued, the slaughterhouse didn't have a name for him. April left that to me. Sometimes I knew right away, but with him, nothing felt right. So instead, I called him my lost boy.

He would tell me his name when he was ready.

Once I arrived home, I instantly missed the fresh air. If I could, I would move outside the city and live near Snowfield.

My father refused to allow it, always keeping his precious omega daughter under his boot. The only reason he continued to let me work at Snowfield, rehabilitating horses, was that it looked good in the press.

Anything to secure a vote. And now that he was leaving the Senate to run for governor, optics were everything.

During his last senatorial re-election campaign, I was in my first year of college and freshly presented as an omega. I hadn't been completely surprised, considering my mother was one, but I didn't enjoy how he paraded me around like some prized pony to win votes.

I was a grown woman, but he knew my weakness. Anytime I talked about moving out, he threatened my mother. I couldn't leave her alone with him. On paper, he plastered on that stupid fake smile, sweetly kissing his precious wife and omega, puffing with pride like the arrogant alpha he was.

Nobody knew the real Senator Sterling, the man who dealt in backdoor bribes and left bruises on his daughter.

I took care of myself, but my mom had faded in the last few years, her light dimming more every day. Without me around, I was afraid of what my father would do to her. And he knew that, twisted that, and manipulated me into doing whatever he wanted.

With less than eight months until election day, he was insufferable, dragging me from event to event. Protesting proved pointless. The only times I was free were at the farm with my horses or snuggling forgotten puppies at the pound.

Not mine, really. The horses were April's. She owned them, but she gave me free rein to care for them. Maybe someday I will have one of my own. They were expensive, and my dad refused to waste money on something so frivolous.

Apparently, the Rolex on his wrist didn't count as wasteful.

Feet pounded on the stairs leading to the kitchen, and I grimaced. I stared at my half-eaten leftovers, debating whether I could slip out the back door without him realizing I had been here, but it was too late.

The pungent scent of his cologne preceded him, stinging my nose. I don't know why he wore that. His alpha scent was a light citrus and cedar, pleasant enough. Yet, he insisted on hiding it beneath a cloying Dolce fragrance, because it was the best.

Even though it made me and Mom gag.

"Good evening, Willow," he said, with that saccharine tone that was sickeningly disingenuous. "I'm glad you are home."

I didn't respond. He only ever acted like that when he wanted something.

"I was worried you were still at that manure field."

"It's a farm, Dad. I have volunteered there for years. It's not flattering and won't win you the rural vote to pretend you don't understand how farms work outside Boston."

Dad had lived his entire life in and around Boston, and more than one article expressed concerns he wasn't a viable candidate for governor because he didn't understand the needs of all of Massachusetts.

A vein in his temple throbbed as he sucked a sound through

his teeth. I hid my smirk, enjoying the sore spot I had successfully prodded. Fingers flexed and knuckles turned white as he straightened his tie.

"I have a private meeting I would like you to attend with me."

A snort puffed past my lips as I rolled my eyes. The whole ruse of him framing his commands like questions got old years ago.

"When?"

"We need to leave now. Hurry and put something appropriate on," he sneered, raising a brow at my muddy jeans and torn t-shirt. "Meet me outside in twenty minutes."

They were my farm clothes. I didn't bother to change when I got home, heading straight for the kitchen for some leftovers.

And of course, everyone ran on his schedule. Not like I was exhausted and wanted to crawl into bed with a book. Instead, I had to spend my night making doe-eyes at some rich prick while Dad tried to woo a big donation out of him.

Ignoring him, I pushed away my picked-over dinner and went upstairs. I closed the door behind me, doing my best not to slam it. Once I entered my nest, my body slumped as the subtle scent of honey hit my nose.

It wasn't anything fancy. Nothing like the lavish nests I saw in magazines, but it was mine, and no one was allowed in it without my permission.

Despite how much of a jerk my father was, his alpha restrained him enough to respect an omega's nest. Sheer silks hung over the posts of my bed, overflowing with fluffy blankets and plush pillows.

My omega longed to burrow into fluffy blankets. It had been a long day at Snowfield, and while I loved every minute, I was tired. Who knew how long this meeting was going to last?

Hopefully, it wasn't some old, handsy alpha that I had to pretend I enjoyed having paw at me.

I wondered what would piss off Dad more—going downstairs in my muddy clothes or taking longer than twenty minutes to get ready?

At least when he was preoccupied with me, it meant he left Mom alone. All the stress of politics wore her down. Over the years, her omega retreated so far inward that her scent was almost nonexistent anymore.

Someday, she wouldn't have to deal with this anymore.

I'd get us out.

How?

No idea.

But anything was possible.

I slipped into a flattering sundress, the cotton smooth against my skin as it hit my knees. The lilac color highlighted my tanned skin. It skimmed the line between conservative and flirty. Hopping out the door, I tugged on my flats, nearly tumbling down the stairs.

The sooner we left, the sooner this would be over with.

Outside, Dad leaned against his sleek BMW. His eyes flicked over me before jerking his chin toward the car. A seal of approval from Senator Sterling, lucky me. Cool leather brushed against my bare legs as I slid into the passenger seat.

I leaned against the window, watching as we maneuvered through the one-way streets toward the south side of town. The tightly packed row houses gave way to an expanse of greenery, a sprawling lawn with lush gardens flanking a massive estate peeking out from behind a wrought iron gate.

Holy shit.

Who the fuck were we meeting? Tom Brady?

The car slid to a stop, and my dad rolled down the window, pushing a call button. Two men strolled over the manicured lawn, pistols tucked into the waistband of their trousers. I was only slightly freaking out. It was fine.

I stared, wordlessly, praying that they were well-armed security for some rich family, but they looked rough.

Tattoos covered their hands, their square faces framed by thick auburn beards. The gate groaned as it creaked open, rocks rumbling under the tires as Dad tapped the car forward a few feet.

Blood coated my tongue after chewing my lips raw. While I didn't mind the repercussions from pushing Dad, these men were different.

If I stepped out of place, I might end up with something far worse than a few bruises. My heart raced as I eyed their weapons. I clasped my hands in my lap, catching the alphas' scents wafting into

Kaelen

the car on the breeze.

My nostrils twitched. Smoke and bergamot. Not for me, but not rancid.

"Senator Sterling." The taller of the two alphas spoke, his silky timbre roughened by a prominent Irish lilt. "To what do we owe the pleasure?"

"I need to speak to Kaelen Finnegan. I have an offer for him. One I think he will be very interested in."

Chapter 2

KAELEN

Sweat slicked off my brow, clinging to my bare chest as I tossed the barbells onto the mat with a dull thud. Bass thumped from the speakers, shaking the mirrored walls in my private gym. It'd been two hours, and I still wasn't finished. I wouldn't stop until the lingering rage faded, refusing to give in to the caged animal trapped inside me.

If I hadn't worked out the last of my aggression, I would have done something rash. And acting on instinct wasn't a luxury I was afforded. As the head of my family, I couldn't lash out. Every action needed to be meticulously crafted with the ramifications accounted for.

Fuck.

The last thing I wanted right now was to be logical. I wanted to paint the pavement outside the Rossi mansion with blood.

Outside my brothers, Torin was my most loyal man.

Family was everything. And Torin was family in everything but blood.

I never doubted that he would take a bullet for me, and now that he proved that. I wanted to throttle the bastard. Fucking idiot, jumping in front of me like that. The kid who shot at me had poor aim; it would have grazed my arm at best.

Torin was still alive, but in critical condition in the ICU. I needed to blow off some steam before I did something stupid. The Italians were really pushing my buttons. If Vittorio Rossi didn't get a handle on his trigger-happy younglings, I was going to do something far more dangerous than sending the head of the guy who shot Torin to his front step in a box.

I grabbed a towel, wiping sweat from my face as I walked toward my bedroom in the opposite wing. After one more set, I accepted that retribution was enough for now. We were on the brink of war with the Italians, and I didn't want to push us over the edge.

Not yet anyway.

The house was quiet. Most of my men were at our pubs or casinos for the night. Aileen puttered away in the kitchen, cooking a meal that almost made me forgo a shower if I thought she wouldn't scold my arse. My housekeeper was sterner than my Ma had been, and that woman could make a grown man cry.

I paused, leaning into the cool granite on the island, trying to peek at what she was cooking. The tiny woman spun, her gray-streaked, braided hair falling over her slender frame. Flames from the stove reflected in her hazel eyes as she narrowed them at me, her lips pursed.

"Kaelen, take a shower. You smell like the pigs after a rain." She scowled, shaking a wooden spoon at me.

Aileen didn't put up with my bullshite. She was the only one who could talk to me like that, and she knew it. Give her a gun, and I'd take her at my side over most of my men.

"Yes, ma'am," I relented, running a hand over my beard.

"Once you wash up, I'll bring supper up to your office. You want something sweet?" she asked, her voice warmer and more matronly.

Even as a kid, I always had a sweet tooth, and I was weak for Aileen's apple cake. At least a few nights a week, I took a slice with my whisky. Before I could respond, she waved me away, returning her attention to the pot on the stove.

"I'll bring the cake," she said, and I relaxed for the first time in days.

After my shower, I slipped into a white button-down, rolling the cuffs. I checked my cell as I sat in the leather chair behind my desk, looking for an update on Torin. My brother Liam was at the hospital with him, protecting his room in case the Italians acted out after they received the head of their man.

What I did was just in our world, and if Vittorio Rossi were smart, he would leave it alone. Based on Liam's latest message, Torin was stable and expected to make a full recovery. I sent off a quick email to the CEO at Boston General, ensuring that all of Torin's expenses would be covered by me.

I poured myself an overfull glass of whisky.

A knock echoed across the room, and I grumbled, surprised to see my other brother, Aidan, standing there instead of Aileen with my supper. His hazel eyes looked like Mum's.

Sometimes, I swore her ghost visited us whenever I looked at him.

My brothers were both younger than me, Aidan sandwiched between me and Liam. Aidan was the steady one who always thought through every scenario. The calm to Liam's storm.

Regardless, they were loyal and put family first, determined to solidify the Finnegan name in Boston. I trusted them with my life.

Aidan and Liam lived with me, staying in the other wing of our family estate. A few of my men also had residences on the premises—some of the single, most trustworthy ones, who handled protection details on the grounds if they wanted them.

When our Da passed away three years ago, I took over all operations for the Finnegan name at only thirty. We owned a string of legitimate pubs throughout Boston. They bolstered our more questionable line of underground casinos. After Ma passed, his alpha didn't want to be without his mate.

He wanted to make something for our family here in Boston. But without his omega, he faded away, leaving me as the head of our family.

Aidan lowered himself into the chair on the other side of my desk, the gun in his jacket flashing under the sunlight streaming in through the window behind me. His expression was unreadable as he tried to decipher mine.

"What?" I snapped.

"How is Torin?" he asked, unaffected by my tone.

I schooled my features. It was interesting that he still liked to pretend Torin meant so little to him. Liam told me that Aidan hadn't left his side, until today when the nurse kicked him out.

So be it. I'd play along until they were ready to open up about their relationship.

"Recovering. Expected to pull through," I said. I swore I aged ten years in one day. "Has our gift been delivered to the Rossi residence?"

A half-smirk pushed against his cheeks as he leaned forward, his elbows resting on his spread thighs.

"One decapitated head and a love note delivered."

I nodded, swirling the amber liquid in my glass.

Initially, I assumed the reason for Aidan's visit was that he wanted an update on Torin. Given that his arse was still planted in my chair, I suspected there was more to it. He usually spent his nights at our most popular casino, hidden in the secret tunnels under Fenway.

"What else?" I prodded, narrowing my eyes.

"Senator Sterling is outside, saying he wants to speak with you. Has an offer for you."

I grumbled, and my lip twitched. Politicians. Slimy and backstabbing, the whole lot of them. At least with someone like Rossi, I knew what to expect. He would attack me from the front. Someone like Senator Sterling made my skin itch. They were brash enough to try something stupid.

Even if I was intrigued about what he wanted, he had some nerve to show up unannounced and expect to speak with me.

"Get rid of him, Aidan. I don't work on the senator's time."

"He's insistent. Has a pretty, young omega with him."

That piqued my curiosity. Did he think that by bringing a girl with him, I wouldn't put a bullet in his head? Messy. All of it. I wasn't wasteful and wouldn't take a life unless there was a reason for it. But I was pissed enough after today to do it.

Presumptuous bastard, showing up here. My thumb flicked the condensation from my glass, wondering how I would deal with the aftermath of killing a gubernatorial candidate.

"I can see your mind working," Aidan said, raising a brow. "You can't kill him."

"Piss off. Any inkling of what he wants?"

"Nope. I have some guesses."

So did I. A career politician like William Sterling didn't get where he was by playing fair. He was polishing his resume, looking to add governor for a potential presidential run in the next decade.

"Bring them up to my office in thirty minutes."

An amused look flicked across Aidan's face as he nodded, leaving the room. I stood, sipping my whisky and looking out the window. My hand drifted to the gun in my desk, tucking it into the waistband of my trousers.

I didn't trust the fucker.

After exactly thirty minutes had passed, there was a knock.

As the door to my office groaned open, the sweetest, most fragrant scent greeted me. It smelled like wildflowers, honey, and summer rain, reminding me of the rolling hills in Ireland where I grew up. My dick twitched, a possessiveness stirring within me.

My alpha begged to be let loose.

Aidan showed the senator and the girl into my office as he stood out of the way, leaning against a far wall.

I squinted, recognizing the young omega from the charity event last week. My hand clasped the tumbler in my grip, almost shattering it before I lowered it onto my desk.

Those pretty blue eyes had haunted my dreams since Saturday. The cute omega disappeared before I could introduce myself.

The Fates must have been pleased to deliver her to me.

Enclosed in my office, all I smelled was her, and I was close to losing it. Aidan had the audacity to smirk at me, his alpha apparently not as affected as mine was.

I prided myself on my control. Omegas didn't affect me, not like other alphas. I didn't lose my mind when they entered the room.

When I presented, my father taught me to control my instincts.

An omega-drunk alpha couldn't be the head of the most prominent Irish family in the country.

For the first time since I turned eighteen, I was close to succumbing to the sweetest-smelling omega I had ever met, giving in to a primal desire to woo her, to get on my knees and worship her.

I've fucked plenty of omegas and betas. There had even been one female alpha who had been as tough as my men. Despite that, I never once lost my composure.

But now, there was this captivating omega, smelling like sin with sapphire eyes that twinkled like crystals, making my dick harder than stone. One look at her, and my alpha roared, ready to throw everything I had worked for my entire life away.

Her eyes widened, casting a silent glare at the senator that had me suppressing a snort. Whoever she was, she was pissed at him. Blue highlights shone on the underside of her glossy black hair when her head snapped to the side. A line of freckles spread over her sun-kissed cheeks, and I wondered if there were more of them under the sexy as hell sundress she was wearing.

I moved to the front of my desk, pressing my hips into the custom oak and gripping the edge behind me. The girl was unreadable, keeping her pretty eyes glued to me, assessing me. Her expression fell when it landed on my gun, some of the color draining from her face.

Instinct told me to comfort her, to hide my gun so she wouldn't be nervous, but I assumed if I made any movement for it, it would only make her more nervous.

Instead, I forced my attention back to the man beside her.

Silence stretched on between us as I tracked my eyes over him, wondering how long he would stand there before squirming. It wasn't long. A minute later, he shifted, eyes darting from me to Aidan.

"Senator Sterling," I said, flicking a bead of condensation off my glass. "I don't usually take unannounced private meetings." A smarmy smile slid across his face, and I debated shooting him in the shin. "Why are you here, and what is this offer that couldn't wait?"

Whisky stung my throat as I took a slow drag of the fifteen-year Midleton. Sterling straightened, trying to look taller. His suit may have been crisp and tailored, but he looked greasy and unkempt.

"I would like to introduce my daughter, Willow Sterling."

A disgusted grimace tugged at her lips as he wrapped an arm around her waist. The gesture looked anything but affectionate, and I had the urge to break his fingers for touching her.

Some primal desire pulsed beneath the surface, my alpha already protective of the omega.

Now I recognized her. I remembered seeing her forced grins in a couple of newspaper articles next to her father.

As she turned away from him, the overhead light caught a glimpse of a crescent scar beneath her eye, along with a slight discoloration of her tanned skin.

Anger surged from some ancient place within me, my alpha commanding me to seek retribution for *my* omega. Blood rushed south, my trousers uncomfortably taut.

No.

Not mine.

Just an omega.

Aidan narrowed his eyes, rocking off the wall, sensing the shift in my patience.

I relaxed my frame, trying to make my features less intimidating as I faced his daughter, Willow.

"Pleasure to meet you, Miss Sterling," I said, dipping my chin. My Ma would come back from the grave and haunt me if I ever disrespected a woman. "I am Kaelen Finnegan."

She flashed a tight grin that was more a grimace as she glared at her father. While she may have agreed to accompany him, whatever he was planning, she wasn't privy to.

"Mr. Finnegan," she said, stiff and uneasy.

"Wonderful." Senator Sterling beamed, clapping his hands together. The motion set me on edge, making my teeth grind. "As you know, Mr. Finnegan, I am running for governor and I am finding myself in need of some assistance from your organization."

Aidan didn't bother to hide his snort, paling slightly when I glared at him. If the senator were coming to me, he wanted more than a simple donation. My fingers brushed over the rough grip of my gun, and I enjoyed watching sweat bead off his brow.

"What *assistance* are you looking for?" I asked.

"Your influence. Your connections. Maybe my opponent has a secret mistress. I'm sure you understand."

"Dad," Willow hissed, scowling at him. "Are you mad?"

"Quiet," he spat at her.

No one should talk to her like that. If she were mine, I'd rip him apart. *Shite.* I was on the verge of doing something rash. My eyes snapped to Aidan's, his expression tight. Willow was undeterred by her father's admonishment, growling at him like a tiny lioness.

A rare glimmer of amusement twinkled in Aidan's eyes, but he stayed out of it.

"And why should my family do this for you?"

A smirk tugged at my lips. Willow's eyes widened, her scent perfuming in the room as she stared at the tattoos on my exposed forearms. That thick, beautiful scent almost sent me to my knees. My vision blurred as I struggled to remain upright.

"I propose an alliance," Sterling's grated voice cut in. "A marriage with my daughter, an omega, for you."

"What?" she shrieked, the pale pink in her cheeks turning a frosty white.

"I don't deal in people," I snapped, pushing off the desk and towering over the other alpha.

Omegas were a delicacy to savor. And of course, this fucking weasel had a daughter who wasn't only an omega, but smelled like mine, sweet and floral and summery. Everything that was far too good for a bastard like me.

Except maybe she wasn't so sweet. A scowl bloomed on her beautiful features, and her scent burned with indignation and fear. An unfamiliar emotion urged me to take her in my arms and purr for her.

She thrashed in his arms, clawing at his face and cursing him. *Good.*

He deserved it, and I wanted to see my little omega tear him apart. How dare he have something so precious and try to barter it away. I needed to protect her, claim her.

"I'm not a whore for you to give away," she hissed, spitting at him.

No, you aren't. Good girl.

Spit dribbled down the stunned senator's face. Pride swelled in my chest, my alpha beaming at our omega.

Fuck.

I ignored the inappropriate thoughts. Maybe it was her father who needed protection. She was a feral thing. My dick stirred in my trousers, and I adjusted myself.

"Behave," Senator Sterling said, curling his fingers around his daughter's slender throat and slapping her across the face.

I saw red. The girl crumbled to the ground, clutching the bruise already blooming on her cheek. Aidan crouched beside her, pulling her away from the impending scuffle. In two long strides, I was in the senator's face, gripping his shirt collar and slamming him into the wall.

Photos shuddered at the contact, one falling to the ground, the frame shattering. Glass crunched beneath my shoes. He glared at me, his alpha demanding him to fight back. But the man didn't. He knew better than to test me.

Especially if he wanted something from me.

"Don't fucking touch what belongs to me." Blood vessels bulged in his eyes, the color receding from his sallow, sunken cheeks as I slammed his head into the wall, accentuating my point. "Don't ever treat a woman like that in front of me." He tried and struggled to swallow past my grip. "Say yes, sir, and I'll let you leave with all your limbs intact."

"Yes, sir," he coughed.

I released him, smirking as he crumpled to the ground. He stroked his neck, sucking in gasping breaths.

"Good boy. Now get out. I never want to see you again."

Nodding, he stumbled to his feet, reaching out for Willow, who was still on the ground with Aidan. I stepped into his space, shoving him.

"She stays."

The words escaped before I could stop them.

"You're not going to kill her, are you?" he asked, and for one brief second, I believed it was out of concern for his daughter.

But no, the slimy bastard was worried about losing his leverage.

"Why should you care? You traded her away like a baseball card. Get. *Out*," I said, drawing my gun and pointing it between his eyes. "You have ten seconds or I will paint the walls with your blood. One."

He sprinted from the room before I could utter the number two. What had I gotten myself into? I needed to protect her from everyone, and that included her urchin of a father. I may be a monster, but I couldn't let her leave with him.

How many other people would he have tried to sell her to?

When I turned around to find Willow, I wasn't sure what I was expecting to find. Maybe tears would stain her swollen cheeks, or perhaps she would be withdrawn.

She was neither of those things; the spirited omega from earlier had returned.

"Let me go," she demanded, her gaze glacial and unrelenting.

"No," I said.

"Fuck off."

The flat of her palm connected with my cheek. A sting radiated across my face, making my eyes water.

Impressive.

I smirked, rolling my head to the side and cracking my neck.

Willow glared, harsh, angry breaths puffing out her cracked lips.

For a split second, I imagined those lips wrapped around my cock, and I groaned.

Aidan's brows raced into his hairline, his eyes wide and disbelieving.

"You're either brave or stupid, Omega."

Without a word, she raised her hand to strike me again. I closed my fingers around her narrow wrist, stopping her mid-swing. She balled her fist, her tits straining the thin fabric of her sundress with each ragged breath.

"Fight me all you want. The answer will still be no."

All at once, she went still, her hand limp in mine. I released it, watching the fury in her body fade as resignation took root. Despite the indignation burning in her cheeks, a glassy hue glimmered over her eyes, dulling the lustrous shine that drew me in.

"Listen, sweetheart," I said, doing my best to keep from barking at her. "The moment you step out that door, I can't protect you. Your father will play dirty to get what he wants. If you think he'll let you live your life unbothered once he realizes I released you, you are naïve."

My words snuffed out the last flickering flame of indignation in her eyes as her scent soured, a burned edge to the spring florals.

She was pissed that I was right, and hurt.

Chapter 3

WILLOW

Heavy breaths choked me as I stared up at the imposing alpha towering above me. The same man who captivated me at the gala. This was the alpha I couldn't stop thinking about. And now he was to be my jailer.

The other man, who crouched beside me, walked into the hall, leaving us alone. Once I brushed off the shame he forced me to face, a different, unfamiliar emotion swirled in my abdomen, my omega perking to life.

His scent filled the room—fresh espresso and whisky.

I craved it, wanted to chase it and drown in it.

It was foreign.

I had never been so enticed by an alpha's scent. At worst, they tended to be putrid, making me want to gag. At best, they were tolerable, but nothing I sought out. I closed my eyes, squashing the primal need to please the man who had effectively taken me prisoner.

Most alphas didn't affect me, but this one was dangerous. And not because of the gun tucked in his pants.

Sunlight glinted off his jeweled eyes, making the jade twinkle. A red mark bloomed on his cheek, standing out against his fair, freckled skin. I licked my lips, following the path of colorful ink on his forearms that disappeared under his rolled sleeves.

His muscles strained against the expensive fabric. My omega luxuriated at the idea of stripping it from him and tracing the lines with my tongue.

Despite the throbbing under my eye, I willed away the unhelpful thoughts. I should be shocked by what my father did. Disgusted.

I wasn't.

It was a step up from his usual games, sure. But William Sterling was nothing short of a selfish bastard who would exploit his own family if it meant he would win an election.

Kaelen Finnegan.

I had no idea who he was, but now he owned me. And he didn't seem like the type to relinquish his possessions. Still, maybe he could be convinced that I wasn't worth the burden.

No one else seemed to think so.

"No?" I echoed, a sting lacing through my swollen cheek, making me hiss.

I clutched the bruised spot, wincing at how tender it was. Bile churned in my belly, and I wished this sensation were unusual. Tenderly, I tapped my fingers over the sensitive flesh, groaning.

Dad hadn't held back.

I would be lucky not to have a black eye.

A shadow swam in my vision.

The mountain of an alpha crouched in front of me. Thick thigh muscles pressed against his pants as a rough hand cradled the uninjured side of my face.

Almost too gently, he stroked my freckles, the touch at odds with the fire spitting in the depths of his eyes.

I stared at his gun, sweat clinging to my nape.

When he didn't respond, the panicked whir grew worse. My omega preened under the touch from the gruff alpha, but I knew better. He held my life in his hands.

I sensed that the longer the silence stretched on, the less likely it was that I would leave this place alive.

My dad was an ass, but this man was something else entirely.

"Please," I murmured, hating the pathetic tint to my voice. "I didn't do anything. Don't hurt me."

The air in the room shifted, dense with his scent. It was tinged, not as sweet and smooth as it had been even a few minutes ago. Veins throbbed in his hand as it fell from my face.

I immediately regretted my words, swaying slightly when I chased his touch. I wanted it back.

"I would never hurt you," he said, nostrils flaring.

"Then let me leave."

"You can't leave. You won't be safe."

Safe was a relative term.

I went from the frying pan into the freezer, and neither option was going to end well for me. I had read stories about the crime families in Boston, assuming that it was all blown out of proportion.

Hard to believe that now, when I was staring into the eyes of a Dublin devil.

Wood groaned behind me, and the man from earlier reappeared. A washcloth sat in his outstretched palm. He handed it to Kaelen.

Without a word, he moved my fingers away from my face, pressing the cloth to my cheek. The initial sting of the ice on my flushed skin made me jump, but my body sagged, relaxing as it soothed away the pain.

"Do you want me to find the senator?" the other man asked.

Pinpricks skittered across my arms, making the hairs stand on end.

"Don't kill him," I begged.

Kaelen's eyes narrowed, his fingers flexing. Only an idiot would bargain with a demon. Yet, here I was.

"My mom is sick. She needs him. I'll do anything you want."

As much as I hated to admit it, my mom was frail, and without my dad, there would be no one left to care for her. I was in no position to help her. My father orchestrated it so we needed him. If he died or left, we would get nothing. I didn't work; he didn't let me. I volunteered and that was it.

No one knew what was wrong with her, but she needed constant care and doctors' visits. Her omega had retreated so far in on itself that her scent had almost completely vanished. Most thought she was a beta.

If Dad was gone, and I was trapped here, who knew how long she would last?

Kaelen scratched his ear. "Leave it, Aidan. Go keep an eye on The Ruby Slipper. With the Sox in the playoffs, the place is going to be a madhouse tonight, and I don't trust Rossi not to pull something. He's hotheaded enough to do something stupid."

"On it," Aidan said as he left.

Quiet minutes ticked by, neither of us saying anything. Kaelen dropped to a knee, moving the makeshift ice pack aside to assess my face. I closed my eyes, not wanting to see what was in his.

Strong fingers gripped my chin, angling my head. The touch drew a whine from me and I tried to muffle the inappropriate sound.

A quiet groan slipped past his lips. Two hands bracketed my hips, pulling me upright with him as he stood. Like most omegas, I was tiny, but he dwarfed me unlike other alphas I'd been around. All six-plus feet of him.

He placed the now half-melted icy cloth on his desk, fiddling with one of the drawers before handing me two small pills.

"What is it?" I asked, my heart plummeting into my stomach.

I didn't want to lose my senses.

"Ibuprofen," he mumbled, scratching a hand through his thick beard. "To help with the swelling and pain."

"Oh," I whispered, taking the pills dry.

His mouth fell open as he ran a hand through his auburn hair, careful not to muss the bun tied at the back of his head.

"What kind of heathen does that?"

"What?" I asked.

"Take pills without water."

I shrugged. I'd always been able to do that. It wasn't that odd. After the brief exchange, another uneasy silence settled between us. I shuffled, scanning the books that lined the shelves behind his desk, curious about what he read.

Not fantasy, that was for certain.

The tension in his body eased as he leaned into his desk, his eyes roaming over me, assessing for weak points.

I couldn't stand it anymore.

At least back home, I knew what to expect.

Based on what my dad had said, Kaelen Finnegan wasn't a mere businessman. And the gun in his pants hinted at something far more ominous.

Something that terrified me.

"What do you mean it's not safe for me? How am I safer here than back at home?"

Based on the fury flaring in his beautiful eyes, I pissed off what appeared to be the head of the Irish mafia. I instantly regretted my big mouth, wishing I could pluck the words from the air and choke them back down.

His knuckles turned white as his nails dug into the supple wood, scratching the surface.

"Here, you won't get beaten."

Blood receded from my fingertips, leaving them cold. My omega curled up like a contented cat in a sunspot at the implications of the alpha's words. His tongue swept along the points of his teeth as he rocked forward, seeming to lose a battle with himself.

A callused palm slid along my smooth face, the touch threatening to burn me from the inside out. His thumb feathered over my lips, barely brushing them before resting on my cheek and trapping me in his hold.

He spoke again, not giving me a chance to say anything. The delicate Irish lilt to his commanding voice was sweeter than melted chocolate, and dangerously decadent. If I weren't careful, I would become addicted to him.

"If you went home, what do you think your father would do? Leave you alone? His plan with me didn't work. Who's to say he wouldn't try to sell you off to the Russians or the Italians? Trust me, sweetheart, I may be the most terrifying man in Boston, but the Irish revere their women. I can't say the same for the Bratva or Casa Nostra. Do you want to take your chances?"

My brain went fuzzy at his declaration.

To that, I didn't have an answer.

He was right.

Did I really want to risk returning home?

Granted, I don't think I had that choice anymore, even if he were giving me the illusion of one.

An icy chill replaced the comfort from his palm as he removed it, gesturing toward the door.

"I'll show you to your room."

Interesting way to say cage, but I followed him through the eerily quiet halls, the path different from the one I had taken when I first arrived. Plush rugs lined the polished hardwood floors while family photos hung on the walls. It almost looked like a normal home.

Distant voices carried up from the lower floors, and I strained to listen, but couldn't make anything out.

Soon, we stopped in front of a door, and the reality of my situation sapped the final dredges of my bravery. I clasped my fingers at my waist, sucking in a slow breath.

"What about all my things?"

"What do you need?"

The abrupt response took me aback. I expected him to brush me off, to tell me I should be thankful that he hadn't lodged a bullet in my back.

"All my clothes," I started, and then stopped. I never had much. Outside my wardrobe, I had a few well-worn copies of books, my pathetic nesting materials and toys for my heats. "Never mind," I rushed to add.

A dark crimson blush burned my cheeks as I looked away from his intensity. The weight of his alpha pressed down on me, his intoxicating scent demanding that I let him care for me. To tell him what I needed.

I dared to meet his gaze, and the severity in it made my chest tighten. Two massive hands landed on either side of my face, caging me between him and the door. Slick coated my thighs. Instead of rebuffing his movements, I perfumed, my scent washing over us like a spring rain.

Darkness crept in, eclipsing the jeweled hues of his eyes until nothing of the Irishman remained, his alpha entirely in control.

"Omega," he breathed, his nose dragging along my clavicle. I mewled, fighting between the instincts that told me to drop to my knees and my brain, which told me to shove him away. "You should go to bed."

The hazy ridges around my vision blurred, unable to focus. An arm slipped around my lower back, supporting me as he pushed open the door. Once I was stable on my feet, he released me. A hiss whistled through his teeth.

"I will make sure you have everything you need. Now go."

His silky demand hovered on the edge of a bark, and my feet moved of their own accord. I stepped over the threshold, and the door clicked behind me, locking me in my tomb.

Frozen, I didn't move as I scanned over the room.

Objectively, it was lovely.

Two massive windows flanked an enormous bed covered in fluffy blankets and pillows. Evening sunlight illuminated the room in a glow that did nothing to help the icy tendrils of fear splintering out from my breasts.

I crawled through the space, running my fingers over the lacquered wood and plush fabric.

On the far side of the room sat an attached bath. A separate shower and tub filled the space as the smooth marble twinkled in the filtered light. I toed off my flats, hating how luxurious the carpet was beneath my feet.

Eventually, I collapsed onto the bed, curling into a ball.

I grabbed a pillow, inhaling the clean smell. The last of my strength cracked, and tears bled into the silken sheets.

It was a pretty prison, but a cell was still a cell, no matter how many throw pillows it had.

Chapter 4

WILLOW

At some point last night, I passed out.

My eyes were dry and itchy, swollen from crying, while my chest ached from how much I had cried.

All I thought about was my mom. I worried about her alone with my dad, and me not there to keep his attention elsewhere.

I tried to muffle the sounds with the pillows, hoping no one heard me. The last thing I wanted was to appear weak in a place like this. I sat up, smoothing out the wrinkles on my sundress from yesterday that I had slept in.

After opening the closet, I realized I would be stuck wearing the same thing until Kaelen collected the rest of my clothes. I assumed that was what he intended to do when he mentioned making sure I had everything I needed.

Cold sweat clung to my nape. I wiped it away, still feeling tired. My muscles ached, and nothing felt quite right. I blinked, shaking away the haze that clouded my vision.

I sat cross-legged on the bed, hugging a pillow. The silk was soft under my fingers as I played with the decorative ties. I desperately wanted to talk to my mom or Sam.

My best friend always saw the bright side of any situation. It was a bit annoying if I was being honest, but I still loved that about her.

Unfortunately, I left my cell in the car when we came here.

So not only was I stuck in a gilded cage, but I was cut off from everyone I loved. It was a small list, but it still stung. I had no idea how long I sat there until my stomach grumbled, pulling me from my self-pity.

Walking across the room, I half-expected to find the door locked. Except, it wasn't. It opened, revealing an empty hallway. I padded aimlessly through the too-big house, desperately trying to locate the kitchen.

Eventually, I found my way to the entryway I remembered from yesterday.

For a minute, I debated walking out the door and testing my luck. Two bodies moved in front of the frosted glass, dousing the smoldering flames of my hope. In each of their hands, I saw the shadow of a pistol.

Whether they were there to keep people out or me in didn't matter. There was no way I would make it two feet. A sigh puffed passed my lips as I hugged myself, stroking my arms.

Then I was hit with the most delicious aroma.

Bacon.

I followed it, finally finding a glittering kitchen tucked in the back of the house.

A matronly woman with gray-streaked, fiery hair stood beside the stove, working multiple skillets at the same time while she sang a lilting tune. Before I could flee, she spun around and beamed at me.

"Come here, deary," she said, pointing at a stool by the island. "You hungry?" I nodded, settling into the seat. "Anything you don't like?"

"Not really."

"Alrighty. I'll have a full fry-up ready in a few minutes. Tea?

Coffee? Juice?"

Taken aback by the relaxing atmosphere, I didn't answer right away. When I left my room, I wasn't sure what I would find. Based on what I'd seen on TV, I thought maybe bloodied bodies, stray bullets, or an endless supply of drugs and women. Instead, it was the picture of domestic quietude.

"It's rude not to answer a question, deary. Stop daydreaming."

The curtness of her words cut the tender brush of her voice, making me stiffen.

"Sorry, ma'am," I murmured, shrinking at being scolded. "Coffee. Iced, please. Cream and sugar."

A bright look settled on her face, highlighting the lines around her dimples. She gave me a tight nod, turning down the gas under one pan before doctoring my coffee per my request. I ran my fingers through my hair, loosening the knots in the strands. I was too hot, considering it was fall. Beads of sweat dotted my collarbone, and I flicked them away, noticing the flush creeping up my torso.

"Don't worry, Aileen mothers everyone," a foreboding voice said, making gooseflesh skitter along my arms.

Soon, all I smelled was him. Instead of terrifying me, it steadied me. Aileen handed me my coffee. I pressed my lips to the rim, purposefully ignoring the alpha who was now standing beside me.

Sweet espresso hit my lips, and I let out a reedy moan.

Not knowing if it was the taste of it on my tongue or the scent of it pouring off the alpha beside me.

A smooth, vibrating sound hummed next to me. My omega rose to the surface, begging me to make sure the alpha wasn't displeased with us. I put down my coffee, fingers rubbing the condensation on the glass. Gnawing on my lower lip, I glanced to my left, and an unfamiliar sound tumbled out of me.

Holy shit.

People actually looked like that?

Gray joggers hung around his hips, a patch of dark hair disappearing beneath the waistband. A thin sheen of sweat glistened on his bare chest, showcasing the intricate tattoos that covered the span of his torso.

Another surge of flames licked through my body.

"Good morning," Aileen said, pushing a black cup of coffee across the island.

The mug looked so small in his hand as he took a sip, his eyes never leaving mine.

Aileen slid two plates toward us, piled high with food. Neither of us paid any attention, waiting for the other to back down.

Strands of hair fell free from his messy bun, obscuring his piercing eyes when he finally spoke, cutting the mounting tension.

"Eat."

Something inside me preened under the command, my omega adoring the attention of an alpha. I, on the other hand, wanted to tell him to fuck off. But I was hungry.

Rolling my eyes, I stabbed my fork into a sausage, taking a bite. It was delicious. I quickly devoured most of the food, surprising myself. I lived on granola bars and cereal. Mom had been an amazing cook, but with her deteriorating health, she hadn't been in the kitchen for the past few years.

I tried a couple of times, but I was a lost cause, burning rice more than once. So I resigned myself to pre-made foods.

Happy I was eating, Kaelen did the same. Aileen paid us no mind, busying herself tidying up the kitchen and doing the dishes.

I resisted the urge to crawl into his lap, annoyed by how insistent the temptation was. Normally, I had more control. I never devolved like this around an alpha.

"Tell me about your Ma."

"Excuse me?"

"Last night, you mentioned she was sick," he continued, dropping his fork. "Not many people would offer anything to a man like me to spare someone else."

What a cynical worldview. My dad may have been a bastard, but I refused to believe the rest of the world was like that.

The owner at Snowfield, April, rescued the horses that everyone else had given up on. Sam had a heart of gold, regularly putting herself last to take care of others. Maybe in his world that was true, but not in mine.

"I don't believe that," I bit back, narrowing my eyes at him.

The corner of his mouth lifted in a half-smirk.

He tugged his hair free, letting it hang freely, skimming his collarbone. I liked this carefree, almost disheveled version of him. I imagined very few people saw him like this. I crossed my legs, squirming against the unpleasant tightness radiating between my thighs.

"You'd be surprised. When faced with a decision like that, most people will protect themselves. Senator Sterling proved that, running with his tail between his legs, and leaving his daughter with me all to protect his own hide."

Hearing it out loud ruffled me. There had been a time when he loved me, but that man didn't exist anymore. I gulped, washing away the acrid taste. The slight grimace on his lips twisted into something kinder.

His palm splayed over my bare thigh, his thumb playing with the hem of my dress. A purr stirred behind my sternum, slick ruining my panties.

It had been years since someone besides my mom or Sam had shown me affection. A long, slow breath released the tension in my body, and I looked into his eyes, unnerved by the openness in them.

I'd never purred for anyone before, and I found I *really* wanted to for him.

Words fell from me freely as I unloaded nearly a decade of grief.

"My mom has been sick for the last few years. We've been to so many doctors over the years, but they can't figure it out. On paper, she's healthy. But she's frail and barely has the energy to get out of bed most days. The last doctor we saw thinks it might be something with her omega, but they haven't figured it out. I hope she's okay."

I murmured that last bit, more to myself.

"Does he hit her too?" Kalen asked, a cool detachment curling around his words.

"Not usually. That's reserved for me," I said, my voice hollow. "He isn't kind to her, though. I hate her being alone with him. Without me there, I worry he might take out his frustrations on her."

A heavy silence lingered between us as he continued to rub my cotton dress between his fingers. His pinky brushed against the burning skin of my inner thigh, unraveling the last thread of my control.

Wispy strands of hair stuck to my sweaty brow and pinked cheeks.

Realization exploded around me like a hurtling comet.

No.

It was too early. I had weeks.

The stress, exhaustion, and anxiety messed with my cycle. As each minute ticked by, I sank further beneath the surface, pulled out with the swirling tide.

A wail escaped me as I slid off the stool, crawling into the lap of the shocked alpha.

I cuddled into the crook of his neck, inhaling his homey, spicy scent. My omega went lax as his arms wrapped around my waist, anchoring me to him.

"Alpha. *Please.*"

Pitch-black eyes met mine, his dick twitching against my ass.

Oh.

It was glorious. Thick. He would knot me so well, stretch me so well. I circled my hips, grinding into him.

He licked his lips, his nails biting into my hips.

"Knot," I moaned, perfuming.

Strong hands cupped my face, forcing me to meet his stare. I sniffed, trying to pull away, wanting to burrow back into the spot where his scent was the most potent. Why was he being so difficult? Did he not want me? Why did nobody ever want me?

"Omega," he said, his voice smooth like crushed velvet. "*Stop.*"

All at once, I stilled, powerless against my alpha's bark.

My alpha.

Chapter 5

KAELEN

Fuck. I deserved a medal.

For the last decade, I ensured I was never around an omega in heat. Da drilled it into me and my brothers' heads that we were never to spend a heat with an omega unless we intended to marry them, bond them.

In our world, the risk of spending a heat with an omega and becoming bonded to the wrong person was too great.

Omegas were sacred, a delicacy to be protected and worshiped. Also, a weakness. One I had to be certain of before I claimed one as my own.

A sweet, honeyed scent invaded all my senses when those crystalline, sapphire eyes blinked back at me, shining with hurt.

This lush omega sat perched in my lap, and here I was pushing her away. Her arse wiggled, grinding into my stiff cock. My alpha thrashed, demanding that I carry the adorable bundle into her nest and care for her.

Unfortunately, she wasn't mine, and if she were in her right mind, she wouldn't want me. I may have had a shite moral code, but I didn't take advantage of an omega who was in heat, no matter how tempting it was.

"Aileen," I hissed, my teeth grinding so hard they might shatter.

Thank God for her. She swept in, handling Willow as if she were something precious. And help me, she was. Aileen knew how to care for an omega. Despite being a beta, she had two daughters, both omegas who were happily bonded to their alphas with their own children.

While I was busy fighting against my instincts, Aileen escorted Willow back to her room. The panicked omega shot worrying glances back at me while Aileen soothed her.

"Alpha," she whinged, the sound high-pitched and needy.

Cold sweat dripped from my brow, and I was hard as stone in my joggers.

"It will be okay, Omega," I said, doing my best to stay calm. "Be a good girl for me and let Aileen get you settled in your nest."

Wide eyes stared at me, but she nodded, crying quietly as Aileen steered her upstairs.

I stalked down the hall, following the lingering scent of Willow until I found Patrick leaning against the doorframe to my office. He was quiet, but loyal, and most importantly, a beta. Willow's heat wouldn't entice him.

Not like me or my brothers or some of the other men on the premises.

I didn't trust myself not to find my way back to the guestroom. She smelled too good. Dark eyes flicked up to mine. Pat's face schooled in a neutral expression as he took in what had to be a feral look on my face.

"Everything alright, Boss?" he asked, keeping his distance.

Knuckles cracked as I flexed my fingers, shaking loose some of the tension in my muscles.

"I need you to guard Willow's room. You don't let *anyone*—even me—fucking pass. I mean it, Pat. Shoot 'em if you have to. Only Aileen is allowed to come and go until I say otherwise."

"Of course," he said, rocking off the wall and only too happy to get away from my grouchy arse.

Gaelic curses mumbled past my pursed lips. My fingers knotted in my hair as I stumbled into my bathroom.

Water.

Yes.

That would help.

After my shower, I fell onto the edge of my bed, trying to focus and failing. All I heard were the quiet sniffles of a desperate omega, pleading for an alpha to knot her. I was painfully hard between my legs as my alpha imagined sinking into our omega's plush pussy and knotting her.

I shot up, nearly running to the kitchen. What a pretty thing she would be, locked on my knot while I filled her: skin glistening, head tilted back, and my name on her lips as she came. Hissing, I tugged at the placket of my trousers, trying to loosen the taut material.

I stared at the overflowing glass of whisky I had poured earlier before draining it in one burning swallow. I breathed through my teeth, scratching my beard hard enough to draw blood. It was unacceptable. Willow was alone in a guest room, having her heat. She deserved a proper nest and an alpha to tend to her.

Not just any alpha. *Me.* I was her fucking alpha. I knew it. And that would be enough until she figured it out.

Willow Sterling was my scent match.

Even so, I restrained myself from barging into the guestroom, pouring a second glass of Midleton instead.

With my instincts in overdrive, I heard the click of the front door opening, and my head snapped to the source of the sound.

Bags overflowing with blankets dangled from Aileen's outstretched arms. The unease plaguing me quieted, seeing that she had nesting things for Willow.

I stood, about to offer her help when I thought better of it.

My omega deserved more than sterile blankets.

She needed me.

Needed *my* scent.

Rougher than I intended, I tore my dress shirt off by the collar, stuffing it in one of the bags.

The lines around Aileen's eyes crinkled.

"This will help," she said, patting my biceps and heading upstairs.

Over the next three days, I struggled to function.

Aidan and Liam handled our family business while I was indisposed. I was on the verge of a rut and didn't trust myself to make any significant decisions.

It had been a mistake putting my sweet omega in the guest room down the hall from my bedroom.

Every night, I heard her pitiful cries, her raw voice begging for an alpha to knot her.

More than once, I nearly tested the limits of what Patrick would do.

If he had the balls to stop even me from entering her makeshift nest. The man was tough. One of the few I trusted at my side.

However, the beta wouldn't be able to stop a rutting alpha from joining an omega in heat without shooting them.

And despite my order to do that, Pat would never pull that trigger.

Not against me.

I wouldn't put him in that position.

Instead, I locked myself in my room, pacing and wearing a path in the carpet. Aileen assured me Willow had everything she needed to get through her heat, but that wasn't true. She didn't have *me*. Her alpha.

Naked. I lay down on my bed, my cock slapping against my stomach and leaking. Again, the sound of her muffled cries carried into my room.

"Alpha," her raw voice moaned.

"Omega," I panted.

I fisted my dick, stroking it as I closed my eyes. My head fell back into the pillows, and I swore her heady scent filled the room, smelling like sex, spring rain, and honey.

My poor omega. I tightened my grip, slicking pre-cum over my length. I pictured her crystal eyes glazed with pleasure as she bounced on me, taking my knot like the beautiful omega she was.

A minute later, her voice changed, turning high-pitched and frantic until she sobbed as she shattered, coming around some knotting dildo instead of me.

Soon, hot ropes of my spend shot out, coating my fist and stomach as I groaned.

Hopefully, my omega would rest now with my shirt tucked away safely in her nest. I grabbed a tissue from the bedside table, cleaning myself enough, too lazy to shower.

The blankets were like velvet beneath my fingertips as my hands fell back onto the mattress with a dull thud.

Closing my eyes, I envisioned my sweet omega curled up in this massive bed beside me.

That first night, when she spat at her father, flames burned in her eyes, forging those bright blues into glittering sapphires. She wasn't fearless. She was terrified. But that didn't stop her; she raised her chin and walked straight into the line of fire like an anchor in the storm.

My omega was a queen, and if I believed in God, I would have dropped to my knees and thanked Him.

I was utterly fucked.

Willow had blown apart every wall I'd spent the last decade building.

When I woke up, there was a text from Liam saying Torin had been released from the hospital. A half-smile tugged on my lips as I texted him back, telling him to send Torin to my office for a meeting at 10:30.

My forearm fell over my eyes, obscuring the late morning sun.

It was quiet. My omega slept, and I exhaled. It had been four days; she was nearing the end of her heat. I sensed it. I shot off another text to Liam, telling him to find me a contractor.

When he poked, I told him to mind his business. I never considered myself impulsive, but my omega would not spend another heat in anything less than the most luxurious nest. Another suite sat unused on the other side of his closet.

No better use for it than her nest.

Warmth spread through me, calming my raging alpha.

Hot water poured off my body as I pressed my forehead to the wall in my shower. Strands of hair fell over my shoulders, and for the first time in days my dick wasn't heavy between my legs. I dried off, tying my hair back into a neat bun, tugging at the cuffs of my shirt.

As I made my way to my office, I passed Pat, still stationed outside Willow's room. Purple marks hung under his eyes as I tilted my head in his direction. The tough fucker hadn't slept, standing like a sentry at the gates of Hell.

He leaned against the wall.

"I'll have Aileen bring you a coffee," I said.

"She beat you to it. Already had my first one when she brought your girl breakfast. Should be getting my second here shortly."

Your girl.

Good.

They should think that. It was only a matter of time before everyone knew. Every fiber urged me to storm into that room and feed her from my fingers. To tuck that precious omega in beside me while she slept.

"Has she been eating?"

"I think so. Aileen's been dropping off food and water a few times a day."

Oil slipped across my fingers as I scrubbed a hand through my beard. Had Aileen coaxed her to eat and drink enough?

Stubborn omega probably hadn't. Not without my alpha to coax her. That wouldn't do. Next time, I would be there to take care of her.

Reluctantly, I left my private wing and strode into my office, surprised to see Torin already there, perched in my chair like a king lounging over his subjects.

"You think nearly dying means you get to act like a shite?"

A confident grin slid across his lips. Bloody Scotsman pretending to be Irish. He was a pain in the arse at the best of times.

"I figured I'd test my luck. Since you didn't pull your pistol on me, I'd say it was a win."

"Get the fuck out of my chair," I hissed, tapping my waistband in warning.

"Fine, you twitchy-fingered fuck." Torin snorted, moving to the other side of my desk and collapsing into the oversized armchair.

Bandages poked out from beneath his collar.

After years, the man finally dressed appropriately when coming to work.

Apparently, eight years in the Marines taught him nothing. Or he chose to ignore everything. Aidan finally convinced him that a clean t-shirt was not a dress shirt.

At the bar cart, I poured two glasses of whisky, handing one to Torin, who accepted with a dip of his chin.

"How is it?" I asked, pointing at the covered wound.

"Hurts like a bitch, but liquor helps," he said, raising his glass in salute and taking a long drag. His eyes widened, holding the glass at a distance to examine the amber liquid. "Shite. You gave me the good stuff. You must want something."

I put down my glass, crossing my arms over my chest. Noticing the shift in my demeanor, Torin straightened, his expression turning serious as he emptied the last of the whisky.

"I'm assigning you to protect Willow. If I'm not with her, I expect you to be."

"The senator's daughter?"

She wasn't his anything. He didn't deserve to call her his daughter. She was *mine*. Torin's eyes narrowed ever so slightly before a glimmer of understanding flashed across his face.

"Yes. She will be staying here for the foreseeable future, and she will need protection whenever she leaves."

"Aye. Heard she spit on the senator and slapped you across the face. Ballsy omega. Are you sure she can't handle herself?"

Aidan didn't know when to shut up. No doubt that he told Torin everything when the two of them crawled into bed together. Aidan thought that he and Torin were sneaky, but those two were as subtle as a slap to the face.

For the last year, they had danced around each other. I didn't care who they fucked, as long as they did their jobs.

And they were the best, with Liam and Patrick a close second.

It wouldn't be long before people realized who Willow was and what she meant to me. When that day came, she would be a target.

Right now, I was certain she could take care of herself. It looked like she had been doing that most of her life. Once the Italians realized she was mine, they would be out for blood. I needed to keep her safe.

I had an inkling that her omega already recognized me as her alpha. Now, it was a matter of getting Willow to come to the same conclusion. I was a patient man when I had to be. I would wait at the end of the earth for her, just to burn it to the ground afterwards if those brilliant crystal eyes willed it.

Almost forgetting that Torin was still there, I dropped into the armchair beside him, squeezing his uninjured shoulder.

"I wouldn't be surprised if that pint-sized powerhouse could take down a few of my men, but I won't take any chances. She's important to me."

"Then she's important to me," he said, nodding. "I won't let anything happen to her, Boss."

"Good. There's one other thing I need. When you find your way into my brother's bed tonight, have him help you with it."

Torin choked on a cough, all the color draining from his face.

"Sir. Kaelen. It's not true."

I raised a hand to silence him. No one lied to me, especially not my family, and Torin was family. Kin. Even if he wasn't blood.

"Don't lie to me. It's true, and I don't care. I won't tell anyone if you two prefer to keep it quiet. You'll need Aidan's hacking skills to help. I want medical records for Isabelle Sterling for the last ten years."

Torin nodded slowly, still uneasy. Eventually, he would get over it. While watching him and Aidan avoid each other when I knew what was happening behind closed doors had been entertaining for a time, I needed them focused.

Now more than ever.

It didn't take me long to find out who Willow's mother was. Isabelle Sterling had been married to William Sterling for thirty years. For decades, she was active in the society pages, her sleek black hair cascading down her back. Willow looked every bit her mother's daughter.

Then, mysteriously, about eight years ago, she disappeared from social life.

If she had been sick, that made sense, but I hated to see that haunted look in Willow's eyes when she talked about her mum. I knew some of the best doctors in Boston and was sure one of them could figure out what was wrong with Isabelle.

Chapter 6

Cold water hit my face, and I fell on top of the closed toilet seat. I didn't even know what day it was. My elbows fell to my thighs, and I cradled my face in my hands. My fever had broken a day or so ago, and since then, I've slept.

This morning, I finally made my way to the bathroom to try to be a person again. Too tired to stand, I sat on the floor in the shower while lukewarm water splashed over my tender skin.

Back out in the bedroom area, I eyed my nest. I should strip it. Aileen had been so kind to me these last few days. She'd brought me so many blankets and toys to help with my heat.

Three times a day, she checked on me, making sure I ate and drank something. This was my first heat where I didn't feel dreadful afterwards. I always spent my heats alone. While toys helped, they didn't fully replace an alpha. I had no one to care for me, which meant I was usually dehydrated at the end of a long week.

Despite my heat being over, I knew I'd feel foggy for a few days.

I should take it easy, but I wanted to talk to Sam. We had a standing lunch date on the last Saturday of every month. Maybe I could convince Kaelen to replace my cell so I could talk to her.

If I didn't show up, my best friend would worry.

I toyed with the hem of the white dress shirt that hit the middle of my thighs. Even all these days later, it still smelled faintly of him. When I found the shirt mixed in with the blankets, I immediately added it to my nest, calling out for my alpha.

Well, not mine, even if my omega thought he was. I curled my fingers around the collar, hugging it close. My omega slipped into the background—content. Flashes of the moments leading up to my heat played out in my head, and I groaned.

No alpha ever affected me like that, even on the brink of my heat.

I needed to apologize. The last thing I needed was for Kaelen Finnegan to misunderstand my intentions. No matter how much my omega preened in his presence.

The handle was smooth under my fingertips as I tentatively opened the door. Gooseflesh prickled along my arms as my body stiffened, prepared to be shoved back into my cell the moment I stepped over the threshold.

Dark, smudged eyes met mine. My breath caught when I eyed the gun strapped to his torso. He stared at me, his face frustratingly impassive, until he caught what I was wearing.

Pink blush stained his cheeks, and he averted his gaze, clearing his throat.

"Am I allowed to leave the room?" I asked, prepared to slink back inside.

"I was told to stop others from coming in. Nothing about stopping you from getting out."

Odd. Aileen came and went freely the last few days. Maybe Kaelen was worried about other alphas being drawn to me because of my heat. The beta shifted from side to side, tugging at the collar of his shirt. I moved further out into the hall, looking from left to right, trying to get my bearings.

"Do you know where Kaelen is?"

"The boss is in his office. Down the stairs, second door on the right."

"Thanks. What's your name?"

"Patrick."

"Thank you, Patrick, for making sure nobody bothered me during my..." I struggled to say the word. "You know."

"My pleasure, Miss Sterling."

I winced at the title, always hating when people called me Miss anything. It was far too stuffy and formal and made me think of every boring charity event.

The polished wood was cool underneath my bare feet as I padded down the stairs. I burrowed into the plush silk of his shirt, inhaling the remnants of his spiced sweetness. Even though my heat had passed, my skin was still flushed and sensitive. I had tried putting my sundress back on, but it was too itchy. The only things I tolerated were his shirt and my panties.

Voices carried out into the hall as I approached the ajar door.

Tentatively, I pushed it open and stepped inside. All eyes snapped to me, and a thick silence settled over the space.

Two men stood beside each other on one side of the room. I recognized Aidan, but the other man was new. Kaelen's alpha scent dwarfed Aidan's. The other man's scent was muted, and clearly a beta. He was a good head shorter than Aidan. He dipped his chin in my direction, looking to Kaelen.

I ran my fingers through my hair, twirling a blue highlight around my finger.

Kaelen pressed his palms into his desk, rising to his full, imposing height. The tip of his tongue licked over the points of his teeth, eyeing me like a lion about to pounce on a gazelle.

A jacket sat strewn over the back of his chair, his chest taut under his shirt.

My heart beat too fast, drowning out the ambient noise.

Those piercing jade eyes met mine, and I wanted to turn and run. The intensity did something funny to my insides. They were too discerning, and I was too exposed.

"Sweetheart."

Kaelen's commanding tone filled the room, making me slick with want.

"I-I. Um. I shouldn't be here. I'll go."

"Stop," he said, the demand almost a bark. I froze with my back to him, rubbing my sweaty palms on my thighs. "Come here."

The glands on my wrists ached as his deep timbre lathed over me.

I sucked in a shaky breath, looking anywhere but at him as I made my way to his desk. Intimately aware of our audience, I tugged at the hem of his shirt, wishing it were longer. Nails dug into my palm as I itched the spot, wishing I suffered the sundress.

Soon, I stood in his shadow.

Rough fingertips brushed along the backs of my thighs, and I squeaked as my heart jumped into my throat. His well-kempt scruff scratched along my face, his cheek rubbing against mine.

A scent mark. My eyes widened, an omega whine clawing at my ribs.

His lips twitched before he pulled away.

"Are you feeling better?" he asked, his eyes roaming over my body.

"Yes," I said, my voice cracking.

"Did you need something?"

"Um." I rolled my lip between my teeth, dropping my voice into a whisper. "I wanted to apologize. For what happened before my heat. I didn't know. It was early, and I shouldn't have crawled on top of you and done things like that. It was inapp—"

One of his fingers pressed to my mouth, cutting off my ramblings. I resisted the urge to flick my tongue out and taste him. A strand of auburn hair fell free from his neat bun, falling deliciously between his eyes.

"Hush. You have nothing to apologize for. You did what your omega intended."

My stomach flipped as butterflies swirled around, making me feel like a teenager with a crush. I peered at the two men watching us with amused expressions. Two fingers slid under my chin as he angled my face back to him.

"Don't mind them," he added. "Aidan is my brother, and Torin has been assigned as your personal guard."

A spark fizzled behind my eyes as my brain short-circuited.

"My *what?*"

"Come," he said, lacing his fingers with mine and ignoring my question. "We'll get you breakfast. You need to eat." He faced Aidan and Torin. "I want those files on my desk by the end of the day."

All the gentleness seeped from his voice, replaced with something cold and authoritative. The men dipped their chins. I swore I saw Aidan wrap an arm around Torin's waist as we left the office. Kaelen's thumb rubbed across my knuckles as he led me through the house.

Two hands bracketed my hips, lifting and placing me on the counter beside the stove. His chest heaved with slow breaths as his palms splayed over my bare thighs, his fingers skimming beneath the hem, doing terrible things to my panties.

"What do you want?"

Your knot inside me, I thought to myself.

Damn my omega brain, she was still in heat mode.

"You're jumping ahead, sweetheart," he said, nipping at my ear.

Oh, *no.* I said the quiet part out loud.

My cheeks burned as I hid my face in my hands.

Stupid omega.

I tried to slip off the counter. I couldn't be around him.

Everything about him made me act irrationally. Unfortunately, his hands held me still, his earnest eyes pinning me in place from beneath his neatly styled hair.

"Stay. I meant what you wanted for breakfast. Aileen has the morning off."

My shoulders sagged at the change of subject. A hint of espresso mingled with my honeyed scent between us, and my stomach rumbled. The corners of his eyes crinkled as a laugh rolled through him, easing the last of my tension.

Until that moment, I wasn't certain Kaelen Finnegan was capable of that. Unfortunately, my stomach betrayed me. There was no way I could leave now. Not that he would let me, anyway.

"You cook?"

Theoretically, I knew there were men who enjoyed making food. My dad had never been one, preferring to eat takeout once my mom fell ill and couldn't cook anymore. Kaelen didn't strike me as the kind to make his own food. Too busy and too important.

He had an air about him. But maybe I misjudged him.

"My Ma taught when we lived in Ireland."

"And she is?"

"Moved on. About seven years ago now. Died in a car accident, broke my Da's heart. He died two years later of heart failure. Doc said it was a broken heart. He couldn't stand the loss of his mate. My parents were a bonded omega and alpha, had been that way since they were eighteen."

"I'm sorry," I whispered, an ache spreading through me.

I massaged the spot above my sternum. When I was younger, my parents were so in love. They would steal kisses and sneak off into the empty rooms. After I started high school, that all changed. Their interactions were forced, and all the light from my mom's eyes faded until there was nothing left.

It was like her omega had given up, forgotten and abandoned by her alpha.

A shudder shook my tiny frame. I promised myself I would never let that happen to me. That I would never be so taken with an alpha that the rest of my life would stop mattering if they didn't love me anymore.

I couldn't do that. I couldn't become a husk of a person.

So I didn't date alphas. Never been with one. I had two boyfriends growing up, and they were both betas. Betas were safe. There were no bond bites, no forevers, and no chance of getting my heart broken.

Even though it left a hollow feeling there.

Kaelen didn't appear to have the same reservations. He wasn't bonded, but he didn't seem averse to the idea. Based on how he looked at me, his alpha may already be charmed with me. My omega harbored similar feelings that I squashed as far down as I could.

No alphas.

Especially not gorgeous, dreamy-eyed Irish ones who may or may not be in the mafia.

Who may or may not be my scent match.

It was like a bad Lifetime movie waiting to happen. And I would not be the dumb omega all alone at the end.

I made a mental note to Google him the minute I had a phone again. Consequences be damned.

"Don't be. They're together again, like I'm sure they wanted."

Instead of waiting for me to decide what I wanted, Kaelen dug in, pulling out bowls and mixing a bunch of ingredients together. After pouring flour into the bowl, he undid the cuffs on his sleeves, rolling them up and exposing his toned, tattooed forearms.

Words in a language I didn't understand mingled with Celtic knots and a patchwork of flowers and vines. Shifting, I nibbled my lip, desperate to trace my fingers along the lines of art on his muscled arms.

I shoved aside the inappropriate thoughts.

"I would like to meet my friend, Samantha, for lunch in a few days. If that's allowed. We usually get together on the last Saturday of every month. And I know I was out for a few days, but I think that's soon, and she'll worry if I don't show up. It would be for an hour."

Samantha was the kind of omega everyone adored. Kind, bubbly, outgoing, and naturally submissive. Alphas followed her down the street with big puppy dog eyes. She had her pick, yet she refused to settle down, always finding something wrong before the third date.

She'd struggle to put her finger on it, but it always came back to needing more. While she didn't tell me the details, I thought it had to do with her ex. She moved here from South Carolina after they ended things, keeping tight lipped about her past.

The oven timer beeped as he tossed in whatever he had made before closing the distance between us. Despite sitting on the counter, we were still eye level. I wondered how soft his beard was. If it would be silky or coarse when I ran my fingers through it.

"You ramble when you're nervous."

"I'm not nervous," I said, narrowing my eyes at him.

"It's cute."

My mouth went dry, suddenly feeling far too crowded by him. No one called me cute or pretty or anything like that. The walls I had spent years building were slowly crumbling.

"You don't need permission to see your friends. You are not a prisoner here. My only rule is that whenever you leave the grounds, you take Torin with you."

I snorted. Pretty things didn't make this place any less of a prison.

"I thought I was not allowed to leave. Those were the terms. Is 'prisoner' too harsh a word for you? Does it affect your delicate sensibilities? How about 'captive' or 'inmate' instead?"

Anger bubbled to the surface. I palmed his chest, shoving him. The brick building of a man didn't move an inch. Frustrated, I threw my hands into my lap. How dare he smell so good and act so nice.

"My only rule is this," he said, his voice dropping in a menacing whisper. "You can leave. Do as you like, as long as you come home every night and take Torin with you."

"Home?"

My heart did this funny flutter thing as too many emotions vied for dominance at once, making it hard to breathe.

"Yes. This is your home now. I want you here every night where I can protect you."

Every instinct told me to run away. Alarm bells rang in my head. I was so tired.

Ever since I presented seven years ago, when I turned eighteen, I shut myself away. Afraid that I would end up with an alpha like my dad. Kaelen was dangerous. The way he made my omega act couldn't be trusted. I had no idea how long I could resist him.

In the throes of my heat, I hadn't been able to.

If he had been any other alpha, he could have taken that as consent and bitten me. I could have woken up bound and mated. A wave of his scent hit me, and I relaxed. It was too much. I focused on something else, needing a distraction.

"Can I use your phone to text Sam?"

"Yours not good enough for you?" he asked, removing his cell from his pocket and handing it to me without a second thought.

Most men didn't hand over their phones easily, especially men in powerful positions. Dad freaked out the one time I picked up his cell.

There were over 10,000 unread notifications hovering over his email icon. I almost passed out, my eyes nearly bugging out of my head. I opened his texts, ignoring an unread message from someone named Liam, and quickly typed out Sam's number from memory before sending off a note about lunch.

"You really need to hire a secretary or something," I mumbled. "Your emails are atrocious. What if there is something important in those unread messages?"

"It's junk. I handled the necessary ones. You volunteering, sweetheart? I think I like the idea of seeing your pretty arse nestled behind my desk."

"I don't think you could pay me enough."

"We'll see about that." He smirked.

I had a feeling I had poked a very competitive bear who didn't like to be challenged. Quickly, I changed the subject.

"I don't have my phone," I said, answering his question from earlier. "I left it in my dad's car that day." I handed his cell back to him.

"I'll get you a new one."

Before I could interrupt, the stove beeped, and Kaelen removed the most delicious thing I have ever seen. Faint hints of vanilla mixed with apples, making my mouth water. He cut a massive piece of what looked like coffee cake, but not quite, onto a plate. He passed it to me, handing me a fork.

A small moan left my lips as I took a tentative bite. He winked, sliding an iced coffee toward me. Whatever worries I had from a few moments ago vanished as I devoured the apple cake and coffee. Once we both finished, he popped our dishes into the dishwasher, returning to my side.

"I have a bit of a sweet tooth," he confessed, and I stowed away that information for later. "Don't tell Aileen I made apple cake for breakfast, or we'll have to deal with her scolding us for eating dessert before noon."

The warning bells from earlier slipped into the background. He planted a hand on either side of my hips, caging me in. Warmth spread over me, soothing the tension in my muscles.

Being brave, I closed my fingers around one of his forearms,

Kaelen

tracing the lines of Celtic crosses and knots woven with thorny roses.

He didn't pull away, content to let me explore to my heart's content. A phrase was hidden among the roses: *Tá sé scríofa.*

Gentle lips brushed against my cheek. "It's Gaelic for 'it is fated.'"

Chapter 7

WILLOW

A quiet buzz followed me through the estate as I wandered. After my odd impromptu breakfast with Kaelen yesterday, I spent my downtime exploring the vastness of my new home.

Home.

The word felt heavy in my chest. I rubbed a spot between my breasts as I tried to soothe it.

My feet padded along a narrow staircase until I reached a heavy glass door. Polished steel brushed against my fingertips as my hand rested on the handle. Aileen let me know—while she fed me far too much food this morning—that I was free to explore anywhere in the house as long as it was unlocked.

The door opened without resistance. A distant thrum of music and clanging iron echoed in the space. My nose twitched, hypersensitive to the thick scent of sweat and cleaning fluid. But then, an undercurrent of something familiar and comforting cut through the harsher aromas.

Espresso and whisky.

Unmistakably alpha.

Unmistakably Kaelen.

My omega purred and I panicked. Internally, I cursed her, hating how in tune she was with him. Not that I could blame her. My eyes scanned the vast floor covered in mats, landing on a broad figure in the far corner.

A needy sound choked me as I tried to stifle it before I embarrassed myself.

Muscles rippled on his exposed back as he leaned over a bench press. Sweat glistened on his skin, pooling in the small of his back. Swirls of dark ink covered nearly every inch of pale skin, creating a mosaic of artwork.

Quickly, I batted away a speck of drool.

His sculpted arms flexed with effortless grace as he loaded a staggering amount of weight onto the bar. I gasped. I told myself it was just the humidity in the room, but the dampness in my panties told me otherwise.

I was utterly undone.

"Relax," I whisper-hissed to my omega, who ignored me.

A hot flush burned my cheeks. I turned to leave, freezing when that infuriatingly sexy Irish brogue rooted me to the spot.

"Willow."

Damn him.

This was exactly what I wanted to avoid—the sight of him sending my omega and me into a spiral.

He sat at the end of the bench, running a hand through his damp hair before knotting it in another bun at the back of his head. He stared at me, an amused look flashing in his pretty eyes before he ran a towel over his face, giving me a moment to breathe again.

"I-I was just leaving," I stammered.

"Why don't you come over here instead?"

No. Nope. Definitely not. Terrible idea.

Except my omega had other ideas, and for some reason, my feet moved of their own accord, already halfway to where that gorgeous man sat, looking like a Grecian statue.

I ignored his fiery stare, running my finger over the weight plates on the bar.

"Do you want to try?" he asked.

Air whistled through my nostrils as I snorted. "And be crushed to death? Pass." I could count on one hand the number of times I lifted any sort of weight.

He stood, his shadow blocking out the bright overhead lights. I took a small step backwards, needing more space. Thick clouds of his scent lingered in the space between us, making my thighs damp with slick.

"Maybe someday you could handle this weight."He smirked, and I hated how much I appreciated his smile. His pearly white canines were slightly longer than the rest and I instinctively bared my neck slightly. "How about we start out with this?"

Before I could respond, he removed most of the plates, leaving one small one on each side. I tugged at the hem of my sweater, eyeing my less than appropriate workout clothes. His large hand splayed out on the bench, giving it a pat.

My chest heaved with a slow breath as I lay down. Kaelen's hands covered mine, bringing them to the bar and positioning them. Desire shot straight to my center. I closed my eyes, refusing to show how affected I was by his electrifying touch.

The metal bars on the side of the bench rattled as he lifted the bar, holding all the weight while he moved it over me, above my head.

"Now breathe," he instructed, his voice thick and smooth like honey. "Lower the bar down to your chest and then push up. Feel it in your arms. Don't let the bar control you. You control it."

Eager to please the alpha, my omega followed his directions. My arms swayed as I struggled to lift the weight after bringing it down. Slowly, I lowered it again, surprised when I lifted it once more.

"Good girl," he murmured, his accented voice laced with approval.

The praise made me whimper. I bit my lip, happy that he said nothing. Instead, he watched me, straining to finish five reps before my arms gave out, and he placed the bar back into its resting position.

I sat up, rubbing the back of my hand across my brow. Kaelen crouched beside me, now at eye level, handing me a water bottle. My fingers brushed along his, unsurprised by the calluses. When his hand retreated, I missed the closeness.

Silently, I took a sip, not knowing what to say.

Almost as if in slow motion, Kaelen reached out, his fingers gliding along my temple as he tucked a strand of hair behind my ear. The tender gesture was so at odds with his intimidating persona. I enjoyed it. More than I should.

"My Da always said pretty omegas had a way of making you question everything."

"What was he like?" I asked, desperate to change the subject before I did something supremely stupid.

Like asking if I was the pretty omega making him question things.

A nostalgic look came over his face, dulling the sharp cut of his jaw.

"An Irish immigrant who came to Boston with nothing but the clothes on his back and a fierce determination to make a name for his family."

I scooted closer, resting the metal bottle between my thighs, enamored by the fondness in his tone.

"My Ma, she was an anchor. A gentle soul with a will mightier than mountains. An omega with the spirit of an alpha. They were devoted to each other. The kind of bonded mates you read about in fairy tales. Every decision he made, every fight, was for her. For his family. He wanted to build a legacy for their children, a future for the ones he loved."

My head fell.

When I was younger, that was something my dad always talked about. Being a senator, making the world a better place, having something to leave my mom and me. He wasn't that person anymore. The power and corruption twisted him into someone I hadn't recognized in years.

I gave up hope that I'd ever know that man again.

"After his heart attack, my da held on long enough for me to get to the hospital. He told me to carry on our legacy. To protect Aidan and Liam. To be strong. I admired him. Wanted to make him proud."

Emotion curled around his words, his vulnerability startling me. He bared a raw piece of his soul to me. A piece I suspected very few, if anyone, had ever seen.

It was a weakness. It was power.

Power over him, and he offered it to me willingly.

My eyes found his, and I truly looked at him. I saw a different man. Not just an alpha. Not just the head of his family. I saw Kaelen. A man with a burden that made him look older at that moment.

"Originally, he'd told me omegas softened alphas. I may have misunderstood his intentions with those words."

"And now?" I asked, terrified of his answer.

"Now, I'm not so sure." Fingers slid into my hair at my nape, and I leaned into his touch. "Now, I think I've just needed the right omega."

Chapter 8

After our interaction at the gym three days ago, I'd barely seen Kaelen.

I wondered if he regretted his admission, his words playing over and over again in my mind.

The right omega.

His phone had rung then, slicing through the intensity and popping whatever bubble hung around us. He disappeared into his office, and I hid in my room, confused.

Confused about my feelings, my omega, and him. I wanted to trust him. To believe that he wasn't like my dad.

My gut twisted as I tossed and turned that night. Dreams of a handsome alpha with tattoos and long auburn hair played on repeat, making my sleep fitful.

The next morning, his scent lingered in my room, a new iPhone on the end table. Did Kaelen sneak in while I slept? It unnerved and excited me. I texted Sam, happy to see all my contacts were there and the home screen looked exactly like my old one.

My thumb landed on the Safari icon, and I Googled Kaelen Finnegan. No social media accounts popped up, but article after article loaded on the bright screen. Everything from stories about his philanthropic efforts with the Children's Hospital to his businesses.

On the surface, he was a respectable businessman who had immigrated from Ireland when he was fifteen. He owned over a dozen Irish pubs and a handful of nightclubs throughout Boston.

The deeper I dove, the clearer the darker side of Kaelen's business emerged.

One article from two years ago detailed his trial after being arrested for murder. The crime had been brutal. A disemboweled man was found strung up outside an abandoned building. Kaelen had been found not guilty but had earned the moniker of "The Butcher of Boston."

There had been minimal evidence, and it looked to be more a vindictive cop than a solid case, at least according to Kaelen's lawyer.

The jury agreed.

I was more curious than terrified, wondering whether he had done it or not.

I kept waiting for my heart to race, for panic to set it, but it never came. Despite who he was, what he was capable of, I saw glimpses of someone different. Someone I craved and my omega adored.

Maybe not just my omega.

After the sun set, I heard his heavy footsteps pad outside my door before vanishing into his own room. More than once, he stopped in front of my door, his shadow blocking out the muted light from the hall. My omega woke, urging me to invite him in.

Eventually, his figure left, and a hollow ache grew behind my breasts.

The next morning, light flooded my bedroom, making it impossible to sleep any later. I reached for my phone, double-checking that Sam and I were still on for our date.

A sleepy glaze slid across my face when she confirmed. Having lunch with my best friend would be a normal thing. Something I needed when my life had been out of control for the last few weeks.

Like he promised, Kaelen had filled my closet with new clothes, ranging from jeans to sundresses and heels to ballgowns. It was too much. I would never wear more than half of it. Smooth silk and chiffon brushed against my fingertips as I ran them over a fitted sapphire dress with a thigh-high slit.

Crystals glittered on the bodice, and it was probably worth more than anything I have ever owned before. Maybe someday I would have an excuse to wear it.

I glanced out the windows, eyeing the cloudless sky, which gave the illusion that it was warmer than it was. Brightly colored leaves decorated the trees. I tugged on a pair of black tights before slipping into a burgundy dress. The material whispered over my skin as I smoothed my hand over the invisible creases.

Grabbing my phone, I headed down to one of the four living spaces, trying to find Torin. Despite Kaelen telling me I was free to come and go as I wished as long as I took Torin with me, today was the first time I was going to test that theory. I still got lost even though I had spent the last few days exploring the house.

My new home.

Once I realized I wasn't trapped in one room, it felt less like a prison.

Gorgeous, lush gardens sprawled across the expansive back lawn, with a guest house tucked into the corner of the property. I almost enjoyed it, padding barefoot through the grass, until I couldn't ignore the swarms of armed guards patrolling the perimeter.

Finally, I found Torin, lounging in an oversized armchair in a sitting room near the back of the house. A bottle of something strong-smelling sat next to a dirty rag on the coffee table, his pistol in his hands. I cracked my knuckles, and Torin's head snapped to mine.

"Um, hi. Sorry to interrupt, but could you take me to lunch with Sam, please?"

"Aye, Miss Sterling," he said, securing something on his gun with a click before slipping it into his holster.

I wiggled my nose. Only a handful of people called me Miss, and I hated it every time. That term usually preceded some entitled older alpha with too much money putting his hand too close to my ass.

"Willow," I corrected. "Miss Sterling is far too formal."

A smirk curled at the corner of his mouth, making his eyes crinkle.

"Sorry, lass. Willow is too familiar. The boss will string me up if I'm too friendly with you." My eyes narrowed. "Best I can do is Miss Willow. Take it or leave it," he said, gesturing toward the front door.

I shrugged, following him outside. He opened the door of a sleek black car. My nails tapped against the thick, glossy tint on the windows as Torin slid into the driver's seat.

"Bulletproof glass," he mumbled in his thick Scottish burr.

"Is that really necessary?"

"Boss's orders."

Ridiculous.

I crossed my arms, leaning into the cool leather interior. An unfamiliar emotion battled with my anger. Nobody cared enough about me before to assign me a bodyguard or put me in an armored car. As a high-profile senator's daughter, it wouldn't have been out of the realm of possibility.

A lot of senators' families had personal security, but my dad always said it was an unnecessary expense.

Warmth curled in my belly, sending a tingle straight to my pussy.

An alpha cared about me and wanted to keep me safe. My skin prickled, remembering his touch. I picked at an invisible thread on the dress he gifted me. It was too good to be true. What did he want? I had nothing to offer Kaelen Finnegan.

Men like him pursued illustrious omegas who could expand their wealth or influence. In theory, having the omega daughter of the future governor under his control was appealing. And if my father became governor, he might use me to control him.

None of that would matter. My father wouldn't be swayed by anything to do with me. Kaelen could threaten to slit my throat, and chances were my dad would be relieved to be rid of me. Regardless, Kaelen didn't need me. He had other ways of getting what he wanted.

It was quiet as Torin drove through the streets of Boston toward my favorite hole-in-the-wall brunch place that none of the tourists knew about.

"Can you turn on some music?" I asked, unable to stand the stale silence any longer.

"No, Miss Willow. I need to focus while you're in the car. No distractions."

Stuffy fucker.

"Fine."

We arrived at The Nook & Cranny. Torin scanned the area as he opened my door, escorting me into the diner. Hair prickled on my nape at his intensity. Did he really expect someone to attack me in broad daylight? All the tension in my body vanished when Sam's hazelnut eyes landed on mine.

Jumping up, she nearly knocked her chair over. A pinched look flashed on Torin's brow before he fixed his face into a more professional mask. He leaned against a wall close to our table.

"I'll be here, Miss Willow," Torin said.

"Woah," Sam breathed, tugging me into the empty seat beside her. "What's going on with the cutie beta looking like he would take a bullet for you? Did your dad hire you a bodyguard or something?"

I sidestepped Sam's question, sipping on the coffee she had waiting for me.

"Ugh. Don't call him cute. He is a barnacle, at best."

"You're calling that gorgeous beta with that delicious Scottish accent a barnacle?"

I rolled my eyes, watching as Torin ran his tongue along his teeth. Part of me debated telling her a lie, but I couldn't. Samantha was like a bloodhound. Girl knew when I was fibbing before I even opened my mouth.

Two plates laden with roasted potatoes, eggs, and toast rested in front of us. I picked at the bowl of fresh fruit as Sam tossed her thick auburn braid aside. A wave of her strawberry and vanilla scent hit me.

Every time I thought about what kind of omega an alpha wanted, I thought of Sam. She was the quintessential version of an omega: beautiful, charming, and submissive.

When she wanted to be.

To alphas, at least.

Sam tended to say what she thought without thinking, but she usually knew when to zip it.

I was awkward and loud and made alphas uneasy. Which was fine with me. I didn't want an alpha. Even if my omega disagreed. I didn't want to end up like my mother. Bound to someone cruel.

"Sam," I whispered, leaning closer. "If I tell you who he is, you can't tell anyone."

The lines around her mouth faded as she glared at my guard. Her tiny fingers curled around my forearm, squeezing gently. Gooseflesh skittered up my arm, and I relaxed slightly. Outside my mom, Sam was the only person I trusted.

"What's wrong? Are you safe? Do you need me to beat the barnacle up and get you out of here?"

I snorted, and she glowered at me. Not only was my friend as cuddly as a bunny, but she was barely five feet tall. While I didn't doubt she would come to my rescue, I imagined Torin would win.

My gaze darted to the dark corner where he was standing, the crinkles around his eyes giving away his amusement at our conversation.

So as we picked over our meal, I told Sam everything. *Almost* everything. I left out the part about Kaelen being the head of the Irish mob. She would figure that part out on her own soon enough.

Like me, her curiosity would win out.

"Your dad did what?!" she hissed, drawing the attention of nearby tables.

"Shhh," I whisper-shouted. "What part of 'you can't tell anyone' included screaming in a packed restaurant?"

"This can't be real," she murmured, pulling me into a bone-crushing hug. "Are you all right?"

The tears I had been choking back for days fell, staining her sweater. Gentle hands rubbed over my arms as she whispered quiet, soothing sounds until I wiped away the tear tracks from my swollen, puffy eyes.

"Can you check on my mom for me?"

"The fucker won't even let you visit your mother?" she said, tossing daggers at Torin, who looked abashed.

"I'm not sure," I said.

We hadn't talked about it. At the heart of it, I knew he was right. I wouldn't be safe back home, and even going to visit my mom was a risk. Who knew how my dad would react? I could try to sneak in when I knew he wasn't there, but leaving my mom alone would break my heart into a million pieces. It was easier this way, and Sam would take care of her.

"I'll do anything for you, Willow. All you have to do is ask."

"Thank you."

The rest of lunch was a lighter affair. Sam told me about the alpha she spent her last heat with, and how dreadful he was. She was about to take a page out of my book and use toys, tiring of alphas. Yet that didn't stop her from stealing glances at Torin and batting her eyelashes.

"Maybe I could be convinced to bring a handsome beta into my nest if he can see some toys like a teammate instead of an enemy."

She winked in Torin's direction. Pink tinted the tops of his cheeks as he looked away, focusing on the growing crowd in the restaurant.

"You're ridiculous," I giggled, feeling normal for the first time in days.

When the bill came, I reached into the clutch Kaelen bought me to pay for my half. My eyes bugged out of my head. Inside the wallet sat a half-dozen credit cards, including one black AMEX, and an absurd amount of cash. I quickly fished out two fifty dollar bills, tossing them on the table to pay for both our meals and leave a tip.

"Oh, are you spoiling me?" Sam teased.

"Only the best for my girl," I winked and we both giggled.

Torin followed two steps behind us as Sam and I walked arm in arm outside. The bright fall sun landed on my face. I closed my eyes, soaking in the rays before Sam pulled me into a hug, kissing my head.

"Text me. For anything," she said. "Love you."

Slender arms encircled my waist before she pulled away. Torin dipped his chin, opening the door for me. I slid into the car, fiddling with the bag on my lap.

"Torin. Do you know whose cards and money are in my wallet?"

"Yours, Miss Willow." I scoffed, tossing my head back into the supple leather headrest. "The Boss wanted to make sure you had everything you needed."

"I don't need a limitless AMEX. Thanks, though."

Ignoring my outburst, Torin changed the subject. "Home or somewhere else?"

The last thing I wanted was to head back to a place that still didn't feel like mine. I doubted it ever would. The only thing about it that made it less sterile was Kaelen's welcoming scent. But even that had faded over the last few days. I missed him. Or rather, my omega missed his alpha. I refused to believe it was anything other than biology urging me toward him.

"Actually, can you take me to Snowfield?"

Crisp farm air greeted me as my feet sank into the damp earth. I tugged at the hem of my dress, which was hardly work appropriate, but I needed some time with my horses. April waved at me from the pasture, her head tilted at my shadow following me.

When we arrived at the stables, I turned, glaring at Torin.

"The horses here are skittish," I said, my voice dropping low. "They have been rescued. Most have suffered terrible abuse. The one I am working with now is a beautiful black stallion. He doesn't like alphas, but I think he'll be okay with you since you're a beta. No loud sounds or sudden movements. Understood?"

"Yes, ma'am. I won't bother the horses."

Nodding, I walked into the stalls. The stallion's head lifted, his glittering features finding mine almost instantly. He knickered, kicking at the dirt. The polished wood of the brush was smooth under my fingertips as I ran it over his coat.

"Hi, boy. I've missed you. Did you miss me?"

The top of his head nudged me, making me stumble slightly. I realized how far we'd come in only a few months. Someday, I hoped he'd let me ride him. Closing my eyes, I imagined it. The wind blowing in my face, his hooves galloping through the well-trodden trail in the woods around the back pastures.

"What's his name?" Torin asked, reminding me I wasn't alone.

"He hasn't told me yet."

I spent most of the night sitting in the stall with him, feeding him carrots and apples. The sun had set long ago, and the lantern light illuminated the barn in a yellow glow. Torin sat in an old, rickety chair by the entrance, his elbows resting on his thighs.

A sound rumbled in my stomach. It was late. I cradled my stallion's face, nuzzling the top of his head and stroking my fingers through his mane.

"I'll come see you soon, boy."

My knees cracked as I stood. Without saying anything to Torin, I strode back to the car. He followed once he realized I was leaving, trotting to catch up. I half expected him to admonish me, but he didn't.

We rode in silence back into the city, weaving up the long gravel path to the towering estate I would soon have to reconcile as my new home if I wanted to feel any semblance of normalcy back in my life.

Two guards greeted us as we slipped inside.

Hungry, I headed into the kitchen. The potent scent of espresso and whisky hung heavily in the air. My body reacted to him before my mind caught up. A tingle shivered along my back, making the hair on my nape stand on end.

A large figure loomed in the dim light. Kaelen stood hunched over the sink, a tie loose around his neck, and a discarded suit jacket tossed on the counter. Blood dripped from his hand as he poured vodka over his knuckles, hissing.

The dim night illuminated half his face, the other still blanketed in shadow, reminding me of a demon.

Something coiled in my belly as my feet moved forward, closing the distance. His head snapped to the sound of my footsteps, his uninjured hand moving to his gun. When he realized it was me, he stilled, his jade eyes glittering like polished river stones.

"Come here, sweetheart," he said, his voice harsh and gravelly.

Chapter 9

KAELEN

Fuck, I needed a smoke. I tried to cut back, replacing cigarettes with whisky. Right now however, I craved to have the smoke fill my lungs.

The nightlights of the Boston skyline blurred outside the window of the SUV as Aidan drove us past Quincy. Things with the Bratva had been tenuous ever since my Da passed. *Never trust the Russians or the Italians.* It had been drilled into my head since I was old enough to sit in on meetings.

I loved my parents, and my Da was a good man—a good leader. But after I took over, it was clear that warring with the Cosa Nostra and the Bratva only led to our men being killed for no reason. Dealing with Vittorio Rossi was impossible. But in the last year, a new head of the Brotherhood took over, Dimitri Romanov, who was more amiable to negotiations with me.

I agreed to a meeting with him tonight at one of his clubs. A possible alliance that would give him access to our shipping ports, and in exchange, we'd get access to the underground utility tunnels the Bratva controlled.

Patting my suit jacket, I fished out a lighter, slipping a cigarette between my teeth. Liam rolled down the window, but said nothing, and Pat eyed me from the front seat.

We agreed to a small meeting. I would bring only three men, and he promised the same. Aidan parked the car outside of *Scent Allure*, one of the Bratva's above-board establishments, even if I didn't like it.

A scantily-clad omega who smelled like peaches escorted us into a roped off VIP section in the back of the club. My nose twitched, put off by her intensely sweet scent. All I wanted was the subtle, honeyed floral notes of *my* omega.

Every night, Torin updated me on her daily activities. She had yet to leave the house, but that changed today. I chanced a quick peek at my cell, seeing that after lunch, Torin had taken her to a farm on the outskirts of the city. He included a picture of her wearing a fitted dress that hugged her curves.

My cock twitched, and I adjusted my trousers.

I imagined nuzzling her hair, playing with one of those blue highlights. Music thumped in the background, and all I thought about was drowning in her scent. Would she perfume for me again? I hated how busy I'd been. I hope she liked the clothes I'd gotten her. Soon, she would let me spoil her, court her properly.

"Kaelen," a heavy, accented voice boomed.

Dimitri stood, his dark hair framing his even darker eyes. The dim lights of the club cast his olive skin in shadow as a waitress deposited a bottle of scotch on the table. A bright pink collar glistened around her slender neck. Tension tightened at the base of my spine as I realized every woman in the club was a collared omega.

The Bratva and I had very different views on how to handle business. My skin itched, hoping these women were willing and not forced. I shared a look with Aidan, who nodded. Before I agreed to anything with these men, I wanted to understand every part of their business. Both the legal and the more illicit activities.

"Dimitri," I said, meeting his hand in a firm grip before sitting.

"On the house," he said, clapping his hands.

Two omegas appeared almost out of thin air. One with long, fiery hair and another with pale blonde curls and alabaster skin.

"Yours for the night. Which one would you like?"

Neither omega smelled appealing, and their fake, breathy sighs made me stiffen. It was a delicate situation. I couldn't afford to offend Dimitri before we talked logistics. I scrubbed a hand over my beard, and Liam winked.

"If I may," Liam cut in. "My brother prefers to keep a clear head when working. I, on the other hand, have no such morals."

A haunting laugh echoed off the walls as Dimitri nodded, gesturing toward the girls. Liam smirked, guiding the tiny redhead into his lap as he sat. I searched the girl's face for any sign of unease, but the lines around her mouth were relaxed as Liam whispered something that made her giggle.

Liam was a charmer, having the ability to make women, especially omegas, swoon. He splayed a hand over her stomach, holding her close as he took the offered glass of scotch from another server. He nibbled at a spot above her ivory collar, his thumb drawing circles around her navel.

"Now that we are settled. Let us discuss," Dimitri said.

The plush seating cradled me as I leaned into it, listening to Dimitri's proposal. It was simple enough. But I needed Aidan to dig more into what he was hiding before I agreed to work with him. Those utility tunnels would be key for our underground casinos. Right now, we used our pubs to front the casinos. It was a dangerous dance that would eventually bite us in the arse if we weren't careful.

A grating voice cut through the din of music and conversations. I recognized it without looking. Sensing the shift in my demeanor, Dimitri raised a bushy eyebrow at me. I flicked my gaze to the bar, my teeth digging into my lip.

Senator William Sterling sat on a stool with a blonde omega, younger than his daughter, nestled between his legs. Someone with a sick wife and omega at home shouldn't be sloppily pawing at a woman who was neither of those things.

Glass shattered in my hand as I clutched my drink too hard.

Waving off my mumbled apology, Dimitri summoned someone to clean up the mess. I flicked the remnants of liquor off my hand, surprised to see I hadn't cut myself. Aidan followed my movements, sharing a knowing look with Liam and Pat.

"Did he disrespect you?" Dimitri asked.

"Yes," I said, my skin prickling with barely constrained anger.

"Then, as a show of friendship, do what you will, Kaelen Finnegan. I ask that you don't kill him. William Sterling owes me $30,000, and I'd like him to live long enough to repay me. He has exquisite taste in escorts and doesn't always come prepared."

Shocker.

William Sterling was in debt to the Bratva and paid for his pussy. Creases dented my trousers as I leaned my elbows into my thighs. I shared a sidelong glance with Dimitri before cracking my knuckles.

"Thank you. I'll be in touch about how we can work together in the future."

Nodding, Dimitri rose, straightening his suit jacket. He murmured something in Russian to his men, making them scatter.

A tall, slender omega with a periwinkle collar stood beside him as he tossed a thick forearm around her. He nuzzled her curls, murmuring something in Russian that made the girl blush.

"Take the trash outside, friend. Blood stains are impossible to get out. Please be discreet. At the end of the night, I'll wipe any security footage."

I dipped my chin, and Romanov disappeared into the throng of people, his arm slung around the waist of the girl on his arm.

With Dimitri gone, I glared at Liam, who was still cozy with the omega escort in his lap. Aidan coughed, and Liam smirked, whispering something to his companion before sending her away with a tap on the arse.

"Wait for me outside," I said, and Aidan nodded.

"Do you need cleanup?"

"No," I grumbled.

In the last hour, Sterling hadn't moved from the bar, with the omega sitting in his lap, feeding him. A glassy sheen slid over his dull eyes, the liquor clouding the muddy brown irises. If it weren't for my promise to my sweet Willow, I'd rip out his heart.

I imagined it still beating in my hand as blood coated my fingers.

Fuck whatever deal I made with Dimitri Romanov.

With Senator Sterling gone, I'd ensure her mother got the best care. Far better than he obviously was. Aidan was still working on getting me her medical records. Once I had those, my personal physician would review them.

I stalked across the floor, looming over a drunk William Sterling, who only noticed my presence after it sent his paid for omega scurrying away. He sobered up when he took me in, stumbling to his feet.

"Senator," I said, the title sliding off my tongue like a threat.

"Mr. Finnegan. How lovely to see you."

His hands trembled at his side, and I tasted his fear scenting the air. What a pathetic excuse for an alpha. A nickel bounced on the counter under his fingers, his eyes looking everywhere but at me.

Acid corroded the lining of my esophagus. How was I supposed to restrain myself enough to keep from killing him?

"How is my daughter?" he asked, struggling to form the words.

The lighthearted atmosphere around me shifted, a chilly breeze settling over the suffocating heat of the club. My knuckles whitened. The smooth leather of my dagger's hilt pressed into my palm.

"I should gut you," I hissed, pressing the blade into his abdomen. "How dare you ask about *her*. After everything you did. Follow me outside or I'll sink this into your belly."

Sweat beaded off his brow, and a strangled sound fell from Sterling's cracked lips. A primal feeling surged in my veins, my alpha spurring me on, demanding that I avenge our omega. His lower lip trembled as he spoke, and I thought he might piss himself.

"I think I'll stay here."

The man was many things, but not entirely stupid. He called my bluff, knowing I wouldn't risk killing him at a crowded bar.

Venom chilled the air as I glared at him. The last bits of color in his cheeks drained away as he gripped the bar top for stability. I leaned in close, pressing my tongue into the points of my teeth. The sweet stench of liquor-tinged sweat hit me, and it only fueled my bloodlust.

"You owe Dimitri Romanov thousands of dollars. He gave me free rein to do with you as I please and agreed to help me clean up the mess." His body stiffened at the threat, not knowing it was a lie. I dug my knife in, tearing at the cheap threads of his shirt. "Now, come with me, or I'll bury this knife so far into your gut that you will taste it."

Teeth chattered as he gave me a weak nod. My nails dug into his forearm, maneuvering us through the devolving crowd in the club. I shoved him through the metal door in the kitchens out into a back alley, snickering as he stumbled.

I moved forward, stalking Sterling through the shadows until his back was pressed against a stone wall. The senator wasn't small, but I was taller. I caged him in, pinning him in place. I plucked the buttons off his shirt with the tip of my knife, smirking when a trail of piss stained his pants.

"Please," he muttered.

"Please," I mocked. "How many times did your daughter beg you to stop? Did you ever listen?" My lip curled, and I continued. "Actually, she is stronger than you. I bet she never begged. She probably stood there and took it. Don't *ever* speak her name again. Don't *ever* think about her again."

"I won't, I—"

Bone crunched beneath my knuckles as I drove my fist into his face. I didn't care about half-arsed apologies from a weak alpha who wasn't fit to lick my boots. Pain pricked along my fingertips, and it took every ounce of self-control to stop myself from beating him until he stopped breathing.

Blood splattered across the bricks as his teeth cut into my knuckles, opening gashes on the thin skin. I reveled in the pain, a feral sneer lighting up my eyes. Heavy breaths strained my chest as I wiped the mixture of his blood and mine from my hand.

Both his eyes were swollen shut, and shallow breaths fell from his cracked lips.

"Go home to your wife," I said, shoving his limp and bloody body onto the stone. "And I'll go home to mine."

Except she wasn't my wife.

Not yet.

I wasn't a monster.

A demon, sure.

But I wouldn't force her.

Someday, she would see that I was hers as much as she was mine.

I wasn't known for my patience, but for Willow, I'd wait a lifetime.

Chapter 10

Something unrestrained and dangerous glinted in his eyes. My omega spurred me forward when I wanted nothing more than to run away.

It was too intense. *He* was too intense.

I was drowning in his scent—intoxicating and soothing and disarming. My stomach tumbled, and gooseflesh prickled along my arms.

I couldn't help it. I perfumed.

A needy growl grew louder as he placed the bottle of vodka on the counter.

Despite every instinct telling me it was a bad idea, I closed the distance between us. Shallow gashes spanned his knuckles. I reached out, ghosting my fingers over the wound, but not touching.

I hated seeing him injured. I wanted to take care of him.

The backs of my fingers dusted over his well-kempt beard, the hair coarse against my unblemished skin. A raspy breath rattled in his chest as his eyes darkened, tracking my movements like a panther stalking its prey.

We were a duo of contrasts, and yet, I couldn't help but contemplate how we would mold together. The tip of his tongue slid along his lips as the strong column of his throat bobbed. My hand fell from his face, moving to the silkiness of his tie, rubbing it between my fingertips.

It had been days since I'd seen him, and the memory stitched a fragmented part of me. I always knew I was broken. Unwanted and damaged. But how messed up did I have to be to be drawn to an alpha like Kaelen Finnegan?

My heart galloped like stampeding wild horses. Nibbling on my raw lower lip, I dared to graze my thumb over his bloody knuckles. He didn't hiss or pull away, instead, simply watching me.

"Did you kill someone?"

The hushed question fell from my lips, and I realized I didn't really care what the answer was. I already knew what he was capable of. And it didn't scare me. I felt safer with him than I had with anyone else.

A strand of auburn hair fell over his hardened features, and for the first time, I allowed myself the pleasure of brushing it away.

A shiver danced over his shoulders as his face remained impassive.

"Not tonight."

Nodding, I raked my fingers through his beard, and he groaned. The points of his teeth flashed a brilliant white in the yellow glow of the light over the sink. My fingertips prickled, and every hair stood on end. I turned the faucet on, testing the water temperature before guiding his hand into the stream. He didn't resist, allowing me to clean his injuries properly.

"Why waste vodka when there is water right here?" I scolded, gently working debris out of the wound.

"Apologies, sweetheart. Liquor disinfects as well as cleans."

Blood whooshed in my ears, drowning everything else out. I teetered on a precipice I couldn't come back from. Images from the articles I read flashed in my mind. The newspapers hadn't even published the worst of them, from what I found.

All I knew was that Kaelen Finnegan was dangerous, lethal, and *mine*.

I was certain of it.

The anxious pitter-patter in my chest wasn't because of who he was, but rather, who he was to me.

"But you have killed? That man who was found mutilated outside a club a few years ago—that was you, wasn't it?"

Double jeopardy was in play. Whether he confirmed it or not, didn't matter. He nodded, and I sucked in a breath. With his free hand, he tucked a strand of hair behind my ear, his large hand cupping my face.

"My brilliant omega." A shock zipped through the pads of my fingers as he stroked the swell of my cheek. I leaned into his touch, wanting more of it. All of it. "Does that scare you?"

"No." It really, *really* should, but I had seen far more terrifying things. Kaelen didn't hide who he was. All of him was laid bare for me to see. To take. If I wanted it. "What did he do?"

"Are you asking if he deserved it? Would that make you feel better if he did?" I stiffened, and his hand drifted to my neck, his fingers flexing over my drumming pulse. "What if I told you he owed the Family a debt, and when he didn't pay up, I collected from his flesh?"

I searched his face, annoyed by the expressionless mask.

"Seems a bit extreme. Dead men don't pay."

He snorted.

"True." A darkness settled into the recesses of his eyes. His thumb pushed into my chin, tilting my head back until our gazes met. "He raped Torin's little sister. I made it hurt. He screamed and begged for mercy, still alive when I sliced my knife across his gut."

The grip around my throat tightened, his massive hand squeezing ever so slightly. If anyone other than Kaelen held my neck like this, I'd be on the verge of crying. But with him, I relaxed into his touch, letting his massive palm surround me.

My pulse quickened, and my vision blurred around the edges. He swept along my lip before he released me, leaving a hollow feeling in its wake. I licked my lips, relishing the faint taste of him as I aimlessly brushed the cuts on his hand.

"Now. Tell me again, are you frightened?"

Fingertips pinched my hip, pulling me closer until we were flush. His heart beat steadily beneath my hammering one. His eyes bore into mine—warm and molten—making me melt in his hold. I looked away, now nervous for an entirely different reason.

"No," I mumbled.

"You should be."

The water rinsed clear as I poured it over his scraped knuckles. My thumb traced the tiny cuts, the air between us becoming heavy and making it hard to breathe.

"Did this guy deserve it?" I asked, his scarred hand rough under my fingertips.

Kaelen bracketed my hips and walked me back into the wall. I swallowed a lungful of air, the room getting small too quickly. My vision tunneled on him, my palms splaying across his chest and tracing the taut lines of muscle.

His nose trailed over my pulse, making my breath catch. Was he going to scent-mark me? When his teeth grazed the thin skin near my ear, I mewled. A powerful voice was over me, and pleasure coiled in my belly, slick sticking to my thighs.

"He's lucky I didn't slit him ear to ear. I showed a mercy I am not known for."

"Why?" I asked.

For a moment, he froze, his hands slipping up to my waist as he stroked the jut of my hips. Indecision flashed in his gaze, a vein pulsing in his neck.

"Business," he mumbled. "I promised someone I wouldn't kill him."

"Good to know your word means something."

"It is everything," he said, his voice raspy and strained. "You're everything. Precious. Pretty. Strong."

All the air was sucked out of the room, the space between us charged with an electrifying current by his declaration. I was not on the verge of heat. My pheromones weren't clouding his or my judgment. Every nerve in my body crackled with a sudden, surprising energy.

Warm breath fanned over my lips, his mouth hovering above

mine. A desperate longing curled around my heart, my omega yearning for me to relinquish control, to give in to an alpha. An alpha I could trust. A frigid dread seeped into my bones, whispering warnings, pushing all my fears to the surface.

About to push him away, his hands covered mine. His beard brushed against my face, his lips resting on the corner of my mouth.

"Tell me to stop, mo chroí."

My retort died, burrowing into the depths with all my worst fears. I squashed them down, wanting to bathe in his scent and the beautiful burning sensation that he elicited inside me. My fingers closed around the collar of his shirt, daring to tug him closer. A wide grin split across his lips.

"Don't," I whispered, his breath mingling with mine. "Please. Kaelen. *Alpha.*"

My omega crawled to the surface. So often, I brushed her aside, not wanting to give in to her. I liked to pretend she didn't exist. But for once I wanted to give in to my omega, to Kaelen, and trust an alpha to care for me.

I was tired of doing it on my own.

Two hands cradled my face, so soft, I almost forgot who Kaelen was and what those hands were capable of. He tipped my head back as his lips brushed mine. I braced myself for something demanding, something that mirrored the unyielding way he carried himself, but the press of his lips against mine was unexpectedly gentle.

It was a tender exploration as his tongue coaxed my mouth open, sending a tremor through my small frame. His hands fell to my waist, anchoring me, like he was afraid I'd float away.

A long, shaky exhale fell from me, and fingers dug into me more. His tongue licked inside, deepening the kiss.

"My Willow," he whispered, holding me close.

He tasted of chocolate and whisky, pure decadence on my tongue. It wasn't the forceful claim I expected. It was something far more disarming, something that stirred feelings inside me I didn't know existed.

I bucked my hips forward, moaning when his dick rubbed against my thighs. It had been over a year since I had slept with anyone, and never an alpha. Slick coated my legs, imagining his knot. Teeth dug into the swell of my lip, nipping before he pulled away with a restrained hiss.

Labored breaths heaved in his chest, his eyes pure obsidian. My fingers trailed over my swollen lips, a swirl of emotions making me sway.

"Easy, little omega."

Tears pricked the corners of my eyes, the ice from earlier encasing my heart and closing me off. I should have listened. I should have run.

This was a mistake.

"You don't want me?" I murmured, hope splintering as icy fear eclipsed the delicious heat from only moments ago.

"No. Shite," he hissed, stealing a brief, bruising kiss. "Are you mad? Of course, I want you. You're *mine*. But I want to savor you. Worship you. Court you. I won't treat you like some whore."

As if to punctuate his point, his stubbled cheek brushed against mine, something between a purr and a growl lodging in his throat. I melted in his hold, going lax as he marked me with his scent. I sighed, nudging my cheek against his to return the motion.

His fingers slid through my hair, gripping the strands.

"Do you trust me?"

Such a simple question.

One I should have immediately answered, but I froze. If I admitted it out loud, it would be like giving over the last piece of myself. The most important piece. The one that would give him the power to shatter me.

I was already broken, so why not risk it?

"Yes. I trust you," I whispered, hoping I wasn't making a mistake.

Chapter 11

KAELEN

In the days since I kissed Willow, I walked around with a constant hard-on. My alpha craved our sweet, strong omega. But I vowed to treat her like the queen she was. I hated the distance between us. I wanted nothing more than to carry her into my bed and never let her leave.

She needed time to adjust. I didn't want to overwhelm her.

So I focused on work. Dimitri sent along a mountain of contracts, and Aidan finally uncovered Isabelle Sterling's medical records.

On top of that, a contractor arrived to convert the additional room off the main suite that would serve as Willow's nest. My omega would not spend another heat in anything less than luxury. Regardless of whether she invited me to join her or not.

I assured her I wasn't ignoring her. I didn't want her to question what had happened between us. Our situation was delicate.

Instead, I asked her to join me at one of my casinos tonight. The way her eyes lit up when I confirmed it was a date made the dark place where my heart resided thaw.

Stacks of papers were strewn across my desk as I pulled open the top drawer, patting the velvet box. The first of many courting gifts I would lavish Willow with. I expected her to be difficult and try to refuse them.

Too bad that wasn't an option.

Almost every day, Torin took her to that farm on the outskirts of the city. I peeked through my ajar door as she walked by every night, her delectable scent calling to me like a spider's web to a moth.

Fuck.

I would let her trap and torture me for an eternity.

Muddy, form-fitting jeans hugged her curves with an oversized sweater tossed over her slender torso when she padded by my office. I wanted to peel her out of them, unwrapping her like the gift she was.

Part of me hoped she'd see the open door as an invitation to join me, being as bold as she had been after her heat.

A few times, she lingered outside, never daring to enter, unfortunately.

Every evening, Torin reported on her activities. Things had been quiet. No one paid any attention to her. Granted, she didn't go anywhere public outside of that lunch with her friend. No one knew what she was to me, not yet.

That would change after tonight.

I kept my affairs private, rarely flashing my dalliances out in public. *Oh,* how I couldn't wait to show off Willow, gorgeous vixen that she was.

She liked horses. Rescue animals. Abused ones, rehabilitating them. Apparently, she was quite fond of a black stallion. According to Torin, it was gentle and calm with her, but bristled whenever any alphas got too close. In the last five years, she had worked with more than a dozen horses.

Shaking away my wandering thoughts, I stared unseeing at the contracts from the Bratva, pushing them aside and perusing the surprisingly slim records of Isabelle Sterling. I sent a copy of the medical findings to the head of internal medicine at Boston General. Who also worked for me as my personal physician.

I couldn't make head nor tail of most of it. However, for someone who had been sick for nearly a decade with no diagnosis, there was a disappointing lack of testing done. The most recent doctor dismissed most of Isabelle's symptoms as anxiety.

As I dove in, it appeared she always saw the same two doctors, each as incompetent as the other.

After my eyes went cross-eyed staring at the documents, a questioning knock echoed on the door. My dick stirred.

It was *her*.

My men were gruffer. Rising from my desk, I placed my palms flat on the finished oak. A whiff of her sweet spring scent flittered into my office, and my nails dug into the wood, leaving indents in the custom lacquer.

"Come in."

A swirl of sapphire material stepped over the threshold, and my entire body seized, pushing all the air from my lungs. My hands flexed, veins popping on the thin skin there.

Willow strode in, her white teeth burrowed in her lush lower lip, looking shy and uncertain.

That wouldn't fucking do. My omega was a queen, and she would act as such.

The image of the bold omega in the haze of her heat flooded to the surface. I would show her how to always be that. Confident and commanding. My omega could be nothing else. I had seen flashes of it, and it wasn't only her omega who was bold. Willow stood toe to toe against her father, even me, the night she first arrived here.

I would tend to her like the strong flower she was, watering and helping her flourish into the gorgeous blossom that she tried to hide. Maybe it was a learned behavior, something she did to protect herself.

My sweet, sweet girl.

Soon, she would learn that she didn't cower.

No, men would fear her, bow to her word.

As mine, the city of Boston would be hers to command.

My dick ached in my trousers, hard and desperate to be buried inside her. How could it not when the embodiment of Rhiannon stood before me? Willow, a goddess reborn, the essence of strength and resilience.

My goddess. My omega. My *everything*.

My instincts itched beneath the surface, driving me to provide and protect my precious omega.

The light from the setting sun illuminated her in a golden glow, highlighting the line of freckles that disappeared beneath the chiffon hanging off her shoulders. Her dark hair bounced elegantly with each step she took, the ends brushing her collarbone and hinting at the cobalt highlights hiding underneath.

With the desk still between us, she stopped, the silver kitten heels poking out from the long slit that exposed the length of her tanned leg. I wanted to drop to my knees and run my tongue over it before sinking into that beautiful cunt of hers.

Keeping my eyes locked on hers, my lips twitched when she didn't look away. I fiddled with the drawer, removing a narrow case wrapped in black velvet. Her gaze darted to the box as I closed in on her.

The alluring scent of hers invaded every fiber of my body. The corner of my mouth lifted, my tongue running along the points of my teeth. I leaned in, my hot breath sending a pretty flush over the tops of her breasts as I chuckled in her ear.

"You are stunning, mo chroí. If I hadn't promised to take you to the casino, I would take you to my bed instead."

A small sound rolled from her lips, and I couldn't tell if it was a squeak or a moan, maybe both. Whatever it was, it spurred me on.

Silken strands of hair slid through my fingers as I palmed her head, marking her with my scent. She would know she was mine. And so would everyone else.

I nudged the gland on her neck, my dick rock hard as the source of her scent consumed me. I feathered a gentle kiss over her pulse, my arm banding around her waist to support her when her knees buckled.

"What—What does it mean? Mo chroí."

I pulled back, cupping her cheek in my free hand. "My heart."

Despite her attempt to school her features, I didn't miss the slight parting of her lips or the subtle widening of her eyes. Oh, the power that Willow wielded over me was dangerous, if she ever realized it.

I tugged at the cuffs of my shirt, adjusting my suit jacket. The tip of her pink tongue darted out to wet her lips as she eyed the package in my hand, curiosity replacing the apprehension in her jeweled eyes.

"Turn around," I whispered, the command no less imposing as I twirled my finger.

A defiant gleam twinkled in her eyes, and fuck if it didn't make my already hard cock ache more. I wondered whether she would refuse me. Part of me wanted her to.

Pursing her lips, she huffed, reluctantly doing as she was told.

I crowded her back, towering over her. The backs of my knuckles brushed along her arm as I tucked her hair behind her ear. A thick wave of her scent clouded my senses as Willow perfumed. My lips rested against her temple.

"Good girl," I cooed, relishing the keening noise she treated me with. "This is for you."

The latch on the velvet box clicked as I opened it, removing the platinum necklace. The morning after our kiss, after Willow confirmed she trusted me, I went out and bought the present, working with the same jeweler that my father used for decades. I told my omega that I would court and worship her, and I did nothing in halves.

All omegas adored gifts, but I had a feeling my omega would be annoyingly stubborn, and she did not disappoint. I clipped the necklace around her slender neck, my fingers gliding over her creamy skin as I draped the brilliant sapphire stone at the hollow of her throat.

"You can't give me this," she shrieked, tracing over the glittering gem. "It's obscene."

Her face betrayed her words. While she tried to hide it, I didn't miss the way her eyes sparkled. She struggled with the joy it brought her to receive a gift from me, nervous about what it implied.

"Do you think you can tell me what I can and can't give you, Willow?"

"Yes," she said, a furrow creasing between her brows as she glared at me.

Pride swelled within me as I kept my face stone-still, matching her glower. Warmth turned to desire, all my blood rushing south.

There she was. My queen.

Flames danced in her eyes as she crossed her arms, making her tits strain against the delicate material covering them.

Technically, she was not wrong.

Everyone believed omegas were beneath alphas, the weakest of the designations, but nothing could be further from the truth. Anyone who had seen a true mated alpha and omega knew omegas had their alphas wrapped around their fingers.

A bonded alpha would level a city to protect their omega, would drop to their knees to please them.

Willow had never seen that type of devotion. The only reference she had was her parents, and based on what I found, their relationship was abusive. I didn't know if she knew of any other mated pairs. Probably not, given how skittish she was. Not only around me, but all alphas, it seemed. I wish my parents were still alive, so I could show her what it meant to be bonded to your mate.

Bracketing her hips, I spun her around to face me.

"It is a courting gift, Willow. Will you still deny it?"

I had a feeling she didn't connect the two at first. While she didn't admit it, I knew my Willow had never been courted before by an alpha. Every instinct told her to brush away my gift, to refuse it. But once I confirmed what she didn't dare to expect, realization flittered across her features. Her mouth moved, but no sound came out.

"I will be so good for you. That is my promise to you. I will cherish you like you deserve. My scent calls to you, as yours does to me. Don't withhold what you want because you are frightened. You said I didn't scare you."

If anyone found out about me begging an omega to accept me, I would bury them alive. A tiny, hollow laugh fell from her as hair spilled over her delicate collarbone. When her eyes found mine again, they glittered with a beautiful resolve that made my alpha roar with delight.

"I never said that," she breathed, and I arched a brow.

She stepped forward, fusing our bodies together as she dug a finger into my chest.

"I said," she paused, poking me, "what you *did* didn't scare me. *You,* you terrify me. Your scent, your eyes, everything about you is intoxicating, and I'm afraid of what I feel, afraid of what this all means. Afraid of getting hurt."

The last declaration was barely audible as she mumbled the words, her hand falling limp at her side. Tension hung in the air, her scent taking on a slight burned tinge. I tightened my hold on her waist to keep her from running. All the muscles in her body seized, and I did the only thing I could.

I purred.

Never once had I purred for an omega. Willow would be my first and my last. The rumble grew in my chest, my scent thickening.

After a beat, she relented, perfuming as her body went limp in my hold. I pressed my lips to the top of her head, closing my eyes and focusing on the lulling rumble that soothed my omega. Cold hands wrapped around my neck when she murmured into me.

"Okay."

"Okay, what?" I asked, tipping her chin up with two knuckles.

"I'll accept your courting gift."

My hand slid to her throat, my fingers wrapping around it as I applied gentle, reassuring pressure. Nothing in her posture or features hinted at her not liking it. The pad of my thumb slid up to her chin.

"You understand what this means?" I asked.

"It means we're dating."

"*Oh,* my sweet omega. It is so much more than dating. The world will know you are mine. My enemies will see it and know that touching you is stirring a slumbering dragon. My men will see it and will follow your commands second only to my own. And you, mo chroí, you will feel it in the very beating of your heart— the devotion of an alpha who has chosen you."

A bead of sweat trickled off her brow, her pulse pounding against the thin skin of her neck. A heady wave of her arousal cut through our scents, and my alpha demanded that I claim our omega.

Without waiting for a response, I fused my lips to hers, taking what I wanted. Gone was the gentleness from earlier. I demanded entrance, licking into her drinking down her tiny moans. My teeth nipped at her plush lips, leaving them swollen and red when I pulled away.

"Now, let me show off my omega."

I ran my fingers through the silken strands of her hair before threading her fingers with mine. Her tiny hand fit beautifully in mine. As it should. We were made for each other. Our scents blended beautifully, and soon she would know how our bodies molded to one another.

The icy glaze around her eyes melted, leaving a twinkling brightness in its wake. A beaming smile looked up at me as she grasped my hand, following me out to the waiting car.

"Yes, Alpha," she said in a velvety voice.

I was utterly fucked.

Chapter 12

I picked at the skin on my cuticles, watching the city lights reflect off the river. Torin drove while Aidan sat silently in the passenger seat, his hand reaching out for Torin's, making my brows raise. If I hadn't been so distracted, my curiosity would have gotten the better of me.

How long had Kaelen's brother and my shadow been seeing each other?

Instead, my mind raced, every horrible scenario playing out like a movie. How long before Kaelen's mask fell? Now that I had accepted his offer, it was only a matter of time. While I panicked, my omega mewled, sated and pleased with our choice in alpha.

Deep down, I wanted to be as content as my omega was, but being complacent would only get me hurt.

One way or another.

My fingers closed around the sapphire, holding it in place. The smooth gem anchored me to the present. For too long, I had distanced myself from what I craved. I could blame my omega all I wanted, but the truth was, I wanted it to.

Some omegas found relationships with betas fulfilling.

I didn't.

Every time I tried, it did nothing to heal the icy space where my heart was.

Nothing did.

Until I met Kaelen.

It was like the sun peeking through cloudy skies for the first time in years. I almost hadn't realized how much darkness I kept myself in until then—when his scent calmed my ever-present, prickling fear.

It was terrifying how certain my omega was that he was our alpha. Within the first few minutes alone with him, she knew. Maybe someday I would have that certainty too. Kaelen already seemed to. I hoped he would be patient with me.

I had time. We were only courting. Most courtships lasted at least a year or more. I could take things at my own pace. I trusted he wouldn't rush me.

After I begged him during my heat to knot to me, I knew he was different. Any other alpha would have joined me in my nest, taking my omega's pleas as consent enough.

Yet, he didn't.

I vaguely remember the pain etched on his face when he asked Aileen to take care of me. He fought every alpha impulse to claim and protect.

Callused fingers brushed over my thigh, slipping under the slit of my dress and palming my leg. The electrifying touch snapped me from my musing, my heart galloping.

"Deep breath, Willow. You're safe with me. I promise," Kaelen murmured, stroking the sensitive skin, sending a jolt of pleasure to my center. "Have you ever been to a casino before?"

"Are you trying to distract me?"

"Is it working?"

"Yes," I said, secretly loving that he was already attuned with my needs. "And no, I've never been gambling. Do people usually get this dressed up to throw away their money?"

"At my casino, yes. It is exclusive and underground. Every person who steps foot through the door is vetted before being allowed in."

The car stopped in front of a rowdy pub lined with patrons in Sox gear. My eyes flicked to Kaelen, my confusion apparently evident on my face.

"Not everything is as it seems."

Without another word, he threaded his fingers through mine, helping me out of the sedan as Torin opened the door. He stroked the gland on the inside of my wrist, making me shiver.

The streets were loud with the sounds of blaring car horns and distant shouts. Kalen tucked me into his side like I was something precious to be hidden away from the world.

And for a minute, I actually believed it.

Inside the pub, cheers erupted at our entrance. Beer sloshed over overfilled glasses as a sea of people clad in Red Sox garb shouted at the TVs mounted on the walls. Somebody had hit a walk-off home run, and the pub was devolving into chaos around them.

Kaelen hugged me tighter, his massive palm splayed across the span of my ribs as he maneuvered us toward an unassuming door behind the bar. A bleached-blonde beta with long, tanned legs and perky tits slung drinks across the bar, easily fending off handsy, drunk men.

"Mr. Finnegan," she said with a thick Irish lilt, her eyes widening when she caught me tucked under his arm. "And who is this pretty thing?"

A possessive flare overpowered him, even if any real malice was lacking in his gaze. This woman either had a death wish or knew how to push Kaelen's buttons without going too far.

"Carmen," he grumbled, annoyed by her amusement. "This is Willow."

"Pleasure," she said, dipping her chin before cursing at a guy trying to climb the bar. "Maybe you can keep him in line. Have fun tonight, Willow."

Before I could talk to her, Kaelen steered me out of the way of a group of screaming men.

"Who was that?"

"Carmen. She runs all our legitimate pubs throughout the city. Even on her best days, she's bothersome."

"Then why does she work for you?"

"Because she's tough as nails. Doesn't take any bullshite from anyone, and above all, is discreet. She knows how to balance the front of house with the silent businesses in the background. She is also my cousin on my ma's side. So I'm stuck with her, like it or not."

While he rubbed a slow circle on my hip, he pressed his other hand to a scanner by the door. It lit up in a bright shade of green as the sound of a lock clicking echoed over the din of the bar. Kaelen escorted me over the threshold into a dimly lit hallway that eerily reminded me of those last walks I saw death row inmates take in movies.

My pulse jumped. My fingers grew cold, and I hated how quickly I was plunged into a fake reality. Anxiety knotted in my chest, making me believe things that weren't true. I trusted Kaelen as much as I worried it was a mistake. I felt the thrum of it in my heart. Unfortunately, my mind played tricks on me, not allowing me to have joy.

It had to be too good to be true.

At least that's what my traitorous thoughts said. I didn't deserve happiness or peace. So something must have been wrong.

"Willow?" he said, his rich Irish lilt cutting through my insidious musings. "Speak to me."

The command in his voice teetered on the edge of a bark. It should have made the hairs on my skin prickle, but it didn't. His scent thickened around us. The blend immediately calmed the tingling in my fingers.

"It's dark here," I muttered, trying to make sense of what about the space unnerved me.

It was hard to articulate. I wasn't exactly sure, but I had a feeling it was an intended consequence, and that the entrance to his casino was designed to do exactly that.

"Are you afraid of the dark?" he asked, no malice in his tone.

"No. It's just… It's unnerving. Maybe that's your intention, to make your guests on edge before they arrive?"

His heavy footsteps stopped as he turned to face me. Rough hands slid along my face, burrowing into the hair at my nape. His thumb rubbed a spot at the base of my skull, making my body go lax.

"Technically, yes. Only a handful of people can open the door that leads to this hall. Anyone wishing to access this location needs to be screened before they're even allowed entry. I did want to remind them of their place when coming here."

"And is that what you're doing? Reminding me of my place, Alpha?"

I hissed his designation, instantly knowing I had made a mistake. The first alpha I put my trust in, and of course it was the head of the Irish mafia. My heart thumped at the catastrophic choice I made. I was trapped.

No one walked away from this decision.

"Never," he said, his eyes blazing with fury as an auburn strand of hair fell over his brow. "When will you understand, Willow? I would drop to my knees and worship you at your feet. I do not wish to control you. I want to cherish you, revere you. You are the only person in this world that holds any power over me."

Emotion choked me as I tried to speak but failed. I didn't know what to say. My omega wailed a pathetic sound, angry at me for ruining everything... again. I was incapable of letting the icy tendrils of fear around my heart melt completely. I was destined to be alone, moving from one unfulfilling relationship to the next.

Large hands bracketed my hips, holding me steady.

"Mo chroí, I promise, once we get inside, you will feel better. But if you would prefer, we can go home and I will make you dinner and we can watch a movie. I only want you to feel safe in my arms." His voice dropped to a deadly whisper. "And I promise that I will gut whoever made you feel like this."

My blood should have run cold at his words, but instead they emboldened me, steeling my heart and mind, protecting me from myself.

For too long, I had let my fears control me, and I was tired. Even though I wouldn't admit out loud, I had been looking forward to this ever since Kaelen mentioned taking me out. He spoiled me with pretty dresses and jewels. He wanted to show me off, and I wanted to let him.

"I want to spend our evening out. I'm sorry if I ruined it."

The only other times I got to get dressed up and shown off were when my father dragged me to some dinner or charity event, and those were the furthest thing from fun. I expected spending time with Kaelen at a casino to be far more enjoyable.

"Never apologize, Willow. You could never ruin anything, my pretty omega. You make everything better."

He kissed a spot behind my ear, his breath tickling my face. Something primal flashed in his jade eyes, making my insides melt.

At the end of the narrow hall, we arrived in front of a plain door with a towering alpha guarding it. Day-old scruff covered his scarred face, with a gun holstered under his jacket.

"Boss. Miss Sterling," he grunted, dipping his chin as his eyes lit up. "Enjoy your evening."

Kaelen leveled an icy stare at the man.

All the color drained from his face. He stepped aside, murmuring an apology before giving us access to an elevator. I saw the briefest flash of fear in his hazel eyes.

A possessive hand pressed to the small of my back, ushering me inside. There was only one option. I pushed the button, pleased at the warmth returning to Kaelen's features. A tenderness only I ever got to see.

"What did he do?" I asked as the elevator descended lower than I thought possible.

"He thought he could have what's *mine*. No one. Especially one of my men, can be allowed to entertain that thought."

I wanted to scold him for talking about me like some sort of toy he refused to share, but my omega hissed at me, loving the attention. I bit my lip, realizing I liked it more than I cared to admit. Besides, that alpha wasn't interested in me. He was being nice.

Sam always told me that alphas were more needy than omegas. They constantly needed reassurance. Usually, I snorted at her, mumbling something about that being ridiculous.

She may not have been too far off.

"I don't want anyone else," I said, dragging my nails through his thick beard, grinning at the way his eyes darkened. "I only want you, Alpha."

He leaned into my touch, breathing deeply into my palm as he held it in place. I dragged the tip of my nose along his jaw, ensuring he smelled of me. A possessive growl rumbled against my skin.

Lips brushed along the skin as he peppered fleeting kisses along my lifeline.

"It's not you I'm worried about. It's any alpha with a dick or a pussy who catches a whiff of your pretty scent and thinks they even remotely have a chance with you. Anyone who thinks they can take you from me will find out why I am called The Butcher of Boston."

My stomach swooped. Not out of fear, but thrilled at the proposition that someone cared about me enough to do such a thing.

Maybe that made me a demon if I was willing to dance with the devil.

Maybe I didn't care.

Chapter 13

WILLOW

My jaw dropped when the elevator opened. I had never been to a casino before, but I'd seen them in movies. The entrance opened like the maw of a cave, revealing something more marvelous than I had imagined. Exposed brick mingled with polished mahogany. Emerald, velvet-lined, bespoke card tables, each guest seated there more lavishly dressed than the last.

Brass lamps illuminated the colorful space, casting shadows along the vaulted ceilings, making it impossible to tell where the game started and ended.

Waitresses in glittering gowns, draped with diamonds, moved effortlessly through the crowds, handing out champagne. When we left, I worried I might have been overdressed, but nothing had been further from the truth.

Guests wore Dior and Chanel, their jewelry more expensive than most people's mortgages. Familiar faces of actors and athletes filled the space. The sound of chips clinked in the distance as Kaelen whispered something to Aidan before he disappeared into the crowd, leaving Torin with us.

"Where'd you two come from?" I asked Torin, trying to calm my racing heart.

They followed us into the pub, but I hadn't seen them after Kaelen took us through the fingerprint door.

"Industry secret, Miss Willow," Torin winked, and I rolled my eyes.

"Mr. Finnegan. What can I get for you and your guest this evening?"

A pretty server blinked at us.

"I'll take a Macallan. Neat. What would you like, mo chroí?" he asked, his hand drifting to my neck and curling around it possessively.

I nibbled my lip. I rarely drank. Tonight, however, I wanted to indulge, to let go and enjoy myself. Other than going to the farm or the animal shelter, I didn't go out. Not to clubs and certainly not illegal casinos. I couldn't risk damaging William Sterling's *glittering* reputation.

"Something fruity. I don't really want to taste the alcohol," I said, feeling like a child at the request.

"Whatever you want," he whispered, his breath lingering on my skin. "A strawberry daiquiri with half a shot."

The woman nodded, disappearing into the crowd. Aidan returned, passing Kaelen an obsidian, velvet pouch, which he tucked away in the pocket of his suit pants. As Kaelen steered me through the crowds, the sea of people parted to make way for us. Whether out of fear or respect, I wasn't sure.

"What would you like to play?" he asked, the backs of his knuckles ghosting over my arm.

Outside of the slot machines, I had no idea how any of the games worked. People sat around tables while dealers dressed in custom suits slung cards and took bets. Electronic tables lit up as people cheered and booed at a ball skittering around a wheel.

Large stacks of chips filled the tables, some towering dangerously tall. Sweat slid down my back, reminding me how out of place I felt.

"I don't have any money," I said, only expecting to wander around with him and take in the ambience.

A laugh whispered over my skin as he cupped my chin, pulling me in for an unexpected kiss. My body relaxed at his touch almost instantly, my lips parting for him. His tongue slid along mine, taking more and more until I almost forgot where we were.

"Don't worry about the chips, mo chroí. I will handle that part. What game looks fun? What do you want to try?"

"Blackjack," I said, regurgitating the name of the one game I knew. "But I don't know how to play. I don't want to embarrass you."

A shyness burned my cheeks, the blush getting worse when Kaelen flashed a brilliant white smile at me. His fingers tracked a tantalizing trail under my freckles.

"This is my casino. You could never embarrass me. I could shut down this entire floor this instant and have the dealers walk you through every game while I kicked everyone else out."

"Please don't," I blurted, panicking.

"I won't. Instead, I'll show you how to play."

Kaelen led me to a large oak table draped in lush velvet. Everything down to the seating was decadent, catering to the obscenely wealthy. A small sign on the right side of the table noted the minimum bet as $100. I paled, my fight-or-flight instinct taking over. I couldn't lose that much money on one hand.

"Kaelen," I hissed. "You have to be joking. Is there a beginner's table or something?"

"This is the beginner's table," he smirked. "All the others have minimum bets starting at $500 or more."

My eyes widened at the stupid, smug expression on his lips. His beautiful lips that I wanted to drag my tongue over. I internally cursed my omega and her horny thoughts.

Now was not the time, not when I could lose thousands of dollars in minutes.

I ignored the feeling of cotton in my mouth, irritated by the equally amused looks on Aidan and Torin's faces. I glowered at them, and they at least had the decency to look abashed.

"Fine. I'll play one hand."

"No," Kaelen said, his voice a silken demand that did terrible things to my panties. "You'll play as much as you want. Come."

Like some sort of king lounging over his subjects, Kaelen lowered himself into the empty chair at the center of the blackjack table, pulling me into his lap. I squeaked, squirming against his hold for only a second before I gave up my frivolous assault.

I went limp in his hold. A strong hand slid along my navel, palming my belly as his other hand pushed my hair aside, nipping at the sensitive skin there.

Fine.

If he wanted to play king, then I'd be the queen on my sexy alpha throne.

"That's my good omega." I wiggled slightly, and he groaned, his nails digging into my flesh. "Don't," he warned.

A queen with a praise kink and soaked panties.

His hardening length poked at the seam of my ass. I debated teasing him further when the waitress from earlier appeared, handing a lowball glass with crystal amber liquid to Kaelen, and a pretty pink drink to me.

A mix of lime and strawberries danced over my tongue as I took a sip, a quiet moan falling from my lips. Kaelen grinned, enjoying my noises. I wriggled happily, thrilled that I couldn't taste any hint of the rum that hid in the drink.

With a thud, Kaelen deposited the black velvet pouch on the table, fishing out an equally dark chip and sliding it into my palm. My hands felt so small when dwarfed by his.

"If you want to play in the hand, you'll need to place your chip here." He pointed to a small betting circle marked on the table.

Deciding not to argue with him, I placed the dark chip in the spot, grinning up at the stone-faced dealer. Creases formed around his mouth, giving away his hardened façade. The dealer handed out two cards to everyone, including himself, showing one and hiding the other.

"The goal is simple, get closer to twenty-one than the dealer without going over and you win," he said, drawing aimless circles over my navel, distracting me.

Everything about him was distracting. His scent, his voice, his taste—how could I possibly concentrate? The dealer's exposed card was a seven and mine was a nine, putting the odds more in my favor. I sneaked a peek at the hidden card, my nose twitching when I saw an eight.

Kaelen's teeth grazed over my pulse point, his murmur vibrating the spot and sending a thrill through me.

"Now you can ask for additional cards as much as you want, but if you go over, you lose. What do you think, mo chroí? Do you want to hit or hold?"

I liked that he didn't tell me what to do, that he gave me the opportunity to make my decision. If I asked for advice, he'd give it to me, but I wanted to try on my own first. I had a seventeen as it was. If I got another card, I'd probably go over, and the chances of the dealer having a better hand than me were slim.

"I'll stay," I said, shifting slightly and taking another sip of the sweet pink drink.

A few people around the table went over, while the dealer held too. When he flipped the cards, I shrieked, jumping out of Kaelen's lap and giggling when I won. The dealer smiled, pushing me my winnings.

"Well done, Miss."

I turned, beaming up at Kaelen, who stared at me like I was a rare painting to be admired. My cheeks burned, my stomach doing a weird swooping thing.

"Look at you," he cooed, brushing his thumb over the swell of my lower lip, and I debated sucking it. "My brilliant girl."

"Can we do it again?"

"As many as you want, mo chroí," he said, his Irish brogue thicker than usual. "We never close."

I lost count of how many hands I played, growing ever more aware of Kaelen's knot nudging at me. He refused to let me out of his lap, getting me a virgin Shirley Temple after I finished the daiquiri.

It didn't take much to get me tipsy, and I felt it after that drink. I wanted to keep my wits about me. As much as was possible with Kaelen's dizzying touches driving me to the brink of madness. My core burned with need, my thighs sticky with slick by the time we made it to the roulette wheel.

Apparently, I had won more than I lost, because Kaelen kept mentioning how he was going to reward me when we got home. Even if it was nothing more than beginner's luck.

"You are doing so well, Willow," he murmured, his chest against mine, caging me in against the roulette table. "My omega deserves to reap in the spoils of her victory."

"If you don't say yes to him, honey, I will." A drunk redhead winked beside me.

An unfamiliar emotion curled behind my sternum, boiling over until I let out a threatening snarl, my omega at the forefront. I spun on the woman, batting away Kaelen's tattooed forearm like it was a bothersome gnat.

"Don't," I whispered in a voice I didn't recognize. "He is *my* alpha. Do not dare think about what's *mine.*"

A struggled sound choked her as she sputtered on her wine, spilling some onto her Chanel dress that washed her out. Her muddy eyes got too wide for her face before she threw her hands up, slowly backing away. The faint scent of lemon tinged the air, making her smell like a burned tart.

"Apologies. I was only joking."

"Leave," I hissed, vaguely aware of Kaelen's hand on my hip.

He waved the woman off without a word, jutting his chin in Torin's direction.

Torin stepped between us, escorting the woman out of the casino. The people nearby were oddly quiet, everyone watching the scene unfold. My chest heaved with labored breaths, my body shaking with a surge of jealousy.

It felt *good.*

Good to want something so much. To crave him and claim him.

Those dark emerald eyes focused on me, and only me. Kaelen urged me closer, his warm palms ghosting over my ribs before landing on my hips.

"What a good girl, making sure everyone knew I was your alpha," he soothed. "Let me take you home, mo chroí. Let me take care of you like you deserve."

It *almost* sounded like he was begging, pleading with me as I had with him a few nights ago.

My fingers dug into the lapels of his suit jacket, yanking him close enough to taste the remnants of whisky and something sweet on his breath. His tongue swept over the points of his teeth as he disarmed the last of my defenses.

"Alpha," I said, not caring who heard us. "I need you."

Chapter 14

WILLOW

The street lights muddled into a blur as we sped through the city. I barely registered the moment Kaelen pushed the door open, my mind a haze being pulled further under by the thickening cloud of our pheromones.

Without waiting for him, I surged forward, jumping into his arms and wrapping my legs around his waist and my arms around his neck. A hand slid under my ass, holding me as he carried me through the grounds. I hid my flushed face in his collar at the nod from the two men guarding the front door as he walked us inside.

"Needy omega," he said, his teeth grazing my earlobe. "Tell me what you want and I'll give it to you. I'll give you everything."

"You," I moaned, scratching his expensive suit jacket, wanting it out of my way.

"Oh, you have me. All of me, mo chroí."

Something in my belly tightened at his declaration. To the world, I appeared as a sophisticated, spoiled rich girl who mooned over my senator father with pretty doe eyes. Only because that was what my dad wanted people to think.

In reality, I didn't have much to call my own. All by his design.

The truth in Kaelen's words stirred a passion inside me, igniting a spark that caught flame and consumed me like a dying phoenix.

He took the stairs two at a time, making me giggle with his urgency. We passed my room, instead moving through the door at the end of the hall. My mouth parted in a small O when we entered his bedroom.

A muted gray colored the walls, while everything else was adorned in forest greens and rich burgundies. Along the center of the far wall stood a grand four-poster bed, draped in shining silk sheets and heavy damask blankets.

My omega was desperate to burrow beneath the bedding and mark it with her scent.

Above the bed, a chandelier cast a glow, mimicking the flames sputtering from the unpolished stone fireplace.

Kaelen placed me on the bed, and I scrambled to my knees, the skirt of my sapphire gown pooling around my legs and exposing my thigh. He stood there, watching me, like a king surveying his kingdom.

I crawled around the bed, smiling as he followed my movements. Silk slid under my fingertips as I splayed them in the sheets before rearranging the mountain of pillows. They were too tidy and organized, too sterile. I burrowed into one, lighting up at the scent of my alpha. I turned, about to ask him for his shirt to add to it, pausing when his piercing stare pinned me to the spot.

"Are you nesting, little omega?" he asked, crossing his thick, tattooed forearms.

Something twinkled in his eyes, like the early morning sun bouncing off the maple leaves. The hint of a smirk appeared, slowly unweaving the tight coil of uncertainty in my belly.

Outside of my heat, I didn't nest. Not really. Never had the instinct. I was a useless omega. Around this man, however, it became second nature to build the perfect place for us. A cozy spot drenched in our scents where he would knot me and make me his.

"Oh. Um. No. Maybe," I added, freezing with a decorative

pillow clutched between my greedy fingers.

Chuckling at my expense, he crawled onto the bed, the mattress sinking under his weight. I licked my lips, slick pooling in my panties. My pussy clenched, and I choked down a pathetic whine. He gently tugged my abused lip free of my teeth. My chest ached, each breath more painful than the last, with a stabbing need for this alpha to claim me.

A voice in the back of my head told me he didn't want me. Why would he want a broken omega who didn't even know how to build a proper nest?

"Go ahead, mo chroí. Make this place ours. So I can knot that tight cunt of yours until you're screaming my name."

I squeaked, my eyes so wide they watered. His filthy words stoked something primal in me. Shadows from the fire danced along his back, making him look like the devil shrouded in smoke. I would sin at his altar, lay myself bare as my confession until he drained every last drop of purity from me.

"Can I have your shirt?" I asked, already tugging at the collar.

He chuckled, the sound warming me like coffee on a winter morning. He spread his arms wide, like an offering. Taking it as permission, I yanked off his jacket, wiggling my ass as I threaded it into a spot between the wall of pillows.

Blood thundered in my ears as my fingers hovered over the buttons of his shirt. My nipples pebbled, straining against the thin material of my dress. Two knuckles slid under my chin, tilting my head back, his eyes almost black.

"Take it off, Omega," he commanded, his velvety voice almost sinful in the orange glow of the fire.

"Yes, Alpha," I said, unable to deny him anything when he looked at me like I was the reason for the moon and stars.

With shaky hands, I slowly exposed the expanse of muscled, tattooed skin, littered with scars. Some old. Some fresh.

Nesting now forgotten, I pushed the material off him, mesmerized by the stories woven into his skin. His hands rested on my arms, playing with the thin straps there.

"Let me see you," he said, his demand raw and teetering on the verge of desperation.

My anxiety spiked, almost making me forget what hid underneath my pretty dress. No one had ever seen them. My fingers traced over the spot below my collarbone. I always wore shirts when I slept with anyone else, or insisted that the lights stayed off.

It wouldn't help much in this case. Not with the firelight. Best to get it over with. The quicker he realized I wasn't what he thought, the better. It meant less time for me to get attached to him. I nodded, the motion jittery as his fingers found the zipper. He dragged it down, each second more drawn out than the last, feeling like a condemned person on my walk to the gallows.

With the zipper down, he fisted the hem of the dress, pulling it over my head, exposing me to him. I hadn't worn a bra, couldn't with the material. All that was left between me and Kaelen was a pair of black lace panties.

For one hopeful second, I thought he might not notice, that he might claim my lips in a passionate kiss.

But no, I wasn't so lucky.

All at once, the desire on his face twisted into something chilling as his nostrils flared and the vein in his neck throbbed. His fingers flexed, his knuckles turning white as he made to touch the marks below my clavicle.

I shrunk away at the motion, and he froze, the two of us suspended in this bleak reality. I couldn't take it. My eyes focused on the blanket I was shredding between my fingers.

"Feel like you were defrauded?" I chuckled, so I wouldn't cry. "Damaged goods. I'll go back to my room."

Making to leave, I covered my breasts, shame staining my freckled skin. Who was I kidding? How could an alpha like him ever want someone like me?

"No." The weight of his words rattled the pictures on the walls, his bark curling around his words and rooting me to the spot. I froze, my eyes stinging. "Who did this to you?"

Acid burned my throat, the taste metallic on my tongue. My hand splayed over the scars and burn marks, trembling. Every time I tried to speak, nothing came out. I couldn't say it. It didn't matter. He knew the answer.

"Please. Don't make me say it," I whispered, guilt making my voice wobble.

Too gently, Kaelen forced my watery gaze to meet his. He brushed away my tears, his lips resting on my temple as he wrapped his arms around me, holding me snugly against him.

"Please, Omega, let me. He doesn't deserve to live."

Venom and authority clung to every word, his face etched into a beautiful mask of destruction.

My whole world froze as Kaelen Finnegan—The Butcher of Boston—begged for my permission. Deep down, I wanted to tell him yes, to ask him to do it tonight. Sometimes I worried I would never be free of my dad.

"You can't," I sniffed. "My mom, she's too fragile. If my dad died. I don't think she'd survive the severing of their bond. She's too weak."

A mate bond was a powerful thing. When an alpha or omega died, the surviving mate struggled, the bond growing cold in their chest like a phantom limb. Some passed of heartache soon after the loss of their mate if they were older or ill, unable to push forward. Most recovered, but I knew my mom wouldn't be so lucky, not in the state she was in.

And selfishly, I needed my mom.

I wasn't ready to say goodbye.

I'd suffer my father if it meant I got to keep her.

His chest rattled with a divine purr, making me cry harder as I clung to him. An alpha's purr was a sacred thing, shared between mates. When he'd done it after giving me the courting gift, I was too stunned to appreciate it. But now, it made me feel special, treasured in a way I never thought I would be.

"Is that the only thing stopping you?" he asked, tucking a piece of hair behind my ear.

I leaned back slightly, putting enough space between us so I could see his face. Strong hands moved over my arms in confident, soothing strokes. My eyes shifted back and forth as I processed his question. No matter how long I searched, there was no love left in me for William Sterling.

"Yes. But it's a big thing, Kaelen. I won't waver on that."

"I understand, Willow," he said, drawing patterns on my arm.

"If I can find a way to help her, will you allow it?"

"You don't strike me as someone who asks anyone for permission."

"Only from you, Omega. I told you. You own me, mo chroí."

Blood never bothered me. Pain was a spectrum, and I wasn't afraid to give it as much as I got.

When I was younger, I thought making myself small and quiet would get my dad to leave me alone. I was wrong. So, as I got older, I pushed him, slapped him, spit on him, anything to remind him I hated him.

A weird sensation swooped through my stomach, the image of Kaelen making William Sterling suffer even a fraction of what he made me. It would be ironic. The man he tried to sell me to win him the election, snuffing the lights from his eyes.

There was something poetic about it. In a gruesome, Viking Edda kind of way. But maybe if he did, I would finally feel some sense of peace, not always living like I was teetering on the edge of a cliff, afraid of one strong breeze blowing me over.

"If you can ensure my mom is healthy enough to handle the bond being broken, then yes. Kill him."

"Oh, my sweet, innocent omega," he said, capturing my lips in a possessive, claiming kiss. "I won't just kill him. I will torture him for days until he begs me for death. And like the devil I am, I won't grant it to him. I'll drag out his misery until I scatter pieces of him throughout the Charles." The backs of his knuckles traced along my collarbone. "Does that frighten you?"

His lips hovered over mine, his promise hanging in the space between us. Admitting to him I wanted my dad's blood on his hands would push me over the edge of something I could never come back from.

I had my faults, but I never considered myself a killer.

Maybe I wasn't as pure as everyone thought I was.

"No," I said, my voice steady. "It makes me happy." I whispered the confession.

Something dark flared in his features as he tenderly cupped my face. Slick pooled at my center, a whine starting to build.

"Then let me make you happy, mo chroí. Be my good girl and let me absolve you of your sinful thoughts with my tongue between your thighs."

My nails bit into the corded muscles on his forearms.

"Alpha, please."

"You're so pretty when you beg."

A large hand splayed over my belly, gently coaxing me into the pillows. I let him push me down until I was flat on my back, my nipples taut as he raked a slow, assessing trail over my figure as if cataloging every freckle and curve.

My breasts heaved with each strained breath. His knees bumped into my legs, spreading me open. A forearm rested on either of my face, caging me under him. Lips pressed to my cheek before he descended, trailing his tongue over my scars and between the valley of my breasts.

"Made for me. Do you taste as sweet as you smell, Omega?"

The tip of his tongue flicked over my nipple and I let out a keening cry, my back bowing off the bed. He pushed on my stomach, forcing me into the mattress.

"I... I don't know," I breathed. "No one has ever—I mean... I haven't."

"Are you telling me no one else has had the pleasure of drinking from this pretty pussy, mo chroí?"

A finger played with the hem of panties, and I squirmed, canting my hips higher. My body sizzled from head to toe, my omega practically panting at the promise of his mouth on me.

"Please," I begged. "Alpha, I need you."

I wanted to hate what Kaelen Finnegan did to me, bringing my omega urges to the surface. Usually, I fought them. Ignored them.

But it felt too good to give in to them. To submit to my alpha. To let my brain and body rest.

I was always so tired.

"Shhh," he cooed, kissing lower until his mouth rested below my navel, his piercing green eyes staring up at me. Fingers brushed over my hips as he peeled my panties off, the cool air hitting my hot center. "I have you, Willow. I'll take care of you. Can you be patient for me?"

"No," I half-chuckled, half-cried, trying to wiggle my hips.

Nails bit into my flesh, making small crescents appear on the pale skin. I gave up, tossing my hands back onto the blankets and blowing a strand of hair off my face.

The smug bastard had the audacity to smirk at me. A frustrated noise morphed into a whimper as his thumb swept over my clit.

"So responsive," he murmured.

Another retort died on my next breath when he licked his way through my entrance, making my entire body catch fire. He took his time, lazily licking my slick before circling my clit and sucking.

Oh, *fuck.* How did I go so long without this? Whenever death came for me, let it be with Kaelen's tongue worshiping me.

Shit. Shit. Shit.

"More. More," I demanded, not caring if I sounded like a petulant child.

"My lovely omega. You are so good, Willow."

The praise made me gush, and I was too far gone to be embarrassed. He responded to my breathy command by sliding one thick finger into me up to the knuckle. I gasped. The stretch was barely enough to take the edge off. I squeezed around him, and he rewarded me by adding a second digit and curling them.

A shock of pleasure made my entire body seize as he tapped a spot inside that I swore only existed in those raunchy books that Sam loved. He moved his fingers in steady, maddening strokes, growling as he lapped at my slick like it was the most delicious thing he had ever tasted.

Everything burned, the hum more intense than anything I felt in the haze of my heats. My climax heated me from the inside out, the flames of it growing with each torturous motion from Kaelen.

Sweat clung to my brow, my hair sticking to my face.

"Kaelen," I moaned, dragging my nails along his back hard enough to leave marks.

My marks. He was mine. *My* alpha.

"That's it, mo chroí. Say my name while you come for me."

The command buzzed over my sensitive skin and on the next pump of his fingers, I shattered, every self-doubt disappearing as my climax tore through me. A rush of slick coated my thighs and his fingers—the sound wet and lewd.

I sagged, and my body collapsed onto the downy blankets. Kaelen's fingers slowed to a stop as he flicked my clit one final time. Short, ragged breaths stabbed me behind my sternum.

This. This was what omegas talked about when they found their alphas. The passion. The intensity. The *rightness*. Whenever I read stories in magazines about omegas and their alphas, I always rolled my eyes at the absurdity of it all.

There was no such thing as perfect *mates*.

But fuck, if Kaelen Finnegan wasn't doing his best to prove me a liar.

Rough fingers brushed over my navel as Kaelen rested his chin on my stomach. My arousal glistened in his copper beard, his jeweled eyes twinkling with dark specks as he licked my release from his fingers.

"Fucking addicting," he said, never looking away.

My pussy squeezed around nothing, aching at the loss of him. My mind was blissfully blank, my omega at the forefront with a single thought. *Please, Alpha.* I enjoyed it. The lack of responsibility. The lack of anything.

Only pleasure.

Only him.

It had never felt like this before.

Maybe Sam was right—I needed an alpha.

Not all omegas did, but Kaelen's alpha calmed me. And a small—insecure—part of me wasn't ready to acknowledge that it wasn't just Kaelen's alpha, but Kaelen who comforted me.

A shadow slid into my vision, ending my curious musings. Kaelen looked down at me with a hungry, determined stare as his knees settled against my thighs, holding me open. Exposing me. Pieces of hair hung over his face as he sat back on his haunches, straining against his suit pants.

The leather of his belt glided along the fabric as he dropped it to the floor with a thud. Dark-rimmed eyes never left mine as he undid the button and zip, stripping. I tried to ignore the ashy taste as his cock slapped against his stomach.

It was thick and weeping pre-cum. Tattooed fingers curled around the length, fisting it and lazily smearing his arousal down to his knot at the base.

My eyes widened when I saw it, a slight panic growing as I worried about how it would fit. I'd never taken a knot before. With his free hand, he cradled my chin, rubbing my cheek. I perfumed at the touch, and his nose twitched.

"You can take it. You were made for me. Are you ready for my knot, Omega?"

Instinct took over, my omega eager to please.

And so was I. I wanted to make Kaelen feel as good as he made me feel.

My momentary fear was forgotten as my omega demanded that we present for our alpha. I made to roll over onto my stomach when he gripped my hips, stopping me. A pathetic sound trilled in my chest as I clutched Kaelen's arms, still attempting to get on my belly for him.

"No. I want to look in your eyes as I knot your delicious cunt for the first time."

Something malfunctioned in the silence.

I blinked, painfully aware of the ache in my pussy. My omega hissed beneath the surface, and for a moment, I was transfixed on him. I nodded as I scratched my nails through his beard, the coarse hairs grounding me. I reached up, and tugged his bun loose, letting the long copper strands frame his face.

Fuck. He was unfairly gorgeous.

Threads of tension unraveled as I ran my fingers through his hair. He smirked, his eyes glinting with amusement. His tip nudged my pussy, and I squeaked. The next breath stuck in my throat as he sealed his lips to mine.

It started out slow, his motions unhurried and coaxing. I opened for him, the faint taste of my come still on his lips. My hands tugged on his hair, growing more impatient as I tried to take his cock only for him to rock his hips back.

On the next swipe of his tongue, he drew out the final few kisses before nipping at my ear. One hand slid to my nape, holding me while he positioned himself at my dripping core. My legs trembled, my body strung out and needy.

"I want a picture of this," he said, his chest rising and falling with heavy breaths. "You, spread out for me. Glistening with sweat. Sexy as fuck. And mine. Isn't that right, Omega? You're mine."

"Yours," I said, my eyes glazing over.

"Mine," he breathed, sinking into me.

The air was pushed from my lungs as he stretched me. I rocked forward, my head smacking into the solid wall of muscle. He hissed, rolling his hips until he filled me completely.

A string of Gaelic curses fell from him as he stilled inside me, his dick twitching as I fluttered around him. I mewled, his hand holding me to him as I tried to catch my breath.

I was ruined.

There was no way anyone else could ever compare to this.

Kaelen Finnegan destroyed me.

"Willow. I can't… I can't be gentle. You are fucking intoxicating, and I *need* to devour you."

"Then *fucking* devour me, Kaelen. I'm not fragile."

My teeth flashed in a tiny growl, and he pressed a sloppy, fierce kiss to my brow.

"No. You are not. You are strong and ferocious. A banríon."

I didn't know what he called me and I didn't care. I wanted him to move. In one drawn-out movement, he swung his hips back, the head dragging deliciously along my inner walls until only the tip remained.

Then, with one forceful thrust, he sank back in, knocking me back.

"Fuck," I screamed with a broken moan.

"Pretty omega," he groaned, setting a punishing pace that had me digging my nails into the sheets. "So cute when you curse. You feel so good. Like bloody Áine. So tight and warm, squeezing my cock like the greedy girl you are. Is this what you want? What you need? Your alpha stretching this gorgeous cunt?"

Oh, he was depraved. Filthy. And I loved it. Wanted more of it.

My body tensed with each snap of his body, spiraling me closer to a dark abyss I wanted to drown in.

"Are you going to come for me? Take my knot?"

He sounded as undone as I felt.

"Yes. Yes. *Yes*," I chanted, not knowing what I was agreeing to.

Everything coalesced in my abdomen like molten lava, and for one sex-drunk moment I thought I might die from it. What a way to go, at least. When I thought about my death, it was never anything glorious or freeing.

Could someone die from an orgasm?

I might.

It built higher and higher until I exploded with it, detonating around Kaelen like a Fourth of July firework.

I rocked forward, clawing at his back and tugging at his hair. Every muscle in my body seized, my pussy flexing. It spurred him on, his thrusts turning erratic. My legs trembled, cold sweat stinging my skin as his growing knot nudged at my opening.

"Fuck. Yes. Mine," he hissed, slipping between Gaelic and English. "You ready, Omega?"

"Mhhmm," I moaned, still too strung out to form a coherent thought.

"I've got you," he whispered.

Logs sputtered in the fireplace, punctuating the next snap of Kaelen's hips as he sank his knot into me, locking us together. The stretch burned and sparked another climax. I tumbled over the edge, nipping at the Celtic cross tattooed above his heart.

He knocked his head back, his hair spilling down his sweaty back.

Warm ropes of his release spilled inside me. His cock swelled as he chased the feeling, still rocking into me as much as he could as his knot caught on my opening. I whined, falling back onto the bed and shaking.

"Shhh," he whispered, his voice raw as he brushed the sweat-soaked hair off my face.

With us still knotted, he carefully rolled me on top of him, feathering gentle kisses over my brow. He scraped his nails over the column of my spine, making goosebumps erupt on my arms.

He murmured in Gaelic, burrowing into the spot between my collar and jaw. Each word was more reverent than the last. And even though I didn't understand what he said, I didn't need to. I felt each word in the beating of heart, my omega content for the first time.

Ours.

"You did so well for me, Omega," he said, his lips resting on my pulse. Another tiny orgasm overtook me, making me pant a needy sound. "That's it. Such a good girl. Stay with me, mo chroí. Go deo."

"Go deo?" I asked, my heavy eyes closing as I drifted to the sound of his purr lulling me to sleep.

"My heart. Forever."

Chapter 15

KAELEN

Ambient light filtered through the dark curtains as the smoldering ash in the fireplace sizzled. The final dredges of sleep released me, and a slow warmth seeped into my limbs. A small weight lay on top of me. My precious omega slept soundly, her tiny frame rising and falling with every breath.

My dick stirred at the vision, and as much as I wanted to wake her up with me buried inside that sweet pussy of hers, I willed it to calm down. I had too much to do today. Besides, my girl needed to rest. I didn't want to wake her. Not when she looked so peaceful.

Fuck, she was perfect like this. In my bed. Sated from *my* knot.

Careful not to disturb her, I combed my fingers through her hair, pushing it behind her ear. She moaned an adorable, sleepy sound at my touch. Willow's omega accepted me, and I hoped it wouldn't be long before she did too. She was close, but I sensed her hesitation to give in completely.

A snarl bubbled beneath the surface as I remembered the scars on her body. I understood why she was so uncertain around me. I wondered if she had ever seen a healthy relationship between an alpha and omega.

William Sterling was a bastard who abused his daughter.

While I didn't have proof yet, I was confident he was the reason for his wife's health issues. What a pathetic excuse for an alpha, manipulating the omegas in his life. Once I proved it, I would help Isabelle Sterling.

I would care for her like my own mother.

A cold, hard fury settled in my gut, remembering the crisscrossing lines and burns that marred Willow's delicate body. My blood turned to ice, splintering into jagged pieces that made it hard to breathe. A man who was supposed to protect her... injured her, marked her.

My omega.

I closed my eyes, my fists flexing as I pictured his smarmy face. The scowl twisting my features morphed into a violent sneer, envisioning how I'd peel that smirk from him, and watch him piss himself as he pleaded for a mercy that would never come.

He'd bow in front of the devil, and I'd murmur a haunting sound, enjoying his cries of pain.

Eventually, he'd beg for death, and I'd show him the same amount of compassion that he'd shown his daughter.

My heart hammered. I sucked in a sharp breath, burrowing my nose in her hair and drinking in her scent. It doused the blazing rage in my veins like a summer's rain damping a bonfire—still there, but quieter.

A bright blue light lit up on my phone from its spot on the end table. I groaned, easing Willow until she was curled up beside me, tucked safely under the blankets. Immediately, I missed her body snuggled against mine. I left my adorable omega under the comforter while I reluctantly hopped into the shower.

I turned the water a touch too hot, appreciating how it scolded my skin, mirroring my simmering anger. Water dripped off as I slipped into a pair of joggers. I dried my hair, leaving it down as I walked back into the room to get changed.

At my entrance, Willow sat up, her half-lidded eyes roaming

over me. The most beautiful creature ever crafted waited in my bed, the sun haloing her head like the angel she was. Her eyes darkened, nipples tight.

My alpha roared at my omega's approval, and my chest puffed with pride. I never cared about what omegas thought of me, except for Willow.

The blankets pooled around her hips as she stretched with a cute mewling sound, her tits bouncing slightly. Fuck. She was pure sin. And the loose sweats around my hips did nothing to hide how sexy I found her. She giggled the most beautiful, melodic noise, covering her mouth.

"What's so funny, Omega?" I asked, my eyes narrowing as I prowled toward her, my palms pressing into the mattress.

"Trouble, Alpha? Do you need my help?"

A pretty pink tongue darted out to wet her lips and I was tempted to find out how gorgeous she'd look on her knees with my cock in her mouth. Memories of her pussy squeezing my knot made me growl. She'd be my undoing.

My phone dinged again. I hissed, dragging my tongue over the points of my teeth. Reluctantly, I turned my attention away from her, irritation prickling at my nape as I read the message on the screen.

"As tempting as you are, I have to get to work."

Her mouth twisted into an exaggerated frown as she tried to get up. Something pinched in my chest. I gripped her arm, gently holding her in place.

"I'll go back to my room."

My thumb feathered over the swell of her lips, my head shaking.

"This is your room. I'll have Aileen move your things this afternoon. We're courting. You belong in my bed, Willow. Now, be a good girl and go back to sleep. It's still early."

She opened her mouth to protest, but I silenced her, pressing my finger to her lips.

"Make yourself comfortable. I'll be in my office if you need anything. Aileen can make you breakfast, and I'll make sure I'm wrapped up by dinner so I can join you."

For a second, it looked like she might fight me on it. And then the most beautiful thing happened. She smiled—an open and unguarded one. My heart forgot how to beat for a moment, and I felt like a young boy with a crush.

"Okay, Alpha," she said, her eyes shining as she shimmied.

A pale pink blush spread over her chest as she rocked up to her knees. My painfully hard dick jumped. Her tits bounced with the motion, and she reached out, running her nails through my still-damp scruff.

Before I could pounce on her and pin her to the bed, my omega pressed the sweetest kiss to the corner of my mouth, tapped my cheek, and fell back into the sea of pillows.

"Sleepy," she mumbled, tugging the blankets over her breasts. "Is this alright?"

"It's everything. You're everything."

And she was. My lips rested on her temple as she fell back asleep, her chest lifting in slow, steady beats. Visions of Willow naked in my bed every morning rooted in the recesses of mind, making their home there.

Reluctantly, I pulled away from her and dressed.

I messaged Erik, my contractor, to give him the day off. While I wanted the nest for Willow done sooner than later, I didn't want anyone disturbing her while she rested. We were on a precipice, and I had to handle her carefully so I wouldn't spook her.

She may have accepted relocating and turning my space into *our* space. But I had a feeling that if she found out I was having a custom nest built for her, it might send her running.

The house was quiet as I walked into my study. It would be half noon before Liam woke up, and I expected Aidan and Torin would wander around shortly. Both were early risers. Not as early as me, but still.

Aileen had a small suite that she stayed in when she didn't want to go home. After she told me her townhouse was too big for her, I made sure she always had a place here. She was the closest thing I had to a mother since my ma passed. I fiddled with the crucifix around my neck. I was never a religious person, but it was my ma's, and I liked to carry a part of her with me.

My phone buzzed with a message from Robert Sweeney, the

Head of Medicine at Mass General. He was a family friend and agreed to personally look at Isabelle Sterling's medical history for me.

I dialed him back, grunting his name when he answered. "Sweeney."

"Mr. Finnegan, thank you for returning my call so quickly. I have reviewed Isabelle Sterling's records, and unfortunately there is not much to go by. Her results appear to have been tampered with. All that I can deduce from what's included is that she suffers from anxiety manifesting as physical ailments."

"Bullshite," I hissed, slamming my fist. "Sterling is fucking with her."

"Possibly," Sweeney said.

Man had fucking ice in his veins. Most people had the sense to shudder when I raised my voice, but Sweeney wasn't easily intimidated. That's what I liked about him. It also helped that my family donated thousands to his research and hospital annually.

"I need an untainted blood sample to do my own testing. Any way you could bring Mrs. Sterling in for an appointment?"

I ground my teeth. "Not possible."

Not without killing her worthless husband, and I promised Willow.

"I can do without seeing her in person if you can get me a fresh blood draw that I can test. The doctor of record, Angelo Hart, has a host of ethics violations and I can't use anything he's collected."

My nails dug into the supple wood.

"If he has ethics violations, why is he allowed to practice still?" I spat.

"Deep pockets," Sweeney said.

"Mine are deeper. Fix it, Sweeney. Get his license yanked. Ensure that Isabelle Sterling gets seen by a credible doctor."

He sucked in a slow breath, and a vein in my neck pulsed.

"It's not that simple, Mr. Finnegan. He doesn't work for me."

"Make it simple," I cut in, the threat in my tone unmistakable.

"I will work on it," he answered, defeated. "But it will take time."

"Fine. I will see if I can get you a blood sample in the interim."

Without waiting for his answer, I ended the call. Falling back into my chair, I pushed my cell across the desk as I booted up my computer, finding the contracts Dimitri sent over last week.

I spent most of the day digging into all the fine print. I didn't trust him not to sneak something in. After I finished my review, I would send them over to our attorney, but I always liked to do a first pass myself.

I picked at the food Aileen dropped off.

Every so often, my focus drifted to Willow, wondering what she was doing. She was the most beautiful distraction, and more than once I thought about fucking off and finding my sweet omega. My pants tightened at the image of her sprawled out on our bed, naked and reading.

"Fuck," I grunted when I knock at the door interrupted my increasingly filthy thoughts. "What?!"

Unbothered by my outrage, Torin pushed open the door. Standing in front of me, he crossed his arms, his face pinched.

"Boss," Torin said. "Massimo Rossi is at the gate, requesting a meeting with you."

Massimo Rossi. The only son of Vittorio Rossi. Vittorio had a daughter around Liam's age. I rarely heard of her, surprised he hadn't married her off yet. Seemed the type to use his children to solicit his own power.

While Vittorio was a bastard, Massimo had always been respectful in any dealings I had with him. Based on his body language, he didn't always agree with his father's action, but like the loyal son he was, kept his feelings to himself.

At least in public.

"What does he want?" I snapped.

"Said Vittorio sent him to negotiate terms."

Alarm bells went off. Something in my gut didn't sit well with the surprise visit. Massimo wasn't stupid, not like his father. Coming into my home, even if he had an army at his disposal, would mean certain death. And Vittorio wouldn't risk his only heir on some half-arsed suicide mission.

"How many men does he have with him?"

"One."

My fingers stilled as they circled the rim of my glass.

Usually, we'd meet somewhere neutral. It took balls to come to my home with only one guard. I had more respect for Massimo Rossi than for his father. And my curiosity got the better of me. It had been weeks since I had left the head of one of his men on Vittorio's doorstep. What was so urgent now that we had to meet?

"Bring him. Strip their weapons. If he refuses, send him away." Torin nodded, about to leave when I stopped him. "Where is Willow?"

Under no circumstances would I let them anywhere near my omega.

"Last I checked, she was still in your room, reading a book by the fire. Aileen brought her a snack before dinner."

I adored the image of my omega eating in our room while cuddled up by the fire. The only thing that would make that picture better would be me there with her, feeding her. My lids grew heavy, imagining slipping my fingers into her panties to find her hot and wet for me.

"It's her room now too," I corrected, and Torin smirked.

"Yes, Boss."

He didn't even try to stifle his laughter as he left the room.

Bastard.

Chapter 16

KAELEN

Torin left.

I poured myself a double shot of whisky before lowering myself into my chair. I debated checking on Willow.

Last thing I wanted was for these bastards to get anywhere near her. And while I was confident nothing would harm her behind these walls, it still made my skin prickle, thinking of Massimo Rossi and his vermin breathing the same air as her.

Nothing would make me happier than sending Vittorio's heir back to him in pieces if he so much as blinked at my omega.

Lost in my musings, the floor creaked as Aidan and Liam entered, asking me a silent question. I beckoned them in, not knowing what to expect from Massimo.

Whatever it was had to be important to show up on my doorstep unannounced. A small part of me tingled, hoping he had finally decided to overthrow his worthless father and wanted help.

Unfortunately for me, Massimo Rossi was loyal to a fault, and would never betray his blood. Even if it led to his death.

A faint knock echoed. I drained the last of my liquor, relishing how it burned its way into my stomach.

"Come in," I said, my detached voice chilling the room.

Massimo strode in with his broad shoulders thrown back as his obedient hound followed him. He was all tanned skin with dark hair and even darker eyes. Torin closed the door behind them, rocking back into the wall, carefully scanning the room.

Thick tension mingled with the lingering scent of wood smoke from the smoldering ashes in the fireplace. I steepled my fingers under my chin, impressed by Massimo's unflinching demeanor. He was twice the man his father was. It was the only reason I let him in. Vittorio must have known that if he came knocking, I would have turned him away.

"What is so important that you had to show up at *my* home, unannounced?" I asked, my words cutting through the silence.

"I believe you have something that belongs to my father," Massimo said, his tone eerily calm, setting my teeth on edge.

"What could that be?"

The muscle in my neck coiled uncomfortably tight. I licked across my teeth, not having patience for games. If they didn't speak plainly in the next three seconds, I would ruin my custom floors with Italian blood.

"You were seen at The Ruby Slipper with a date," Massimo said. "Willow Sterling."

"Don't," I hissed, the threat chilling the room. "Say my omega's name."

The veins in my hands pulsed as I flexed my fingers, choking down the violent words lingered on my tongue. I'd skin Patrick alive. How the fuck did Italians swindle their way into my casino? I knew being public with Willow would bring the wrong sort of attention to her.

Granted, I didn't expect it so quickly.

Massimo reached into his suit jacket, and all three of my men drew their weapons at once. A smug smirk curled on Massimo's lips as he threw his hands up.

"I meant no offense. There is a contract I wish to show Mr.

Finnegan."

I jutted my chin at Liam, who rocked off the wall, extending his hand. When Massimo didn't move fast enough, Liam snapped his fingers.

"Now," he hissed, impatient and demanding as ever.

Part of me knew I should admonish him, but I found it entertaining. Massimo's eyes narrowed into thin slits as he dragged out a thick envelope sealed with wax. After handing it over to Liam, my brother placed it on my desk before returning to his spot beside Aidan.

A trickle of blood dripped from my thumb as I dug it into the letter opener, staring at Massimo. The expensive fabric of his shirt strained over his chest when crossed his arms, unamused by my antics.

My heart plummeted into my stomach as I scanned the contract.

I reread it three times, schooling my features, refusing to show any emotions.

Finally, my eyes narrowed on the date, a silent, deadened feeling hollowing out a hole where my heart supposedly was. William Sterling signed away his daughter the day after he realized he would get nothing from me.

Without drawing attention to the motion, I quietly opened my desk drawer, removing my da's Claddagh ring and slipping it into place on my finger. Cool metal made my skin tingle as I traced the gold band.

Aidan, Liam, and Torin stood stoically in their positions, their faces flat. The bastard with Massimo was sweating like a stuffed pig in that too-tight suit of his, obviously not used to uneasy quietude. The two didn't stand a chance against us. Massimo was gritty, and there was a chance he'd take out Torin or Liam before I got to him.

I would go to war for Willow, but I didn't have to.

Not yet, at least.

There was more than one way to keep her safe. A way that was more foolproof with less of a chance of blowing up.

Even if she spat in my face for it after she found out.

Slowly, I rose from my chair, my palms splaying across the supple wood. Massimo tracked my movements as I rounded my desk, motioning for my men to stay in place.

"Your father's contract with William Sterling for Willow Sterling is void."

"Why is that?" Massimo asked, a hint of curiosity in his voice.

Whatever reaction he suspected from me, it wasn't this.

I made a show of pointing to the dates on the signature line, the gold band on my finger glinting in the light spilling in through the floor to ceiling windows.

"Last I knew, polyandry was illegal in the state of Massachusetts. Something I would expect a candidate for governor to know."

Massimo clicked his tongue, but stayed quiet. Aidan seemed to catch on to my plan, trying to hide his smirk.

"Willow Sterling was already married when Senator Sterling promised her to Vittorio Rossi."

"What?!" Massimo snarled, color rising in his olive cheeks.

"Willow is *my wife*. William Sterling offered her to me first in exchange for giving him the election."

Marriage would protect her from the Italians and her scum father. It was more than marriage; she would be *mine*. My alpha roared a victorious sound, my chest expanding at the thought of making Willow mine.

I knew she would protest, that this would frighten her.

Even possibly make her run.

But she didn't have a choice. There was no *fucking* way I would allow Vittorio Rossi to ever put a hand on her. And us being married was the most holistic protection I could offer her.

Bleeding Catholics.

Rossi would never offend God by coveting another man's wife, no matter how much he wanted her.

As much as I craved blood. This path was the smarter one. Eventually, Willow would understand. My omega was brilliant; she would see reason once I explained how dire the situation was.

Ever since I was old enough to learn the business, my da taught me the importance of knowing when to fight and when to outmaneuver.

"My father has a signed contract for Willow Sterling, and he plans to collect," Massimo said, running his fingers through his dark beard.

An image of Vittorio Rossi finding out he couldn't have Willow played out in my mind, and I desperately wanted to see the look on his face when his son told him. The man was a coward, always wanting what he couldn't have.

"I don't give a fuck what Vittorio has," I spat, taking a measured step toward Massimo. "Willow is *mine* and has been. If he has a problem with that, I suggest he takes it up with William Sterling directly."

Maybe if I were lucky, the Italians would kill the man for me. Granted, I knew that would upset my omega. At least until her mom was taken care of. Massimo's nose twitched, his guard dog moving as I stepped closer. Liam jolted, pinning the man who was twice his size to the wall with the barrel of a gun buried in his chin.

"Back off," Liam ordered, racking the slide on his glock.

Massimo hissed something in Italian, his dark eyes laced with warning. The man with him threw his hands up in surrender. I called off Liam, who looked put out when he stowed his gun back in its holster.

Despite his playful personality, Liam was lethal, always happy for an excuse to fight.

"Senator Sterling lied to you. Promised you something that was no longer his to give." Not that Willow was ever something for him to barter with. "Do you want a war? Because if you continue to assert some false claim on *my wife,* my omega, I won't show mercy. Take that back to your Capo dei Capi, and get out of my house," I spat.

My threat hung in the stilted silence, no one moving as the words permeated the thick air. Soot darkened the stone of the mantle. I crossed my arms, stretching the bespoke fabric.

With a nod, Massimo splayed a hand over his chest, tipping his head toward his man. Without another word, Liam and Torin escorted the Italians from my office. I fished a cigarette out of my pocket, lighting it and taking a long, slow drag that burned my lungs.

I'd quit again tomorrow.

Aidan had enough sense to keep quiet while I rubbed the frown lines from my forehead. The lit cigarette dangled from my mouth as I twirled the Claddagh ring on my finger. It was relatively plain compared to my ma's, pure gold.

Heavy footsteps made my head snap back toward the door when Liam and Torin returned.

"Maybe she'll slap him again," Aidan mumbled, huffing as he leaned into Liam's side.

"Someone has to," Liam chimed in.

"Nip it," I snapped, glowering at my brothers.

They were right.

My lovely omega was going to be pissed and borderline feral when I told her. A knot sat heavy in my stomach. I had promised her a courtship, a chance to adjust to being with an alpha who would spoil her. A nagging voice inside of me told me I was no better than her pathetic dad, forcing her into something she didn't want.

Except my goal was to keep her safe. Something she wouldn't be with Vittorio.

I wanted to take my time with her. Court her. Woo her. Worship her. After everything Willow had been through, she deserved to take things at her own pace. I wanted to show her how an omega like her deserved to be treated.

Unfortunately, that wasn't a luxury she'd be afforded.

I would gut William Sterling for everything he did to her. Snuffing out the butt of my smoke, I looked to Aidan.

"Call Father Fitzpatrick, have him come this Saturday. Then meet with the town clerk and find out how much money it will take to backdate the marriage license."

Aidan nodded, sharing a look with Torin I didn't bother to decipher.

Sweat stuck to my nape. I wiped my damp palms on my suit pants as I walked to the door. I'd spilled blood, faced the death penalty, and buried my family without losing a wink of sleep.

But now, this trip to tell my feral omega that she would walk down the aisle with me whether she liked it or not, felt like a sentence to the gallows, and she was my executioner.

At least she was the prettiest headsman I'd ever seen.

Chapter 17

Sometime around mid-morning I woke up, content and sleep-mussed, under the thick blankets of Kaelen's bed. *Our* bed.

A delicious ache throbbed between my thighs. My fingers ghosted over the marks he left on the creamy skin there, admiring how much I liked seeing them there. I hadn't slept in that late in a long time or felt this sated ever. My omega relaxed, curling up like a lazy cat on a Sunday afternoon in a sunspot.

Cool silk slid under my fingertips as I glided them along Kaelen's pillow, nuzzling into it and drinking in his familiar scent. I stretched out, splaying out over the massive bed, still not able to reach the sides.

Whatever this was, it was bigger than a king size, and I feared it had ruined me for any other bed ever.

Maybe this was Kaelen's plan. To court me with fancy linens and absurdly oversized mattresses.

It was working.

After last night, I worried I wouldn't be able to deny him anything. At the casino, it wasn't my omega who was jealous of the woman who thought Kaelen attractive. It was me. If anyone asked, I'd blame it on my omega, the alcohol, anything to avoid admitting that I liked Kaelen.

More than liked. I was rather fond of him, enjoying his company a lot more than I wanted to admit.

It meant giving him power over me, the power to destroy me.

Like my dad had done to my mom.

Logically, I knew not *every* alpha was horrible, but a small, niggling part inside of me was terrified that I was destined to find a bad one.

Kaelen Finnegan was lethal and violent, but completely soft for me.

The necklace he had gifted me was lovely, the nicest thing anyone had ever given me. Every omega adored getting presents, and as much as I tried to hide it, I was no different. Afraid of appearing too eager, I squashed down my excitement. Even if I was thrilled to see what other courting tokens Kaelen would present to me.

Eventually, I crawled out of my makeshift nest and took a quick shower. Covered in a fluffy towel, water dripped onto the floor as I tiptoed toward my old room to get changed.

Of course, Aileen caught me, with an amused glimmer flickering in her eyes. Crimson stained my cheeks as I shrugged, holding the knot between my breasts so the cotton wouldn't fall.

"Good morning, sleepyhead."

"Morning," I murmured, wanting to melt into the floor.

"After you get dressed, why don't you go down and have the lunch I made while I move your things."

"You don't... I mean, I can do it."

"Hush. I like to keep busy. I'll be finished before you're done eating. Now get inside before you get permanent water spots on my floors."

"Yes, ma'am," I squeaked, my cheeks hot.

With a crisp nod, I disappeared into my room, quickly throwing on a pair of leggings and a chunky oversized sweater. My hair was long enough now that I could tie it into a braid. I tossed the used towel in the hamper, padding down to the kitchen.

When I passed Kaelen's study, the door was closed, and I fought the urge to go see him. He was working. I didn't want to be a clingy omega.

Even if everyone told me alphas adored that.

I wanted to sit on his lap while he did whatever it was The Butcher of Boston did in there. I had loved it last night at the casino, the feel of his roughened hands brushing over the silky fabric over my dress.

A rush of slick coated my thighs, and I nearly choked on a whine. Kaelen had ruined me. There was no way I could go back to sleeping with betas. Not when I experienced how glorious it was to be knotted. He filled me in a way that left me breathless and content.

Granted, I had an inkling that feeling was a unique experience with Kaelen. If our courtship didn't pan out... Well, I didn't want to dwell on that, imagining spending the rest of my life without my alpha.

Downstairs on the island lay a spread of sandwiches. Two alphas I didn't recognize came in as I sat down with a smoked salmon one. I stiffened, the hair on my arms standing on end. Internally, I cursed the reaction, knowing my scent took on that smokey, fearful hint.

Someday, I'd stop bristling around unknown alphas.

But apparently not today.

"Miss Sterling," the taller of the two said in his thick Irish brogue. "We didn't mean to intrude. We'll leave you to it if you prefer to be alone."

"Yes, please," I whispered, relaxing when I realized they planned on giving me space.

Nodding, both men disappeared the way they had come.

Kaelen

I spent most of the afternoon in our room, unsurprised when Aileen had moved all my belongings over while I ate. Not that I had much. Kaelen splurged on clothes and toiletries along with a few books I asked for. Sam insisted on me reading this particularly filthy one about an omega getting snowed-in with an alpha logger.

Images of Kaelen in a flannel and chopping wood made me giggle.

Flames flickered in the giant stone fireplace, and I slid further into the cushions. Something in my stomach lurched, making my insides somersault. I put my book down, rubbing the hollow spot over my sternum. My nose twitched and I eyed the clock. It was half-past six.

Kaelen promised me dinner, and I hadn't seen him since this morning. Marking my page, I tossed the book aside. Amelia and her pack would be waiting for me later. My skin itched with the need to see my alpha.

Mine.

I hated how much I liked the sound of that.

Maybe not hated.

I tugged at the hem of my sweater, pushing open the heavy oak door to the rest of the house. A couple of men nodded at me as I padded down the hall that led to his office. I paused outside the door, my fingers trailing over the supple wood. Teeth gnawed at my lip as I fought against my instincts to be close to my alpha.

Raised voices echoed from the other side of the door, and I stilled. Silken, accented voices I didn't recognize spoke in that same authoritative tone I equated with Kaelen. I shouldn't snoop, but like all omegas, I was curious.

When I heard the man with the Italian accent say my name, a shock zipped through my fingertips and my stomach twisted in knots.

Uneasiness slithered through my veins. Kaelen's commanding voice sliced through the air and landed squarely on my chest. An icy dread gnarled around my insides like twisting ivy.

"Your father's contract for Willow Sterling is void."

My breath hitched, and my hands went numb as my skin turned cold. Swaying on my feet, I pressed my palm into my temple. I flexed out my fingers, willing the blood to flow there as I paced, digging my nails into my palm.

Italian and Irish voices bounced back and forth, but I caught a few unmistakable words.

"Already married."

"My wife."

"Signed contract. Plans to collect."

I heard enough. Each heavy step took longer than the last as I tried to put as much distance between me and whatever fate awaited me, blood rushing in my ears as if I had been pulled under a swirling tide.

Finally, I stumbled into the kitchen, my hands splaying out on the cool stone countertops. I murmured a quiet prayer to whatever deity listened that no one would find me here. It wasn't exactly hidden, but I knew Aileen was out for the night and Kaelen's men gave me a wide berth—mostly.

I rummaged through the cabinets, eyeing the unopened bottle of vodka. Without hesitating, I wrapped my fingers around the neck, yanking it into my chest like a small child clutching a stuffed bear.

This couldn't be real. I must have misheard. We were supposed to have more time. A proper courtship where I adjusted to the idea of having an alpha. *Damn* my curious omega. I hopped onto the counter, holding the liquor between my thighs as I removed the topper. My nose scrunched at the distinct odor wafting from it.

Before I could change my mind, I took a quick swig, coughing as the sharp fire burned its way into my belly. My brows tilted in toward my nose while I glared at the bottle.

Why did people drink this stuff? It was disgusting. I wavered, trying to shake free the feeling of my skin crawling. Despite the taste, I took another sip, the sting as potent as the first one had been.

I hoped my taste buds would dull soon enough until all I was left with was a floaty haze that made all my problems disappear.

Ah.

Maybe that was why people suffered the clinical, acrid taste. It seemed like a small price to pay to forget. A deal with the devil. Except the devil was going to be my husband. I took another drink, shakily placing the bottle on the counter beside me.

A different heat spread, not as piercing as before, but instead something soothing. The edges of the room blurred, and my limbs loosened. The corner of my mouth quirked as my problems slowly locked themselves away in the recesses of my mind.

It could be worse. I could end up bound to some grouchy bastard who was old enough to be my father. Based on what I heard, that sounded exactly what Kaelen was trying to avoid by claiming me as his wife.

I was still pissed. Not at him. Not exactly, but at everything.

For once in my life, I wanted to have a choice.

And for one fleeting moment, I really believed I would.

I snorted, taking another hit of vodka.

Familiar footsteps grew louder until a broad figure appeared, leaning against the wall. My body tightened, attuned to him. Stupid pretty alpha. His dark green eyes bounced between me and the liquor, his expression frustratingly blank.

God really did have favorites, and Kaelen Finnegan was one of them.

Chiseled muscles framed his inked torso, and his sculpted ass looked like it had been poured into those pants. I bet I could bounce a quarter off it if I tried.

When he didn't move, I raised my drink in salute.

"Hello, *husband*," I slurred, closing my lips around the neck of the bottle and taking another drag, hissing as the liquor burned my raw throat.

Chapter 18

KAELEN

The inside of my palm itched no matter how much I scratched it. My grandmother once said that was a sign of good fortune. I rolled my eyes, shoving my hands into my pockets. The only luck coming to me would be in the form of a tiny terror by the name of Willow Sterling.

Willow *Finnegan*.

A primal, possessive glow bloomed in the hollow of my chest as my alpha beamed with pride. My last name sounded good on her.

As much as I knew Willow would be displeased, that didn't snuff out the peaceful feeling that eased my ever-tetchy alpha. Willow would be *my wife*, and soon *my omega*.

Ever since I first scented her delicious spring scent, I knew she belonged to me. She resisted it, but I knew she felt too, knew I was her alpha.

Our mating *could* wait, even if the idea made my skin prickle.

I roamed through the quiet halls, pushing open the door to our bedroom.

A discarded book sat on the settee by the fire. A half-naked man with an ax winked at me from the cover. My girl liked dirty books. I scratched my beard, disappointed not to find her sleepy and cuddled under a blanket like Torin had mentioned.

It was past dinnertime. I made my way down to the kitchen, assuming Willow got tired of waiting for me and decided to eat something. *Good girl.* She needed to take care of herself. I needed to take care of her.

My brow pinched as I paused, taking in the vision of Willow propped up on the counter. At first, I was entranced by how adorable she looked, dwarfed by her oversized sweater.

Then, I saw the half-empty bottle of vodka clutched in her tiny hand. She swayed, glossy eyes twinkling in the muted light.

Streaks of red stained her cheeks, and her eyes narrowed as she raised the Grey Goose bottle like some sloshed little pirate captain.

"Hello, husband."

Shite.

My temple throbbed. I clicked my tongue, not knowing how much she had heard. Enough that she knew I claimed we were married.

Selfishly, I hoped she heard it all, so I wouldn't have to repeat myself.

Based on how deep my tipsy omega was into the vodka, she may have.

Only one thing in this world frightened me, and that was my omega.

I rocked off the wall, moving slowly until I reached the counter. The points of her teeth dug into that pillowy bottom lip of hers as she unconsciously parted her legs for me. I stepped into the space, caging her in as my palms rested on the marble.

"You lied about being married," she said, her nails tapping on the bottle.

"I did."

Unable to stop myself, I tugged her lip free. My dick thickened when her tongue darted out to lick me.

Fuck. This was torture. I wanted to bury my face in her pussy until she screamed my name and forgot how pissed she was at me.

I curled my fingers around the neck of the vodka bottle, gently prying it away. That amount of straight liquor was enough to put a grown man on their arse, let alone my petite omega who didn't drink much.

She snarled, but I ignored it, placing the bottle out of reach.

Hot skin brushed against my palms as I cupped her face, stroking her alcohol-flushed cheeks.

"How much did you hear, mo chroí?"

"All of it," she murmured, wrapping her slender fingers around my forearms to hold herself steady.

A heavy breath expanded my chest as I nodded. No one had seen her when they escorted Massimo out. She only thought she heard all of it. Her gaze drifted as she traced the lines of my tattoos, and something splintered as I watched her.

For years, she had been held together by sheer determination.

It was cruel. I had dangled hope in front of her only to snatch it away.

I wanted only to protect her. Someday, she would understand. I would kneel at her feet if she wished it. The pad of my thumb aimlessly stroked her freckles when I finally broke the stilted silence.

"The Italians have a few brain cells between them. It won't be long before they figure out we aren't married."

Darkness engulfed her glazed eyes, almost turning them into polished obsidian stones. She tipped her chin up, fighting the slight tremble in her fingers. My heart swelled and shattered at the same time. She refused to show fear, even as it lingered beneath the surface.

"What will happen?"

Her sweet voice came out in a strained whisper.

"They will enforce the terms of their agreement with your father."

All the color in her face disappeared as an icy chill overtook her limbs. Her breasts rose with quickening breaths before she spun out of my hold. Tiny, shaking fingers clung to the sink as she retched, vomiting into the stainless steel basin.

"Shhh," I soothed, running my fingers through her hair and holding it off her face. "I won't let anything happen to you, Willow. I will die to keep you safe."

Minutes passed as she quivered, her stomach finally empty. I filled a glass of water, silently handing it to her. Her pale lips rested on the rim as she sipped, slow at first before downing the entire thing, easing some of the tension in my muscles.

"It will never happen," I said, pushing sweaty strands of hair off her brow.

"But how?" she asked, her words still slurred as her eyes glistened.

"Father Fitzpatrick will be here on Saturday to marry us. The license will be backdated if the Rossis go digging."

"What?! You can't."

Color returned to her cheeks. The streaks of red burned brilliantly with her anger, making my dick stir. I admonished my cock. Now was not the time for him to remember how pretty our omega looked when she was angry.

"I can and I will," I said, my face tight as I held her arms to keep her from falling off the counter. "This is the easiest way. The most foolproof protection I can give you. Making you my wife."

Words lingered on my tongue. Despite the righteous fury blazing in her eyes, I loved the way that sounded. My wife. Willow was mine. And soon, she would be my omega. I wouldn't take that choice away from her. But soon, she'd see that she was mine. That I was hers.

That we belonged together.

"So that's it? I have no say. I'm yours? How could you? I trusted you. You're no better than my dad," she hissed, lashing out and punching my chest. "Made me believe in you. Believe you were different, only to prove to me you're not."

Furious tears spilled from her eyes, her assault frivolous. Air whistled through my nostrils as I sucked in a breath, closing my fingers around her wrists. I didn't care if she hit me, but I didn't want her to hurt herself.

Her words landed like a punch in the gut. They rang true. Copper slid over my tongue as blood coated my lips. I was another alpha stealing her voice from her.

"Let me go," she bellowed.

"No."

For a second, I thought she was going to spit on me. But no. She fought against my hold, mumbling a series of slurred words I didn't quite understand. The intent was clear, however. If I demanded marriage from my omega, she'd think me no better than her father.

I wasn't used to asking for things.

Yet, I had to. I couldn't make demands of my omega. At least not without her consent. If she were to be my wife, my partner in all things, I must treat her as such. I had to trust her to understand.

"Willow," I said, pressing my cheek against hers and marking her with my scent. Her body stilled, a tiny sound of pleasure escaping her. "I believe marrying you is the best option to protect you from Vittorio Rossi. But I will not force you into anything."

A dangerous noise built within me, my alpha disagreeing with me. My hand ran over Willow's messy braid. If she refused marriage, I'd keep her safe. Even if it meant slaughtering every Italian until their blood stained the streets of Boston.

Glossy eyes stared at me as she brushed her cheek against mine. My heart leapt at the gesture; she was marking me. *Fuck.* I really wanted to have this conversation with her when she was sober. I hoped she remembered it tomorrow morning.

"Some butcher. Can't you just kill them?"

A disbelieving laugh escaped me, not sure I had heard her correctly. Was this the same woman who begged me to spare her piece of shite father? While she insisted she didn't mind the blood on my hands, I had a hard time picturing her as someone who relished the idea of death and decay.

My sweet omega was full of surprises. I cupped her chin, fascinated by her beauty.

"The Rossis are a part of the Cosa Nostra, with ties to powerful Italian families as ancient as they are bloodthirsty. If I were to go to war with them, we would have families from Chicago, New Jersey and even Rome at our doorstep. Make no mistake, Willow," I added, seeing her trying to process the information. "I would slit their throats until the Charles ran red with their blood."

"Then why—" she started, when I silenced her with my finger on her lips.

"Because I am a strategist first. I don't needlessly take life. A war between the Irish and the Italians would lead to you being sealed away in some safe house for months or years until the dust settled. Even then, nothing would stop the Italians from trying to claim you."

A shudder rolled through her as she covered her mouth, looking like she might throw up again. My lips found her forehead, resting there as I held her tighter.

"The Italians are good Catholics." She eyed the cross dangling over my chest, and I answered her unasked question. "Irish Catholics like to bend the rules."

The tight lines around her mouth relaxed, and I inhaled a deep breath.

"It means that if the Italians find out you are legally wed to another, and always have been, they will consider the contract void, and leave you in peace. Meaning you can live your life versus hiding away from bloodshed always in fear of one of their men coming for you."

My words hung in the air between us as I tried to calm the slight tremble still coursing through her.

"Willow. Trust me. This is the only way. Do you consent?"

A small, defeated noise rolled off her tongue. She tipped her head back, staring at me, nostrils flared.

"Fine. But I'm pissed at you."

Expected.

"I want something shiny in exchange."

I snorted, knowing sober Willow likely wouldn't request such a gift. But drunken Willow gave in to her omega easier. And I knew the gift to give her.

"I agree to your terms," I murmured, nuzzling the gland on her throat.

It was enough for now.

Granted, I wondered if she'd even remember this conversation come morning. I didn't relish the idea of having to have it a second time with a sober Willow. The last of her strength gave out, and she collapsed onto me. I welcomed the comforting weight of her. Her sweet spring scent surrounded me, calming my alpha.

The tip of her nose brushed along my collarbone, and my arms wrapped around her waist, refusing to release her. She hummed a chorus of breathy sounds, trying to crawl further into me. I smirked, carefully picking her up until she clung to me like a drunk koala—all loose-limbed and heavy and adorable.

Tiny fingers ran through my beard before she pushed a strand of hair off my brow.

"You are unfairly attractive. All muscles and stubble and tattoos. My omega thinks she loves you and that you belong to us."

I froze, taken aback by the sincerity in her words. Her nails scraped along my back.

"Just your omega?" I asked cautiously, walking us up the stairs to our bedroom.

She responded with a noncommittal noise. The tip of her pink tongue slid over my pulse, and I growled. She smelled so sweet.

Like mine.

A moment later, a quiet purr rumbled in her chest as she hugged me tighter.

I doubted she even realized she was doing it.

My omega purred for me. She recognized me as her mate, even if she wasn't ready to believe it.

Sweat clung to her nape as I slipped my hand into the spot, cradling the back of her head. My lips pressed against the top of her head.

"I do belong to you, little omega. Go deo is go brách."

Chapter 19

The tip of a blade dug into the spot between my eyes, twisting until pain exploded out into my temples. At least, that was what it felt like. I groaned, my entire body aching as too-bright light pushed against my eyelids. I rolled to the side, burrowing my face into an unyielding wall of muscle.

A hoarse moan irritated my dry throat as nails scratched through my hair, massaging my scalp. I blinked, nestling further into the scent of my alpha. His presence was a balm to my aching body.

And it didn't hurt in a good way.

Why did anyone get drunk if this was the result?

Nothing outweighed this outcome. Last night definitely wasn't worth it.

Grimacing, I squinted my eyes tighter to prevent any light from getting in.

A quiet laugh rumbled through my frame, and lips caressed my temple.

"Not funny," I hissed, regretting it immediately when pain thundered in my skull.

"Kinda funny."

I swatted at him half-heartedly, and he didn't stop my lackluster assault. Instead, he pushed two pills into my hand along with water. I took them, draining the glass before blinking my eyes open, relieved that the room wasn't as bright as I expected.

"Eat."

A piece of fruit pressed against my lips before I had time to register what was happening. My mouth parted, teeth piercing the supple flesh of the strawberry. My tongue brushed over the pads of his fingers, making his face twitch.

It was oddly intimate. One after another, he fed me until the plate on the end table was clear.

"Good girl."

Slick soaked my panties, and I squirmed. Now that the pulse in my head eased, flashes of the previous night started piecing themselves together.

Unfortunately, it had not all been a cruel nightmare. It was real.

All I wanted was more time.

Except, I wasn't going to get it.

My dad had seen to that.

It was marry the ancient Italian mafioso, who was older than my father, or marry Kaelen. A man whom I cared for more than I'd ever admit.

I wasn't ready.

I needed more time.

Things with Kaelen were good. In the future, I could see mating with him, marrying him, spending a life with him, but I wanted to get to know him better, take things slow… allow myself to trust him—as an alpha.

The alternative was unacceptable.

If I didn't marry Kaelen, I most certainly would end up with an alpha who would treat me horribly.

At least with Kaelen, I knew what I was getting into.

At least, I think I did.

My omega scolded me for dismissing our alpha. He was perfect for us. She knew it, even if I refused to accept it.

It wasn't a refusal, not really.

It was fear.

I was scared.

Scared of being trapped. Scared of being hurt.

Not physically, but emotionally. I saw the torment my dad waged on my mom to control her, and it was worse than any slap or burn.

I rolled over, my legs dangling off the bed as I put my face in my hands. My hands trembled as a bead of sweat dripped down my brow. The mattress shifted, and I figured Kaelen didn't want to deal with me and had gone to take a shower.

A shadow shifted in front of me, blocking the light. Two callused hands covered my own, gently pulling them away. I sucked in a shaky breath, and a knuckle rested under my chin, tipping my head back.

The muscle at the base of my head twinged with the strain of looking up at him. Kaelen towered over me. Tight briefs clung to his muscled thighs, colorful ink flexing on his taut torso as he gazed at me with an unreadable expression.

I tugged at the hem of the t-shirt he must have put me in last night before I passed out. Goosebumps broke out on my legs and arms. His eyes flicked to my mouth, dropping lower before finding my stare once more.

"I'm still mad at you," I murmured, my words from last night coming back in pieces. "You're an over-protective asshole."

Slowly, he dropped to his knees beside the bed, his rough palms caressing the smooth skin of my thighs. My lips parted as I followed the movement, in awe of the most powerful man in Boston kneeling before me.

"And I will suffer your ire if it means you are safe. Someday, Willow, you will understand." His warm breath fanned over my cheek, his next words a reverent whisper. "I kneel for no one. Except you."

Time stopped and I froze. He took my left hand in his, dwarfing it as he rubbed his thumb over my knuckles.

In his other hand, he clutched a small box wrapped in dark, lush velvet.

"I believe I owed my omega something shiny."

Snorting, my cheeks pushed against my eyes.

"I know you wanted more time, mo chroí. And in a perfect world, I would have given it to you. But I never needed it. I have known from the moment that I saw you. I'm sorry it's happening like this. Not because I don't want it, but because I know you are conflicted."

I sucked in my bottom lip, not allowing the brimming tears to fall. Too much emotion choked me, making it hard to breathe. He popped open the lid of the box. Inside a stunning ring glimmered, nestled in blue silk.

A shiny sapphire sat between two golden hands with a diamond-encrusted crown above it. It was gorgeous without being gaudy.

Without a word, he plucked the ring from the silk, slipping it onto my left finger with the heart pointing out.

"It's a Claddagh ring. Traditional in my family. The heart is for love. The crown for loyalty, and the hands for friendship. With the heart pointed out on your left hand, it signifies an engagement. When married, it will point inward."

I nodded along, my eyes glued to the golden band on my finger. The weight eased my skittering pulse for some reason. I expected when he put it on that I would panic.

But the feeling never came.

"It's beautiful," I whispered.

"It pales in comparison to you."

At that moment, I believed him. Believed that he cared for me. That he thought me more beautiful than a precious stone.

Maybe this was fate.

My fingers curled around his forearm, tracing the Gaelic words I had once asked him about.

Tá sé scríofa.

It is fated.

Maybe fate wasn't a bad thing.

Before I could overthink it, I closed the space between us, fusing my mouth to his. His lips quirked as one of his hands slid to the small of my back while the other burrowed in my hair at my nape.

Confident lips melded with mine, slowly coaxing them open. He didn't take more, keeping it light and gentle before pulling away and kissing the corner of my mouth.

"This doesn't mean I forgive you," I murmured against his lips.

"I know," he said, brushing his hands over my ribs. "I will find ways to make it up to you. Unfortunately, I have to leave. Liam and I have a meeting, and I won't be home until late."

An unfamiliar feeling bubbled up and my breaths came out fast and uneven. Stinging cold made my fingers go numb as I searched his face for any signs of uncertainty. I struggled to voice the words out loud, but I was worried.

"Shhh, omega," he soothed, holding my face. "I have a scheduled meeting with Dimitri Romanov to discuss contracts. Nothing more."

I nodded, nuzzling into him and breathing in his intoxicating scent. Letting my omega lead, I rubbed my face against his, marking him with my scent. If he was going to be out with others, I wanted everyone to know he was *mine.*

Something close to a groan rumbled in his chest, and I grinned. Pleased with his reaction. He offered me the same, blending his scent with mine on my skin. After a long, quiet pause, he spoke.

"Aileen is down in the lounge, working on putting things together for Saturday. Why don't you sit with her? Pick out your dress."

The change of subject made me stiffen. Logically, I knew we were getting married on Saturday by a priest, but it was only now that I realized he intended for it to be a real wedding. One with a dress and flowers and all that other nonsense I never thought about.

Except for one thing.

Whenever I pictured my wedding, there was one constant that was always present.

"My parents. My mom. Can she come?"

A long breath loosened from him, and he slumped. He pressed his forehead into my belly, his hands anchored on my hips.

"I'm sorry. No. If your mom attends, so will your dad. He will know we haven't always been married, and would tell the Italians. It's not safe, mo chroí."

"So no one," I bit back, anger and pain lacing through my chest like shards of broken glass. "I'll have no one at this farce of a wedding."

It wasn't necessarily his fault, but I wanted to be mad at someone. I reared back, about to slap him when his fingers wrapped around my wrist, stopping me. I hissed, glaring at him.

"Careful," he warned.

"Or what?" I snapped, trying and failing to yank my arm free. "What will Kaelen Finnegan do to his wife?"

His jaw worked as he ground his teeth together, rising back to his full height. I stood with him, forcing myself into the space between us and the bed. If he thought he could intimidate me with his mountainous body, he was wrong.

"Curse Áine for giving me such a mouthy omega for a wife," he said. I glared at him, and he released me. "But I wouldn't change a thing. I like that you're feisty. I wouldn't have you any other way."

Confused by the sudden change, I blinked. Kaelen had the audacity to chuckle, cradling my chin and pulling me in for a chaste kiss before hopping in the shower.

After Kaelen left, I wandered down to the sitting room. Aileen sat on the sofa, sipping her tea as she pushed around magazines with flower arrangements and dresses. My throat started to close, and I did the only thing I could.

I ran, colliding with a solid figure that made me stumble.

Two hands bracketed my arms, catching me.

"Woah, now."

"Aidan," I breathed, relaxing instantly when I saw it was him.

Aidan had a calming effect everywhere he went. He wasn't like other alphas. Despite being the middle child, he didn't act like that. He exuded a reassuring, confident demeanor that put everyone at ease, including me.

"Ahh, my future sister," he said, his voice even. "What has you sprinting like a mad person?"

"Where's Torin?"

He palmed the back of his neck, a slight pink dusting the tops of his cheeks.

"Still asleep in my bed. Is something the matter?"

"I need to get out for a while."

His eyes narrowed for a moment before he inclined his head, understanding what went unsaid.

"I'll go wake the terror and then we'll take you wherever you want."

"Thank you," I murmured.

"Anything for my baby sister," he said, kissing my cheek and disappearing down the hall he came from.

I liked that he called me his sister. After growing up as an only child, I always wondered what it would be like to have siblings.

Chapter 20

An hour later, Torin appeared with Aidan, looking more haggard than I had ever seen him. His auburn hair hung in messy waves on his face and a bruise peeked out from under the collar of his t-shirt.

I stifled a giggle, looking away before my wide eyes gave me away.

Usually, it was Torin who guarded me. It was odd to see Aidan with him as well. Maybe now that I was to be Kaelen's wife, I warranted extra protection.

That, or the whole thing with the Italians meant I needed two burly Irishmen guarding me.

Well, technically, one burly Irishman and one Scotsman.

Regardless, I found the two of them endearing.

Alphas rarely had committed relationships with betas—at least not outside of a pack setting. If anything, it was a quick fuck before parting ways, but Aidan cared for Torin. I saw it in the way he hovered and held his hand when he thought no one was looking.

In the car on our way to the shelter, my curiosity got the better of me.

"How long have you two been together?"

"About a year," Aidan said, meeting my eyes in the rearview mirror.

Aidan stroked the nape of Torin's neck while he drove. Affection warmed my belly. They were part of Kaelen's family.

Soon to be my family too.

As we pulled onto the street that led to the shelter, Aidan and Torin's demeanors shifted, their eyes scanning every passerby.

People said Roxbury was unsafe, but I found it charming. My bodyguards did not share my sympathies as they practically swaddled me, leading me through the entrance. The animal shelters in places like Back Bay and the South End had plenty of volunteers and donations, but spots like these—off the beaten path—got forgotten.

That was why I kept coming back. Someone had to protect these babies.

"So what warranted the additional escort today? Kaelen going all overprotective alpha? Or does it have something to do with the Italians?" I asked, noticing how Aidan's hand twitched above his concealed pistol.

The men shared a look. A blush tinted Torin's neck while Aidan shifted from side to side.

"Is it so horrible that I wanted to spend some time with my beta?" Aidan said, rubbing a small circle on the inside of Torin's wrist.

Oh, they were adorable. I almost didn't notice the girl nearly bouncing behind the counter at my approach.

"Hi, Lily," I said, getting the attention of the frantic girl behind the desk.

"Oh, Willow. Hi. I'm so glad you're here. Maybe you can help."

The joy in her eyes faded. A knot dropped into the pit of my stomach, heavier than a leaden weight. A lot of the animals in the shelter struggled to adapt, but there were always cases of abuse or neglect that needed special attention.

"What's wrong?" I asked.

"We brought in a new resident three days ago. Black lab mix. She's young. Somewhere around fourteen weeks, the vet thinks. She's completely withdrawn. Won't eat or let anyone near her."

"What happened to her?"

Aidan and Torin leaned against the wall, listening while scanning the room.

"Somebody tortured her," Lily whispered, frowning. "She's in decent shape all things considered, but all the fur on her tail is singed away like someone set her on fire."

A whispering snarl echoed behind me and I spun, unable to tell if it was Torin or Aidan who had made the noise. If Torin strained any harder, the vein in his neck would burst.

"I'll see what I can do," I said, steeling myself for the worst.

Lily handed me a pouch of treats. "She's in the kennel at the end of the hall. The yard's empty if you can convince her to go outside."

I pocketed the baggie, walking across the stone floors lined with kennels that felt more like prison cells. An uneasy feeling slithered around my limbs. I hated it. How cold and detached this place was. After one too many fights with my dad about donating more money to the shelter, I gave up.

The only hope for most of these animals was that someone would adopt them or a well-funded rescue would take pity on them and pull them out. I knew it was impossible to save them all, but that didn't stop me from trying.

I was never allowed to have a pet. Even though I really wanted a dog, I would have settled for anything. But my dad refused, not letting me have so much as a fish.

A pair of footsteps followed in my wake, but I ignored them as I closed my fingers around the latch to the last kennel. Curled up in the corner sat a pitch-black puppy.

Her poor, bare tail was tucked between her legs as she trembled on the cold stone floor, refusing to use the cot in the corner. A food bowl filled with kibble sat untouched in the corner. Slowly, I crept into the space, sitting on the floor as far away from her as I could.

Lily didn't mention she was aggressive, but after everything she had been through, it wouldn't have surprised me.

"Hey, sweetheart," I said, my voice quiet as I jiggled the bag of treats. "Are you hungry? Is it okay if I sit with you?"

One of her floppy ears twitched at the sound of my voice, and I wiggled the pouch again. When she didn't react, my heart plummeted into my stomach.

"It's okay, honey," I whispered, inching slightly closer, careful not to make any noise. "I'll never let anything happen to you again. We're not so different, you and I. I have burn marks too."

Someone snarled again, and this time I was certain it was Torin. "They'll heal."

At the sound of my voice, she turned her head, still resting her muzzle on her paws. Her large, dark, soulful eyes met mine, and I wanted to cry. In the last few years, I had sat with more abused dogs than I could count, and each one reacted differently.

Most wanted nothing to do with me. Some ate when prodded, but this beauty did something that stole my breath away. She stood, moving across the kennel, never taking her eyes off mine until she curled up in my lap.

My mouth fell open as she nudged at the treats with her nose. Afraid I might spook her if I reacted too loudly, I opened the pouch and hand-fed her pieces while stroking the singed fur along her back. The slight shake in her body returned, but she didn't leave my lap.

We stayed like that for hours until Lily arrived, giving me the spare key to lock up when I was ready. For the time being, nothing else mattered. My entire focus was on the puppy in my lap, who reminded me so much of myself.

Tiny, scared, and alone, even if she tried to hide it.

I admired her bravery. Despite feeling those things, she trusted me enough to take a chance on me. Something splintered in my chest, my omega cooing at the thought of our alpha. If this puppy could face its fears, maybe I could too.

She saw something in me, something that made her fears appear less scary. Even though I didn't want to admit it, I felt the same way when I was with Kaelen. He hadn't given me any reason not to believe in him.

The wedding had to happen, regardless of whether I wanted it to or not. I didn't have a choice, even if Kaelen tried to give me the illusion of one. I imagined being ripped away from him, forced to marry and bond with some pot-bellied alpha old enough to be my dad.

A sob squeezed my lungs, and I quieted it before either of my guards could ask me what was wrong. My omega paced. She wouldn't survive the loss of Kaelen. And a small part of me knew I wouldn't either. I clung harder to the sweet puppy, relieved when she didn't pull away.

"Miss Willow," Torin's gruff voice called. "Time to go home. It's getting late."

"I can't leave her."

They whispered behind me. I scowled at them before bringing my attention back to the puppy.

Hours later, the tiny black dog slept in my lap, trembling against my chest. My head started to droop. Every time, I snapped it up, forcing myself to stay awake. If I fell asleep, I knew they would carry me out and make me leave.

I wouldn't.

"Willow," a silky, familiar voice called.

My body reacted instantly, attuned to his commanding presence. The knot in my stomach loosened, and my omega perked up, delighted that our alpha was here.

Bastards.

Of course, Torin and Aidan ratted me out to their boss.

"Kaelen," I said, squaring my shoulders and looking straight ahead.

"It's late," he murmured, his footsteps cautiously moving into the kennel.

Luckily, the puppy didn't seem bothered by his presence, or at least, didn't react to it. Shadows darkened above me as he crouched. A heavy hand rested on my waist, and it immediately calmed me.

"So?"

"So you should come home and rest."

He kept his tone even. I expected him to be frustrated, to yank me away. He continued to prove all my fears wrong.

Maybe I could do this. Maybe I could be happy.

"She needs me," I whispered, nuzzling into her fur as he came to stand in front of us.

And maybe I needed her.

"I see that. Come on then."

One massive hand extended towards me. My gaze darted between that and his oddly serene eyes. They looked gentler than I had ever seen them. I wanted to call them beautiful. Call him beautiful.

Instead, I retreated further in, not quite ready to give up the high ground.

Even though he was towering over me like a giant.

"What are you doing?" I asked.

"Bringing my soon-to-be wife and our puppy home."

"Ours?"

"Yes, mo chroí. I'm sure the shelter won't mind. It seems like she has found her person."

My heart skipped a beat. If I weren't holding onto my precious bundle, I would have jumped into his arms and kissed him.

I struggled to stand, still holding the shaking puppy to my chest. She didn't recoil when Kaelen reached out and went willingly into his arms as he held her. At fourteen weeks, she wasn't tiny, but looked like it, cradled in his thick forearms. Nestling the puppy in one arm, he offered his free hand to me.

Rough fingertips brushed against my smooth ones as he tucked me into his side. As we walked out, he dropped a wad of cash on the counter.

"What's that for?"

"Adoption fee," he said, threading his fingers with mine in his free hand.

His thumb rubbed over the sapphire ring on my finger. My stomach lurched, my omega pleased with our alpha's claim on us. Even if she wanted more. She craved his mark. His bite. The only thing that would make us his—completely.

"It's like a hundred dollars. That was way too much."

"I'm bad with math," he said with a shrug. "It's close enough."

"Did you just make a joke?" I asked, swatting him with our still-laced hands.

"Why do you sound so surprised? I'm funny."

A pair of stifled snickers broke out behind us. Apparently, I wasn't the only one amused by Kaelen. While there were times I glimpsed a more relaxed side of him, that was when we were alone. When he was working or around his men, he remained stone-faced.

I thought back to the terrifying image of him on the first day I met him. When my dad slapped me. I didn't imagine many people found Kaelen Finnegan funny.

"Do men usually laugh when you threaten them?"

I'd meant for the question to come out more like a joke instead of an accusation. I expected the mirth on his face to vanish. The opposite happened, and his mouth spread in a wide, twisted smile that would frighten anyone else.

"No," he whispered. "But I do. If I'm the one carving them to pieces, it's because they did something unforgivable, and I enjoy watching them beg for mercy."

A dark part of me loved the idea of it. I knew Kaelen was dangerous, but he wasn't wasteful. For so long, too many people were allowed to be cruel without repercussions.

Maybe I was twisted too, because I liked knowing that Kaelen was waiting in the shadows to punish anyone who dared to hurt anyone he cared about.

I trusted my alpha. I trusted Kaelen.

Even though it terrified me to do that.

"Scáth beag," he whispered, lifting the puppy so he could kiss the top of her head.

"What's that mean?" I asked as we slipped into the back seat together.

"Little shadow."

I grinned, watching as our little shadow snuggled into Kaelen's lap as content with him as she had been with me. After a minute, she stopped shaking, her chest rising and falling with steady breaths. Kaelen splayed a hand over my thigh, giving it a squeeze.

Pieces of hair fell free from his bun, lying between his brows. I reached up, pushing them off his face. A vibration grew in his chest as his eyes darkened.

Kaelen

"Thank you," I whispered, kissing him. "You have no idea how much this means to me."

"Anything for you, Willow."

I believed him.

Chapter 21

WILLOW

After we got home from the shelter, I stayed in bed with Kaelen and our little shadow. It was almost as if everything that happened to her vanished. She jumped onto the bed, nuzzling into the expensive duvet before falling asleep.

Kaelen snorted, unconcerned about the dog in our sheets. Careful not to disturb our new bedmate, he stripped down to his briefs, taking me down to my panties before tucking me into him. I lingered on the edge of sleep as he stroked my hair.

"Alpha?" I whispered, keeping my face burrowed in his neck.

"Hmm?" he groaned as I dragged him from the precipice of sleep.

"Could you ask Aileen to make any necessary decisions for the wedding? I'm not picky, and I'm overwhelmed."

The premise of marrying Kaelen wasn't as terrifying as it had been even a few hours ago. But I still wanted nothing to do with planning it. Some girls spent their whole lives dreaming about their weddings.

For me, all it did was make acid crawl up my esophagus.

Propping himself up on his elbow, he cradled my face.

"Are you sure? What about your dress?"

"No cupcake ballgowns. But yes, I'm sure. That's my only stipulation."

Unconsciously, I played with the ring on my finger, the sapphire cool to the touch. He brought my ringed hand up to his lips, kissing it. I perfumed, and his nails dug crescents into my ass as he pulled me closer.

"Sleep, Omega."

I reluctantly obeyed, wishing we'd do more than sleep.

Saturday morning came, and my skin crawled. I spent most of the previous day hidden away in our bedroom while Kaelen worked in his study. At some point, he had moved me into our bed after I passed out reading in a chair by the fire.

Something hard poked my bum. I rolled from side to side, acutely aware of the dull ache between my thighs. I wanted to wake up like this every morning. With my alpha's solid chest pressed against my back.

I rocked my hips, grinding into him.

A raspy moan blew over my ear, and my omega preened. What started out as sexy turned into funny when he tugged at the bunched duvet by his feet.

"Blasted beast, stealing my side of the bed, hogs more of the blankets than you," Kaelen grumbled as Shadow sprawled out her legs near his pillows.

"I don't hog the blankets," I pouted, even as I was cocooned in the oversized throws.

"When you lie, at least try to hide the evidence."

"Alpha," I murmured as his thick length twitched against my ass.

Flames erupted over my arms, slowly spreading out to my fingertips until I was almost ablaze with it.

It wasn't my heat. It was him. It was my alpha, and how badly I wanted him.

"It's bad luck to see the bride on the wedding day," he teased, enjoying the furrow of displeasure between my eyes.

I let out a squeaky sound, wrapping my slender fingers around his wrist as much as I could while trying to force his hand where I wanted it.

"And you've already seen me. So what does it matter if you give me an orgasm? Alpha. Please," I said, my voice jumping up an octave. "You can't leave me like this."

Colors shifted in his eyes as his pulse thumped beneath my fingers while he weighed my proposition like some ancient emperor waiting to levee judgement.

"Shadow," he said, patting the pup on her bum. "Go down to the kitchen and have Aileen spoil you rotten."

"It's not like she'll understand you."

As if to prove me wrong, Shadow stretched out, and then hopped off the bed, nudging at the door before Kaelen let her out. I rolled my eyes, crossing my arms.

"Careful. Bratty omegas don't get to come."

A sharp inhale hissed through my teeth as I snapped my mouth shut. Without moving, his eyes roamed over me as his length strained against his briefs.

All the angels and whatever gods there were had crafted him from marble.

I was sure of it.

Crafted him for me.

Thick forearms stretched over his inked chest as he took pleasure in making me squirm. I sat up on my knees, sinking lower until I could grind my panty-clad pussy on the blankets. His eyes darkened as he stalked closer, circling me like a cornered rabbit as the scent of my arousal thickened in the room.

The bed sank under his weight as he knelt on the edge, crawling over me until I was caged under him. His tongue circled a sensitive spot right above my pulse, making me buck.

"So responsive. Such a good girl," he murmured.

I nodded, digging my nails into the sculpted muscles on his back and dragging them down. A possessive sound vibrated in his chest as his nostrils flared, and he crashed his lips into mine. I opened for him, letting him take all of me. He pushed aside my panties, sliding his fingers through my soaked center.

"Wet for me, Omega?" he groaned, gathering up my arousal and toying with my clit.

"Yes. Yes. Yes," I chanted, each word more broken than the last.

He didn't pull away, trailing kisses along my skin until he licked and sucked a mark into my neck. My eyes rolled back into my head as a tingling sensation grew hotter in my veins.

Kaelen pinned me down with his knees on either side of my hips.

Too slowly, he sank one finger into me up to the knuckle. A long, shuddering breath rattled my ribs. He smirked into my skin, pulling back and adding a second finger on his next thrust.

"Made for me," he groaned, dragging his teeth over the gland on my neck. "Look so good stretched around my fingers."

Words failed me as I tried to speak. It might have looked good, but it felt even better. He curled his fingers, tapping that spot behind my clit that made slick drip from me. The pad of his thumb brushed over my clit and my legs trembled.

"That's it. Relax for me. Give it all to me," he cooed, setting a steady pace that made my vision blur.

Heat stretched across my abdomen as the pleasure grew, getting tighter and tighter with each stroke of his fingers until my body was on the precipice of shattering. His lips dusted over the shell of my ear.

"Come for me. Be my good girl and soak me with it."

"Alpha," I panted, clawing at his skin hard enough to make it bleed.

On the next curl of his fingers, I came undone. My release crashed down on me with so much force I thought I would pass out. My legs quaked as a sheen of sweat clung to my flushed skin.

My lips parted with a silent cry. Kaelen slid two fingers into my mouth, and I sucked hard, desperate for something to distract me from the delicious fire devouring me. A primal, possessive glare stared at me as he worked me through the crests of my orgasms, pulling his hand away with a wet, lewd noise that made my cheeks burn.

"Shhh, sweet omega," he soothed, closing his lips around his fingers and sucking them clean.

Once the haze clouding my vision cleared, I tugged at his hips, frustrated that he didn't budge.

"Knot me," I demanded.

A lazy smirk pushed against his cheeks as he wiped the long hair off his face.

Infuriatingly smug bastard didn't move, merely grinned at me.

If he wasn't going to fuck me, I'd do it myself. I slipped my hand into his waistband, gripping his cock. A groan rumbled in his chest before he pulled my hand away, securing both my wrists in one of his hands.

"What about you?" I asked, my chest still heaving.

"Don't worry about me," he said, cupping my chin and resting his thumb on my tongue. "Tonight, mo chroí. I will claim my wife. Knot her tight cunt until she is begging me to stop."

Despite the remnants of my last orgasm still lingering, I already wanted another. I was turning into a greedy, needy omega.

I kind of liked it. At least with Kaelen. He looked at me like I hung the moon.

"You're evil," I pouted.

Even if his filthy promises of what would happen tonight sent a skitter of pleasure through my abdomen. Like most omegas, I reveled in instant gratification. And it appeared Kaelen was content to drag out my torment.

"Only sometimes," he mused, playing with the hem of the t-shirt I slept in.

I sat up on my knees, ignoring the sticky feeling between my thighs. Two massive hands palmed my hips, holding me steady.

"I'll leave you to get ready. Aileen should be up shortly to help."

Before I had time to panic, he pressed his lips to mine, holding my face in his large, roughened hand while the other anchored my waist. The tip of his tongue coaxed my mouth open, kissing me until I tasted the tiniest hint of whisky that must have lingered from the previous night.

"Nothing to fret, my pretty omega. I'll always take care of you."

And with that, he left the room, leaving a swarm of butterflies taking flight in my stomach.

Chapter 22

After Kaelen left, I stared at the blank door for I didn't know how long before slinking into the shower. The hot water sprayed against my face as I shampooed my hair. My lips turned down in a frown at how dull the blue streaks in my hair had gotten.

I made a mental note to text Sam. She was the only one I trusted with my hair. Despite not being licensed, she had been dyeing it since I met her.

When I padded out into the bedroom with a fluffy towel wrapped around me. I expected to find Aileen waiting for me.

Yet, the room was empty. My stomach twisted as uneasiness slithered around my heart like gnarled ivy. While I may have reconciled myself to Kaelen being my alpha, our looming marriage made new levels of anxiety stick to my ribs.

The bed sank under me as I sat on the edge, twirling my fingers in my lap while water dripped ominously from my hair.

A quiet knock echoed on the door, and I paused. It was Aileen with my dress, coming to help me get ready. Despite my arguing that I didn't need a dress, she and Kaelen insisted. So I gave up the fight. I fidgeted with the ring on my finger, hating how pretty it looked.

"Come in," I finally mumbled, spinning away to face the vanity.

"Surprise!" a familiar high-pitched voice called.

My head snapped forward, and I jumped to my feet.

"Sam," I shrieked, wrapping my arms around her waist as she fussed with the heavy garment in her arms. "What are you doing here?"

"Well, two gorgeous men with even prettier accents came to my house last night and told me you were getting married. How could I say no to being here for my best friend? It also helped that I was sandwiched between that sexy Scottish and Irish brogue," she said, winking.

My eyes crinkled. "Did they tell you what was going on?"

"Only after I pestered them endlessly. Don't worry. I whittled them down."

While telling me all about how pretty Torin and Aidan were, she maneuvered me into a chair after discarding the garment bag on the bed. I nibbled on my lip, loving how enamored Sam was while she pulled out hair dye, makeup, and a curling iron.

The tightness in my muscles unwound as she worked on my hair, letting the dye sit while she leaned over me, doing my makeup.

"Then they had the audacity to threaten me if I told anyone."

Logically, I knew Kaelen would never allow his men to harm Sam, even if she spilled the beans. It would be an accident if it ever happened. But she wouldn't.

"What did you tell them?"

"That I would claw their eyes out. For some reason, Torin's dick twitched when I said that."

I snorted, sputtering on a cough. Tossing the used brushes aside, she moved to drying and styling my hair. The levity in the room vanished, sucked out all at once as she clung to me and I covered her hand with mine.

"Are you okay, Willow?" I nodded, and her eyes thinned in the mirror. "I mean it. We'll run away."

"There are armed guards everywhere. We wouldn't make it past the gate."

Turning off the curling iron, she moved around until she was between me and the mirror. She crouched, taking my face in her hands as her expression hardened.

"If you don't want this, Willow, I'll find a way to get you out of here."

Every emotion I had stuffed away for the last few weeks came rushing to the surface before I could stop them.

"But I do," I huffed, staring at her through glassy eyes.

"Oh, babe. Then what's wrong?"

"I'm scared," I whispered.

A small voice inside me chanted that fear didn't mean danger. My muscles twitched as my breath came in quick stutters, making my chest burn. I could do this. I could be like Shadow. I could push through my fear and find happiness.

"Of Kaelen? I mean, he is The Butcher. The title is only slightly unnerving. He's never hurt you though. Right? Seriously, I'll murder his ass. I don't care who he is."

"No. Never. That's not it."

"Then," she paused, her eyes widening as her lips parted in a wide O. "Willow... you love him."

It wasn't a question. She saw it. I had never been able to hide anything from her. Sam knew all my secrets, from the burns on my skin to every horrific thing my dad did.

My fingers splayed across my breastbone, trying to soothe the ache there.

Growing up, everyone told me I would just know when it was right. That answer always frustrated me. How was that even possible? Now, sitting here with Sam looking at me with such a tender expression, I realized maybe that was exactly how it happened.

"I'm not sure. Maybe."

"Oh, babe!" she squealed. "You deserve it. Kaelen is gone for you."

"Have you ever even talked to him?"

Kaelen

"I don't need to," she said with a dismissive wave. "I can see it. The way he looks at you. It's intense. It's the way an alpha is supposed to look at their omega. Like they'd burn the world for them. And then give them the ashes on a silver platter."

I sucked in a sharp breath, sitting in silence while she continued to work.

Sam fluffed out the curls into romantic waves. As she unplugged the curling iron, her fingers lingered over the outlet, and she whipped out her phone, snapping a photo of the empty outlet.

My lips quirked. I never judged Sam. No matter how much she tried, sometimes she couldn't shake the feeling that something was wrong. She'd gotten better over the last few years, asking for reassurance from me less.

In the year since she moved from South Carolina, her OCD flared up, making it hard for her to even leave the house. I was so proud of her.

I would always be there for her. Just like she was for me.

"Pretty," she said, kissing my cheek and helping me stand. "Do you want to see it first?"

Dainty fingers clung to the garment bag as she wiggled it, a playful gleam shining in her eyes.

"Surprise me," I said, turning away from the mirror.

It wasn't a frilly, poofy gown, and that was all that mattered.

The garment bag landed on the floor with a thud, and Sam tapped my ankle. I stepped into the pool of silk at my feet, keeping my back to the mirror.

My heart still thudded like wild rhinos.

"There," Sam whispered as she dusted her hands over my arms. "You're gorgeous."

Her hands rested on my hips, spinning me. My brows raced into my hairline, and an unfamiliar sound rattled around my ribs. It was unlike anything I had ever seen.

Pure ivory satin hugged my curves, accenting every dip as it whispered over my flushed skin. The swooping asymmetrical neckline wrapped around one side of my bust while the other was tastefully covered in illusion fabric adorned with Swarovski crystals.

They glittered all the way down to my wrists, making me look like some garden fairy.

Sam hugged me from behind.

"Don't ruin my work," she said, her eyes lighting up in the mirror. "I'll be right beside you the entire time."

"Thank you."

As Sam left me to walk down the makeshift aisle, I tipped my head back.

Hues of purple and pink splashed against the sky as the sun set. It was unseasonably warm.

I stood underneath the gazebo that led into the ground's gardens. Aileen was worried it would be too cold for an outdoor wedding, but the weather held out.

A handful of chairs sat on either side of the grassy path lined with stunning arrays of fall florals. My fingers trembled around the brocade velvet on the handle of my bouquet. Aileen had done an amazing job in only a few days. I swore the woman was part superhero. That was the only explanation.

That, and Kaelen's influence.

People said money didn't buy happiness, but it definitely made things happen.

Music rang in the distance, and I had a feeling that was my cue. My feet stayed rooted to the spot.

A weight grew between my shoulder blades as a large hand rested there, snapping me out of my wandering thoughts.

"Looks like you need an escort. May I?"

Dark hazel eyes met mine—soft and welcoming. Liam offered his arm, and I wrapped my fingers around his forearm. He was the closest to my age, and the more chaotic of Kaelen's brothers.

A bit of a wild child, even by mafia standards.

But in that moment, I saw him as a brother.

A steady force that wouldn't let me tumble.

I always hated growing up without siblings. Most alpha and omega bonded pairs had big families, but unfortunately, my family hadn't been so lucky. I looked forward to having two new brothers. Three if I counted Torin.

Liam's hand covered mine and we started to move.

Afraid to meet Kaelen's gaze, I stared at my silver flats poking out from under my dress with each step.

"Look up, Willow," Liam said, his voice gentler than I had ever heard. "I promise you, it's alright."

Long fingers patted my hand. Dragging my lip over my teeth, I tilted my head up. On the left stood Sam with a tiny bouquet clutched in front of her dress. Ignoring how my heart hammered, I finally dared to look at him.

Aidan clutched Kaelen's arm, whispering something in his ear.

A purr whispered against my lips as my eyes found his. The bright green glimmered in the setting sun, looking like dewy morning moss. He followed my every movement, his calm façade cracking ever so slightly. My omega preened, and a swell of emotion choked me.

Father Fitzpatrick nodded as Liam placed my hand in Kaelen's. His crystal eyes twinkled under his half-moon glasses.

"My gorgeous omega," Kaelen whispered, pecking my cheek as he stroked my ring.

I barely registered what was happening until Father Fitzpatrick directed me to turn Kaelen's Claddagh ring while he did the same with mine.

"I now pronounce you husband and wife. You may kiss the bride."

Two palms cradled my face, rubbing my cheeks with so much reverence. I covered his hands with my own, allowing him to angle my head how he wanted it. Warmth burrowed into my heart when I met his unguarded gaze, so full of longing and passion.

It was like Sam said; he looked at me like I was the center of the universe.

I almost blurted out those three words. But before I could make a fool of myself, his lips slotted with mine. Our few assembled guests broke into applause. Kaelen slid a hand to my nape, gripping it while his other fell to my hip, tugging me closer.

Father Fitzpatrick cleared his throat as Kaelen slid his tongue past my lips.

Desire burned beneath my freckles. Kaelen chuckled, palming my head and pressing it into him.

"Sorry, Father," he murmured. "Got carried away with my blushing bride."

Chapter 23

KAELEN

As we settled around the table for dinner, I kept touching Willow, refusing to hold back. I tucked her hair behind her ear, staying as close to her as possible. My gaze flicked to Aidan and Torin, who had Sam tucked between them, showering her with attention.

Goosebumps broke out on Willow's arms as I nuzzled into her, drowning in her intoxicating scent.

For weeks, I'd restrained myself with Willow, nervous that I would spook her if I approached her with the full force of my alpha. But now, she was my wife. Fucking *mine.* And nothing would ever change that.

Soon, I would bite her. Claim her in every possible way.

By the time her heat came, she would be ready.

I would bond her.

At the shelter, I saw something shift. Her scent blossomed, and the shell that surrounded her dissipated. My brave girl. Her omega had accepted me that first night, and now Willow had too.

Even if her heart still hammered like a hummingbird every time I got close.

I secretly adored the effect I had on her.

In between talking over Liam, who got louder with each glass of whisky, Willow leaned into me, flicking her tongue over my ear. I dusted a knuckle under her chin, and a nervous bumble of words spilled from her painted lips.

"What if they had looked before the wedding? There are a few days when they could."

It took a second, but I finally realized what she had asked. My girl was nervous the Italians would figure out when our marriage actually took place.

And come to collect.

I did nothing by halves.

Especially when it came to the well-being of my wife.

While the city clerk had been less than amenable to our advances at first, he relented eventually. I had mistakenly believed money would have been enough to convince the clerk to backdate the license and close up the offices in the interim.

Unfortunately, the clerk was one of the few people in government with any morals. In a civil servant position. It shocked me. It had slowed things slightly. Luckily for us, after some digging, Aidan found payments to a mistress the clerk didn't want his wife to know about.

So much for morals.

In the end, it worked out for me. Blackmail was more effective and saved me money, with the added benefit of keeping my omega protected.

"Bad luck. City clerk's office has been closed all week. They'll never know the difference. I promised you would always be safe with me."

A series of emotions flittered across her features before landing on a sort of reverence that made my chest swell with pride.

Everyone made pleasant conversation over the delicious meal Aileen cooked. Me, on the other hand, counted the minutes until I could sweep my wife away for the evening and show her the courting gift I had been most desperate to give her.

My body ached at the prospect of being buried in her sweet pussy. I edged myself into oblivion all day. I wasn't usually a sadist, but, fuck, for some reason, knotting my omega the morning of our wedding didn't sit right with me.

Now I sat at this table, squeezing her thigh. On the verge of a rut. Desperately in need of release. Ideally, buried inside her.

It didn't help that I fucking smelled her arousal underneath that pretty gown of hers. I licked my teeth, already imagining peeling her out of that silky fabric and revealing her gorgeous tits and curves.

Sweat glistened on the delicate column of her throat as she pushed a piece of cake around with her fork. I didn't notice any distress in her scent, and my hand crept higher up her thigh until she squeaked, releasing her fork with a clatter.

Everyone except Sam ignored her outburst. The woman narrowed her eyes at me, only relenting when she connected why Willow had reacted that way. She pressed the rim of her wineglass into her lips, giving me a tiny nod of approval.

"Eat, Omega," I commanded, lifting a piece of the cherry sponge to her lips.

"Yes, Alpha."

Fuck.

She was so sweet when she wanted to be. I rewarded her by moving my hand slightly lower, groaning as her lips closed around my fingers. That sweet pink tongue darted out, taking the sugary treat. Her lashes fluttered as her eyes twinkled.

Siren. She knew what she was doing to me.

I was seconds away from sending our guests away and tossing her over my shoulder like an unhinged alpha.

And maybe I was.

Willow made me crazy.

Soon, Aileen retired to bed with a glass of wine while my brothers filtered out one by one. Sam kneeled beside Willow, giving her a big hug, saying Torin and Aidan agreed to drive her home. I leveled a stern glare at the pair of them.

Both were honorable, but I silently commanded that absolutely no fuckery happen between them and Willow's best friend. They were in a committed relationship, and I never saw them bring another into their bed, but Aidan's glazed expression gave me pause.

He clutched his chest and dipped his chin. My shoulders dropped as I sent him away with a subtle wave of my hand.

Now that we were alone, I refused to wait a moment longer.

"Come," I said, extending my hand. "I have a gift for my wife."

At the prospect of a present, my omega perked up, an adorable squeak shaking her slim shoulders. That sight undid me as her tiny hand slid into my larger one. Soft skin brushed against my callouses as I entwined our fingers, bringing her knuckles to my mouth and kissing her ring.

A pretty flush crawled up her chest. Instead of letting her walk, I slid my arm under her knees, cradling her like the precious parcel she was. Something that sounded like a squawk echoed around the room. She wrapped her arms around my neck as I carried her up the stairs, careful not the step on her dress.

"Kaelen. Alpha," she hissed, the slight lilt in her tone giving her away. "Put me down."

"No."

I nipped at her chin, and she moaned the prettiest noise. The wooden door to our room groaned as I backed into it, kicking it shut harder than I intended. Books rattled on the shelves, and my omega grinned at me with dark, playful eyes.

"Patience, Alpha," she cooed, running her nails through my beard. "Where's my present?"

My teeth dug into my tongue as I guided her to the floor, resting my hands on her hips. I adored her like this, unguarded and wanting. While the gown hugged her beautifully, I needed to feel her skin under me as I teased and wrung pleasure from her trembling body.

"Needy thing," I said, spinning her.

Her chest rose with a tiny, indignant huff, her breasts straining against her dress.

When Willow first started staying in this room, she asked me what all the loud construction was behind the door. I shrugged it off, telling her it was another closet. Luckily, she let it go after that, not the least bit interested in another room for clothes.

I walked her toward her gift, and she looked at me, a cute V nestled between her brows.

"A closet?" she asked, unable to hide the disappointment in her tone.

"No, mo chroí," I said, opening the door and gesturing for her to step inside.

It was important that I didn't intrude on her space. I stayed a respectable distance away as she stepped inside. An omega's nest was special, and only when she invited me to join her would I step all the way in.

I leaned against the doorframe, tracking her movements.

After some persuasion, I made sure Willow's nest was completed before today. Granted, I still hadn't physically seen the finished project. My contractor sent me photos after having it professionally cleaned to remove all lingering scents.

With her back to me, I couldn't see her face. After taking a few short steps, she froze, her head moving as she took in the entire space. Pale slate gray covered the walls, while floor to ceiling windows stood along the side opposite the door.

In the center of the room, an oversized bed draped in sheer silk canopies sat covered in thick, brightly jewel-colored blankets.

She toed off her flats, digging her toes into the plush carpet as she ran a finger over the end of the jacuzzi tub by the windows. During her heat, the tub could be adjusted to a cooling temperature that would soothe her.

When she reached the bed, her head fell forward. Her torso shook with the sobs she couldn't quiet, and my alpha demanded that I help our omega. Acid burned my esophagus as it felt like shards of glass stabbing me in my chest.

"Invite me in, Omega," I said, struggling to keep the bark out of my tone.

It had to be her decision. I couldn't compel it. My nails dug into the supple wood of the doorframe, my entire body tightening.

"Alpha," she whispered, her voice thick with emotion as she faced me with glassy eyes. "Please. Join me. I need you."

Those three words were a balm to my panicked alpha. In three long strides, I closed the distance between us. My arms curled around her waist, turning her to face me. Her lip wobbled as her eyes darted between me and the bed.

"This is mine? My nest?"

A tentative purr started in my belly, soothing my sweet girl. Her shoulders fell from the pinched position by her ears. I ran my fingers through her silky hair, gently nudging her face to rest in the crook of my neck.

"All yours. If there is anything you don't like, we can change it."

"Oh, God. I love it," she whispered, her voice cracking.

Tiny fingers clung to the lapels of my suit jacket. I continued to run a hand along her back, calming the frantic thrumming of her heartbeat, which finally evened out. She took a step back, looking up at me from under wet lashes.

"But we're married now. Isn't the courtship over?"

Taking her face in both my hands, I kissed her forehead. My thumbs stroked a familiar path over her freckles, shaking my head.

"Oh, my innocent little omega," I said, tucking a piece of hair behind her ear. "Until my mark is here for everyone to see, we are courting. And even after, I will lavish my omega with all things exquisite, shiny, and special, because she deserves no less. Do you understand?"

No matter how long it took, Willow would know how treasured she was. I would devote myself to her happiness. The worry lines on her face vanished as she stared at me.

"I think so," she said, still looking uncertain. The tip of her nose wrinkled. "It doesn't smell like us."

"Not yet," I said, cupping her chin. "We can fix that. Do you want that?"

"Yes, Alpha."

"Good girl," I said, nearly drunk on the scent of her thickening arousal. "Turn around so I can peel you out of this gown and drown your nest in our scents while I knot you."

Chapter 24

WILLOW

A cold bead of sweat trickled down my temple as I let out a shaky nod. I still couldn't believe that this was *mine*. My nest. Growing up, I never had a separate space for one. After I presented, I turned my closet into a makeshift one during my heats.

My heart quivered like some magical fairy while I tugged on my fingers. Roughened hands brushed over my clavicle.

"So beautiful," he murmured, expertly undoing the illusion buttons on the back of my dress.

I traced the crystals on the bodice as the corset loosened. All I heard was the sound of the zipper crawling down my back and my ragged breaths. The smooth silk slid off my shoulders, puddling at my feet. My nipples tightened, and my pussy throbbed.

"Made for me," he said, trailing his fingertips across my exposed skin, leaving goosebumps in his wake. "Did you know that, Omega? That you were crafted especially for me. And I was made for you.

To make you feel good. To take care of you."

His lips closed around my clavicle, and a keening cry escaped me. As my knees buckled, his arm banded around my waist, holding me up.

"No," I breathed.

"I'll have to show you then."

Inked fingers skated over my stomach, toying with the hem of my panties. I moaned, my head falling back onto him. A hand slid between my breasts, and I bucked my hips, desperate for him to touch me.

"Please," I begged. "Alpha."

Ignoring my request, he lifted me as if I weighed nothing, tossing me onto the bed covered in plush blankets. He scrubbed a hand over his beard, his eyes darkened as they followed a path across my body.

"On your knees, hands on the headboard."

The smooth command wrapped around me like spun silk. I eagerly complied, my omega almost in full control. My nails dug into the velvet on the headboard as I looked over my shoulder, watching him.

Slowly, he shrugged off his suit jacket, tossing it onto the foot of the bed. Long fingers worked open the buttons of his shirt, sliding the expensive fabric over his muscled body. A needy sound fell from my lips, making his eyes darken as he stripped down to his briefs.

The mattress sank under his weight as he crawled toward me with all the lethal grace of a panther. My omega keened, wanting to please our alpha.

"I want my pretty wife to make a mess for me," he said, the filthy words sliding effortlessly off his tongue.

His hand cupped my pussy, and I gasped, rocking forward. He chuckled, the sound breathy and ominous.

"Such a good girl. All wet for me."

The praise went straight to my center, making another wave of slick drip down my legs. Soon, the sound of tearing lace filled the room. Kaelen tore my panties off me, tossing the scraps of material aside.

"I liked those," I pouted.

They were ivory lace that Sam brought me with my dress earlier that morning. The delicate material molded to me perfectly, hugging my bum and making it look delectable.

"I'll buy you more," he groaned, adjusting his stiff length in his briefs.

My eyes narrowed, and Kaelen winked, dropping onto his back. As I was about to ask what he was doing, he palmed my thighs, spreading me open and positioning his face between my legs.

"Kaelen," I said, my eyes widened as I tried to scoot away, feeling too exposed.

Nails dug into my thighs, keeping me anchored in place. A chuckle vibrated close to my clit, making me moan.

"Willow," he said back, dragging his teeth over the sensitive flesh of my inner thighs, making me tremble.

"What are you going to do?"

All I saw were his mossy green eyes staring up at me. He lifted a brow, holding me tighter as he sucked a bruise onto my skin. I rocked, letting out a tinkling moan.

"Oh. My innocent omega. I am going to drink from you like the fountain of youth until you're begging me to stop. Until my wife makes a mess of my face with her sweet come."

Fuck, I wanted that. My omega panted with unrestrained need, clawing at me and demanding that I give in to our alpha. That I present and let him take anything and everything. Instead, the only response I mustered was a small, unsteady nod.

A sly grin slid across his lips as he peppered kisses along my thigh, pausing near the spot I needed him most. My eyes closed, and my head fell back. A sting skittered across my leg, making me hiss.

"Eyes on me, Omega. I want to see how beautifully I make you fall apart on my tongue."

The rumble of his words settled in the pit of my stomach, sending a burning passion searing through my veins. My mouth parted with a heavy breath as I did exactly what he said. His tattooed hands curled around my legs, cementing me to the spot.

Completely at his mercy.

"Don't let go, or I'll stop."

Part of me wanted to challenge that, to see if he'd really leave his omega a needy, panting mess in their nest. When his tongue swept over my clit, all thoughts of rebelling vanished. A thread snapped into place, turning my entire body rigid as pleasure swept through my center.

Kaelen licked again, circling my clit before sucking and making me sob. The tip of his tongue trailed lower than his nose nudged against me. My vision clouded. Tingling heat consumed me, burning brighter until it felt like flames shot from my fingertips.

A devious chuckle sounded between my legs. Sweat tangled my hair and my chest heaved with each broken breath. My hands almost flew off the headboard, desperate to run through his long hair and tug.

But I wanted to come, and I was afraid he would make good on his promise and stop.

Strands of hair stuck to my neck while the headboard rocked against the wall. Kaelen continued fucking me with his tongue, alternating between sucking and licking until I was babbling incoherently.

A thread tightened around my waist, and my body quaked. He steadied his pace on my clit, determined to make me fall apart.

And I did. I came with a shattered cry, digging my nails so hard into the headboard that they might break.

"Fuck!"

A mumbled moan vibrated against my clit, drawing out my release as Kaelen leisurely licked me while my legs continued to twitch.

"You're cute when you curse, Omega," he said, holding me against his tongue.

"Alpha. Please. I-I can't. It's too much."

Despite my half-hearted pleas, I circled my hips, rocking back and forth on his face. The last of my orgasm shuddered through me, and another began to build, turning me to ash like a phoenix.

A plush, possessive sound rolled over my sensitive center, and Kaelen dragged the flat of his tongue through me in one long, languid lick that stole my breath. For a moment, he stopped, looking up at me from between my thighs.

Short, shallow breaths escaped my cracked lips, and for a second, I believed he'd let me rest. Then a devilish, twisted smile slid into place. He circled my clit, and I bucked, trying to crawl away with no luck.

A sting skittered across my bare thigh as his hand connected with it in a warning slap. I hissed, glaring at him.

"I always finish my meals, wife, and respectfully, I don't give a fuck if you're shaking."

"Kaelen. Alpha, you ca—"

Two thick fingers slid into my pussy, the sound lewd as he stroked them in and out.

"Give me another, mo chroí."

Hazy rings blurred my eyes. My traitorous body chased his fingers, meeting him thrust for thrust. My head fell onto the headboard with a thud. I tried to speak, but nothing came out.

Kaelen twisted his wrist and tapped a spot that instantly made me fall apart, slick rushing from me as my body contorted in a way I didn't think was possible.

"Good girl," he said, coaxing me through the last of my release before removing his fingers.

My pussy clenched around nothing, missing the fullness of him inside me. Somehow, I still clung to the headboard, needing it to keep me upright. Kaelen's alpha tone broke through the cloud consuming me.

"Come here," he said, gripping my waist and sliding me back until I straddled his hips.

I squeaked, adjusting to the movement. My release glistened in his beard, and my cheeks stung from embarrassment. Strands of hair hid my face as I tucked my chin into my chest. He smacked my ass playfully.

"Lift, so I can I fuck you properly, Omega. Watch you collapse, sated and sleepy on my knot."

Heat coiled into pleasure as I sat up on my knees, and Kaelen slipped out of his briefs. Death loomed. This man was going to kill me, but what a way to go.

It was a pretty dick—thick and heavy.

Like everything else about my alpha, he was objectively gorgeous.

He squeezed his length, fisting above his knot. My body buckled, and he steadied me with a hand on my hip, dragging the tip through my entrance.

As he lowered me onto him, my eyes rolled back into my head. Nothing had nor would ever feel as glorious as Kaelen stretching me.

The tiny part of me that regretted pushing his buttons earlier that morning disappeared, wanting to feel him fill every part of me. It was delicious and made a rightness thrum in the spot below my sternum.

He hissed, drawing small circles on my waist as I tentatively bounced on his cock, too tired to set any type of pace. My hands splayed over his chest, and my brow furrowed.

"Alpha. Can't," I cried, on the verge of collapsing. "Help."

Seeming to understand what I failed to say, Kaelen banded an arm around my waist, rolling us until I was under him. Shadows from the fireplace crept up his back, making him look like some sort of dark angel, kidnapping me from the crystal gates to take me to his lair in hell.

His elbows rested on either side of my face, caging me in.

My hand wobbled as I reached out, unsuccessfully pushing his loose auburn hair out of the way. Something wicked and possessive ignited in his gaze, and to punctuate it, he slammed into me. His lips fused to mine, muffling the inhuman noise that tried to escape.

His knot swelled, catching on my entrance with each thrust. Nipping at my lip, he pulled away, peppering kisses over me until I was breathless.

"Come for me, Willow."

My nails curled into the ridiculously expensive bedding, and my back arched off the plush blankets. Something exploded, the intensity of it slithering around my limbs.

"Fucking perfect," he breathed, sinking his knot into me, stretching me to the brim and locking us together. "*Mine.*"

"Yours," I murmured, weakly clawing at his back for purchase as he emptied himself into me.

He continued to twitch and swell, while smaller orgasms rolled through me, making whatever was left of my reservations melt away. Kaelen whispered sweet words in my ear, brushing my sweaty hair to one side as he positioned me on his chest while we waited for his knot to go down.

A purr vibrated in his chest, his breaths labored as he scent-marked me.

Oh shit.

Sam was right.

I was his, and I wanted him to be mine.

I was in love with my husband and wanted him to be my alpha.

Chapter 25

WILLOW

After two days of keeping Kaelen a prisoner in my nest, he finally convinced me to let him leave. I reluctantly agreed, burrowing further into the plush blankets that smelled of the ideal blend of espresso and honey—of *us.*

Now, I had to figure out how to ask my husband to claim me. I tried to stay in the moment the last two days, keeping my mind from wandering to how to tell him I loved him. I wasn't a teenager anymore. My omega snipped at me, annoyed at me for not presenting for our alpha and confessing our love and devotion.

I snorted, ignoring her ridiculousness for the time being as I inhaled his lingering scent on the pillow. My nose twitched, irked that it was already fading. Like some crazed little thief, I crept into our bedroom, raiding the laundry before Aileen cleared it, stealing his shirts to add into our nest.

Kneeling on the bed, I wove his clothes in between the blankets, rearranging the shirts and pillows for far too long before I was satisfied. With both me and my omega content, I fell back asleep.

Eventually, I woke up when the sun was too bright to ignore anymore. After I showered, I wandered into the bedroom to get dressed, smirking at Shadow, lazily dozing on our bed. I crawled in beside her, scratching a spot behind her ears.

My lips turned down in a frown when I eyed the burned patch on the tip of her tail. Kaelen had found a vet and booked an appointment for Shadow in a few days. Hopefully, they would offer something to help encourage the fur to regrow there.

I hated the idea of her having to wear a permanent reminder. Subconsciously, my fingers drifted to my own scars.

After another hour of dozing with our puppy, I finally slipped into a lilac sundress, the silk whispering against my skin. The house was unusually quiet as I padded through the halls. A note accompanied the serving of soda bread on the counter.

Aileen insisted that I was still too skinny and needed to eat more. Kaelen said she told everyone that. Even Patrick, who ate enough protein to last a lifetime.

I rolled my eyes, picking at the loaf before plopping into an oversized chair in one of the sitting rooms. Unease prickled under my skin. I tried to watch something on TV, but nothing held my attention. A quiet voice echoed in the back of my mind, telling me to go find our alpha.

The more I ignored my omega, the louder she got.

"Fine," I hissed out loud. "You're turning into a real bitch, you know?"

Before I knew it, I was standing outside his study, my hand hovering to knock on the door. I gnawed on my raw lip. My heart jumped as I second-guessed everything. The sapphire on my Claddagh ring shimmered in the light.

It had only been a few hours since Kaelen had left the nest. I shouldn't be so dependent on him that I was already seeking him out. The needy omega thing would stop being cute real quick if I continued to interrupt him when he was working.

My hand fell, and I spun, about to retreat to my nest and burrow into the blankets where his scent still lingered.

"I can smell your sweet cunt, little omega," he said from the other side of the door. I squeaked, my cheeks stinging. "I want to see you, Willow. Join me."

Ignoring the pounding in my ears and the stickiness on my legs, I pushed open the heavy oak door. It closed behind me with a click, and a moan slipped past my lips. Kaelen always looked good. Usually, straining the fabric of bespoke suits and custom-tailored button-ups.

His eyes lit up when he caught me gawking at him. Dark jeans clung to his muscled thighs while a black t-shirt stretched across his chest, showing off his tattooed arms. This was my new favorite version of him.

There was something debauched in his casualness.

Staying quiet, he crooked two fingers at me, beckoning me closer.

My feet moved on their own until I stood beside him behind his desk. A single strand of auburn hair broke free from his bun, hanging over his face.

A rough hand followed the curve of my ass, and a high-pitched whine filled the space.

"No panties," he groaned, nails digging into my skin.

I sucked in a harsh breath, trying to hide behind my hair.

"None of that," he said, pinching my chin, forcing my gaze to meet his. "I want you desperate. My greedy omega is wonderful, panting for her alpha to take care of her. And I will. I'll knot you and keep you full and sated. Strung out from so many orgasms that you can no longer move. I'll worship and protect you always."

"Alpha," I mewled.

"Come here," he said, voice hoarse and commanding as he wrapped an arm around my waist and tugged me into his lap. "What do you need?"

Denim brushed against my bum as I struggled against his hold, unable to get comfortable. The emptiness ached with a need to be filled. I breathed in the hints of whisky and espresso like an addict.

And maybe I was.

When I didn't answer his question, Kaelen grunted, tugging on the zip of his jeans, freeing himself. In one motion, he lifted me, sliding me onto his length. Something between a moan and a scream left my lips as all the air rushed from my lungs.

The burn of him stretching me quickly morphed into a delicious fullness that made me dizzy. Tentatively, I circled my hips, rubbing his crown against the spot that made me melt into a pliant, needy thing.

A warning slap landed on my thigh, and I hissed.

"Don't move, Omega," he said, mischief mixing with the intensity in his eyes. "I want you to sit still and keep my cock warm and snug in this pretty little pussy of yours while I finish reviewing this contract."

"What?! You can't be serious."

"Deadly," he murmured, ghosting his fingers over my abdomen. "If you can be my good girl and do that, I'll knot you afterwards."

"Sadist," I panted.

"Only for you, mo chroí."

The bastard had the audacity to wink at me. He twitched, and I groaned, my nails digging into his thighs. Minutes or hours passed. I had no idea how long it had been. I swore he had finished reviewing the paperwork on his desk long ago and was enjoying stretching out my torment.

A knock echoed around the room, and I scrambled to get off him.

"I didn't say you could move," he said. The authority in his voice made goosebumps break out over my arms. "Stay still."

Terrified, I did my best to fluff out the hem of my sundress, grateful for the desk hiding us mostly from view.

"Come in," Kaelen called, and his tip nudged against a sensitive spot, making me flutter around him.

Kaelen groaned and I smirked, loving that I wasn't the only one unraveling at the seams. The door opened, and Aidan stepped in. His eyes flicked between me and Kaelen, his tongue pushing into the points of his canines.

"I didn't mean to interrupt," he said, the emotionless, businesslike mask in place on his face.

Kaelen's grip on my waist tightened. I prayed Aidan was unaware that I was impaled on Kaelen and staining his jeans with my come. I kept quiet, afraid that if I opened my mouth, I might moan.

"Just spending time with my wife," Kaelen said, brushing the backs of his knuckles over my cheek. "Isn't that right, Willow?"

Fucker. After Aidan left, I was going to kill him.

"Yes," I said, hating how my voice cracked.

The smallest hint of mirth flashed across Aidan's face, gone as soon as it came. He cleared his throat. I wished he would hurry because I didn't know how much longer I would last without begging Kaelen to fuck me.

And the last thing I wanted to do was plead for my alpha's knot in front of my new brother-in-law.

"I only came to let you know that Dimitri agreed to amend the contracts to include exceptions to allow for the use of the tunnels in cases of life or death without prior approval."

The last thread of my willpower melted away. My hand curled around the back of Kaelen's neck, and I scratched hard, smirking when he bared his teeth.

"Good," Kaelen grunted. "I'll have the final amendments finalized shortly."

Now acutely aware of our foreplay, a blush crept up Aidan's face as he backed toward the exit.

"I'll leave you two to it then."

"You're a prick," I hissed, barely waiting for the door to close behind Aidan.

Saying nothing, he stood, lifting me off him and leaving me empty and positively debauched. Air rushed back into my lungs. My bare feet landed on the lush carpet, and before I got my bearings, Kaelen splayed a hand between my shoulders and shoved my breasts into his desk.

"I love it when you're feisty," he whispered, covering my body with his own as he hiked up my dress around my waist.

"Maybe stop talking and start f—"

A sharp sting bloomed across my ass, rushing to my clit, turning my threats into moans. His rough palm rubbed soothing strokes over the spot he had slapped. Warm lips pressed to my pulse, sucking.

Almost too slowly, he filled me in one intoxicating thrust that made me forget why I was mad at him.

"Fuck," he hissed, wrapping a hand in my hair and tugging enough to send a pleasant pressure over my scalp. "You're like the finest aged whisky. Smooth, fiery, and leaving me wanting more. I'm addicted to you, Willow."

A million thoughts raced through my mind, but I was too drunk on the feeling of him to make any sense of it. My hips knocked into the desk with every punishing thrust. Bruises had already formed, but I didn't care as my orgasm rushed to the surface.

Long fingers collared my throat in the gentlest of caresses. A contented moan rose inside me at the feeling, leaning into the grounding touch.

Those three words lingered on the tip of my tongue. I *refused* to blurt out that I loved him like some teenager with a crush while he fucked me. Pressure built as a delicious feeling vibrated in my veins.

"Kaelen," I breathed, sending his papers flying off his desk. "Please."

"I love my name on your tongue," he groaned, struggling to form the words as his knot swelled and caught with each stroke of his hips. "Choking my cock with this tight cunt of yours."

This wasn't the reverent lovemaking of the previous night. This was passionate. Primal. Claiming. Kaelen fucked me within an inch of my sanity.

A wave of heat tore through me, catching fire until I was screaming his name, begging my alpha to knot me. And soon, he was, his knot locking us together as he spilled inside me. My legs gave out, and I was thankful for the expensive mahogany desk supporting me.

Strong arms encircled my waist, carefully pulling me onto his lap as he lowered our joined bodies into his chair.

"Sorry about your contracts," I murmured, limp against his sweaty frame.

"Fuck 'em," he said, rubbing his cheek against mine and scenting me.

Chapter 26

WILLOW

My omega settled enough over the next few days that I didn't whine whenever Kaelen left. Despite that, he still stayed close by. Instead of traveling in and out of the city to complete business, he worked mostly through Aidan and Liam, doing what he could from his office.

We established a routine, one that included Kaelen waking me up with his face between my thighs and his tongue buried inside me until I came, screaming his name.

I dragged myself out of my nest, smiling at Shadow curled on our mattress. She stretched out, splaying her paws in the blankets, completely ignoring the massive, fluffy bed Kaelen got her.

After getting dressed, she followed me down the halls and into one of the sitting rooms. I plopped onto an overstuffed armchair, grinning when Shadow crawled into my lap. It wouldn't be long before she couldn't do this anymore. She was getting big.

My nails scratched through her fur, running her tail through my palm and lingering on the burned section on the tip. At the vet the other day, they confirmed Shadow was overall healthy, but the burn might never heal and that the nerves were dead.

For some reason, it stung like a knife to the chest. I hugged Shadow closer. Kaelen stroked my hair, whispering soothing words to me in between talking to the vet. Kaelen got a second opinion, and that vet told us the same thing.

I felt like I had let Shadow down, leaving her with a constant reminder of the pain she had suffered. My hand paused, aimlessly petting a spot on her belly. Now we both were marked with burns that would never go away.

Maybe I secretly hoped that if I healed her, in a way, it would fix that part of me I always thought was broken.

Fidgeting, I turned on a movie and moved to the couch, Shadow following me. I dozed in and out of sleep, plagued by my thoughts of Shadow and the looming dinner with my parents.

Kaelen informed me last night that my parents would come for dinner on Friday. I had no idea how he convinced my dad to come here after what happened that first night, but based on the smug look on Kaelen's face, it hadn't been an option.

Anxiety bubbled in my stomach, adding a burned tinge to my scent that Kaelen was determined to fix.

A sound pulled me from my thoughts, and I saw Torin standing in the doorway, a pinched expression tight across his face.

I still wasn't used to the two versions of Torin. The carefree beta boyfriend of Aidan and the serious, in-command soldier. This one unsettled me, the tension hanging over him, catching me off guard.

"Something wrong?"

"I was going to ask you the same thing, Miss Willow."

Still with the whole Miss Willow thing.

"We're married now. Can't you call me, Willow? Surely, Kaelen isn't going to have some primitive response to you addressing me by my name?"

A single brow rose into Torin's hairline. Giving up, I tossed my head back onto the couch cushions. Who were we kidding? Now that Kaelen and I were married, the intensity around his alpha had doubled. I loved and hated that he snarled at anyone who looked at me for more than a few seconds.

He had been extra growly since our wedding.

"Mrs. Finnegan, if you prefer," Torin said, mirth twinkling in his words.

Mrs. It made me feel old, even if I liked the Finnegan part.

"You take that back," I hissed, and Torin threw his hands up in surrender.

The knot in my chest loosened. He sank onto the other side of the sofa, staying a respectable distance away. I hated the pitying look that crossed his features, gone before I was certain it was there. His dark eyes swept over my face, cataloging my expression before landing on the place where Shadow slept in my lap.

"You've been keeping to yourself the last few days. You haven't left the house."

"So?" I asked, realizing that Kaelen probably sent Torin to question me under the guise of being a *friend.* "Tell Kaelen he can talk to me himself if he's worried."

"Kaelen didn't send me. You're family now, Willow." My eyes raced into my hairline at the use of my name. "We take care of our blood."

I offered a weak shrug, wanting to deflect the serious conversation that loomed between us. Aidan and Liam technically were my brothers now, but I didn't doubt that Torin felt the same way as the other two alphas.

Sensing there was no avoiding this conversation, I stroked along the length of Shadow's back.

"It's Shadow," I confessed, not willing to admit that it was maybe something more. "The vet said it's not going to heal any more. The nerve damage is too extensive. It'll always be like this."

The tiny black puppy in my lap wiggled, burrowing further into me. I scratched behind her ears, relaxing when she leaned into my touch. Quiet understanding sparked in Torin's demeanor. His body straightened as he shifted.

"How could someone do something so barbaric," I hissed, acid wrapping around my icy words. "And they got away with it. They always do," I continued, my voice getting louder with each word.

"Even if they get caught. They get nothing more than a slap on the wrist. Meanwhile, she'll be scarred for the rest of her life. People abuse animals because they are too weak, pathetic, and insecure to do anything else."

If Torin picked up on the true meaning of my speech, he didn't let on. My usual nurturing omega instincts flared into a protective rage, mirroring a mother bear with her cubs. Shadow was *mine,* and someone had hurt her. It was my job to protect her.

Silence stretched on between us, the clock ticking ominously in the background. A muscle twitched by Torin's eye, his face fixed into an unreadable expression.

"There are other kinds of justice," he whispered, the words so quiet I questioned whether I really heard them.

"What are you saying, Torin?" I asked, afraid I was about to step over a line I could never come back from.

He nodded, a slow, deliberate movement as he rocked forward, resting his elbows on his thighs. Dark eyes glimmered like polished obsidian when he looked at me.

"Kaelen built this family on loyalty, Willow," he said, his Scottish burr getting thicker. "On protecting our own. And you, lass, you're family now. My loyalty to you is as strong as my loyalty to him. Do you understand what I'm saying?"

Warmth spread through me, replacing the cold fury from earlier that choked me. My head fell forward, overwhelmed with the unwavering support. A pledge of devotion. Not something formed from love or bonds or instinct. Rather one from a brother, determined to protect his sister.

"Someone hurt her, Torin. That can't be allowed," I murmured, my voice thick with a command I didn't recognize. "Can you find who did this to her?"

"I can find them."

My breath hitched. This was it. The line. The choice. My omega grew protective and held Shadow closer. The more primal side of me took control, and my morality recoiled.

"Can you make it hurt?" I asked in a raw whisper.

The question hung in the air with unspoken meaning. Torin's eyes—dark and knowing—met mine. Something predatory flared to life as the corner of his mouth lifted.

"Aye, lass," he responded, his voice a chilling rumble. "I can make it hurt."

Something dark twisted inside me. Something foreign. Something powerful.

"Don't kill them. I want them to suffer. I want them to remember what they did to her every single day for the rest of their lives."

Torin inclined his head, covering his chest in a silent vow. Without another word, he rose, his broad back disappearing through the doorway, leaving me alone with my racing thoughts.

Later that night, I curled into Kaelen, counting the thumps of his heart as he stroked my hair in my nest. If Torin told him about our agreement, he said nothing, instead distracting me with his knot until I fell into an uneasy sleep.

Two days later, Torin entered the den where I was curled up with Shadow, tossing a burned match onto the coffee table. I arched a brow, confused when I saw none of his usual playfulness.

"What's that?" I asked.

"The match I used to light him up."

"Is he... dead?"

"No, lass. He only wishes he were."

With a tight nod, Torin exited the living room. A cruel pleasure alighted in my veins, brimming with a darkness that mingled with the very fiber of my being.

Chapter 27

KAELEN

My alpha paced, unhappy with how sad our omega was. A distance lingered in her eyes, her scent not as sweet as it usually was. After our visit to the vet, all she did was cuddle Shadow, fidgeting with her scarred tail.

I didn't try to placate her, giving her space to talk to me if she wanted.

While I tried to ignore the feeling, I knew it was more than Shadow. Inside, she was grappling with a lifetime of abuse she suffered at the hands of her father along with her own marks. I wanted to hold her close, tell her that those burns on her skin, on Shadow's, strengthened them.

Unfortunately, this was something Willow had to come to terms with on her own.

In her own way.

And me springing on her that her parents were attending a dinner with us this weekend didn't win me any favors. I tried to spin it as an opportunity to see her mom, which made a light spark in her jeweled eyes.

I hated forcing her to spend time with that piece of shite. Yet it was the only way I could get close to Isabelle Sterling. All I had to do was get my mother-in-law alone long enough to convince her to let my private nurse take a blood draw.

Then I would send it to Robert Sweeney for a diagnosis. Once I knew what was wrong with Willow's mom, I could help her.

Not just Willow's mom, but mine too. Isabelle Sterling was my blood, and I wouldn't allow her to suffer a moment longer. And once she was taken care of, I'd crush William Sterling like the fucking maggot he was.

The door squeaked open, and my eyes shot up to it, only now realizing someone had been knocking for the last minute. Torin loomed in the entrance like a cryptic shadow. My jaw stiffened as I leaned back in my chair.

Torin was family in every way that mattered. I trusted him as much as Aidan or Liam. The anger clinging to him reminded me faintly of the night he came to me after his sister had been raped.

He moved across the room, standing stone-still at the edge of my desk.

"Willow asked something of me," he said, his tone tight and emotionless.

My fingers toyed with the ring on my finger. I debated replacing it with something new, still wearing my da's since I used it that day to trick the Italians. Instead, I took comfort in something from the past, tying me to the present.

I trusted Torin to protect my wife, my omega. I intended him to keep her safe, but it seemed my sweet girl wanted something more from Torin. Something he was uniquely capable of giving her, if his demeanor was to be believed.

Blood. Revenge.

Torin never went into too much detail of his time in the Marines. However, he had been open when we first met, ensuring me he was uniquely qualified to make people disappear without anyone noticing.

"Are you asking permission or telling me?"

The steeliness in Torin's features faltered for a second, struck by my words. Side-stepping my question, he continued, "She wants me to find the person who tortured Shadow, and extend them the same courtesy they showed the pup."

A darkness hid beneath the surface of my gorgeous omega. Pride swelled in my chest at her protectiveness. If she rallied so fiercely for a rescue puppy, I imagined how intensely she would care for our children.

Images of her pregnant with my child filled my every thought, and I growled.

Torin mistook the reaction for anger, stumbling slightly.

"Boss. Apologies. If you would prefer I leave it, I'll tell her I couldn't find the guilty party."

I waved a dismissive hand, standing. Color returned to Torin's already pale cheeks when he dropped his shoulders from the pinched position by his ears.

"Do whatever Willow asks of you."

Curiosity weaved into my thoughts, wondering why my omega asked Torin and not me. It didn't take long for me to realize that what Willow had asked Torin probably stirred up too many emotions.

Guilt. Confusion. Grief.

Grief for the person she was versus who she has become.

A queen capable of ordering death and destruction.

It wasn't only Torin. Any of my men were at her command. And the sooner she understood that, the stronger she would be.

Regardless, I was so fucking proud of her. But I wouldn't force the issue. She would tell me about Torin and this request when she was ready. Until then, I would spoil her and keep her close.

Footsteps receded as Torin left. I pulled open the bottom drawer of my desk, taking out the wrapped box.

The size didn't quite encompass the scope of the gift in my hands, but ever since I saw her curled up in that tiny kennel with Shadow, I knew exactly what to gift my wife. I shoved it into my pockets, unsurprised to find my omega dozing in her nest, snuggling with one of my dirty shirts.

Fuck. My dick hardened, and I willed it to go down.

Quietly, I padded into our bedroom, hiding her gift in my end table. Shadow kicked in her sleep, looking as peaceful as a hellhound. The menace decidedly claimed our bed as hers, too good for the overpriced dog one on the floor.

I rolled my eyes, hating how easily I was wrapped around a puppy's paw. Someday, it wouldn't only be a dog. I was already at the mercy of my omega, even if she didn't realize it. And once we had a child, my daughter or son would own me just as much.

Careful not to wake Willow, I slipped into her nest, a quiet purr vibrating my ribs as I tucked her into my chest. Sweet, sleepy noises fell from her, and she unconsciously snuggled closer, burying her face in my neck.

I traced a spot over her pulse, the place where I'd make her mine with my mark.

Two days later, Torin told me it was done. It didn't take him long to find who had hurt Shadow. Fucker boasted about it on social media, and Torin enjoyed making him scream for mercy.

I paid personally for the arsehole's care, ensuring that he survived.

The rest of his life would be spent with crippling burns marring one side of his body.

With that knowledge from Torin, a weight lifted from Willow. A light twinkled in her eyes, different from what used to be there. Something glacial gleamed in her sapphire eyes, hardening her in a way that made me ache to fill her.

While eating breakfast, I tugged her onto my lap, moaning at the beautiful, carefree giggle that rang almost melodically around the room.

"I have something for you," I said, fishing her present out of my pocket and placing it in her lap.

The silk of her tiny top was smooth under my fingertips as I stroked her stomach. She wiggled, dragging her bum over my dick in tantalizing movements that had me groaning in her ear. My hand drifted from her belly, down to her bare thighs, caressing the sleep-warmed skin.

A minute later, the tone shifted, and my girl turned cold, sniffling in my arms.

"I did a bad thing," she whispered, her hands shaking around my gift.

I had a feeling what this "bad thing" was, but wanted her to tell me, so I could prove to her how wrong that belief was. What she'd done was necessary. If left unchecked, that prick would have continued to hurt animals, escalating to people eventually.

What she did was a service, and therapeutic for her. Once she accepted that, the easier it would be.

Now I understood why she was conflicted about her dad, if this happening to a stranger tormented her so much.

"Nonsense," I said, tucking a strand of hair behind her ear. "You are my good girl."

"I asked Torin to hurt the guy who injured Shadow."

The bright light faded from her face, and I pinched her chin, forcing her to look at me.

"And?" I prodded.

Her brows pinched, a tiny frustrated sound rumbling under her sternum.

"*And* it's my fault that someone will spend the rest of their lives suffering. Omegas are supposed to be sweet, quiet, and loving. Not orchestrating pain and murder," she said, her last few words so quiet I barely heard them.

Such bullshite propaganda.

Everyone assumed omegas were quiet and submissive, and to an extent they were. But at the heart, they were powerful and protective, more so than most alphas. Their maternal instincts were terrifying when unleashed.

Willow was beautiful and venomous, like lily of the valley.

"Oh, mo chroí, you are wrong."

She hissed, and I chuckled.

"Everyone wants omegas to *believe* that they are fragile, tender things that need an alpha to protect them and take care of them. And that is because alphas egos are so delicate they cannot accept omegas true nature."

My hands slipped into her hair, holding her attention.

"Omegas are fierce, unyielding, and protective of anyone and anything they deem pack. Shadow is *yours,* just as I am. You protected her when no one else would."

A stilted silence hung around us, and slowly, her burned scent shifted, returning to those sweet, floral notes that drove me mad.

"Willow," I said, making her eyes widen with the intensity of her name on my tongue. "My men are at your command… as am I."

My words landed, and before she questioned it, I fused her lips to mine. She relented to me, allowing my tongue to slide into her mouth, her body soft and supple. I grinned when she raked her nails across my back.

"Good girl," I crooned, my lips hovering over hers.

Smirking, she stole another biting kiss, and the fire I loved about her erupted in her gaze.

"I needed to hear that. Thank you."

"Don't thank me," I said, nudging the forgotten box in her lap. "Now open."

The lightheartedness from earlier reappeared as a broad smile split across her swollen, kiss-bitten lips. My adorable omega wiggled in my lap again, and I choked down the inappropriate thoughts flashing in my mind as she tossed the lid away. She unfurled the piece of paper inside, her eyes narrowing as she reread the legal document multiple times before pouting at me.

"What is it?"

"A deed for fifty acres outside of the city."

A cute furrow nestled between her brows. I rubbed the wrinkles away, kissing the spot before explaining.

"The permits for an animal rescue and sanctuary on that property have been approved. Construction will begin next week. You can be involved as much as you want. A beta from Georgia has agreed to relocate here to handle the running of the rescue. She has the knowledge and experience."

"Kaelen," she breathed, knocking a plate full of eggs to the floor as she scurried into my lap.

"Ooof," I grumbled, surprised by something so tiny knocking the wind out of me.

My arms instinctively wrapped around her. Unshed tears glimmered in her eyes, and my alpha preened at how happy we made our omega. It wasn't pain or grief in her gaze. It was pure joy. And I put it there. And I would for the rest of my life.

The sapphire on her ring was smooth under my fingers as I brushed it.

"Sorry," she squeaked, eyeing the spilled food as a pretty blush colored her cheeks. "This is… It's… I can't believe it. This will help so many animals."

All the blood in my body rushed south, and I hissed internally for my cock to relax. Now was not the time. No matter how Willow's nipples tightened against that silky sleep top, or how her cute arse shimmied in my lap.

"*Anything* you want, is yours," I murmured, kissing her temple.

An intoxicating cloud of honey, wildflowers, and fresh rain blossomed around us. I kissed my girl and she perfumed so prettily for me. She mewled, trying to crawl into my skin, and I traced the notches on her spine.

Finally, I think she understood what I was willing to do for her, and now, she was strong enough to accept it.

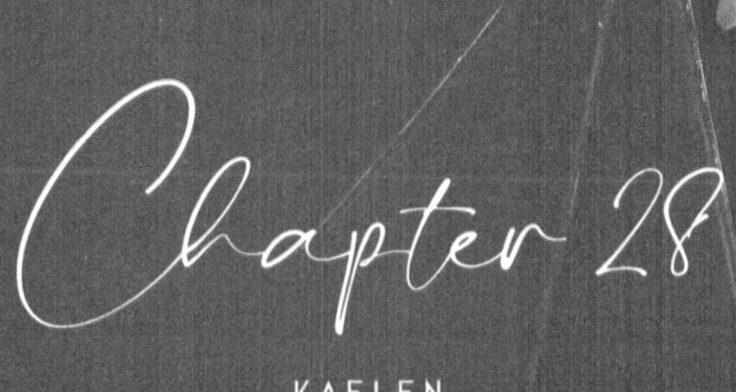

Chapter 28

KAELEN

An eerie calm hung around Willow as she stared in the mirror, smoothing her hands over invisible wrinkles in her sweater. The oversized cream-colored cable knit drooped off her shoulders, showing off the expanse of the collarbone I wanted to lick.

I stood behind her, catching her gaze in the reflection. My hands rested on her hips, and I murmured praises to soothe the nervous energy that she tried to hide.

"Such a stunning omega." She blushed prettily, and I grinned into a spot on the underside of her face. "You have nothing to worry about tonight. Patrick is picking up your parents, and your mom is excited to see you."

When I invited her parents to dinner, William had been less than thrilled. As expected, he prattled on about how his wife was too sick to leave. Based on what Willow told me, Isabelle struggled with fatigue, but always moved mountains to show up for her daughter.

And when I leaked a story to the papers about the candidate for governor and his wife having a private dinner with their daughter and her new husband, he couldn't refuse.

Unless he wanted bad press.

Her hair bounced as she nodded along, hands splaying over her legging-clad thighs. Quiet sighs made her chest heave. I reached over to the table, plucking the necklace I had gifted her weeks ago, and gently clasped it around her neck.

She fiddled with the glimmering sapphire.

"He will never hurt you again, mo chroí," I said, my nostrils flaring.

"I know," she said, covering my hand with hers. "You'll keep me safe."

The admission sent a tendril of heat coiling around my ribs and squeezing until it was hard to breathe. I spun her around, tipping her chin. Like the brave omega she was, she leaned in, brushing tentative lips along mine.

My hands fell to her arse, urging her closer. Her eyes crinkled, and the sweetest giggle grew between us.

"Ready?"

"Ready," she echoed, stealing another kiss before slotting her hand in my much larger one.

The honeyed undertones in her wildflower scent intensified as we arrived in the dining room, and a raspy sound left my lips. She squeaked, hiding her face in my chest. I relished the quiet moment alone, dancing my fingers over her freckled skin.

A throat cleared nearby, and I palmed the back of Willow's head.

Beaty, muddy eyes glared at me, and I wanted nothing more than to watch the life drain from William Sterling. The hair on my arms prickled, and based on Willow's reaction, my scent soured.

"It's okay, Alpha," she whispered, dragging her nails through the wispy hairs on my nape.

Fuck. How did I get so lucky? I was a vile bastard and didn't deserve the sweet thing in my arms, but I would cherish her until my dying breath. My purr grew, and I buried my face in her hair.

"Thank you, mo chroí."

Looking up, I ignored William, my eyes landing on the thin, pale woman beside him. Isabelle Sterling flashed a tight, tired grimace. I tapped Willow on the hip. She turned, sprinting across the room, and gingerly hugged her mom.

Despite the gauntness around Isabelle's cheeks and the sallow tinge to her skin, it was easy to see Willow inherited Isabelle's beauty. Both had dark hair and piercing blue eyes. However, if I didn't know Isabelle was an omega, I wouldn't believe it. Her scent was so muted it was almost impossible to pick the subtle hints of vanilla and peaches.

"My precious girl. You know, I'm sad I didn't get to be at your wedding."

"Sorry, Momma," Willow said. "It was a bit of a whirlwind."

Isabelle leveled a glare at me that made my stomach curdle with more fear than any man with a gun.

"Apologies. We have some pictures we can share with you."

"I'd like that," Isabelle said, threading Willow's arm through hers.

Sweat glistened on William's brow. He plopped down, ignoring his wife and daughter as he poured himself a glass of whisky. I pulled out Isabelle's chair, carefully helping her sit.

"A gentleman. How surprising," she said.

I shoved down my simmering anger. Any alpha that treated their omega poorly deserved to be tossed in the Charles, but there was a special place in Hell for William Sterling. A place I would *personally* escort him to when the time came.

"Yes, ma'am. Would you like a glass of wine?" I asked.

She answered me with a weak wave. "Water is fine, please."

After filling her glass, I sat next to Willow, eyeing the half-full wineglass in her hand. A pretty blush appeared under her freckles, and I whispered in her ear.

"Not too much, little omega."

Nodding, she took a sip, avoiding eye contact with her dad. I didn't care if Willow drank or how much, but I knew she would feel like shite in the morning if she had more than a glass or two. Granted, with the terrible hangover she had after her escapades with straight vodka, I doubted she'd drink much ever again.

Dinner was a stilted affair, the thick tension hanging over our group. I helped Isabelle with her plate when William did nothing to assist her, and this time I couldn't stop the anger that hissed through my teeth.

The fucker had the sense to freeze, fingers shaking around his glass.

Good.

"He seems like a nice boy," Isabelle said, looking at her daughter, the words almost as frail as she was. "How did you two meet?"

Of course, William didn't tell his wife that he had sold their only daughter like a piece of cattle. If not to me, then to the Italians. Willow bristled beside me, the color draining from her face. My hand covered her thigh, squeezing it under the table.

"At the animal shelter in Quincy," I said, bringing our joined hands to my lips.

"What is it you do, Kaelen? Your home is… impressive," Isabelle asked, pushing the food on her plate around.

Unfortunately for us, Willow's mom was perceptive, and she didn't believe an ounce of our bullshite. Someday, we'd tell her the truth, but not now. She was family and deserved to understand our relationship.

My alpha recognized Isabelle as blood, as someone to protect, and I'd do anything to ensure her safety.

"I own a string of successful pubs throughout Boston. I have been lucky to have a lucrative business," I said, leaving the rest unsaid.

William snorted, and I swear I saw the moment blood turned to ice in his veins when I glared at him. Bold for a man who had a clock counting down his demise above his head.

As we worked through the roast and dessert, Willow relaxed, telling her mother about the rescue I'd gifted her. That seemed to win me bonus points with Isabelle Sterling. While she barely touched dinner, Isabelle ate a heaping portion of pudding.

Placing my napkin on my plate, I stood, pressing a kiss to the top of Willow's head.

"The gardens are breathtaking this time of year. I'd love to show you the flowers. My ma planted them before she passed." Sadness brimmed in Isabelle's eyes. "Would you honor me with your presence, Mrs. Sterling?"

A half-hearted growl fell from William's lips, but faded as quickly as it came. Willow stiffened, and her scent turned almost acrid with fear.

"I think I can only handle a short one," Isabelle murmured, taking extra time to stand. "But that sounds lovely."

"Wonderful," I said, tilting my chin in the shadows. Aidan and Liam emerged, William blanching at their approach. "My brothers can join Willow and William and get to know him better."

Once Willow understood I wasn't leaving her alone with him, the tightness in her limbs faded. Aidan and Liam plopped less than elegantly into the empty seats on either side of Willow.

"Hi, sis," Liam said, pecking her on the cheek and glaring at William.

I joined Isabelle. The faint scent of peaches and freshly baked bread shifted, lined with the barest touch of fear. My alpha reacted, trying to ease the omega who was now my mother-in-law.

As we stepped out onto the lawn, I wrapped her arm around mine. A light breeze rustled through the treetops, carrying the scent of honeysuckle with it. We strolled down the cobblestone path, my pace adjusting to match hers.

A subtle tremor twitched Isabelle's fingers as she caressed the flower on a nearby hedge.

"You take care of her," Isabelle said, patting my forearm.

"On my honor, ma'am," I said, plucking the rose and tucking it into Isabelle's hair.

We reached a secluded bench nestled beneath a willow tree. This had been my ma's favorite place. On her last day, she sat out here for hours with my da. Ma always said willow trees represented resilience and rebirth. Told me they gave her hope.

My Willow was all those things. Strong. Tenacious. Unyielding. I watched her grow in the last few weeks, blooming into the fearless omega she had always been. My gaze landed on Isabelle, and it was easy to see where Willow had gotten her strength from.

Isabelle swayed but didn't falter.

I gestured for her to sit, and she looked thankful for the

opportunity to rest.

"Isabelle," I began, my quiet voice laced with a serious undertone. Her eyes narrowed, a flicker of apprehension in their depths. "I'd like to help you."

"I'm fine, Kaelen."

"No, you're not. You're an omega, but your scent is barely visible, and Willow told me the doctors continue to downplay what's happening with you."

Her gaze dropped to her entwined fingers on her lap.

"Nothing to worry about. Getting old."

The shaky break in her tone told me she didn't even believe what she said.

"You're not old," I said, leaning forward. "Something or *someone* is making you sick, Isabelle. I can help you. I have a private physician who has agreed to investigate your results, but he needs a blood sample from you first."

Every muscle in her body went rigid, and she refused to look at me.

"I-I can't. William wouldn't allow it. His campaign, and I..."

"Shhh," I whispered, rubbing her arm. "You don't have to go anywhere, and William will never know. I have a nurse here who can take it right now, and all he will know is that you and I went for a stroll in the gardens where you threatened me if I hurt your little girl."

A hollow laugh made her cough, and she finally looked up at me.

"You really think you can help?"

Hope illuminated her tired words. I took her small, delicate hands in mine, surprised by how cold they were.

"I do. All I need is your permission, Isabelle."

If this woman was anything like Willow, I expected her to fight me. But then I saw it, the moment clarity settled in her eyes, making the blue crystal clear. Her body slumped.

"I couldn't protect her."

My heart dropped into my stomach.

"He made it so you couldn't."

I didn't know how, but I knew he had something to do with

Isabelle's condition. And I was going to find out. All I needed was her permission. She blinked away a stray tear, resolve glistening in her features.

"Okay."

"Okay," I echoed.

Without letting go of her hands, I fished my phone out of my pocket, sending a text. A minute later, a young beta girl appeared, crouching in the grass by Isabelle. The woman was exceedingly gentle, talking Isabelle through every step before sealing the blood sample and packing away her supplies.

"Doctor Sweeney will be in touch soon, Mr. Finnegan."

"Thank you, dear," I said, and the girl disappeared the way she came. "Ready?"

After escorting Isabelle back to the dining room, I was pleased to see Willow completely at ease with Aidan and Liam. And I was even happier to see a vein in William's head about to throb out of his temple.

He jumped to his feet upon our arrival.

"Time to go home."

I patted Isabelle's hand, pecking her cheek before she and Willow said their goodbyes. Liam and Aidan offered to drive William and Isabelle home, and I chuckled at the green color rising on William's face.

Once we were alone again, Willow stepped into my space.

"Alpha," she whispered, the sound listless and needy.

A coil of hair wrapped around my finger as I tucked it behind her ear. She came to me, her alpha, and I'd take care of her. I slipped an arm under her knees, sweeping her up and against my torso.

"You did such a good job today. Do you want to curl in front of the fire and watch a movie or cuddle in your nest?"

"Nest?"

"Yes, Omega. My good girl. Let's go to your nest. I need to reward you."

Chapter 29

KAELEN

The first hint of dawn pressed against my eyes, but it wasn't the light that woke me from a dreamless sleep. A warm pressure glided across my chest, moving lower. I groaned, the sound sleep-roughened. The musky scent of arousal clouded my senses, mixing with overwhelming notes of honey and wildflowers.

With my eyes still closed, I slid my hands into Willow's silken hair, urging her closer. A gasp brushed over my lips as her fingertips dipped into the waistband of my briefs. I licked my lips, lifting my arse as she slid the tight fabric down my thighs.

Tiny fingers encircled my shaft, making my head fall back into the pillows. The pad of her thumb stroked over the slit, catching the bead of pre-cum there and dragging it down my cock.

"Omega," I moaned.

Instead of saying anything, she giggled a tantalizing sound that made me harder than stone. Those velvety lips wrapped around my tip, and white-hot pleasure moved like molten liquid through my veins. My nails scratched at the blankets, and I swore I saw God as she took me into the back of her throat.

She swallowed around me, and a string of Gaelic curses hissed through my teeth. My balls tightened, and too quickly I was emptying myself in her hot little mouth.

I finally opened my eyes, the muscles in my abdomen rolling as I emptied the last of my come. Her lips curved as she flicked her tongue over the head, making it twitch.

"Morning, Alpha," she said seductively, her husky voice sending a coil of need slithering around my limbs.

Hair hung around her face as she hovered over me, her sapphire eyes twinkling in the morning light.

Her knees pinched on either side of my hips as she sat up, licking the remnants of my release from her swollen lips. I wrapped a hand around her throat and took what I wanted. The taste of me still clung to her lips. I held her there, sliding my tongue along hers. She gave in to me, letting me take more until I pulled away, both of us breathless.

"Come here," I grunted, my voice still heavy.

My fingers dug into the supple skin on her thighs, rolling us over.

"What do you want this morning, mo chroí? My mouth or my fingers?"

I grinned, my touch making her squirm.

"Both?" she said, sucking on that plump bottom lip.

"Greedy omega," I said, smirking as I palmed her cunt.

"Please," she breathed, rocking off the bed.

"Only because my good girl begs so prettily."

The mattress bounced under me as I dropped to my stomach, slipping my arms under her legs and pulling her until her wet pussy was only an inch away from my face. Fuck, she smelled like ambrosia.

Tiny tremors seized her muscles as I languidly licked through her slit, gently flicking her clit. I started slow, wanting her pleasure to build until it exploded from her like a dying star. She was all the stars in the sky.

All of *mine.*

Her core grew impossibly snug as I slid one finger in up to the knuckle, pulling out and adding a second. A desperate, whining sound trilled from her as she took me deeper. Her honey coated my face as I fucked her hard, tapping that sensitive spot that made her cry out.

"Kaelen. Alpha."

"That's my omega," I crooned, rotating my wrist and making her sob as I sucked on her clit. "I want to feel it. Soak me with your delicious come."

A long, wailing cry rumbled in her chest as sweat glistened on her sun-kissed skin, making her look like an angel as she came apart for me. Delicate fingers knotted in my loose, long hair, tugging me where she wanted me as she rode out her release on my face and fingers.

"Shit," she panted, going limp as her drenched pussy finally stopped convulsing around my fingers.

Carefully, I crawled over her, holding myself up on my elbows and pushing the sweaty strands of hair off her face.

"Well done, wife," I whispered, stealing a quick kiss. "Would you like to join me in the bath so I can clean you up?"

"Down boy, you insatiable creature," she chuckled.

"Me? You're the one that woke me up with your pretty pink lips on me."

"Semantics. Besides, I have a meeting with Caroline about the new rescue in about an hour. If I take a bath with you, I will be late. So, no. You can stay here while I get ready."

With another shove, she pushed me aside, and I fell backwards into her nest. The tip of my tongue pressed my teeth as I watched her cute arse walk toward the bathroom. I groaned a rattling moan, willing my half-hard cock to settle.

Reluctantly, I left her to get ready while I slipped into our ensuite in the bedroom after giving Shadow her obligatory side-eye at her sprawled out figure all but claiming our bed. Water dripped from my hair as I tugged out a pair of dark trousers.

Tiny hands slid over my bare waist, nails trailing deliciously over the lines of muscles on my abdomen.

"You're a terrible tease."

"You love it," she giggled, her lips warm against my back.

Three words almost spilled from me. Instead of saying them, I shrugged on a white button-down.

From the moment Willow walked into my office, I knew she was my omega. What I hadn't expected was to care so fucking much. To care beyond my alpha's need to please and protect.

It wasn't a biological imperative turning me soft.

It was Willow. Beautiful. Brilliant. Tenacious.

I controlled Boston with a snap of my fingers, yet Willow could have me on my knees with one look if she willed it.

And now that she realized it, I was utterly fucked.

Utterly devoted.

Utterly in love.

I loved Willow Finnegan, my wife.

I belonged to her.

"Bye, Alpha," she said, pulling me back to the present with a kiss.

I wrapped my fingers around her hair, tugging enough to make her gasp, taking more of her. My hand cupped her bum, grinning at the shocked expression.

"Goodbye, Omega," I said, letting my lips linger on the corner of her mouth.

Color appeared high on her cheeks as her delicate throat worked. She wavered slightly, giggling like a flustered schoolgirl as she left. I snorted, running a hand through her hair before adjusting my tight trousers.

Fuck.

I was going to be hard for hours, and it was entirely my fault.

Clouds rolled in, darkening the afternoon sun as I struggled to focus on the paperwork on my desk. It was bureaucratic bullshite regarding permits and liquor licenses. Usually, Aidan dealt with this nonsense, but I wanted to get my eyes on the legal side of business for once, already regretting my decision.

My fingers tapped on the polished glass in my hand, swirling around the early afternoon whisky when my phone rang. Robert's name flashed across the screen. I hissed, taking a large sip before answering the call.

"Sweeney. I assume you have Isabelle Sterling's results?"

After a brief pause, Robert's calm, measured tone broke the silence.

"Mr. Finnegan," he started, and I scrubbed a hand through my beard. "The results are concerning."

My knuckles whitened as I gripped the phone. "How concerning?"

"The levels of suppressants in her system are dangerously high. Far beyond prescribed therapeutic doses to manage heats. It's a sustained, aggressive regimen that's poisoning her."

The depravity made my blood run cold. Dead air echoed on the phone, Sweeney not daring to interject my thoughts. Only a few unmated omegas with unmanageable heats went on suppressants. I never heard of anyone being on them as the side effects were dangerous.

Every time I thought I had found out the most disgusting thing William Sterling had done, he proved me wrong. I repressed a snarl, digging my nails hard enough into the polished wood to scuff the surface.

"How long?" I asked, hissing again when he didn't answer quickly enough. "How fucking long has this been going on?"

"Difficult to say precisely without an accurate baseline," Sweeney said, his tone careful as he spoke each word. "But given the accumulation, I'd estimate years. At these levels, it mimics the pain of some late-stage cancers while keeping an omega compliant. In essence, she is too weak to do anything but please her alpha."

A bitter taste flooded my mouth. Why? The only reason that made sense was that William Sterling wanted sympathy for his sick omega. And while he poisoned his wife, he tortured his daughter.

"What's the prognosis? If she stops?"

"If the suppressants are immediately discontinued, she should begin to see improvement within a couple of weeks. Omegas are resilient," he said with a fondness that settled my frantic alpha. "Within a few months, she could be back to normal, provided there are no underlying conditions that have been exasperated."

I worried the band of my ring as I contemplated what to do. It was never a question of what I would do for Willow. But after spending one evening with Isabelle, I was as committed to protecting her. The older omega had burrowed into a dark part of my heart that had been empty since my parents died.

"Mr. Finnegan?"

The silence lingered as I tried to plan out how to deal with William Sterling. Willow's only stipulation before anything happened to him was that her mom was safe.

"And what about her bond with her alpha?"

"Isabelle Sterling's omega isn't just dulled, but their bond is weakened. While not common, we have seen an increasing amount of alphas managing their omegas through suppressants to make them more malleable. The suppressants have stripped the bond down to its final frayed threads."

"Could she survive if the bond was severed?"

I heard the man swallow, the intent clear behind my words. Only one method existed to destroy a mate bond between an alpha and an omega.

Death.

"Once she's off the suppressants. Yes. In fact, it would be safer and allow an easier recovery for her. While the physical effects can be addressed, the mental ones may linger. I can recommend someone who could help with that as well."

Relief washed through me. I released a shaky breath, only half hearing what he said.

"Thank you, Sweeney. That will be all."

I ended the call, my mind racing. The situation was delicate. I had to coordinate a series of meticulously timed steps, or William Sterling would be on the evening news accusing me of kidnapping his wife.

And while I trusted my attorney to get me out of sticky situations, I wasn't confident there was any way out of that one. I texted Liam and Aidan to meet me in my office, settling into the oversized leather chair by the fireplace, running through scenarios while I waited for them.

Twenty minutes later, they arrived, their scents sharp. Aidan's eyes swept over the room, narrowing on me before sinking into the chair opposite me. Liam stayed standing, leaning against the wall. Between ourselves, I was confident that we could quietly intercept the deliveries of suppressants and swap them with placebos.

"Aidan. I need you to find out how William Sterling is receiving his omega suppressants," I said.

My brother growled. His dark eyes narrowed and his nostrils flared, understanding the implications behind my words. Aidan was a strategist, calm under pressure and calculating. If something was hidden, he'd find it. The only other time I'd seen his alpha react was after the attack on Torin's sister.

The man nearly ripped my head off when I ordered him to stay put while I took care of it. He was too emotional and would have done something stupid.

"When I find them, you want them replaced with fakes?" Aidan asked.

Nodding, I smirked as Aidan pulled out his phone, not wasting a second at getting to work. It only took twenty minutes with the senator for my brothers to hate him almost as much as I did. My eyes flicked to Liam.

He scratched his beard, unusually quiet. His gaze finally met mine, and an intensity blazed there, boding well for me and not so much so for Sterling.

For as playful and annoying as Liam was, he was bloody terrifying, taller than me and built like a stone house.

"Liam," I said, my brother tipping his chin higher. "I want two men on him at all times. His house. His office. I want to know if he so much as sneezes. When he realizes Isabelle's omega scent is returning, I suspect he'll become erratic."

Liam cracked his knuckles. "I'll have me and Pat keep an eye on him."

"Don't let Sterling see either of you," I said.

"You never let me have any fun."

I pinched the bridge of my nose, too tired to spit back.

What I wanted… was my omega. I checked my watch, contemplating texting Torin and telling him to get her cute arse back home. I wanted to worship every freckle on her skin with my tongue and drown away this day with her scent.

"And if the senator tries to get replacement medication when he pieces together it isn't working anymore?" Aidan asked, not looking up from his phone.

"Intercept those too and notify Liam. If he attempts to harm Isabelle, I want you to intervene and notify me immediately. Secure Sterling until I arrive, and make sure Isabelle is safe."

Aidan remained buried in his phone, pacing until there was a worn spot on the floor. Liam stood, watching the flames lick at the stone. Every piece had to move in sync with the others. If we pulled out Isabelle too soon, we risked not being able to sever her bond with Sterling.

If we waited too long, that piece of shite might do something rash, and my omega would be heartbroken.

A knot ached at the base of my neck. I needed her in my arms, in my bed, where I could show her how much I loved her.

At least until I figured out how to tell her.

Chapter 30

WILLOW

Fresh rain glistened on the leaves, mud thick under my boots as I walked around the grounds. I'd spent hours at the site for the rescue every day for the last week. Contractors came in and out, meeting with Caroline. The beta was almost as intense as Kaelen, snapping at everyone and giving directions.

At first, I thought I'd be in Caroline's way, but she seemed indifferent to my presence. Based on her rigid attitude, I'd take that as a win. I sat at a table in a small trailer, reviewing the scope of work, and it was a massive undertaking.

Some acreage was slotted for play yards and others for housing for large and small breed dogs. Before I knew it, Torin slunk out of the shadows, snorting at my hunched figure.

"You'll develop a hump if you keep sitting like that."

Rolling my eyes, I saluted him with my empty cup of coffee. "I guess Kaelen will have to banish me to the bell tower then."

"Come on, lass."

"Lass? No more Miss Willow?"

"No."

Deciding not to push it, in case he ended up calling me Mrs. Finnegan to make me mad, I left it alone. Kaelen greeted us at the front door of the contractor's trailer, his hands in his pockets.

"What?" I asked.

"Come. We're going out to dinner and you need to get ready."

Butterflies swarmed in my belly as I let him lead me into the backseat of the car with him. My omega was delighted to spend time with our alpha. And I was excited, looking forward to a night out with my husband.

My husband.

A man I loved.

Grunting, he placed my legs over his thighs, caressing my calf as we drove through the suburbs and into the city. Once back home, he followed me into our room, his palm an anchor against my lower back.

My eyes roamed over him as he shut the door behind us. Dark suit pants hugged his thighs, with a white shirt stretched across his chiseled chest. Someone carved him out of marble. That was the only explanation of how one man could be so handsome.

"You know you don't need to take me anywhere fancy. I'd be happy with a burger at one of your pubs."

Smirking, he silenced me with a kiss, grabbing my hips and pulling me into him. I grinned at the combined headiness of his scent and his hands. A thumb brushed over my freckles, tucking a strand of hair behind my ear.

"Someday you'll learn to enjoy it when I spoil you, mo chroí."

Threads from his ridiculously expensive shirt slid under my fingers as I pushed him down onto the bed. His knees collapsed against the edge before he landed with a quiet thud.

"I enjoy you in jeans and a tight t-shirt," I winked, crawling on top of him.

"Feral thing," he chuckled, pinching my hip. "You, saying you don't like my suits."

I shrugged, sitting up on my knees and tracing a line of tattoos visible under his shirt. "It has a certain appeal."

Truthfully, I loved the way his muscles flexed under the material, and the way his body molded to the fabric. Every version of him was made for me, and my omega keened when I gave in to that realization.

A sting made me hiss as he swatted my bum.

"Get dressed, Omega."

"Yes, Alpha," I said, unable to ignore how much I liked it when he tried to boss me around.

A thrill zipped up my spine as Kaelen's hand settled on the small of my back, guiding me over the threshold into the restaurant. His potent blend of whisky and espresso expanded as we moved inside.

Silk brushed against my fingertips as I tugged at the hem of the custom Marc Jacobs dress Kaelen insisted I wear. Beside him, I felt like a movie star. Every eye in the room landed on us. I leaned in closer, resting my palm on the lapel of his bespoke suit jacket.

I didn't belong in a place like this with someone like him. As if sensing my unease, he tucked me into his side and purred—a velvety, decadent sound that made me want to do the same.

Lips rested on my temple as he drew circles on my hip.

The touch steadied me, reminding me of who I was.

I was Willow Finnegan. The most powerful woman in Boston. I belonged here. I belonged with him.

And he belonged with me. My hold on his forearm tightened. I swore something akin to pride glittered in the dark specks of his eyes.

A tall man with a pointed nose greeted us, shrinking under Kaelen's unrelenting glower.

"Reservation for Finnegan."

For a second, it appeared the host forgot how to breathe, nearly choking and bowing so low I thought he might snap in half. The man wordlessly gestured for us to follow him through the lavish dining room. Kaelen threaded his fingers with mine, bringing my knuckles to his lips and kissing them.

Blush burned my cheeks as every head turned, eyeing us before quickly snapping away. Hushed murmurs followed our footsteps, and my heart raced. Soon, the whispers melted into a reverent silence, some people dipping their chins in our direction.

Unease pitted in my stomach as I instinctively nestled further into Kaelen's hold, chasing his sinful scent. The odd combination of awe and fear among the guests made my skin prickle. Kaelen, however, thrived in it.

With an arm slung around my waist, his palm splayed possessively across the jut of my hip.

Lips brushed over the shell of my ear, and I sighed, almost forgetting my discomfort.

"It's alright, mo chroí. Embrace it. This is your power now. Mine and yours. Let them see it. Let them fear it."

The quiet affection resonated in my gut, sending a different warmth through my veins. *Trust.* Something stirred within me, willingly accepting the power Kaelen was offering. The power of belonging, and the satisfaction that I wielded as much of it as he did.

My chin lifted almost imperceptibly. Kaelen let out a pleased groan that did terrible things to my panties.

"Good girl," he cooed.

"Can we go home?"

"Needy thing. No. I haven't finished spoiling you yet."

"You spoil me plenty."

"Not even close to enough," he said, lightly collaring my throat and tipping my chin back with his thumb. "Not until you're naked in my bed with priceless jewels adoring your body."

I squirmed, another needy sound whispering from me. We arrived at a secluded table in the depths of the restaurant, illuminated by candles and brass lamps on the walls.

"Mrs. Finnegan, if I may," the host said, gesturing to a chair.

I offered him a reassuring smile, only for Kaelen to slap his hand away.

"Mr. Finnegan. Sir… Apologies. I did not mean to offend."

Kaelen dismissed him with a half-hearted wave of his hand, pulling out my chair for me instead.

"That was unnecessary," I said, rolling my eyes as I sank into the cushioned seat.

"No one takes care of my omega except me," he said, pushing my chair in and kissing my pulse point.

Despite my best efforts, I secretly enjoyed the possessive claim from my alpha. Kaelen made me feel safe. *Safe.* It was an odd sensation. It wasn't until now that I realized I had spent the better half of the last decade feeling anything but that, constantly in a stage of fight or flight.

Kaelen settled in beside me, touching and kissing and whispering until I wiggled in my seat, making him chuckle. The backs of his knuckles dusted over my arm when our meals came out. I leaned further into him, and he gently pinched my chin, sending a rush of arousal to my center.

"Eat, Omega."

The warmth of his alpha command seared over my skin. I speared a scallop, moaning at how it fell apart on my tongue.

"You can't make those noises," he grunted, squeezing my thigh under the table.

"Trouble, Alpha?" I asked, sweeping my tongue across the tines of my fork.

"You're the one who is going to be in trouble, *wife*," he said, his voice hoarse as he drained his wine.

Dark green eyes watched me as I ate, taking pleasure in my movements. A faint smile ghosted over his features. I savored each bite, surprised by how tender the steak was.

Over the years, I had attended at least a dozen fancy dinners for my dad's re-election, but nothing tasted this good.

The waitstaff were courteous and slightly terrified as they cleared our plates and brought out dessert. I shimmied, almost giggling at how pretty the chocolate pastry looked. I had no idea what it was, but knew it was going to be delicious. Kaelen breathed a raspy sound, digging his fork into the dessert and bringing it to my lips.

Before I tasted it, an acrid scent, like stale cigar smoke and spoiled fruit, made me gag. I winced, shaking my head. My omega bristled, and Kaelen dropped the fork with a clink, digging his nails into my hip.

"Kaelen Finnegan and his wife," a rough, grating voice said, cutting through our reverence. "What a pleasant surprise."

A metallic taste danced along my tongue as my teeth dug in hard on my poor lower lip. Two men and a young girl stood in the entryway to our tucked-away table. Far enough to be respectful, but close enough to leave me and my omega uneasy.

Kaelen's scent shifted, a burned edge corroding the usual cozy notes.

Both men were undeniably alpha, the older of the two gray-bearded and pot-bellied. A seedy sneer spread across his lips, revealing yellow teeth. My stomach flip-flopped, and Kaelen's grip on me tightened. The younger of the two men remained unnervingly neutral, his face giving nothing away.

"Rossi," Kaelen said, his free hand drifting to his gun, while holding me tighter. "I will kindly ask you to keep your eyes *off* my wife and omega."

My breath hitched. I tried not to panic. I didn't want to show fear, not in front of the man who had been too close to marrying me. I retched, imagining a world where I was bound to Vittorio Rossi.

Wood scraped against the floor as Kaelen rose. Even in a room full of alphas, his towering figure dwarfed everyone else. I clung to his hand, my pulse thudding in my ears. Vittorio gave me a look that hovered between placating and predatory.

The younger alpha placed a heavy hand on the young omega's shoulder, prepared to jump in front of her if needed. Kaelen stiffened, giving my hand a reassuring squeeze as his chest heaved with labored breaths.

Chances were we were a few seconds away from Kaelen's alpha bursting free, sending the restaurant into chaos. I trailed my finger over his tattooed knuckles, trying to push out as many calming pheromones as I could.

"Willow Sterling is such a charming creature. Can't say I'm surprised you scooped her up," Vittorio said. "I still believe she was promised to me first."

"Finnegan," Kaelen corrected, the vein in his neck throbbing. "And she is not *yours*. Willow is *mine*. My omega. My wife."

Vittorio gave a clumsy bow, a hand splayed over his chest.

"Of course. My sincerest apologies. Please forgive my rudeness, Mrs. Finnegan," he said, his raspy voice thick with his Italian accent.

"Don't. Talk. To. Her," Kaelen snapped, his green eyes almost black.

The younger man beside Vittorio shifted. Unsettled. He murmured something in Italian to Vittorio, making his beady eyes narrow. Vittorio's face pinched as he waved off whatever the other man said. The younger man shot a subtle look at Kaelen, something urgent in his gaze.

Kaelen's hand drifted, and for a second, I thought it was to his gun. My throat constricted. I debated hiding under the table when the shadows in the dimly lit room shifted. Torin emerged from the darkness, with no playfulness in his features.

Soon, Aidan and another man I didn't recognize appeared, the men flanking me and Kaelen.

"What are you doing here?" Kaelen asked.

"Simply a happy coincidence," Vittorio said. "I was enjoying dinner with my son and daughter when we saw you. The polite thing is to say hello. Is it not?"

"Not in this case. Leave."

The younger man gently hid the young omega with dark eyes and even darker hair behind him, trying to move her out of harm's way. Vittorio's son sneered. Not at Kaelen, but at his father, hissing loud enough for us to hear.

"Padre, per favore. Non addesso."

Torin moved from the side of the table, now in front of it, blocking me with his hand resting on the hilt of the gun on his hip.

What color remained in Vittorio's gaunt cheeks vanished. He glowered at his son but relented, dipping his chin.

"Of course, Kaelen. My apologies. A misunderstanding,"

Vittorio said, his eyes landing on Torin before drifting back to Kaelen like he had been trying to steal another glimpse of me.

My skin crawled. I buried my face in Kaelen's stomach, feeling safe when he palmed the back of my head.

"We'll leave you to your dinner."

Vittorio reached out, attempting to pull his omega daughter to his side. His son snapped, placing himself between his father and his sister, murmuring something in Italian to the young girl. Sad eyes stared up at him.

An expression I was familiar with. One of resignation.

I struggled to see around Torin, only hearing footsteps fading into the distance. The tension in the room slowly dissipated. The hushed murmurs from the main dining room, carrying back in. Our table was secluded enough that other patrons only heard raised voices, not seeing everything that unfolded.

"Keep an eye on the Rossis," Kaelen said, his tone cold and detached. "Vittorio is up to something."

The unfamiliar man nodded, leaving us alone as Torin and Aidan made their way back to wherever they had been.

Once the two of us were alone again, Kaelen crouched beside me, running his rough palms over my thighs. I shivered, a mixture of residual fear and heat from his touch. He cupped my cheek, holding me steady.

"Are you alright, mo chroí?"

I nodded, still shaken. My omega swelled with pride at how well our alpha protected us. I ran my nails through his beard, scratching as he leaned into my touch.

"Okay. A bit of shock."

My gaze landed on the forgotten cake-like pastry on the table, and my stomach twisted in knots.

"Alpha. Can we have dessert to-go?"

"Anything you want," he said, brushing his lips against mine in the shadow of a kiss. "I'll have them deliver one of every dessert on the menu. Come, wife."

Standing, he slipped his hands under my knees, cradling me against him. I squeaked, wrapping my arms around his neck.

"Kaelen, you can't carry me out of here like this."

"Watch me," he said, and I buried my face in his neck.

Chapter 31

WILLOW

The next morning, everything ached. I barely remembered crawling into my nest with Kaelen when we got home. He tried to feed me bits of chocolate, but I shrugged most of it off, falling asleep faster than I thought possible.

Fingers brushed over the thin silk covering my navel as I stirred. Kaelen's arm around my waist tightened, pulling me snug against his firm chest. I rested my hand over his, tracing the ink on his knuckles.

"Good morning," he said, his sleep-roughened voice blowing over my ear.

"Morning."

I turned around to face him, smiling as his hand slid to the small of my back, rubbing against the dimpled skin. Even half-awake, his face was fixed in a hard line. I scratched my nails through his beard, melting at how easily he gave into me.

Kaelen Finnegan may have been the most feared man in Boston. But with me, he showed a different side, something fierce, protective, and undeniably gentle. The sapphire on my ring caught the dappled sunlight, glinting prettily with a kaleidoscope of color.

I loved this man. I wanted to spend my heat with him. I wanted him to bite me. Claim me in every way possible.

A small flicker of fear remained, but mostly, I was happy.

I trusted Kaelen with my life.

After everything with my dad, I thought I'd never trust an alpha enough to ask him to bond me. Yet here I was, those words on the tip of my tongue when his baritone interrupted me.

"I have some news about your mom."

All the joy from seconds ago faded as I clutched Kaelen's forearm.

"Shh. It's alright. I wanted to tell you sooner, but you've been so preoccupied with the rescue, and then last night when we got home you were out almost instantly."

Some color returned to my cheeks at his reassurances, the warmth trailing over my freckles.

"You should have told me sooner."

"You're right, mo chroí, please forgive me. I was waiting for more information from Aidan and Liam before relaying it to you."

I nodded, knowing that whatever was going on with my mom wasn't simple. I knew Kaelen would never jeopardize her or me, so I sucked down my initial anger. Instead, a heavy weight rested in the pit of my stomach, making me queasy.

"What is it?" I whispered, terrified to know the truth.

"Your dad has been dosing her with high levels of suppressants."

"Why?" I hissed, launching up until I teetered on my knees.

A blaze ignited in his carefully controlled features. He snapped his eyes shut for a second before opening them again. The brief flash of heat from seconds ago disappeared, replaced with a serene glow.

"Sympathy from voters, maybe. Most likely to control her. Some alphas need more power. Inadvertently, though, he's weakened the bond with your mom this way. We've replaced the suppressants with placebos. I've spoken to a doctor. We should be able to sever the bond without any injury to your mom. She should have a full recovery."

I swayed, falling on my ass as I tried to process everything Kaelen said. Since I turned ten, my mom had been sick. I barely remembered the vibrant woman I had grown up with. Part of me accepted she would always be that way, frail and unable to do most things.

A whole future flashed before my eyes. One where she was happy, spending weekends at the beach house down in the Cape she loved so much. One where we went shopping, smiling without a care in the world.

It was almost too much to hope for. My hands trembled, and Kaelen took them in his own, pressing them over his thumping heart. It beat steadily. I tapped my fingers in time with the thudding in his chest.

My gaze met Kaelen's. Dark rings pushed against his green eyes as he looked for something in my own.

"*Please.* Allow me. Give me your permission, mo chroí. I will end all of this."

My heart skipped a beat as something sharp cleaved through my chest.

All the pain, grief, and anger I had been silently carrying around for over a decade broke free.

Kaelen stayed quiet, releasing my hands and guiding me into his lap. He didn't prod me for an answer.

The choice hung ominously between us, and something steeled within me. I knew what I had to do. It wasn't really a decision at all. Blood already stained my hands. What was one more? The man who hurt Shadow deserved all the pain he got and more.

And William Sterling had a lifetime of sins to atone for.

My mom and I deserved peace.

"Kill him, Kaelen. Kill William Sterling for me, Alpha."

"I am yours to command, wife. Let me serve you."

He claimed my lips in a fiery kiss, leaving me breathless.

After making me come on his tongue three times, Kaelen regrettably left me a sated mess in my nest. A sigh hummed from me as he pecked my forehead before leaving with Aidan for a meeting.

High from the dizzying orgasms he gave me, I simply nodded along, half-asleep in the bundle of blankets and pillows. It wasn't until about noon when I pulled myself out of my cocoon.

Despite still feeling tired, I wanted to spend some more time at the construction site for the rescue. Caroline sent me a bunch of documents laying out the build locations along with proposed partnerships with local shelters and some high-kill ones in the southern states.

I wanted to be involved.

Whether that meant shoveling dirt, or making phone calls, I'd do it.

The messenger bag Kaelen gifted me bounced against my legging-clad hip. I padded my way into the kitchen where Aileen arched a brow at me while whisking batter in a bowl. I shrank under her intense, silent glare, wondering what I had done to earn her ire.

"Eat before you leave," she said, pushing a sandwich in my direction. "You skipped breakfast."

Her eyes narrowed, and I swore she knew exactly why I had missed breakfast. I hid behind my hair, falling onto the stool by the island as my face flushed. The hard lines around Aileen's mouth faded as I took a bite, pushing a glass of water my way.

"Do I have to tell your alpha you're not taking care of yourself?" she asked.

My eyes widened, and her gaze twinkled. The last thing I needed was Kaelen showing up and forcing me to eat. Besides, it was his fault I had been distracted this morning.

"No, ma'am."

After finishing lunch, I found Torin with his nose buried in his phone.

"Can you take me to the rescue site?"

Color spread high over his cheekbones, and he quickly shoved his cell into his pocket. He offered me a tight nod. I tilted my head to the side, curious about what I had caught him in the middle of that had him so embarrassed.

"Did Aidan send you a dirty picture?"

"What?! No," he sputtered, trying to shoo me toward the front door.

I giggled. "Then what has you so frazzled?"

Torin huffed, rubbing a spot between his brows before opening the car door for me. My nails tapped on the bulletproof window glass, debating whether to put him out of his misery or to poke more.

I always wanted a younger brother to needle.

"It's a girl. An omega. Aidan and I both like her, and we're trying to figure out how to ask her to dinner with both of us."

"Oh. Does she know you're both interested? Is she open to a pack dynamic?" I asked.

One girl from high school was part of a pack now. I'd seen all the photos she posted online. The omega absolutely glowed around all her alphas. I remembered being so confused at first when I found out.

Packs weren't uncommon, but I couldn't fathom trusting one alpha enough to be bonded to, let alone multiple.

She was the only omega, and she had three alphas in her pack. But I'd see all sorts, mixes of alphas, omegas, and betas. So hearing that Aidan and Torin had a crush on an omega only made me curious.

"We're not sure. Hence, dinner," Torin said, palming his nape.

For such a tough guy, he sure looked nervous. It was endearing. Aidan and Torin made an interesting pair. For an alpha, Aidan had an unusual level of control over his instincts. Still strong and imposing, but with more restraint. Then there was Torin, lean and playful.

I imagined the two of them would be the right partners for someone if that's what they wanted.

"How could an omega not be interested in you two?"

The muscles in his face relaxed as he revved the engine and pulled out onto the street. Traffic was relatively light for lunchtime. I yawned. The leather headrest was soft against my scalp as I leaned back and eyed Black and Brew on the corner.

"Can we stop at the coffee shop on the way there?"

"Aye."

After putting the car in park, Torin opened my door. I shielded my eyes from the sun, watching as he tapped the gun hidden under his jacket. A bright blue head of hair floated behind the counter as the barista bounced between four different things.

Torin leaned against the wall by the entrance, eyes scanning as I placed my order. I slid the black AMEX Kaelen had given me through the card reader, and picked up my cold brew from the other side.

I shoved the drink into Torin's hands, snorting at his bemused expression.

"No, thanks," he mumbled.

"I wasn't offering. Hold that for me while I go to the bathroom."

Torin followed close behind me, standing outside the door as my palm pressed against the plywood door.

"Seriously? You're going to stand out here while I pee?"

"Yes," Torin said, his Scottish brogue slipping through his gruff tone. "Be thankful Kaelen doesn't make me go inside with you."

I rolled my eyes. "Have fun. I'll be back in a second."

The first toilet was empty in the small two-stall bathroom. I sat down, admiring the pretty pair of flats in the stall beside mine. My nostrils flared, surprised by the strong alpha scent filling the space. Female alphas were rare, and the other woman in the room with me smelled distinctly of lavender and freshly mown grass.

After I finished, I went to the sink to wash my hands. The tall, tanned alpha came up beside me.

"Hi," I said.

When she didn't return the gesture, I shrugged, ripping off a paper towel and drying my hands.

An arm wrapped around my chest, dragging me backwards. I flailed, fighting to no avail.

"You are sweet. No wonder he wants you. Now hush."

Her honeyed voice chilled me. A thick cloth soaked with something covered my mouth, muffling my screams. I yelled again, calling out for Torin, but no sound came. I kicked and clawed at the arm holding me until my nails were bloody.

My vision blurred, all the colors clouded in the brightly lit room. My omega cried out. We needed our alpha. I never got to tell him. He needed to know I loved him. My thoughts muddled as my limbs turned heavy.

Everything went black.

Chapter 32

KAELEN

The hair on my nape stood on end while I fidgeted. I didn't fidget. Something was wrong and I didn't know what.

I scrubbed my hand over my brow, rereading the text from Liam for the third time.

William Sterling knew the suppressants weren't working. Liam tapped a phone call that morning from the senator's phone to his crooked doctor, rambling about Isabelle's scent returning, and how bright and energetic she was.

Liam asked if he should take Isabelle now. I said no. It was too risky to kidnap a sitting senator's wife. It would be a shitestorm and draw too much attention. When we took Isabelle, it had to be at the same time we were ready to deal with William.

While my wife had given me permission, I had to ensure Isabelle's health and safety first. According to Sweeney, she needed more time for the hormones to clear her system, making it safer to sever the bond with Sterling.

Instead, I told Liam to intercept the new shipment of suppressants and replace them with placebos.

I tossed my phone onto the desk and rolled my shoulders. A wave of Willow's sweet scent wafted off my shirt collar. I groaned, my eyes closing as the honeyed morning rain soothed whatever uneasiness prickled beneath my skin.

My dick twitched at the image of our pretty omega—our wife—safe in our arms, snuggled under the blankets in her nest. My alpha demanded that I hide her away from the world, uneasy that she was still unbonded.

I loved my wife, my omega, but I was a patient man when I had to be. And if she wasn't ready, I would wait. I would wait a lifetime for Willow. I was at her command. Her dutiful servant. All I wanted was to please her. Love her.

And I would spend an eternity worshiping at her altar to prove myself.

A pain throbbed between my eyes as I tried to focus on the calendar. My fingers hovered over the dates on my computer while I tried to count out the days since Willow's last heat.

It had been a breakthrough one, so we were both uncertain if her next one would occur on its usual schedule or if it would follow a new schedule based on the heat she had when she first arrived.

Part of me wanted to text Torin, ordering him to bring her home. I still hadn't told her the depths of my feelings, not exactly certain of why. I told myself it was because I wanted her to be ready, that I didn't want to frighten her, but that was only partially true.

Something buried deep inside that I refused to face, worried about our omega rejecting us, rejecting me and my alpha.

Nothing in this world scared me... except that.

I didn't know whether I would survive the loss of Willow. Marriage only went so far. If she refused my bite, my bond...

I snarled, cracking my knuckles, shaking away the unpleasant thoughts.

Tonight.

Tonight, we would talk. I would show her how devoted I was. Tell her how much I loved her, how I worshipped her and wanted to make her mine.

Torin's name lit up on my phone, and my face pinched as I immediately answered.

"What?" I snapped.

"Boss," he started, his tone detached and slightly off. "She's gone."

All the color drained from my face. My blood went cold, not daring to believe what I was hearing. Torin was with Willow. They were off to visit the rescue site. My omega had been spending all her free time there while I worked.

"Who's gone?"

The pointless question slid from my cracked lips, already dreading the answer I knew was coming. A throat cleared on the other side of the phone, and Torin's whispered voice barely echoed over the line.

"Willow. She's gone."

I stood, my chair toppling over with a loud thud as I banged my fist on the desk. It was impossible. Torin was the best. How the *fuck* did this happen?

Rossi.

Anger bubbled in my gut, the burn of it tearing a hole through my stomach as my alpha howled.

That bastard took *my* omega.

My wife.

It was him. Vittorio Rossi. It had to be. I had a lot of enemies, but he was the only one who made sense.

I spat back at Torin, texting Aidan at the same time to come to my office now.

"What the fuck do you mean 'gone?'"

"Someone took her from the café bathroom."

Frozen, I listened as Torin explained. They had stopped at a coffee shop on their way to the rescue. Willow used the bathroom, and when she was gone for too long, Torin investigated, only to find the stalls empty.

The only evidence of what happened was the ajar window and signs of struggle. Torin mentioned broken porcelain from the sink and beads from a necklace scattered around the floor.

Kaelen

My little omega fought.

Hard.

Torin's voice cracked—high-pitched and unsteady.

Outside the window, he found two sets of footprints. However, one looked more like drag marks.

Based on what he said, it sounded as though someone had waited for Willow in the bathroom, hoping on the off chance that she would come in.

And when she did, they subdued her and snuck her out the window before Torin noticed.

Someone had been trailing my wife, looking for the opportune moment to snatch her.

I'd find her. I'd burn the city to ashes if I had to.

"Get your arse back here now!"

I ended the call, tightening my grip around the cell until it shattered in my hand. Shards of glass from the screen pierced my palm, sending blood streaking down my arm. I stared unseeing at the fireplace, hearing only the sound of my heavy breaths and the quiet trickle of my blood pooling on the desk.

Chapter 33

WILLOW

I groaned, coughing as the stench of decay hit me. For a long moment, I refused to open my eyes, convinced that I was trapped in the middle of some vivid nightmare that I would wake up from any second.

Blood slid along my tongue as I bit into my bottom lip, willing myself to reappear in my nest with Kaelen curled protectively around me.

Alpha.

I gagged at the metallic scent. I wept, palming the matted hair at the base of my scalp. An insistent stabbing pain throbbed there over and over again until I opened my eyes.

Dim lights flickered overhead, barely illuminating the dark, dank room. Concrete surrounded me on every side. The threadbare blanket at the foot of the squeaky mattress fell to the floor as I tried to stand, only to collapse when my legs gave out.

Panic clawed at my insides. I wrapped my arms around my

waist, hugging myself tightly, wishing it was Kaelen. I tried to sift through the fog.

The last thing I remembered was getting coffee with Torin.

I winced as my bladder twisted. My eyes widened and I glanced around my cage. This was a true cell, unlike the one I imagined when I first arrived at Kaelen's. I wobbled to my feet, pressing my fingers into my temple as I steadied myself. I desperately needed to pee.

A massive metal door stood imposingly along the far wall. Cool steel met my hand as I spun the handle, unsurprised when it didn't move. My head hit the sterile steel. Nausea rolled in my belly.

Kaelen would find me.

I knew it.

My alpha would come for me. He would burn the fucking world down to find me.

I needed to survive.

"Hey, I need the bathroom!" I shouted, banging hard enough to make the door shake against the concrete.

Eerie silence followed my words, and after the third time, I gave up.

In the corner, I spotted a tin pail. Sweat clung to palms as I itched the sensitive skin around my wrists. I bit my lip, walking over to the pail and reluctantly pulling down my stained leggings, finally relieving myself.

After dripping dry, I sat back on the thin mattress, snuggling the ratty blanket against my chest. My omega whined, nearly sobbing for our alpha. The lingering scent of whisky and espresso still clung to my sweater. I snuggled into the collar, seeking any semblance of comfort I could find.

My breathing started coming out faster, and I closed my eyes, laying down. I kept hoping for a distant sound to break through the suffocating silence.

Anything.

A creak.

A drip.

But nothing came.

Minutes stretched into what felt like hours.

Instead of focusing on the aching emptiness in my chest. I thought of Kaelen. My alpha. Unconsciously, my hand slid to my neck, fingers grazing the unbroken skin. I blinked away quiet tears, wishing now more than ever I had his bite.

If I did, he'd be able to find me.

A mated alpha was an unstoppable force, able to find their omega through their bond. I sniffled, wanting Kaelen's bond more than anything. I loved him. Unequivocally. He was mine and I was his. Regret weighed heavily on me. I wished I hadn't been so frightened.

That I had told him I loved him while I still had time.

I worried I might never get that chance now.

An unpleasant thought slithered into place.

One where I never got to tell him that. One where my husband didn't know I loved him. One where my alpha suffered because he had lost me.

I shoved my hands into my lap, huffing.

No.

Fuck that.

I was Willow Finnegan.

The most powerful woman in Boston.

All I had to do was buy time. Kaelen would come for me.

Or maybe find a way out. I suspected they'd open that door at some point.

I dozed in and out, ignoring the hunger pangs in my stomach. A sudden, jarring sound rattled on the other side of the door. I sprang upright, splaying a hand over my sternum, trying to calm my racing heart.

The door clicked, and the metal scraped against the cinder block. I swallowed the viscous taste coating my tongue, feeling like shards of glass were poking their way down my trachea.

A figure emerged in the doorway, silhouetted against the bright lights in the hallway. My nose twitched, and I gagged, met with the distinct scent of mildew, spoiled fruit, and musty cigars. My hand flew to my mouth, afraid I might vomit.

Even in the dim light, I recognized Vittorio Rossi. My blood ran cold, freezing in my veins. He stepped into the room, sucking what little warmth remained with his presence.

A looming shadow followed behind Rossi, the man's face obscured by shadow. My eyes scanned over their frames, looking for their weapons, not the least bit calmed by the fact I didn't see any.

Rossi's thin lips curled, revealing dripping canines. He silently tapped his breast pocket in an unspoken threat. His Armani suit hugged his hulking body. I crawled back onto the bed, gasping when my back hit the icy wall.

A terrifying sound echoed in the darkness, his smirk not quite reaching his eyes as he stepped closer. Every nerve ending sizzled, urging my body to run. I panicked when my mind caught up, realizing there was nowhere to go.

"Ahh. My omega is awake," he said, his voice a silken whisper.

"I'm not your anything," I hissed.

The meaty man beside Rossi lunged forward, his hand disappearing into his jacket when Rossi stopped him with a stiff arm to the chest.

Fiery defiance swam in my belly. An intensity that refused to be extinguished. I wouldn't give Rossi the satisfaction of being the compliant, submissive omega he craved. I tilted my chin, glaring.

Rossi took another step closer, his man standing like a sentry by the door, completely blocking the exit, making escape impossible. The subtle scent of expensive cologne hit my nostrils, struggling to mute the man's foul alpha stench.

His ring-clad fingers slid along the edge of the mattress as he bent over me until his face was only a few inches from mine. I sneered, gathering a bitter mouthful of saliva, spitting on his face with all the contempt I could muster.

"Bitch!" the guard bellowed.

Vittorio raised a hand, quietly commanding his man to stand down. I glowered at him, my lips narrowed as the glob of my spit slid down his cheek.

For a moment, he stared at me, letting my spit splatter onto the bed.

The silence stretched on, suffocating me until I almost forgot how to breathe. I braced myself for an explosion, for Vittorio Rossi to unleash his fury on me.

But it never came. Instead, something dangerous rumbled in his chest, a mix between a chuckle and a growl.

"Feisty," he murmured, his eyes glittering with something unsettling. "I can see why Finnegan is so enamored with you. You are quite the prize."

My stomach twisted, pulling taut until it was painful. I grimaced, choking down the bubbling plea for my alpha.

"I like that," he said, flicking my spit from his face as if it were a speck of dust. "It will make breaking you that much more rewarding."

My heart dropped into my stomach as he leaned in closer, eyeing the ring on my finger.

"That means nothing you know. It doesn't bind you. Not truly."

"Y-You would offend God?" I stuttered, grasping at straws, remembering how Kaelen spoke of the Italians' beliefs.

With a dismissive wave of his hand, Rossi returned to his full height.

"He will forgive me for my sins. Besides, you're not bonded. Finnegan hasn't truly mated you. Married or not doesn't matter. So that means you're mine to claim."

Dread spread through my limbs, leaving my fingers numb. I clasped my hands in my lap, trying to stifle the small tremor before it became noticeable. The points of his teeth dug into his lip as a chilling look settled into his features.

I wasn't sure when my heat was due, but unless Kaelen found me before then, this man would bite me, forcing a bond into place.

Nausea rolled in my stomach, and hot acid burned in my chest.

"I have something for you," Vittorio said, shoving a hand into his pocket and removing a dark vial swirling with liquid.

My eyes widened as my body screamed at me to run, to fight, anything. Except I couldn't, paralyzed by fear. With a curl of his fingers, Vittorio beckoned his guard closer.

"No!"

The word tore from me, irritating my raw throat. It was a pathetic plea, barely echoing in the silence in the room. I tried to scramble away, kicking my feet, my nails clawing at the expensive shirt covering the man's torso. I thrashed my head from side to side.

Vittorio laughed a hollow sound as his guard closed his hand around my neck, pinning me to the bed and halting my meager assault.

"Let go of me!" I shrieked, scratching hard enough to draw blood.

Ignoring my protests, the man clutched harder, cutting off my air just enough to make me panic. I gasped as he took the vial from Vittorio. His teeth bit into the cork, unstopping it before spitting it across the room.

"Be a good girl and open your mouth," Vittorio said, his eyes glowing as he closed one hand around both my wrists.

I snapped my mouth shut, my nostrils flaring. My gaze locked with Vittorio's, and his bright yellow teeth gleamed at me as his dirty nails bit into the sensitive skin around my wrists. His guard brought the vial close to my face, and a foul smell wafted from it. I closed my eyes, internally chanting for my alpha, praying Kaelen would burst into the room any second.

But we were out of time, and I couldn't overpower the two alphas restraining me.

"Something to get my omega ready for me," Vittorio cooed, the dark promise gnarling around me like rotting ivy.

The hand holding me moved, and Vittorio's guard tilted my head back, forcing my mouth open until I thought he might snap my face in two.

Searing hot liquid poured down my throat, burning like molten tar. I gagged violently, my body revolting against the foreign substance. I protested as my limbs trembled and my body bucked.

The man snapped my mouth shut, pinching my nose, ensuring I swallowed every drop and that it stayed down. Vittorio's guard finally released me, returning to his sentry post by the exit.

I coughed, the strength of them shaking me with each one. I bent over, resting my elbows on my thighs and dry heaving.

Hard stone dug into my knees as I collapsed onto the floor, wanting to vomit, but unable to. A too-familiar need started to spread through my body, coursing through my veins like wildfire.

No. No. No.

It couldn't be.

That was impossible.

My vision swam, everything in the room blurring. A pain thrummed behind my eye, and my head spun. My hands clutched my stomach as an involuntary, needy whine stung my raw throat. I bawled, my body betraying me as it succumbed to the insidious symptoms of my heat.

Vittorio stepped closer, his shadow falling over me.

"There now," he said, his voice unnervingly gentle as he brushed his fingers through my hair and over my back. "That wasn't so bad, was it? I can make you feel go—"

"Fuck you," I snapped, not wanting him to finish that disgusting sentence.

He crouched beside me, too gently cradling my face in his hand. I resisted the urge to spit on him again, a heavy heat weighing me down and making me want to sleep.

"Don't worry. Soon, I will, Omega. I'll claim your tight little cunt and make you mine permanently."

My stomach rolled.

A flurry of curses died on my lips as the two men left, locking the metal door behind them with an ominous click.

My back hit the bed as I fell onto my ass, my head falling back on the mattress. I wrapped my arms around my waist, imagining Kaelen's thick arms holding me. Protecting me.

I closed my eyes, calling forward memories of his scent.

"Alpha," I breathed, afraid I'd never see him again. "Please. Please help me. Don't let them hurt me. I want you. Only you. I love you."

Hot tears slid down my cheeks as I curled in a small ball on the bed, wishing I had told Kaelen sooner. Told him how much I loved him, how much I needed him. I had no idea how long before my heat consumed me.

Based on the slick ruining my panties, and the burn in my belly, not long.

Soon, Vittorio Rossi would bite me, mating me to him for life.

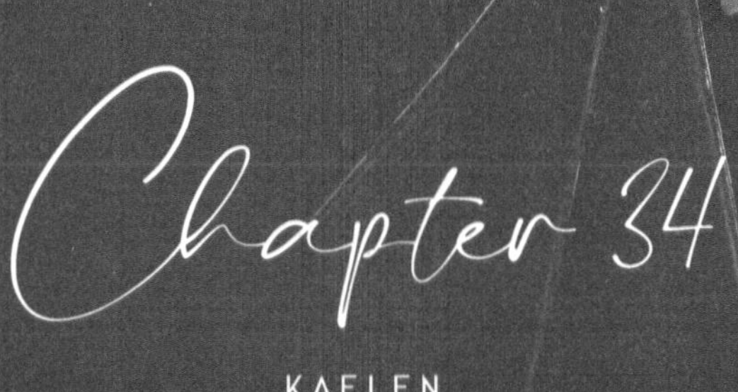

KAELEN

The glass tumbler shattered against the stone fireplace with a deafening crack, shards exploding outwards like shrapnel. A pained sound tore from me, shaking the pictures on the wall.

I scrubbed a hand over my face, fishing the burner phone from my pocket before shooting off a text to Liam while I waited for Aidan and Torin to arrive. Part of me wanted to recall Liam, but instead, I did something borderline stupid, sending him a two word message.

Do it.

Based on everything he'd seen, Isabelle had recovered, meaning we could take Sterling. I ground my teeth, my nose twitching at the pain shooting along my jaw. A few days ago, Aidan worked with Doctor Sweeney to concoct records showing William Sterling died of a massive coronary.

For all I knew, that might end up being true by the time I was done with him. A muscle pulsed in my neck, remembering the burn marks on my beautiful omega's skin. I ran a hand through my hair, the strands mussed and loose.

The only marks that should be on my wife are *mine.* My bite.

After I got Willow back, I planned to take my time with the senator, drawing out his pain until he begged for death. Until he pissed himself and his heart gave out.

If he hadn't ever tried to sell his only daughter like cattle, Vittorio Rossi wouldn't have come looking for her. I knew it was him. It had to be. He was the only one stupid enough to take my wife—my omega—in broad daylight.

My alpha roared again.

I spied another text from Liam, confirming that by the time the sun set, a shackled William Sterling would be in my basement and Isabelle secured in the guest house on our property.

Something dark ignited within me. Something cruel and twisted that made my mouth lift in a barely there smirk.

An icy chill slithered up my spine, quickly dousing the small reprieve from worrying about Willow. I spun the Claddagh ring on my finger, running through every conjured scenario of where she was and how to get her back.

Every second mattered.

First, I had to figure out if Vittorio Rossi had taken her, and where he was keeping her. This wasn't a case of him wanting something from me and using my wife as ransom. What Rossi wanted was *my* omega. I foolishly believed that, being a Catholic, he'd respect a marriage bond.

But no, the only thing that protected my girl now was my bite, my alpha bonding us together for an eternity.

Shame settled in the pit of my stomach. I failed my omega. It was my duty and honor to keep her safe. To protect her.

And I failed. If she had my mark, none of this would have happened. She would be adorable in her nest, mewling contented sounds as I held her.

During her first heat, she had been here only a day. I wasn't sick enough to force-bond an omega. But Rossi was. I needed to find Willow before her heat arrived. My skin prickled, and the heavy oak door to my study groaned open.

Aidan strode in, his face stoic as he tucked his phone into his pocket, silently dipping his chin in my direction. Behind him, Torin moved inside, closing the door to my office with a click.

Something primal seized my senses, my instincts overtaking me. Before I could stop it, I lunged, wrapping my hand around Torin's throat and smashing him into the wall beside the fireplace with a loud thud.

The plaster cracked as the air pushed out of Torin's lungs with a wheezing gasp. Those blue eyes widened as I retreated further until my alpha took full control. I trusted him with my wife. My heart. And he fucked up.

How could I forgive him?

A terrifying, unfamiliar growl rose from Aidan as his calm demeanor shattered. Gold flecks glinted in his predatory eyes. Aidan's nostrils flared as he battled with his instincts to protect his mate and his loyalty to me.

"Kaelen," he snapped. "Release him. Now!"

Of the three of us, Aidan had always been the collected strategist, rarely letting emotions get in the way of his decisions. It made him good at his job. It made him lethal in a way Liam or I never mastered. He found people's weaknesses and exploited them.

But right now, Aidan wasn't my brother. A bloodthirsty, possessive alpha roared in my direction. Ready to fight me to protect his mate.

I blinked. Torin's bright eyes watched me as he stayed markedly quiet, his eyes flicking from mine to Aidan's, trying to soothe his alpha.

Slowly, I unfurled my fingers, releasing Torin and taking two steps back.

Heavy breaths heaved in my chest and I ran both hands through my hair, tugging at the roots. Torin coughed, rubbing at the bruises I'd left. A thick purr rumbled in Aidan's chest. He pulled Torin into his arms, rubbing his fingers over the purple marks, scenting him.

It didn't matter that Torin was a beta. Aidan loved him, and his alpha claimed him as much as he would any omega.

A stilted silence lingered. I pulled my hair into a bun at the back of my head, leaning into the edge of my desk. This was the man who almost died for me. The man I considered family.

"Torin, I'm…"

He held up a hand, shaking his head. "Don't. It's my fault. You trusted me to protect her and I failed."

Another threatening growl fell from Aidan.

"No one could have expected her to be taken from inside a bathroom. You didn't fail. Ever since Sterling promised Willow to Rossi, he wanted her. Craved her. It was only a matter of time until he did something reckless."

"You're sure?" Aidan asked, his voice raw.

"Almost positive. Vittorio Rossi plans to bond my wife."

The thought lingered like a piece of poisonous fruit, rotting from the inside out. I felt unleashed and lost, not knowing what to do or where to start. I looked at Aidan, hoping that big brain of his had a plan.

Even if I had attacked his mate.

Keeping one hand notched on Torin's hip, Aidan flicked through his phone furiously, his brow pinched.

"What is it?" I snapped, ignoring the glower Aidan shot my way.

"Someone is at the gate requesting entrance."

"Who?"

"Massimo Rossi."

Chapter 35

KAELEN

My knuckles cracked. Aidan looked up at me from his phone. An uncomfortable silence settled over us, only interrupted by the steady popping of logs in the fireplace.

From what I knew about Massimo Rossi, he was calculating, loyal, intelligent, and above all, ruthless. That night at the restaurant, I sensed tension between Massimo and his father.

Perhaps he always knew what Vittorio planned to do.

Perhaps he disagreed with it.

"What does he want?" I asked.

Aidan's lips thinned, eyes scrolling over some unseen message on his phone. "He's saying he has information about Willow."

Without thinking, my fist collided with the drywall, pieces of it splintering onto the floor. Both men eyed me but stayed quiet. My chest heaved, blood dripping from my knuckles as a dust cloud hovered nearby.

Nothing good could come from this, but it confirmed my suspicions—that Vittorio Rossi took my wife. My omega. Staring into the distance, I ignored the pointed stare from my brother while I tried to compose myself.

I was no good to Willow unless I got my shite together. Having Massimo Rossi on my doorstep didn't bode well. The Rossis knew the rage I'd be in trying to find her. Vittorio likely sent his son to feast on that, luring me into a trap.

Regardless, I couldn't send him away until I heard what he had to say. I might regret it otherwise.

"How many men are with him?" I mumbled, grabbing a cloth from my desk and wrapping it around my knuckles.

"None," Aidan said.

"None?" I asked.

"None. He came alone. He told the guard he is willing to come in unarmed to prove his motives are purely to talk."

"Have them remove his weapons and then bring him up."

Aidan nodded. I moved behind my desk, yanking open the top drawer and removing my gun. After securing a fresh clip, I tucked the pistol into my waistband. A knock sounded on the door. Aidan and Torin stood off to the side, and I leaned into the edge of my desk.

"Come in," I barked.

The door opened, revealing Seamus with Massimo Rossi at his side. I dismissed Seamus, and Massimo took two careful steps inside before meeting my glacial gaze.

An impeccably tailored suit clung to his broad frame, his dark hair styled cleanly atop his head. A flicker of something I couldn't quite decipher slid over his usually indifferent features. He inclined his head, and a feral snarl tore from me.

To the man's credit, he didn't flinch.

Shadows shifted behind me, Aidan and Torin's hands resting on their weapons. My muscles tensed as I struggled to contain the rage burning a hole in my chest.

"What do you want?" I spat.

"I've come to talk," Massimo said, his accented voice quiet and serious.

I eyed him, my alpha screaming at me to tear him apart for daring to touch our omega.

"Then talk. You'd be wise to choose your next words carefully."

A twisted part of me debated holding Massimo as ransom in exchange for Willow. The heir to the Italian crown sat a few feet from me, unarmed.

Unfortunately, I wasn't confident Vittorio would surrender her in return for his son.

As fucked up as that was.

I schooled my features, refusing to give anything away, even as aching pain clawed at my ribs. Ignoring the burning sensation in my chest, I glared at Massimo. For a second, the façade on his face fell and he ran a hand through his hair, looking much older than he was.

"My father took your wife."

A roar worked its way up my throat as I took a prowling step into Massimo's space. The other alpha didn't retreat, despite the subtle flare of his nostrils that he quickly stifled.

"She is being kept in one of the older safe houses, beneath the industrial district. It's decommissioned, but still functional. He intends to force-bond her, claim her. He has procured something that is said to induce heat in an omega when ingested."

Black spots blurred my vision. The veins on my hands bulge under my tattoos. The metallic tang of blood coated my tongue as I licked away the dripping spot on my lip from where my teeth had pierced the flesh.

Unlike his father, Massimo Rossi had always shown himself to be loyal. Something didn't sit right. It felt like a trap. I didn't trust it, and I would never trust him.

"Why?" I started, glaring at him. "Why should I trust anything you say? Why would I trust a man so quick to betray his family?"

That elicited the first genuine reaction I had seen from Massimo since he had arrived. His eyes narrowed into thin slits as a quiet growl slid past his lips. I tilted my head, finding the reaction curious.

I offended him.

Under normal circumstances, I would have expected him to lash out when anyone questioned his loyalty to his family. But given the information he offered, I found the pinched expression on his face out of place.

The brief glimpse of emotion in his eyes was quickly hidden behind something cold and unyielding.

"Not my family," Massimo seethed. "My *father.*"

Interesting.

"I am loyal to my blood, my sister. I promised my mother I would protect her with my last breath as she took hers."

My gaze slid to Aidan's, whose expression was as impassive as always. I knew Massimo had a younger sister, but like most daughters in our world, she had been sheltered. That night at the restaurant was my first glimpse of her.

"My father is the one who has betrayed us by stealing your wife and bringing war to our doorstep. In his madness, he has also promised my sister to an alpha in Rome who is almost sixty. I will *not* allow it. I vowed to keep her safe. And *that* is the oath I am keeping."

In the years I had known him, I had always held more respect for Massimo than for his father. His words only proved it. With Vittorio gone, Massimo would step in as the head of the Italian family in Boston.

Business between us would be less hostile if we dealt with him instead of his reactive father.

"What are you suggesting, Massimo?" I asked, the room quiet enough to hear a pin drop.

A dimple appeared at the corner of his mouth, and he covered his chest with his hand.

"I know the location he's keeping your wife in. I will share it with you, along with all pertinent information about security in exchange for you agreeing to kill my father. With this, I can protect my sister and you get your wife and omega back."

Hold on. I'm coming, mo chroí.

old sweat stuck to the back of my neck. I lost all sense of time, trapped behind these stone walls. I rubbed at the irritated skin on the inside of my wrist, not knowing if it had been three days or three hours since Vittorio had forced that sludge-like liquid down my throat.

I toyed with a loose thread on the thin blanket he had graciously brought me, like some grand offering to *his* soon-to-be omega. I tried to banish the unwanted image. The last thing I wanted was to belong to *him*.

Silent tears slid down my cheeks. I trailed my thumb over the ring still on my finger. Surprisingly, Vittorio hadn't stolen it from me. Either he hadn't noticed or hadn't cared. Or maybe he let me keep on purpose, getting some sick satisfaction out of seeing me wearing it when he planned to bite me.

I buried my face in my hands, wiping the beads of sweat off my brow. With my eyes closed, I tried to remember Kaelen's scent—

whisky and coffee.

The memory enveloped me, staving off the dampness in the air. My hand spread over my sternum. A dull ache throbbed in the pit of my stomach, a thrum I first dismissed as anxiety.

But it morphed into something familiar, something unsettling. The knot in my belly unfurled. A prickling sensation erupted over my body, dragging across my sensitive skin like sandpaper.

Soon, a series of cramps twisted in my abdomen, and I cried out, curling into a ball on my pathetic excuse for a bed.

Everything that was happening felt wrong.

Usually, in the days or hours before my heat, my body tingled with anticipation, a joyful urge dulling some of the more unpleasant symptoms. This time, however, a foreboding doom hung over me.

My body screamed, resisting every twist and gush of slick.

"No. No. No," I whispered, sniffling and hating how my biology betrayed me.

I only wanted to spend my heats with one person.

Kaelen.

My husband.

My alpha.

"Alpha," I moaned into the dim light.

Alpha. Alpha. Alpha.

The words chanted over and over again in my head, followed by a chorus of *mate, mate, mate.* I kicked the blanket away, my nesting instinct hidden under my fear.

This wasn't a nest, wasn't *my* nest.

It was a cage.

Images of Kaelen's tattooed arms wrapped around my waist, pulling me into him in our nest filled my mind. The phantom scent of fresh espresso rose to the surface.

I imagined stroking my nails through his beard, tugging his hair free from its well-styled bun at the back of his head. I'd run my fingers through it while he groaned a pleased noise, scenting me.

A grating sound cut through the guttural silence, and I crawled as far away from the noise as I could. The scrape of metal on stone echoed in the small space as the door creaked open.

The now familiar scent of cigar smoke and rancid fruit greeted me, and I hissed. My omega protested the wrongness of it all. Vittorio's broad silhouette filled the entryway. A slow, predatory glimmer alighted in his features as he shut the door behind him, leaving the two of us alone.

Pressed black trousers hung around his slightly protruding stomach. The older alpha was showing his age. His bloodshot eyes narrowed as he rolled the sleeves on his shirt, stepping closer with precise movements.

Each one stole more air from my lungs, my eyes darting around the room. The walls closed in around me, making my chest constrict as I gasped for air.

"You're close," he said in a gravelly voice that made my hands tremble. "I can smell your cunt from the hallway. Your omega is calling out, desperate to be bred and bonded, needing your alpha. Don't worry. I'm here."

He pounced with surprising speed, pinning me beneath him. My heart hammered against my ribs, the blood rushing in my ears drowning out most of the garbled words he said, his hot breath fanning over my flushed cheeks.

I needed an alpha. *My* alpha.

Not him. Never him.

"Fuck you," I hissed, scratching his face.

Pinpricks of blood dripped over his olive skin, and I smirked, the victory fleeting. His knees dug into my hips, his yellowed teeth flashing in the muted light.

"Stronza," he howled, slapping me across the face.

A different kind of heat from the one curling around my insides spread over my cheek, the pain slightly overshadowing the cramping in my belly. My hands flew up to my face, but Vittorio caught my wrists, securing both my hands in one of his above my head.

With his free hand, he caressed the backs of his knuckles over the blooming bruise. The gentle motion was so at odds with the rest of him. I bucked and fought, but to no avail.

He laughed, the sound harsh and unnerving.

"I like it when you fight. You will look so pretty, round with my baby. I'd like another son."

Realization made what little warmth remained leech from my cheeks. Truthfully, I'd never given much thought to children. Unlike other omegas, it wasn't something I dreamed about.

If I wanted anyone's babies, it was Kaelen's.

Not like this.

"Don't worry," he cooed, licking a spot over my pulse that made me fight harder. "Soon you'll be begging for me, omega. Begging for your alpha to fuck you and bite you."

The grin on his face elongated. I didn't want to be scared of him. I didn't want to be weak.

No, I refused to give in to fear. A queen bowed to no one. Except her king. And Rossi was a jester at best.

The sound of crashing glass echoed above us, followed by a chorus of shouts and gunfire. A jolt of electricity shot through my veins, and I was almost too afraid to be hopeful.

Then I heard it, the lilting voice of my alpha telling someone to *move*, followed by another gunshot and a roar. Relief doused the building panic tightening around me like a vise. He was *here*.

He came for me. My husband. My alpha. *Mine.*

I only had to hold off Rossi a little longer.

"Kaelen! Alpha!" I screamed, praying he heard me. "I'm down here!"

Another roar rattled from upstairs, and I swore I heard his voice call out for me.

"Quiet! Fuck. No matter," Vittorio hissed, releasing my wrists and angling my head to expose my neck. "I'll bite you now. You're primed enough for my bond to take, Omega."

I thrashed. If Vittorio sank his fangs into my flesh, nothing could save me.

In his death, the bond could be severed, but it was dangerous to do with a fresh bite. If the alpha didn't tend to the mark, infection usually took root, and omegas succumbed to the sickness.

Even if Kaelen found us, it would be too late.

Sharp teeth grazed the thin skin over my pulse, and my body reacted. I threw a hand out, but he was too fast, too strong. He grabbed my wrist, rolling us over and twisting it painfully behind my back. I yelped, my face pressed into the dirty mattress.

A long, thin knife glinted by one of my eyes—Vittorio flashing the blade in front of me in warning. A power built within me. Something that had always been there. Something that bloomed with the love I had for Kaelen. For the love he had for me.

We may not have said those words, but I felt them in every thrum of my heart.

That's what I was to him. What he called me. *Mo chroí.* My heart.

Omegas weren't weak. And neither was I. I refused to be a victim of fate. Determined to make my own.

A breath expanded in my chest, and I gathered all my strength.

Quickly, I flung my head back, smashing into his face as hard as could.

My vision blurred with the stinging pain that pulsed at the base of my neck. A strangled gasp fell from his lips, his body slipping off mine. The knife clattered to the floor with a deafening thud.

Chapter 37

The coordinates on the navigation blinked ominously in the quiet of our car. My eyes trailed over the map while Torin drove through the abandoned warehouse complex, with another one of our SUVs following behind us.

According to Massimo, the safe house had minimal security since it had been out of commission for almost a decade. His father had, however, enlisted at least a dozen men to secure the property.

With that, I knew we had to be discreet. Along with Aidan and Torin, I brought another dozen men. While I wanted Liam and Patrick with me, they were otherwise occupied, dealing with the senator and securing Isabelle.

That left fifteen of us—split between two cars—to handle Vittorio and a dozen of his men. While I was confident every one of my men could handle two of his, I would have preferred to stack the odds more in our favor, but needed to avoid drawing attention.

We planned to silently invade the safe house and take out

Vittorio's men one by one. And then, I'd make my way to the basement where he kept Willow.

At least that was what Massimo conveyed. I still wasn't certain if I believed him, but his story about his sister compelled me. I put a lot of stock in my ability to read people, and I knew Massimo wasn't loyal to his father.

He loved his sister and would do anything to protect her.

For now, that had to be enough.

I had to get Willow before the bastard claimed her.

If I got there too late... I banished the image from my mind, refusing to let it fester. My alpha paced, a beast begging to be unleashed. And I would. I would let the most unhinged parts of me break free and tear Vittorio Rossi to shreds for daring to take what is *mine.*

He would understand why they called me The Butcher of Boston.

After taking a steadying breath, I closed my eyes. If I gave in to the rage, I might miss a crucial detail. I might get us all killed. And with that, damn Willow to a life bound to an alpha who would treat her no better than his dog.

My nostrils flared. Willow was a fucking queen, *my* queen, and nothing would stop me having her in my arms that night.

I scanned the faces of my men, all of them grim but determined. Aidan rested a hand on Torin's thigh, squeezing lightly. Metal heated under my fingertips as I grazed them across the barrel of my pistol.

The warehouse complex loomed ahead, and I jerked my head at Torin. He nodded silently, turning off the headlights while the car behind us followed. Our vehicles pulled into an abandoned parking lot before we exited, moving like ghosts through the damp alleyways that led to our destination.

Shadows shifted in the darkness, and I raised my hand in quiet command. My men stilled, eyeing the building where Willow supposedly was.

And then, I smelled her.

It wasn't the comforting scent of sweet summer rain and wildflowers.

No.

It was an explosion of heady, overwhelming honey and mist-soaked flowers. I clutched my chest, almost dropping to my knees with the force of it. I stifled my burning growl, not wanting to give us away. My vision blurred and my cock hardened.

My teeth ground together as I refused to give in to my rut. Into the primal haze to fuck my omega—to breed her and fill her. My omega, who was on the verge of heat. A sweet aroma that should have only ever been for me.

A hand landed on my shoulder—firm and grounding.

"Kaelen. Focus," Aidan whispered, his tone cutting.

"She's in heat," I said, blood thundering in my ears.

"I know. But if you go in there like this, you'll get yourself killed. He wants you to be reckless. Think, Kaelen. She needs you. Think of her."

My heart plummeted into my stomach, the reality of his harsh words hitting hard. They broke through the haze of my rut. A tiny pinprick of sanity.

Aidan was right. I couldn't bust in there. We had to be methodical. The need to save my wife, my omega, was the only thing more powerful than my instincts.

I was more than her alpha. I was her mate. Her husband.

My devotion to Willow ran deep, deeper than I ever thought possible. Because of that, I would leash my anger, harness it into something powerful. A weapon that I would use to sever the head off the serpent who threatened the woman I loved.

Love.

The clarity of that word curled around my thrumming heart, soothing it with the rightness of the meaning. I loved Willow Finnegan and would cherish and worship her until my dying breath.

My senses sharpened as my nostrils flared. Two of Rossi's men flanked the entrance to the warehouse, automatic rifles resting in their meaty palms. I recalled the blueprints of the building—the ones I had spent the entire day memorizing.

Besides the main entrance, an old delivery tunnel remained hidden and in disrepair in the back.

Kaelen

"You two," I said, nodding at the two men behind me. "Go with Aidan and Torin and sneak in through the back tunnels. Dispatch any you come across silently. We need to avoid drawing attention and gun fire. Luke, you come with me. The rest of you wait here until my signal. Luke and I will take care of the guards at the front."

Aidan moved with the others, quietly maneuvering to the back of the building while Luke and I removed our knives. I shared a look with Luke, and he nodded. With that, we slid along the cold stone walls buried beneath a layer of moss and grime.

The two men guarding the front door murmured, slurring words as they huffed at some obscene joke. If they were drunk, it would be much easier. They hadn't heard or seen us approach.

"Now," I whispered, in a harsh breath.

Luke moved with me, dragging his blade across one man's throat while I did the same with the other.

Blood spilled from them, pooling on the ground in a puddle. Their eyes bulged, their mouths falling open in silent screams as their hands scrambled to cover their fatal wounds. With gurgling breaths, both men collapsed on the ground, dead without a sound.

I let out a whistle, signaling the rest of my men, who joined us. Crimson brushed along my fingers as I wiped the remnants of it off my blade, shucking it towards the ground with a flick.

The metal door groaned as I pushed it open, greeted by muted yellow lights.

Another wave of my omega's scent stole the air from my lungs as I stepped inside, shocked by how potent it was. Fuck.

A thud echoed behind me, and I snapped my head in its direction. Surprised to see another one of Vittorio's men falling to the ground at the hand of Eric.

Labyrinthine pathways of steel pillars and pallets snaked through the warehouse. We moved room by room, eliminating the few guards who wandered among the dimly lit corridors.

I still hadn't seen Torin or the others when a muffled cry carried down a long, dark hallway. The sound set fire to the last vestiges of my control, burning it to ashes. I didn't stop to think.

I ran.

A series of footsteps followed me, echoing ominously in the

shadows. Another mountain of an alpha—almost as tall as me—stood like a sentry before a massive steel door.

Without thinking, I plunged my knife into his throat, slicing a gash across his artery. I wiped the blood from my face, drowning in the intoxicating scent of my omega nearing her heat.

I didn't bother wasting time looking for a key, instead smashing into the door with my shoulder, ignoring the bite of pain with each thrust. On the third strike, the wood frame splintered, and the door flew open.

I almost fell to my knees at the heady scent, consuming me in the thick cloud of her heat. My alpha roared, demanding I tuck her away safely in her nest and tend to all her needs while filling her over and over until she was sated and my seed took.

A single bare bulb hung from the ceiling, casting a sickly glow across the concrete floor.

In the middle of the room, I saw them.

A contorted grimace twisted on Rossi's face, creases tight around his mouth. A hand clutched his groin as he knelt on the ground, moaning a pathetic sound.

And standing over him, my beautiful mate.

Her lips trembled with short, stuttered breaths. Beads of sweat glistened on her pinkened skin. The scent of her heat hung heavily in the air, but beneath it, I scented her determination, her defiance. My brave girl.

In her hand, a silver knife glittered, the point of the blade barely pricking the skin of Vittorio's jaw. A fire blazed in her blue eyes, illuminating them like brilliant sapphires.

Something cold sparked in her gaze. A ruthlessness that I had never seen from her before. A look that promised destruction.

Pride swelled in my chest as I stilled, watching the scene unfold. Her head snapped up, large doe-eyes finding me. A flash of pure relief appeared in her irises, but her hand never wavered. I saw the raw strength in her stance, the unshakeable resolve in her steady hand.

My omega. My *wife* hadn't just survived. She fought.

And won.

The firestorm that had brewed in my chest settled into a

rumbling snarl. My strong mate. She hadn't needed saving. She saved herself.

"Alpha," she breathed.

"I'm here, mo chroí."

Chapter 38

WILLOW

The sound of the knife hitting the concrete made my heart stutter. Time slowed. My body froze in the contorted position. Rossi's strangled, agonized gasp echoed off the walls. He fell to the floor, his knees crunching into the stone.

Adrenaline pumped through my veins, barely dulling the inferno swirling in my belly. I spun, pebbles digging into my palms. Blood stained Rossi's teeth, dripping steadily from his broken nose as he groaned, trying to stem the bleeding.

My eyes darted to the forgotten blade, now lying on the floor a few feet away, its gleaming surface catching the flickering light. I hissed, the sting of pain from the rough stone against my knees a minor inconvenience.

All that mattered was the knife. I needed it if I wanted to have a chance of escaping. I scrambled, my fingers brushing over the worn handle. Hope melted away the worry, my muscles sagging.

Yes.

Kaelen

"*Stop*, Omega," he barked.

No!

The alpha command slid into the depths of my mind, straightening my spine. I cried out, unwilling to submit to him. Unwilling to allow him that control. I jerked, whining against the guttural order that I refused to obey.

Yet my omega twisted in confusion, fighting against me. My omega wanted—*needed*—to relinquish to the primal command, but I refused. The poison Rossi fed me spurred on the unnatural heat, betraying my body against me.

However, it also filled me with a strange, fierce determination to fight.

To fight for *my* alpha.

Rossi barked again, demanding that I stay. Like a *dog.* Any respectful alpha only used their bark in the throes of their omega's heat, and only to keep them healthy. Most omegas refused to eat or drink during those days, focused only on their alpha's knot.

Again, Rossi barked a command, spit flying from him and mixing with the dried blood on his face. The bark brushed against my mind, a cold, alien touch, but it didn't take hold. I simply shoved it aside.

I didn't obey.

I didn't freeze.

Instead, the frayed leather hilt of the knife settled in my palm. The weight felt comforting in my hand. My body trembled, but not with fear.

But with resolve. With strength.

I had always thought of myself as a broken thing with a talent for healing other tattered souls.

Even if I was broken, I wasn't defeated. I would not be the quiet, submissive omega Rossi or my dad expected.

I pushed myself to my feet, ignoring the sharp sting of pain behind my eyes. Cramps seized my abdomen as slick slid down my thighs. The points of my teeth dug into my lips, and I squeezed my legs together, willing the ache to go away.

"Aww, poor, weak omega. You're nothing without an alpha to help you. Come to me. I'll take care of you," Rossi cooed, smiling with blood-stained teeth.

The words burrowed into the hollow spot behind my sternum, feeding the powerful rage fueling me. It fought for dominance with the heat turning into a consuming, blinding need.

My fingers went numb as my grip turned unrelenting on the knife.

"Fuck off. I don't need you for anything."

The sinister glint in his dark eyes faded along with his fleeting smile. Amused, I drove my bare foot into his half-hard dick. A string of Italian curses hissed through his strained jaw.

At least, they sounded like curses. Definitely weren't terms of endearment.

"Vaffanculo!"

An indignant glaze slid over his yellow eyes, and I darted out of the way of his wandering hand. I ran behind his kneeling frame, pushing the tip of the blade into his throat, the sharp point barely dimpling the skin.

An empty, unsettling chuckle rumbled from Rossi, and I pushed the knife deeper, a trickle of blood staining the steel. I knew what I had to do, but my hand shuddered.

I saved puppies, cared for horses… I didn't… I wasn't a murderer.

Morality existed in shades of gray. If Kaelen had taught me anything, it was that no one was ever truly bad or good. Most people existed somewhere in the middle.

Maybe I was capable. Torin destroyed a man's life at my word because I wanted to avenge Shadow.

Could I do the same to protect myself? Could I end a life?

The knife trembled violently in my grip. However, I wasn't afforded the luxury of questioning myself. If I did, Rossi would sense my hesitation and strike.

Air whistled through my teeth when the door flew open, screws from the hinges rattling on the ground. My head snapped towards the sound. A tall, broad-shouldered figure filled the doorway. The familiar scent of espresso and sweet whisky enveloped me.

My breath hitched. My eyes found his strained ones, swirling with pain.

Kaelen. Alpha.

Sprays of crimson painted his freckled cheeks, a terrifying mark across his pale skin. I gasped, relaxing only when I realized the blood wasn't his. He wasn't hurt.

A grimace slid across my lips.

"Alpha," I called out, the purest form of relief melting over my taut muscles.

Seeing him dulled and heightened me in equal measure. My fear receded, yet the heat ignited in my body, doubled. The muscles in my stomach contorted, threatening to send me to my knees.

A whine hissed through my teeth, my chest heaving as Kaelen snarled.

"I'm here, mo chroí," he said, his sweet, possessive voice soothing something in the furthest reaches of my soul.

"Finnegan," Rossi said. I'd almost forgotten about him. "Come to watch me claim your wife?"

A sudden, bone-deep resolve bloomed. Rossi tried to stand, and panic rose, choking me. Kaelen stood frozen, eyes darting between the weapon in my hand, me, and Rossi.

It was up to me.

This was my body, my life, and I had to fight for my mate.

I had to fight for myself.

Sharp stings zapped in my stomach, my palms cold with sweat. The knife started to slip. I summoned the last shred of my willpower.

I'd always thought I was pure.

That omegas were destined to be quiet, sweet beings, but I knew that was wrong. Like Kaelen had said, we had a hidden strength. A power that few understood.

And in this moment, I had power over Rossi. He had underestimated me. Tried to steal everything from me.

With all my strength, I drove the blade into Rossi's neck in a single, brutal stroke. The blade slid in, a sickening, wet rip, making my stomach lurch. Vittorio's head fell back, his eyes wide and blank. Hot blood sprayed over my hands.

"Good girl," Kaelen whispered, pride and praise lacing his words.

The last bit of light flickered out, dull eyes staring, unseeing.

With a wet breath, the old alpha's body fell to the floor with a thud. Frozen, I turned the bloodied blade, my eyes blank as I stared at it.

I dropped to my knees. The muted heat rushed back—cloying and consuming. My vision clouded, feeling unbearably empty.

A high-pitched whimper stung my ears as I dropped the knife, curling in on myself and rocking slightly.

Powerful arms encircled my waist, guiding me up. A comforting, familiar scent filled my lungs. I leaned into Kaelen, burrowing my face in his chest, unbothered by the sweat and blood staining his black t-shirt.

I breathed, letting the steady thrum of his heartbeat ease my frantic one.

"Willow," he said, his voice rough and tired.

"Kaelen," I murmured back.

Callused fingers gripped my chin, tipping my head back. He rubbed his cheek against mine, scenting me. I relaxed further into his touch, wanting to smell only like him, wanting every remnant of Rossi washed from my skin.

My hands still trembled as I gripped his biceps. I leaned into his touch. His lips found mine, brushing gently against the cracked skin. He kissed me gently, swiping his tongue along mine.

I moaned, drunk on his taste. My nails dug into the corded muscles on his arms. The room blurred. A jumbled mess of half-formed thoughts battled for dominance. The last dredges of my lucidity wavered. I didn't have long before I fully succumbed to my heat.

To my needs. To my omega.

He had to know. I had to tell him.

Weakly, my fingers scraped over his temple.

"Alpha. Please. Bite me. Make me yours," I whispered, the words a broken plea.

Fire licked through my limbs, igniting in my veins. I needed him. I needed his knot. He had to help me. I wanted to be his. Forever. I wanted my husband. My alpha. My mate.

He nipped at my bottom lip, pulling back. A tiny V formed between his brows, his hand sliding along my face as I nuzzled into his palm, scenting him and marking him as mine.

Kaelen

"Omega."

His voice was a guttural whisper. Something between a vow and a prayer. But the undercurrent of his restraint cut through everything else, making a different fear gnarl behind my sternum.

"Please. *Please.* No one else's, only yours. It hurts," I said, raking my nails through his beard.

A long silence stretched out between us as his nostrils flared. The pad of his thumb trailed over my freckles, making flames follow in his wake.

"I know it hurts. Shhh, little omega. I'm here now. I've got you."

I struggled to connect two thoughts. I loved his touch, his comfort. *Him.* But I needed more. I needed to feel his heart beat in mine. I wanted to bond with him, to connect our lives in the most intimate, complete way.

Why didn't he understand?

I hissed, clenching my thighs when another cramp sliced through my abdomen. I needed... I needed... help. My alpha needed to help me. Complete me.

"Knot," I said, tugging at his waistband. "Mark me."

His sharp gaze stung me, a silent protest. "You don't mean that. Not like this."

The claim cut across me like a blade—an agonizing hurt. I chewed on my lip, seeing the truth in his eyes. He was being noble, assuming I was a victim of my heat. That my omega was in control and begging for a mark that I didn't want.

But I wasn't.

I was strong.

This was me. Not my omega.

Not *just* my omega.

I knew what I wanted.

I loved him. And nothing would ever change that.

"Don't tell me what I mean."

His eyes widened, something dark and determined appearing in the slight lift of his lip.

Voices echoed above us. Familiar, yet I couldn't quite place them.

I gazed up at him, willing him to see me. *Me.* Not my omega.

I claimed the last dredges of my lucidity, hoping Kaelen would understand. The heat was a rising tide, but the next words I spoke echoed in the depths of my soul.

"I love you, Kaelen Finnegan. I want to bond with you," I paused, whispering the next words, afraid they were true. "Unless you don't want me."

My confession hung in the air, making me feel exposed. Trying to calm my racing heart, I traced my fingers over my sternum. Opening myself up to someone, to an alpha, to someone I trusted to protect and love me like I deserved, terrified me. A vulnerable part of me wanted to steal the words back and pretend I never said them.

But it was too late.

All of me was laid bare to Kaelen.

To claim or reject.

Every second felt like a lifetime in the silence that followed.

I was right on the edge and ready to fall.

Trembling, I finally faced him, unprepared for what awaited me.

His gaze softened, looking like a lush forest after a rainstorm. My fear dissipated when I saw adoration replace the worry that had been there. Rough fingers traced the line of my throat, a featherlight touch that sent a jolt of pleasure to my core.

"Mo chroí. My heart. I have always loved you. My heart belongs to you. I would be honored to make you mine. To be yours," he murmured, the fierce mix of Gaelic and English like a balm to my frayed nerves.

His fingertips twitched along my pulse. Another sharp pain shot through my side. I sobbed, succumbing to the unnatural heat. Kaelen's hand rested on my hips, holding me up. I whined, a needy, keening sound of want, the noise harsh against my raw vocal cords.

"It's okay, my love, I've got you." Arms slipped under my knees, lifting and cradling me against him. "Let me get you into your nest. Where I can take care of you and make you mine."

My alpha spoke with such gentleness. My omega was pleased with the promise of our safe place. The place where our alpha would claim us. Where he would love us and mark us as his.

"Nest?" I whispered.

The last of my clarity faded, a lost light in the storm of flames.

Chapter 39

WILLOW

The last hour passed in a blur. I barely remembered Kaelen carrying me through an abandoned warehouse with Torin and Aidan flanking us along with half a dozen other men. At some point, he settled me in his lap, in the back of a car with Torin and other betas I didn't recognize.

I clung to Kaelen's shirt, nuzzling and scenting him, unbothered by our audience. Sweat glistened on my skin. My body ached, and the empty spot between my thighs demanded to be filled with my alpha's knot.

"Alpha," I murmured over and over again, uncertain he was real.

"Omega," he whispered, gently stroking his fingers through my damp hair.

Lips brushed over my temple. A rumbling purr grew in Kaelen's chest, getting louder the tighter I held him. The heaviness of the soothing sound lulled me.

Comforting arms lifted me, swaying me gently.

Through my hazy vision, I saw Aileen—her face drawn and lips turned down. I tried to offer her a weak smile. Unfortunately, it came out more like a tired grimace. I burrowed my face back into Kaelen, inhaling his heady scent.

A door clicked behind us, and I lifted my head.

"We're home," he said.

Carefully, Kaelen righted me. I wobbled. Hands flew to my hips, steadying me. In the center of the room sat my nest, my omega sighed.

"Let me clean you up, and then you can get settled."

A noncommittal sound trilled in the back of my throat. Despite the incessant need swirling inside me, I wanted nothing more than to scrub any lingering scent of that place and that man off my skin.

I wanted to smell only of us—of *my* alpha, of *us*.

Cold marble pressed into my bum as he placed me on the vanity. Turning, he ran the tap in the shower. After testing the water, he stood between my thighs, running his hands over my sides before cupping my face.

"I love you, Willow."

Those three impossibly perfect words quieted the roaring in my blood. The open sincerity in his declaration made everything *right*. For the first time, the constant whir of intrusive thoughts stopped.

Instead, all I heard was *him*.

Of how right he was for me and I for him.

Lips pressed to the tip of my nose. Then he claimed my mouth in an unhurried kiss. The coarse scruff rubbed against my cheek, his lips against my jaw.

"Love you," I breathed.

With a peck on my temple, he pulled off my dingy sweater and bra—a possessive purr growing with each second. Helping me to stand, he removed the rest of my clothes.

A shuddering sigh rattled my ribs at the immediate relief. My skin itched and burned, everything far too sensitive.

Keeping his gaze locked with mine, he slowly removed his belt, the leather gliding through the fabric. My mouth turned dry, fascinated by the veins in his hands as he tugged the t-shirt off his muscled frame.

Whoever created my alpha, hewed him from stone. A sculpture for me to admire.

I moaned, shamelessly drinking in my husband. Dark ink covered his pale torso, his heavy cock slapping against his abdomen.

Auburn strands hung loose around his face as he tugged the hair free from its confines. A burning throb ached over my clit. My nails mapped a path over the hard planes of his abdomen before I gripped him in both hands, huffing a tiny, impatient growl.

I imagined the weight of it against my tongue as I sucked and licked at him before he gave me his knot. As I started to sink to my knees, he stopped me, urging me towards the glass ensconced shower instead.

"No. Knot," I grumbled, unbothered by how petulant I sounded.

Why was my alpha denying me? He said he loved me. How was this love?

"Omega," he said, his voice on the edge of a bark. "Wait. We'll wash off and then get you in your nest where I can take care of you."

A tug pulled behind my sternum, my omega urging me to please our alpha. Resignedly, I stepped into the shower, delighted when cool water met my flushed face. I closed my eyes as my alpha trailed a soapy cloth over me, gently washing away the blood and grime.

Water mixed with swirls and brown and red slithered down the drain as he washed my hair, massaging my scalp. I arched into him, grinding my ass over his knot. My alpha was everything.

And he was mine. All mine.

"Omega," he said, and I grinned at his crumbling restraint. "Can my good girl be patient for me?"

I perked up at the praise, spinning in his arms to face him.

"Yes, Alpha."

"So sweet, listening to your alpha."

With that, he finished washing the blood from his face and turned off the water. Carefully, he wrapped a fluffy towel around me. I squirmed, finding the material too itchy.

"It's okay. Just for a minute. Come on," he murmured, carrying me into my nest.

Instant relief consumed me as the towel fell away from my skin.

Kaelen

My alpha stood beside my nest, his eyes blazing with desire.

Passion.

Love.

I sat up on my knees, and my brow furrowed. Something wasn't right. This place wasn't ready for my alpha to knot and mark me.

Huffing, I crawled around the bed, shifting pillows and fluffing them. Kaelen stood out of the way, a glimmer of amusement playing across his features as I scurried across the room, collecting more blankets and clothes from the hamper.

It needed to smell of *us.*

A rush of slick stuck to my thighs as I weaved our clothing between the pillows. Another needy whimper escaped me. I collapsed, curling in on myself, burrowing into the back of my nest.

I writhed, wordlessly reaching out for my alpha.

"Invite me in, Omega," he panted, a vein in his neck pulsing.

"Alpha. Please. Come here. Now. Don't leave me alone."

Responding with another growl, the bed dipped under Kaelen's weight.

"Never. Never alone again. I'm here for you always."

Firelight danced along his back, casting him in shadow. A frown tugged at my lips as I eyed my nest, worried I hadn't done a good enough job.

My alpha deserved a perfect nest. My hands fumbled as I frantically tried to rearrange the pillows and blankets. Kaelen's hand covered mine, stilling my movements. Warm lips rested on my cheek as he brushed my hair over my shoulder.

"Shhh. It's lovely. It's perfect because *you* made it."

"Do you like it?" I asked.

Long fingers carded through my hair. He maneuvered me until I was sitting in front of him. His hand slid under my chin, his thumb brushing over my lips.

"Such a pretty nest. You did such a good job. Do you want me to fill your sweet cunt here?"

"Please. Please. *Please,*" I babbled.

My nipples tightened and flush spread over my cheeks, fighting for dominance with the need burning me from the inside out. Kaelen grabbed something from the end table.

"Drink, little omega," he ordered, holding a water bottle to my lips.

I pushed it away. "Knot."

"Soon. After you've had something to drink and eat," he said, his voice quiet but no less commanding.

Glaring, I relented, parting my lips. Cool liquid slid down my throat, coating the sore spot. A quiet moan escaped me at the sweet relief. I drank the entire bottle, smiling at Kaelen, eager for his praise.

"My good omega. Now, eat."

He reached for a bowl of berries, his scarred fingers brushing against a blackberry. My omega keened at the primal, intimate act as he brought the fruit to my mouth. The juice stained my lips as I licked the remnants from his fingers. A dark, possessive look settled in the depths of his blown pupils, making pride swirl in my chest.

I did that. I unleashed my alpha.

I rocked my hips, eagerly accepting the food he fed me until he was satisfied I had enough.

"Now. Alpha. Knot?"

"Almost, sweet omega," he cooed, laying me down into the pile of blankets. "Need to get you ready for me first."

"I'm ready," I protested, closing my slender fingers around his thick length.

A pearl of pre-cum glistened on the head. I swiped at the bead, bringing it to my lips and sucking it clean. It tasted of him, of my alpha. My omega clawed at me, desperate for control. I was on the verge of letting her have it, wanting to give in completely.

Kaelen's nostrils flared, his knees pinning me in place on either side of my hips. His mouth crashed against mine.

Gone was the tenderness from earlier.

This was a claiming, bruising embrace that made stars explode behind my eyes. He growled into the kiss, his hands brushing along the underside of my breasts.

My back bowed into the touch, an electrifying current scolding me. Rough fingers plucked my nipples, and I moaned, my hands burying into the blankets beneath me. With a nip on my bottom lip, my alpha moved lower, trailing hot kisses and lashing his tongue across my skin.

Lips closed over my nipple, suckling and flicking. I whined at the exquisite torture of it all, running my fingers through his hair and tugging.

"Alpha. Please," I begged.

A dark chuckle escaped him as he descended, his fingers digging into my thighs. He spread me open, and the cool air stung along my burning core.

A slow breath rolled through me.

His eyes found mine from between my legs, unyielding as he nipped and marked my flesh. The pad of his thumb trailed through my slit, gathering the slick there and circling my clit, making me gasp.

"Such a pretty pussy. My omega is so wet for me. So needy."

Before I could say anything, he licked a languid, teasing swipe through my entrance. Words failed me, feeling as though my body wasn't my own. Everything caught fire, the intensity devouring me. Kaelen gripped my hips, holding me in place.

I clenched around him as he slid a finger inside almost too easily. His dark green eyes found mine again, and I couldn't look away. The intense look burned into my very soul as he added a second finger, curling them and tapping that spot that stole the air from my lungs.

A series of stuttered breaths choked me with the dizzying pleasure overpowering me. Kaelen was unforgiving, thrusting harder.

His mouth closed around my clit and I screamed, yanking hard enough on his hair to make him unleash another feral sound that threatened to send me over the edge.

"Good girl. That's it. Doing so well. Come for me, Omega. Come for me and I'll give you my knot. Fuck you like you deserve."

Those words unraveled me, undoing the tight coil in my belly. His tongue circled my clit and his fingers curled deliciously. I came with a broken cry, my come coating his hand and staining the blankets.

My chest heaved with heavy breaths.

"Shhh. There you go, sweet girl. Deep breath."

My thighs trembled as my orgasm rocked me, sending me into some fiery oblivion with the intensity. The heat in my body faded for only a moment, the relief short-lived as my omega demanded more.

Demanded my alpha.

Demanded his knot.

"More. More. More. Knot me."

Kaelen removed his fingers, shining with my release. I licked my lips, impatiently waiting for my alpha to give me what I wanted. He brought his fingers to his mouth, sucking them clean with a possessive groan that made my pussy flutter.

He settled between my thighs, pushing them open with his knees. Sweat dotted his brow, his cut jaw glimmering in the dim light. I had no idea what time it was. He fisted his length, stroking it, notching the tip at my core.

Smirking, I pressed my feet into his sculpted ass, urging him to take me. Stubborn alpha didn't move, however, making me pout. He smirked at my eagerness, collaring my throat with his free hand and bringing my lips to meet his. I softened at the possessive touch, feeling safe and protected in my nest with my alpha.

With his lips still fused to mine, he sank into me in one heady thrust. My teeth grazed along his bottom lip, nipping the flesh as my nails dug into the corded muscles along his back. The stretch was otherworldly; nothing had ever felt more complete.

My entire body tensed.

"Harder," I breathed into his kiss.

"Anything for my omega," he said, snapping his hips.

I cried, clawing at his body, desperate for something to hold on to.

The pleasure tunneled my vision until I saw only my alpha. Flush colored his cheeks, the tattoos on his chest and hands glinting in the light from the fireplace. I saw now why people thought him to be a demon.

In this moment, he looked every bit of one. But he was mine.

My demon.

My alpha.

His pace turned punishing, each snap of his hips more determined than the last. Every nerve in my body burned with exquisite bliss. My legs quaked and my body trembled. With each thrust, his growing knot caught on my entrance, spiraling me higher. He thickened, his impending release spurring on my own.

"That's it. You're taking me so well. Come on my cock," he moaned, his voice cracking.

I sobbed, my chest squeezing as I detonated around him like a dying star. My cunt flexed around him, taking him deeper with each subsequent stroke of his hips. As waves of my climax destroyed me, his knot slid into place, and he came, warm ropes of his release spilling inside me.

With us locked together, everything quieted. My mind quieted, and my body stilled, the heat from earlier abating. Kaelen positioned my sated form on his chest, stroking my hair and caressing my curves.

"I love you. My pretty girl. You did so well. We fit so beautifully together, don't we?"

"Yes, Alpha," I whispered, peppering sleepy kisses over his pulse. "Will you bond me now?"

"Soon," he soothed.

I didn't try to hide the disappointment on my face.

It wasn't long before his knot deflated enough for him to slip out of me. I whimpered at the loss, my pussy clenching longingly around nothing. Moments passed before flames licked across my flesh again, need commanding me.

The desire to be filled by my alpha overtook every thought.

"Alpha. More," I pleaded with a tiny growl that my alpha appeared to find endearing.

"I will give you everything you desire, Omega. Worship you. Serve you. Cherish you. Now. Present for your alpha," he commanded, gently slapping my ass.

Chapter 40

KAELEN

God above, she was the prettiest thing I have ever laid eyes on. I wasn't sure what I believed. What I knew was that I was blessed with my beautiful mate. Those sapphire eyes glimmered at me like sparkling crystals. Her raven hair—thick with sweat—fanned around her like a halo.

I twined a strand of blue streaked hair around my finger, giving it a light tug. She gasped the sweetest sound, her bright eyes large and fixed on me.

My omega quickly obeyed, rolling onto her belly and thrusting her plump arse into the air. Face pressed into the blankets. Lips parted. Eyes wide.

Needy.

Mine.

Fuck.

Everything ached, already hard again and ready for my omega. And I would continue to be, for however long her heat lasted. I would rut and knot her, making her come on my tongue, fingers, and cock until her body relented.

Until my wife was sated and safe in my arms.

My alpha roared in delight, filled with relief at the joy of caring for our omega in her nest.

"Alpha," she whinged, wiggling her cute arse impatiently.

I gave it another swat, smirking at the angry pout on her lips. The tip of my tongue pressed into my aching canines, imagining my mark on her. Soon. When she was lucid enough to enjoy that moment with me, I'd bond her.

Mark my wife as *mine* forever.

In one fluid stroke, I filled her. Something between a moan and a snarl vibrated in me at the intoxicating squeeze of my mate's cunt fluttering around me. Nothing had ever felt more right in my life than at this moment.

She rocked into me, chasing her own release as I thrust to meet her. The creamy skin of her thighs was lush under my fingertips. Syrupy sounds fell from her, muffled by the pillows.

"Good girl," I cooed, leaning forward to cover her body with my own.

"Close," she panted.

"I know."

My balls tightened and my dick swelled as my knot grew. A mix of her slick and our combined release dripped from her wet pussy, the noises from between us lewd and filthy and positively deranged.

That's what this woman did to me. Turned me feral.

The points of my teeth dragged over her pulse, and I stopped myself from piercing her soft flesh.

Not yet.

I had to wait.

"Mate. Mate. Bite me. Bite me. Now. Please. Alpha," she begged, her voice a dry rasp.

"It's almost time, Omega," I whispered, not wanting to distress my sweet girl.

My fingertips traced her constellation of freckles, soothing her as her body shuddered. With each thrust, her hungry cunt hugged me tighter and tighter. I roared, slotting my knot into place as she came undone for me again. Her limp form collapsed in my arms. I held her up, emptying myself in her, groaning at the delicious softness of her pussy milking me.

Gently, I laid beside her, tucking my omega into my chest as another, smaller orgasm rocked her while I continued to come. My alpha quieted, comforted by having our mate so close. I stroked her navel.

Willow was a wild, fierce creature. And suddenly seeing her pliant and slow took my breath away.

Images came into focus.

Ones of her belly taut beneath a thin shirt, round with our child. Ones of her skin glowing as she spread her bare feet out in the grass, reading one of those dirty books she loved.

Nothing in my life was soft. Except for my wife. My omega.

My hand covered the curve of her flat stomach.

This was the most precious thing I'd ever been entrusted with.

I silently vowed to devote myself to the love and protection of not only my omega, but our entire family.

She wriggled, a cute yawn stretching her jaw, breaking me from my reverence.

"Rest, Omega."

Each day drifted into the next, blending until I no longer knew when or where we were. I had no idea how long it lasted. It was a cloud of knotting, making my omega come, and forcing her to eat and bathe.

Something she stubbornly fought against.

More than once, my wild omega nipped at my fingers while I tried to feed her, leading to me knotting her hard and fast. I swore she pushed me on purpose, smirking like a feral kitten when I gave her what she wanted.

Water dripped from the cloth in my hand, and I gently caressed it along Willow's curves. Since she refused to get in the bath—saying she needed our scents on her—I have enjoyed cleaning her while she rested.

Those pretty, sleepy eyes blinked open, and my heart threatened to burst from me. The glazed expression that had covered them for the past days wasn't there. Instead, I saw my wife staring back at me.

The delicate column of her throat bobbed with a tentative swallow. I leaned over her, brushing the backs of my knuckles along the freckles that decorated her tanned skin.

"Hi," she whispered, the greeting a faint rasp.

Golden morning light spilled in from the windows, making my omega glow like the goddess she was. It was a small reprieve from her heat. My alpha prowled, pacing, urging me to seal the bond.

Bite. Bite. Bite.

"Hello, mo chroí. Do you feel it?" I asked, resting my palm over her heart.

"Yes. Is it time?"

I closed my eyes, trailing my nose over her pulse, relishing her delightful scent. It smelled entirely of her. Of summer rain, wildflowers, and fresh honey. I cradled her face in my hands, knowing I could spend an eternity drowning in her presence.

"If you are still sure?" I asked, praying to whatever deity who would listen that she'd say yes.

Her tiny hand covered mine. My heart stuttered at the brilliant smile she granted me. My still half-hard cock sprang to life, slapping against my stomach. She perfumed, drowning us in sweetened wildflowers.

A muscle jumped in my jaw as I barely held myself back.

Once I marked her, her scent would change. A flawless blend of morning coffee and wildflowers. Honey and whisky.

Her hand pulsed in mine—steady and sure. She traced my knuckles, following the inked, flowering veins covering the skin.

"I'm sure. I want this, Kaelen. Alpha. Please."

And with those words, my alpha tore free like an unleashed

beast. I crashed my lips to Willow's, lifting her and sliding her silky cunt down onto me while I kissed her.

This was it, the moment in my life I was certain I'd never have. My world was too dark and twisted for anything good. Here in my arms sat the most beautiful, stunning creature I'd ever met. And she was mine. She wanted me as much as I wanted her.

I'd found my queen.

The woman I'd worship until my dying breath.

The points of my teeth elongated, preparing to make my wife my mate.

Chapter 41

WILLOW

I shuddered at the fullness, wrapping my arms around his neck. We faced each other, me in his lap as he slowly—maddeningly—rocked his hips. I breathed into him, sliding my tongue along his, wanting to taste all of him.

The decadence.

The depravity.

The devotion.

Everything burned. The film of my heat may have lifted, but it hadn't completely dissipated. Flames still licked in my blood, and my pussy clenched, trying to take more of Kaelen. I tangled my fingers in his hair, loving the feel.

The tip of his tongue lashed over my skin as he trailed his mouth to the juncture of my neck.

My head rolled to the side, submitting to him. I gave all of me to him, willingly. My omega might have quieted, but she was still in control and commanded me to submit to our alpha. I released a keening sound that broke the last of his restraint.

"Omega," he breathed, his voice a husky whisper. The points of his teeth grazed my flesh. "You're mine."

"Prove it," I hissed, the sound morphing into a moan as his knot stretched me.

The next words died on my lips. A sharp, brief pinch pricked on the side of my neck. It wasn't the painful, agonizing bite I had expected. Instead, it was a quick, searing pain that soon gave way to something otherworldly.

My stomach coiled and then snapped as I came with his knot and his teeth buried inside me. My head fell back, sweat sticking to my flushed skin. Large, callused hands gripped my waist, holding me still on his lap, forcing me to *feel* everything. He came with a roar, the sound muffled as his teeth sank in further.

Every cell in my body sang with the sensation. The lingering burn of my heat vanished. The firestorm swirling within me quieted into a gentle warmth, lapping at my limbs until I was euphoric with the feeling. My omega settled, purring like a contented kitten basking in the afternoon sun, finally at peace in the presence of her alpha.

Our alpha.

A heaviness grew behind my sternum, the bond settling into place.

It was *him.* It was Kaelen.

It was his passion, his desire… his love… for me. Tears welled in my eyes. The intensity of it was too much, but also not enough.

This was what I thought I would never have, and now that I did, I almost didn't believe it.

The teeth in my throat receded, and his tongue lathed over the wound in tender strokes. I sighed, and he nuzzled the mark, caring for it as we both rode out the high of combined release and our new bond.

It was subtle, but it was there. Kaelen was there, the beat of his heart pulsing with mine. When I was younger, I worried a bond would be too distracting. How wrong I'd been. This was glorious. The most brilliant sensation.

I *knew* Kaelen loved me. That all the things he had promised me were true. His vows played on repeat with each thump in my chest, reminding me of my alpha's words.

Devotion. Love. Protection.

I'd never question my feelings for him again.

Not when the strength of it made our bond glow like a full moon on a cloudless night.

He shifted, his hands moving to cup my face. His thumbs stroked my cheeks with a tenderness that made my heart ache. Instinctively, I wrapped my legs around his waist, rubbing my face against his, marking him with my scent.

Although the nest smelled of us, I needed more. I needed my alpha to smell of me.

Gently, he tipped my head back, and his eyes met mine. Flecks of obsidian glimmered in the jade. They were the color of emeralds, shining under the moon at midnight.

With the tips of his fingers, he flicked the tears away, his lips hovering over mine.

"Mine," he whispered, his vow thrumming in our bond. "You are mine, Willow. My omega. My mate. My wife. My everything. Just as I am yours."

"Mine," I murmured back, running my fingers through his beard. "Will you add something for me? Here?"

My nails trailed over the swath of un-inked skin near ribs.

"A willow tree for my heart," he said, sealing his lips to mine in a coaxing embrace.

I clung to him, a pliant and willing thing. A simmering warmth curled in my belly, a different kind of fire. Gone was the intense need. Instead, it was a soft blend of intimacy and passion.

After his knot deflated, a hollowness remained, my omega not quite satisfied. I whimpered, holding his face in my tiny, shaking hands.

"Alpha. More. Please."

"All of me belongs to you now, Omega. Come here."

With that, he pulled me into his chest, my tight nipples brushing against the corded muscles. I groaned as he lifted my calf, resting it over his hip. His mouth closed around his mark, and I moaned. He slid into me, his chest vibrating with his purr.

It was a heavenly sound. And it was only for me.

In only a few slow strokes, I shattered, coming with his name on my lips as he knotted me again.

Kaelen held me close, moving with a reverence that took my breath away. I dozed in and out, succumbing to the intensity of my heat and our new bond. When I was awake, he caressed me, murmuring words of love and adoration that I felt echoed in the bond.

Now, he could never hide from me or me from him. There was no doubting his commitment. I was foolish to ever think he was anything less than worshipful. Any uncertainties I harbored disappeared.

Kaelen was my alpha.

He was my home.

My everything.

My sanctuary and salvation.

My mate. My love.

My eyes fluttered, lost in the rhythm of his body, the scent of his skin, the caress of his rough fingers. I sank into a blissful sleep, one lulled by the hum of my alpha beating in my chest.

When I woke, the smell of fresh bread and the dulcet purr of his voice greeted me. The afterglow of my heat still muddled my senses. I reached out, spreading my fingers in the mussed blankets of my nest, cocooned by the scent of my alpha. My other hand rested on the ridges of his stomach, my head on his chest, listening to the steady beating of his heart.

His hand covered mine, gently stroking my knuckles, bringing them to his lips and kissing them.

"Good morning, mo chroí."

"Is it? Morning, that is?"

"Yes. You have been in and out for the last two days."

A sleepy, content look glazed my expression, and my hand drifted to my throat. My fingers danced over the raised mark. I loosened a disbelieving breath. It was real. It hadn't been a heat-fueled daydream. The bond glowed in my chest, radiating love.

As if answering my unspoken thoughts.

I glanced at Kaelen, his eyes twinkling in the morning light filtering through the sheer curtains. He brushed over his mark, and I shivered. He reached behind him, closing his fingers around a glass.

"Drink," he ordered, bringing the rim to my lips.

"Bossy alpha," I said, still doing as he said.

"Stubborn omega," he bit back, a quiet laugh softening his retort.

The cool water slid down my throat, and I nearly moaned, forgetting how good water tasted. He continued to feed me, his touches constant and reassuring until I pushed him away, too full to eat anymore.

I basked in the brilliance of our bond, touching him as much as he touched me. Eventually, we'd have to leave my nest, but for a little while longer, it was just us. I burrowed into him, flicking my tongue over his pulse, making him release a possessive sound that made my pussy contract.

After what felt like an eternity, he shifted, rolling onto his back and settling me on his waist. I squeaked, his tip nudging me. A wolfish grin slid into place, making him look even more dangerous. The tip of his tongue pressed into the roof of his mouth, his palms caressing my curves.

"Let's get you cleaned up, Omega," he whispered, his voice still rough with sleep.

My heart lurched, my omega nervous about leaving our nest. Every instinct screamed for us to stay in our haven. The tired creases around his eyes faded, and he lifted my chin with a gentle finger.

Our bond hummed behind my sternum.

"Don't worry, sweet omega, it's still us. After our bath we can curl back into this nest, and I can lick that pretty cunt of yours until you're screaming for your alpha."

I breathed a delighted sound, enticingly rocking my hips against his length until he hissed, nails biting into my hips to stop me. A cloud of my scent thickened as I perfumed, and Kaelen snapped. Sliding out of the bed, he lifted me in his arms, carrying me toward the bathroom.

"Patience," he said, more to himself than me, it seemed.

The cool air in the ensuite stung my flushed skin. Kaelen sat me on the vanity while he busied himself running the bath. I greedily drank in the vision of his toned, muscled legs flexing as he crouched.

Saliva coated my tongue when I imagined running it over the lines of every tattoo decorating his chest. I wiggled slightly, releasing a breathy sound. Turning, I faced the mirror, shocked by the image staring back at me.

Pale pink colored my cheekbones, a flush still warm on my chest and neck. Rough skin bounced under my fingers as I feathered them across my lips. My hair was a knotted mess. All that aside, I couldn't stop staring at the raised mark at the juncture of my collarbone.

Kaelen turned, steam rising from the tub.

"It's very pretty," he said, his eyes dark as the backs of his knuckles grazed over the sensitive skin. "Just like my omega."

Another blaze of love alighted in our bond, and I splayed fingers between my breasts. Lips pressed against the underside of my jaw as he lifted me, lowering us into the bathtub.

Water sloshed over the sides, lavender bubbles curling around my toes.

My back leaned into him, his legs bracketing my hips. A soapy cloth trailed over my arms, melting away the tension that had been suffocating me for days. My eyes closed. The gentle caress of his hands lulled me into a light doze.

Fingers slid into my hair, shampooing and massaging my scalp. The motion made me moan, and he prodded the small of my back.

"Needy alpha," I teased.

"Only for you," he murmured, his tongue flicking over his bite.

We stayed in the bath until the water cooled, the last of the steam billowing into nothingness. Rivulets of water cascaded along the divots of his muscles as he stood, eyeing me like a starving lion. The tattoos on his hand flexed as he extended it to me, helping me out.

Wrapping an oversized towel around me, he carried me back to our nest, gently laying me in the mountain of blankets and pillows that smelled like *us.*

Strong arms curled around my bare thighs, his fingers dimpling the skin there as he dragged me closer. He sat on his knees, illuminated in the afternoon sun. My core fluttered. He teased my opening, and my back arched.

With a feral growl, Kaelen fell to his stomach, burrowing his face between my thighs. The tip of his tongue followed the path his thumb had taken, the ecstasy blinding.

"Mine," he said, lapping at me until my vision blurred. "Already so wet. Taste as sweet as you smell. Going to come for me, Omega?"

"Yes. Yes. Yes," I chanted, yanking on his hair and bucking into his mouth.

A moan vibrated against my clit and I came with a broken cry as my release tore from some unfathomable place in my core that I didn't know existed.

"More," he rasped, slipping two fingers into my pussy.

"God," I whimpered.

"He's not here, mo chroí. He has forsaken you. Left you with the devil. I'll be your god."

"Fuck."

"Yes," he growled. "I will fuck you. Corrupt you. Sin for you."

He unraveled me. Ruined me. I came two more times, once with his mouth and fingers before he sank into me, stretching me in the most devastating way.

"Knot," I gasped, clawing at his sculpted shoulders with each snap of his hips. "Alpha. Husband. Please."

"Again," he said, kissing my neck. "Say it again."

"Alpha," I begged.

"No. The other one."

His knot inflated, catching on my entrance with each thrust. It was so close. I was so close. I barely registered what he demanded of me until he stilled and clarity crashed down on me.

"Husband," I whispered, my throat raw as I slid my tiny hand over his cheek. "My husband. Only mine."

And he was.

This gorgeous, protective, ruthless alpha was mine.

He belonged to me.

"Wife," he murmured, rocking his hips and locking his knot

into place.

The thread in my abdomen snapped. My omega was a melted, sated kitten as my release rolled over me in slow, sweet waves. Each peak crested and lapped at my frayed nerves, other small orgasms shaking my tired body as Kaelen came, spilling his seed.

"Nothing means anything without you," he said, fusing our lips together in a languid, consuming kiss. "Everything I do from this day forward until my last breath will be for you. Thank you, Willow."

"For what?"

He smirked, pressing another chaste kiss to my lips. "For letting this demon corrupt you."

My hand landed on his forearm, tracing the words etched there.

Tá sé scríofa.

It's fated.

And we were.

"You didn't corrupt me, Kaelen. You showed who I was always meant to be."

Chapter 42

WILLOW

For hours, I slipped in and out of sleep. Kaelen stayed close, tending to his mark. The bond thrummed with his attention, my heat done and my omega content. I wanted to spend every heat like this, curled up with my alpha, safe in our nest.

A sleepy smile crinkled my eyes, knowing that was exactly what every heat would be like.

Once the sun set, my stomach grumbled. Kaelen rose from the bed, pulling on a pair of sweatpants. The lines of his muscles and tattoos disappeared under the waistband.

It was unfair how gorgeous he looked.

My omega whined, the sound reedy and high-pitched.

Despite my heat being over, our bond was still fresh, and neither me nor my omega wanted our alpha to leave.

"Alpha. No," I pleaded, reaching for him. "Don't."

I hated the neediness in my tone, but it was too soon for him to go. A warm palm slid along my face. I leaned into the touch, holding his hand in place.

"Shhh, sweet omega. I'll be right back. I'm getting more food for us. Ten minutes. I promise. Can you be my good girl and wait here for me?"

I nodded, my eyes still wide as my fingers clutched the nearest blanket. He pressed a reassuring kiss on my forehead, saying so many unspoken things.

At that moment, he wasn't Kaelen Finnegan, head of one of the most feared families in Boston. He was my husband, my alpha. The man I loved, who loved me. Someone fiercely dedicated to my protection, his devotion clear in the brush of his lips.

His retreating form moved, and I stared a little too long at his firm ass as he walked away. It was like he had been poured into his clothing. Sweatpants, suit pants, jeans… it didn't matter. Anything he wore highlighted how stunning my alpha was.

True to his word, Kaelen returned a few minutes later, carrying a tray filled with fresh fruit, buttered toast, eggs, bacon, sausage, and something else I didn't recognize. My mouth watered, and my stomach lurched again.

During my heat, Kaelen tried to keep me fed, but it proved to be an impossible task. Now that I was lucid again, my body reminded me how hungry I was.

"Breakfast? Isn't that a bit odd for nighttime?" I asked.

"Nonsense," he scoffed, placing the platter on the edge of the bed and sitting behind me.

He positioned me on his lap, feeding me a piece of bacon followed by a few blueberries. I licked his fingers, smirking at his unhinged noises. His desire flared in our bond and I shimmied in his lap, grinding on his dick.

A sting radiated over my thigh as he swatted me, making me squeak.

"Be good, Omega," he said, his voice almost a bark. "You need to eat."

I huffed, but he wasn't wrong.

"What's that?" I asked, pointing to a blackish cake in the corner.

"Black pudding. My favorite. Try it."

Those large fingers broke off a piece, bringing it to my lips. My nose twitched, unsure about the coppery scent. Tentatively, I closed my lips around it, taking a small bite that I immediately regretted.

An earthy nuttiness tainted with the tart tang of blood lingered on my tongue even after I swallowed it. Spinning in his lap, I glared at him as if he had betrayed me. This was supposed to be his favorite.

I felt as though I had licked sausage off a lamppost.

"You like this?"

"It's an Irish delicacy. We had this every Saturday morning growing up."

"You must have ruined your tastebuds," I said, finding the water bottle on the table and draining it to rid the taste lingering there.

"You'll learn to love it."

"Doubt it," I grumbled, scarfing down all the strawberries to make the taste disappear.

After spending hours lecturing me on the importance of black and white pudding in an Irish diet, Kaelen pulled me down onto his chest. A fondness hung around his words as he told me more about what it had been like to grow up in Ireland.

They'd lived in a quiet village surrounded by rolling valleys. Every year, they celebrated Samhain, Imbolc, Beltane—something Kaelen missed. His mother had been the one to organize all the holiday events when they moved to Boston.

After she passed, no one else took up the mantle to continue with their traditions. I made a mental note to poke Liam about it. I had a feeling he'd be more than willing to help his new sister breathe some life back into their home.

While I didn't see myself ever enjoying black pudding, I was willing to try the white one. Everything else sounded lovely. I'd never traveled overseas before. Ireland sounded like a beautiful place, and I wanted to know everything about Kaelen.

Where he'd grown up was a big part of him. Of his family. My family now.

"Maybe you can take me there someday to visit? I'd like to experience those things with you."

Flecks of silver moonlight glittered in his green eyes, his hands bracketing my face.

"I would love nothing more," he said.

At some point, I fell asleep, drifting off to the steady sound of Kaelen's decadent purr. Bright morning sun spilled in, pushing against my eyes. I grumbled, burrowing further into my alpha, wiggling when I scented him.

"Grumpy, omega," he said, his voice thick with sleep. "You're cute when you're still tired."

"And you're brave to poke a testy omega."

"If I die, tell my men I fought valiantly," he said, his smirk narrowing his eyes.

I shoved at him, annoyed when he didn't budge.

That stupid, strong, handsome, immovable wall of alpha. His fingers curled around my wrist, keeping my hand anchored to the spot.

"I can think of no better way to go than in the arms of my beautiful omega."

His tongue swept along the seam of my lips lazily. I opened for him, sighing into the tender press of his lips to mine.

This was my future.

Quiet mornings with my alpha. Passionate, satisfying heats. Protection. Love. Adoration.

I don't know how long we lay like that, holding, kissing, and petting each other. Long enough for the sun to rise high in the sky, the bright light showering the room. The glazed softness on Kaelen's face shifted, contorting into that mask he wore so frequently.

Sitting up, the blankets pooled around my waist and I stiffened. He ran his fingers through my hair, the gentle touch sending a tingle over my arms. He palmed the back of my head, holding me close.

The quick change in his demeanor set me on edge, my entire body rigid.

"Before we found you, Liam secured your mother. She is safe and staying in the guest house on the property. She is doing well."

All the worry of a few seconds ago melted away. My cheeks hurt from how happy I was. I wanted to see her. See her healthy and happy like she used to be.

"And we have William Sterling. I want to be sure, my love. So I will ask you one more time. Do you want this? Do I have your permission?"

He stroked over the burn marks near my collarbone, a snarl hissing through his teeth.

At the mention of my father, everything that happened before my heat came rushing back, the assault of it dizzying. I sucked in a rattling breath, rubbing a hand over my chest.

I raised my hands between us, rotating them to see them clean and unblemished. Visions of the blood that had stained them kept flashing, reminding me of the life I took with these same hands.

Something close to grief blossomed in my belly.

Not for Rossi, but for myself.

That one moment had changed me. Hardened me.

I wasn't weak. I was strong. While I didn't enjoy the idea of ending a life, it was a necessity. I grieved the person who I thought I was. A version of myself that never truly existed. There had always been sparks of my true self, even if they were muted.

In a place where it was me or my alpha or someone else. I would always choose me. Him. Us. Family. Every time.

William Sterling fell victim to his alpha, allowing his instincts to corrupt him. When I was younger, I tried to rationalize his behavior, not wanting to accept that my dad didn't love me like he once had. I framed it as him trying to protect us.

But no, he tortured and abused us. William always craved power, and that power clung to all the worst parts of him, infesting him before twisting him into something grotesque.

He took pleasure in controlling his omega, suppressing her. My mom deserved to be free. I'd suffer a thousand lifetimes as long as she was happy. If he continued to live, she would always be beholden to him, to their bond.

I knew what we had to do.

And I would feel as much remorse for it as William Sterling felt for everything he did to his wife and his daughter.

"Willow," he whispered, tracing the apples of my cheeks. "What

Kaelen

is it?"

"Nothing. Truly," I added at his pinched expression. "End it, Kaelen."

His forehead rested against mine, his large hand collaring the side of my throat.

"With pleasure, mo chroí."

Chapter 43

KAELEN

I lamented leaving Willow's nest. I had never experienced anything as fulfilling as spending a heat with my mate. My entire life had been spent working, reviewing finances for the pubs and casinos, guarding our interests, protecting my family.

For a few days, none of that existed. Willow—my omega—had been my focus, my reason for breathing.

As we wandered through the house, I kept her tucked into my side, unable to stop myself from grazing my fingers across my bite mark. Every time I touched it, my alpha beamed with pride. And it seemed the touch affected Willow as well, an endearing quiver shaking her tiny frame whenever I showed attention to the spot.

An unnatural quiet drifted down the halls. I kissed the top of her head. My strong girl continued to impress me. I was honored that she chose me. That her omega found solace with my alpha.

I found what I had always wanted. What my parents had. Something I wasn't sure I was destined to have. Willow was a queen—*my* queen. Powerful and steadfast.

Delicate fingers ran over my fitted black t-shirt and I purred louder for my omega.

A surge of happiness flared over our bond, and I tangled my fingers in her hair, tugging her head back. I claimed her lips in a bruising kiss.

The bond was a two-way street. A constant stream of emotions moving fluidly between us. Her contentment sang in the bond, eliciting a flare of protectiveness from me.

It wasn't until we arrived in the living room that I heard the distant clang of pots in the kitchen that usually followed Aileen.

As much as I didn't want to leave Willow, I made a promise to her. One I was happy to satisfy. I stopped, turning to look at her.

No matter how often I gazed at her, I'd never stop being in awe of her beauty. Immediately, my hands found her face, holding her like the precious treasure she was.

"Why don't you go find Aileen? She can get you something to eat. And then Liam can take you to see your mom. I have work I need to do. I'll find you tonight."

Part of me wondered if there would be regret or hesitancy there, but no. The most brilliant resolve glittered back at me.

"I'm not very hungry after a certain alpha fed me this morning," she beamed, playing with my hair.

I hadn't tied it back yet, knowing how she loved to play with it. If anyone else did it, I'd snatch their hand away. However, I quite enjoyed it when my mate did it. I traced the freckles on her cheeks, mapping the constellations with my fingers before kissing the tip of her button nose.

"Beautiful."

A pretty pink flush colored her cheeks, and I must have been the Grinch, cause I swore my heart swelled three sizes.

"I think I'll spend some time with mom. I don't need an escort to the guesthouse in the gardens."

"Probably not, but Liam has grown fond of Isabelle. He'll take any excuse to say hello."

Rocking up on her tiptoes, she pressed a kiss to the corner of my mouth.

"Tonight. It'll be done?"

The warmth of her love in the bond brightened the darkness corroding my flesh. While I wanted to draw out Sterling's pain, I wanted to be back with my omega even more. Besides, with what I had planned, he likely wouldn't survive more than a few hours.

Despite being an alpha, he was weak with no honor. I gave him minutes before he begged for mercy. Mercy I wouldn't give. And then, after an hour or two, he'd beg again.

But this time, it would be for death. Too bad for him, demons weren't merciful.

"Yes, mo chroí."

As if I could deny her anything.

"Later then," she murmured, disappearing into the kitchen.

I licked my lips as my gaze roamed over her delectable arse flexing in those tight pants. Leggings should be illegal. My dick twitched, clearly disagreeing with me and wanting to see our omega in more tight, skimpy things.

Rolling my shoulders, I scrubbed a hand over my face. I shook off the love-drunk look, replacing it with something harsh and indifferent.

The air grew colder as I descended the stairs into the basement. A metallic scent permeated the damp, dank space. Mixed in with it was the faint burned edge of fear. I refused to stop the sinister sneer sliding into place, enjoying the way it stretched across my lips.

Patrick stood by the door, offering me a silent nod as I slid past him. Cool metal stung my palm as I pushed the door open, closing it behind me with a loud click. My brow furrowed at the oppressive stench of sulfur corroding the air.

An iron chair sat bolted in the center of the room, William Sterling restrained in it. Dark bruises marred his cheeks, thin cuts caked with dried blood under them. Impulsive as he was, I wasn't surprised Liam took a few swings.

A shadow of the arrogant man stared up at me, his dark eyes emotionless. No longer did a powerful senator grace my presence. Instead, a broken, pathetic monster trembled under my glare, anticipating what was to come.

Beady eyes tracked my movements as my boots echoed over the stone floor. On the small metal tray sat a pair of pliers, a lighter, some cigarettes, and a few of my other favorites Liam knew to leave for me.

I pocketed the lighter and cigarettes, moving until I stood in front of Sterling.

Without a word, I tore his dirty shirt from his body, the buttons raining over the concrete. The other alpha snarled, yanking his bound wrists. The metal restraints dug into his skin, making blood drip onto the floor.

My hand shot out, pinching his chin, my nails biting into the flesh.

"Why? Why did you torment your daughter and wife?"

Silence.

I didn't expect an answer. Men like Sterling didn't have a reason. At least not one they'd ever admit out loud. Because it'd be admitting they were weak.

The flames from the lighter danced in the dim room as I lit a cigarette, Sterling's eyes bulging. I twirled the Marlboro around for a moment, admiring it before I snuffed it out on his chest, under his collarbone.

A piercing howl mixed with a sob rang out as he bucked. The acrid scent of melting skin burned in my nose. I ignored it, burying the butt deeper into his flesh, smirking as ashes floated to the floor.

Once done, I tossed the cigarette aside, lighting a second one.

Sweat clung to my nape, my heart oddly steady despite the rage coiling inside me like a flaming serpent.

Every fiber inside me demanded vengeance. Commanded me to gut him, to make him pay for the things he did to *my* wife. I sucked in a breath, pushing the cigarette into his skin. I rotated my wrist, urging it harder into him.

"St-Stop. Stop," Sterling babbled, still thrashing uselessly in his bindings.

Freezing, I gave in to the white-hot anger. I burrowed my hand in his greasy hair, yanking hard.

"Tell me, Senator. Did Willow cry and beg for you to stop?"

He stayed quiet, with only the sound of his ragged breath

cutting through the silence.

"No. I suppose not. Because she's strong. Stronger than you. My wife probably stayed stoic, waiting for you to leave before showing any signs of distress. She's a warrior. And you're a coward."

More screams filled the air, reminding me how much of a demon I was. Satan reveling in the screams of his condemned. The metal pliers sat heavily in my hand. Pure fear blazed in Sterling's eyes.

And I fucking laughed. Grinned like the demon I was, bathing in the flames of hell.

Hours later, and still an endless stream of adrenaline fueled me. Discarded, bloodied teeth and nails littered the floor, Sterling's face covered in blood, snot, and tears.

"Plea—please. Kill me," Sterling slurred, both his eyes swollen shut.

"You're lucky I miss my wife," I hissed.

He lasted longer than I believed he would.

Time lost meaning in the dark, soundproof room, but I guessed the moon had long since risen. The bond beat with a residual warmth. My omega was pleased. Content. And I wanted nothing more than to clean up and join her, holding her close while I licked my bite.

"You only ever did two good things in this world, Sterling. Fathering Willow and bringing her to me."

His lips parted, and the blade in my hand sliced cleanly across his throat, blood pooling in a wet puddle at my feet. The senator slumped over with a final, gasping, wet breath. His body twitched before going limp.

Turning away, I removed my cell, texting Sweeney.

Tomorrow morning, a story announcing William Sterling's

heart attack would run in the paper.

Patrick eyed me, unbothered by the blood streaking my beard and skin.

"Take care of that," I ordered, jutting my head towards Sterling's body. "I need my omega."

Chapter 44

WILLOW

Despite the calm façade I showed Kaelen, an anxious feeling made my heart tumble into my stomach. I knew what "work" he had to do today.

And while I was certain it was what I wanted, I was still human. I still felt remorse. I wondered, did my choice make me as bad as him? Was I as dark and twisted as my father?

In response to my wandering thoughts, our bond glowed with pure adoration, quieting my worries. No. I wasn't anything like him. If we allowed him to live, I'd never be safe. My mom would never be happy.

Forever trapped in a bond with an alpha who drugged her and stole a decade of her life.

It needed to be done.

Liam leaned against the French doors leading to the gardens, his thick forearms crossed. He rocked forward, his normally close-cropped hair getting long.

"Hey, baby sis."

"I'm older than you, Liam," I said, rolling my eyes.

"Semantics. You're technically shorter," he said, waving his hand dismissively. "That bite looks good on you."

"Thanks," I said, blushing and touching the mark. "I don't need a bodyguard out in the gardens."

"Who said I was coming along because of you? It's time for my daily visit with Momma Bella."

I snorted, knowing how much my mom detested anyone calling her that. *Twilight* had ruined that nickname for her. Shrugging, I opened the door. Cobblestones clicked under my feet as we moved down the winding path flanked with an array of flowers.

Just then, a figure appeared in the doorway of the guest house. My breath hitched, and I covered my mouth, not believing what I saw.

She was beautiful. Glossy black hair cascaded down her back in thick waves, glittering in the sunlight. Gone was the sallow tinge in her skin. Instead, a pale pink blush colored her tanned cheeks.

Her hips didn't jut out, and her face was full and brimming with life. In front of me stood the woman I grew up with. The one I remembered.

Despite the vast improvements, a hint of fatigue still lingered, the thin skin under her eyes darker and rimmed. A pang stung behind my sternum, and I wondered if her body still recovered or if the bags under her eyes were more from the emotional toll of the last few weeks.

Pushing the heavy weight aside for now, I smiled.

"Momma," I whispered.

I ran the last few feet, slowing myself before twining my arms around her waist. A twinkling laugh that sounded like wind chimes greeted me. When her fingers stroked through my hair, I felt like I was a child again, being soothed by my mom.

The scent of fresh baked bread and peaches encircled us, and I beamed. Her omega was vibrant. Strong. I leaned back, putting enough distance between us so I could see her face.

"How are you feeling?" I asked.

"Wonderful. Kaelen and Liam have taken very good care of me.

Hello, Liam," she added, still hugging me close.

"Lovely to see you, Bella," he said, an amused smirk tugging on his lips.

I didn't have to look up to know the glare my mom gave him. I remembered it well. He gulped, and I giggled.

"Sorry, ma'am," he mumbled, sounding like a thoroughly scolded child. "I'll give you two some time alone. I'll be inside if either of you need anything."

After Liam left, Mom ushered me inside the quaint cottage. She busied herself in the kitchenette, making tea while I settled into a plush armchair by the window. The frayed thread on my sweater was rough between my fingers.

Bright beams of sun illuminated the warm space. Tons of plush blankets hung atop overstuffed furnishings. It was exactly the kind of place I'd always pictured my mom living. An omega's den.

Unlike the cold, sterile home where we lived for so long.

With two cups of tea in her hands, she sauntered back, handing me one before sitting in the chair opposite mine.

"You look well, my sunflower."

My chest swelled at the sound of the name she hadn't called me since I was nine. This was how we always should have been. When things first started getting bad, Dad insisted all he wanted was to keep us safe.

In the beginning, that was true.

Dad had endorsed a couple of controversial bills, which led to a series of threats against me and Mom.

But soon, what had simply been an overprotected alpha twisted into something nefarious. He learned how sympathetic voters were to his sick omega wife and his innocent omega daughter, and eventually, that greed and thirst for power corrupted him.

Chamomile sweetened with honey coated my tongue.

"You too, Mom. You look… You're—" I choked, struggling to find the words. "I love you."

"Oh, Willow," she said, lowering her teacup, taking my free hand in hers. "I love you too. You have always been my daughter and I'm sorry I couldn't do more to protect you from him."

"No. It's never been your fault."

I refused to let her blame herself. She was as much a victim as I was. There was only one person to blame, William Sterling.

Instead of responding, she simply smiled, her chest rising and falling with carefree breaths.

A comfortable silence settled around us as we drank our tea, enjoying the company. My empty cup rattled on the side table as I deposited it, no longer able to ignore the churning in my gut. I hoped she already knew about Dad.

There had been a time when she loved him, cared for him. They were mated.

"Do you… Do you know about Dad?" I asked, picking at my cuticles.

She clicked her tongue, gently stilling my movements.

"I know what Kaelen has planned, yes."

I took my first full breath in the last few minutes. Of course, Kaelen had taken care of everything, not leaving anything for me to handle. It was those things that made me love him more.

"And you're okay with that?"

After a long pause, she said, "Yes."

Her delicate hand covered the long-faded bond mark on her throat.

I scanned her posture for any signs of distress, but found none. Like me, I think she realized that there was no way to move forward with William Sterling still in the picture. Outside of the bond with Mom, he would always try to use me.

Smiling, my mom tossed a blanket across her lap, eyeing the mark on my neck.

"You found a good one, Willow. You have an alpha who will love and respect you."

"I'm lucky."

"Oh no, he is the lucky one. He has you, after all."

And I have him.

The sun had long set by the time I left the guest house. We spent hours talking. Sometimes, simple things, like new books or movies. Others, more serious. Mom planned to sell the house after the papers confirmed Dad's death, not wanting anything to do with it. Kaelen had asked her to stay with us, but she refused.

Even when he offered to buy her something far too lavish, she insisted on taking care of herself. She was the strong, independent omega I remembered. She promised to find a place close by after I worried she might move across the country.

After hugging her goodnight, I wandered back into the den.

Shadow sat curled up on the sofa, wagging her tail when she saw me. I snuggled in beside her, resting my head on her thick coat. A subtle scent of freshly mown grass lingered on her coat. I wrapped a blanket around both of us, grabbing my dogeared copy of *Little Women* from the coffee table.

I had barely finished my chapter when heavy footsteps padded into the room. Delectable waves of whisky and fresh espresso settled nearby. My fingers splayed over my sternum, lighting up with the serenity my alpha pushed through our bond.

Fringe hung over my eyes, obscuring my vision as I looked up, pleased to see Kaelen staring at me like I was the reason for the moon and stars.

His eyes softened as he sat beside me, careful not to disturb Shadow. Two callused fingers tilted my chin back, his lips brushing against mine in the shadow of a kiss. They slowly moved southward, pausing at his mark, tending it with reverent licks.

A purr vibrated his chest, and I leaned into him, practically crawling into his lap. Damp, loose tendrils of his hair hung around his face, fresh from the shower.

"Is it done?" I asked, my face buried in his shirt.

"Taken care of."

The grief I expected never came, only relief. My dad was gone and so was Vittorio Rossi. With Kaelen's work, I suspected the inherent dangers that came with that, but knowing the two bigger ones were handled made my breath come easier.

I laced my fingers with his. The pad of his thumb rubbed over my Claddagh ring as sparks sputtered in the hearth.

"Come to bed with me, my little omega," he said, sweet and gravelly in my ear.

A tingle danced down my spine, making me shudder.

"Tired, Alpha?" I cooed.

"No," he grunted, standing up and effortlessly tossing me over his shoulder.

"Hey," I squeaked, swatting at his back.

Laughter spilled from me, dampening my protests. Aileen eyed us from the dining room, both brows arched as Kaelen carried me up the stairs. I blanched, hot crimson burning my cheeks, but Kaelen didn't care, taking the steps two at a time with those massive tree trunk legs of his.

A whine fell from me, imagining those strong thighs pinning me in place while my alpha knotted me.

Two hands gripped my waist, tossing me on top of a mountain of plush blankets and pillows. I giggled, scooting back and admiring my husband.

Without looking away from me, Kaelen ripped off his t-shirt by the back of the collar, his tattooed torso on display. Like the greedy thing I was, I ogled my alpha and how his joggers clung to his hips.

I sat up on my knees, curling a finger in Kaelen's direction— beckoning him.

"Come ravish me, Alpha," I whispered.

"As my omega commands."

Chapter 45

KAELEN

A dull pain lingered behind my right eye as I finally looked away from the computer screen I had been staring at for the last hour. No matter how long I reviewed the financials for the pubs, they never made sense.

Everything to do with the pubs was strictly legitimate, and as such, needed to be pristine. I trusted our accountants and Aidan, but I preferred to give them a look myself at least once a year after one of our managers had been caught funneling money from the Quincy location three years ago.

I sat in my office, the glow of the monitor the only light in the cavernous room.

It was late, and I hadn't bothered to turn on a light.

Things had been quiet for the last month. Quiet enough for me to have time to go mad staring at reports where all the numbers and names blurred. With Massimo as the new head of the Italians, a tentative peace had formed with them.

Most of the men loyal to his father had been killed when we found Willow, leaving his ranks to mold as he wished. And as I suspected, Massimo remained true to his word, looking to forge new alliances between our families.

Sweeney doctored Sterling's medical records, and no one questioned when the papers announced his passing after a heart attack.

The sound of quiet footsteps echoing down the hall pulled me from my thoughts. All the coiled tension in my muscles unwound as my omega's intoxicating scent preceded her.

My wife's shadowy silhouette stood in the doorway, illuminated by the hall lamp.

"Why are you sitting in the dark like a vampire?" she asked, flicking on the light.

I hissed for dramatic effect, grinning at the tight scowl on her porcelain face. My wife was the most breathtaking creature in existence, especially when she was pissed at me. I rather enjoyed pushing her buttons. Her dark hair skimmed the tops of her shoulders, the blue highlights fresh and twinkling.

Closing the laptop, I pushed back from my desk. I wordlessly tapped my thigh. My stubborn omega rolled her eyes, but joined me regardless. Her cute bum slid over my cock and I groaned, banding an arm around her stomach.

She wiggled and I swatted her thigh, enamored by the melodic sound of her voice.

"Be careful, mo chroí, vampires bite."

I burrowed my face into the delectable curve of her neck, inhaling her honey-dipped scent. A quiver shook her slender frame as I kissed the delicate skin along my bite.

This was my peace. My sanctuary. My forever.

I bowed to no one.

Except with her. With her, there was no fight. Only surrender. An absolute, total, and willing surrender.

I belonged to her and she owned all of me.

"Why aren't you in bed?" she asked.

"Wrapping up a few things. How was your day?"

While I had been busy with reports, she had only just gotten home, having spent all day at the rescue. She shifted slightly, getting more comfortable in my lap, tossing her arms around my neck.

"Exhausting. We had to dig a few more trenches for the drainage system in the north pasture. The rain last week made a mess of it. And we finally got the new fencing up. It's a good six feet high, so the horses have a lot more space to run now."

My heart swelled with her passion. There were more than enough people to dig trenches and mend fences, but my girl would not stand by while others worked. She loved being in the thick of things and wasn't afraid of hard work. And I would spoil her, reward her for everything she did.

Every time I bought her a gift, she waved me off, begrudgingly accepting it. I never tired of the bright light illuminating her gaze whenever I did, however. She couldn't hide how much she adored my presents. Even though she tried.

"We also got plans finalized for separate facilities. We'll have a barn for the horses, with stalls that are a bit bigger. Then, on the other side of the property will be yards and kennels for the dogs. We also have three vets on staff we've hired."

I listened, the thrum of her voice a balm to my weary soul. With each word she said, I saw it all. The horses running free. The dogs chasing balls. Cats curled up in the sun. It was her dream. And I would give her all of it. I would build her an empire of rescue animals for her to protect from the world.

"I'm so proud of you," I said, scent-marking her cheek. "You must be tired."

No matter how often I did it, she never got used to my compliments. Pale pink rose high on her cheekbones, and my fingers chased the flush.

"Thank you. It's worth it. They deserve a second chance. They deserve to be safe and happy."

The double meaning of her words were not lost on me. I had never been one to believe in second chances. Even if she never believed me, Willow Finnegan was my second chance.

A chance at the life I never believed I deserved.

The one my parents had that I thought I'd never find.

"Let's take a bath and then go to bed," I offered, taking her tiny hand in my much larger one.

Fragrant soaps filled the steamy water as I stripped, drowning in the beauty of my omega. She eyed me just as greedily, her nipples hard as she licked her petal-soft lips, her burning gaze making me harder than stone.

Water sloshed over the sides of the tub as I slipped in, helping Willow nestle between my thighs. Instantly, she relaxed in my arms. I gently trailed a soapy cloth over her arms, purring for my omega.

She was so delicate. And yet, she was the strongest person I had ever known. A survivor. She withstood the abuse and neglect of her father, and still somehow managed to come out on the other side.

I closed my eyes, focusing on her sweet little purr rumbling in time with mine. My entire life was condensed to this moment, with her in my arms. I only needed this. Everything else I had… it was meaningless without her.

Before my da died, he urged me to build something better than he did. And so I did. I devoted myself to building an empire. A kingdom built on blood and loyalty. I had believed it was my destiny. My birthright. The legacy my da wanted me to leave behind.

Except now, I realized I might have misunderstood what my da meant when he said, *build something better.*

Better was love. It was Willow.

An angel wandering through a world of demons. And I had captured her. Stolen her away to a place where the sun hid behind clouds and every kindness came with a price.

She changed me, her light illuminating the darkest depths of my soul. At first, I thought I had corrupted her, damned her to a life of shadows.

But I was wrong. She brought me into hers. A world of quiet strength, compassion, and love.

I was a demon who stole an angel, and I was never letting her go.

Epilogue

WILLOW

ONE YEAR LATER

The late afternoon sun beat down on my face and cast long shadows across the freshly turned earth in the pasture. A gentle breeze blew by, carrying with it the scent of cut grass and wild clover.

"Ooh," I gasped, the sudden kick in my abdomen surprising me.

My hands curled around the subtle swell of my stomach. It wouldn't be long before I'd no longer be able to hide it. It was a secret we had kept to ourselves for weeks now. But I suspected Aileen and Torin knew, each catching me multiple times struggling with bouts of morning sickness.

And if Torin knew, it was certain Aidan knew. Chances were that Aidan had also told Liam.

So I had a feeling that our secret wasn't as mysterious as Kaelen thought.

Cosmo gently bumped his head into my belly, resting it there, and I giggled. It seemed like so long ago when I had first worked with him at Snowfield. The scared black stallion that now let me cuddle him and feed him from my hand.

I laid my head on top of his, running my fingers through his mane. He towered over me, his magnificent black coat gleaming in the sunlight. A quiet nicker left him as he nosed my tiny bump, making the baby kick gleefully.

The rhythmic puff of his breath against my palm calmed me. I trailed my fingertips along his velvet skin. Cosmo was among the first horses we rescued. Technically, the rescue hadn't been opened yet.

But when Snowfield reached out, asking if we would take him, I couldn't say no. He belonged with me. With us.

Cosmo was still skittish, a fear for everyone except me and Kaelen. Every time I stared into his dark eyes, I couldn't help but wonder what horrors led to him being tied up in a warehouse. Alone and wounded. Aidan and Torin promised to find who did it, but it had been months and they still hadn't found any leads.

It had taken weeks for me to earn Cosmo's trust. Hard fought hours of me sitting in the pasture, waiting for him not to sprint away whenever I appeared. Eventually, I started joining him in his stall, but only when Kaelen was with me.

My alpha worried that Cosmo might lash out and kick me. Not on purpose, but out of fear. After a week, he took an apple from my hand. Day by day, he opened up more, letting me touch his neck or brush his mane.

Something in him called to me. A kindred spirit. I recognized his pain, and he saw mine.

My gaze drifted to the west, where the mountains rose in a rolling wave against the horizon. It was quiet here. Peaceful.

So different from the city.

I was different.

The last year has changed me. On the day my dad brought me to Kaelen and tried to sell me to him, I snapped at him like a frightened animal.

The scent of coffee and whisky carried on the breeze, and my lips curved before I even turned around. I didn't need to look. I knew that scent. The scent of my alpha.

A man who worked in a ruthless world, but with me, he remained tender and worshipful.

Two thick arms banded around my middle. My back collided with a wall of muscle. Kaelen rested his chin on my shoulder, his purr singing for me. I carded my nails through his scruff.

A massive, callused palm curled around my stomach. He drew slow, reassuring circles around my navel. A glow of black fur raced past my feet, Shadow sprinting happily around the pasture, chasing tufts of grass and yellow butterflies.

Despite being uncomfortable around most people, Cosmo was content with Shadow's presence.

Kaelen's lips brushed against my ear, his teeth grazing the lobe, making me wiggle in his hold. I had become increasingly needy the last few weeks, regularly yanking my husband into our bed or whatever secluded spot I could find, begging for my alpha's knot.

Pregnancy hormones.

He didn't seem to mind, though.

"How are my two favorite girls?" he murmured, his timbre a possessive staccato that did nothing to help the damp panty situation between my thighs.

I leaned my head back against his chest. His eyes twinkled as they gazed down at me, the hand not holding my stomach, moving higher and gently collaring my throat.

"We're good. Your daughter is very active today. She likes Cosmo."

"How could she not?"

As if he understood, Cosmo nickered, kicking at the loose dirt of the ground and prancing in a circle. Kaelen bent at the waist, his lips meeting mine in a long, languid kiss that was both a question and a promise.

A question of what I needed, and a promise to always give it to me.

When he finally pulled away, my lips were swollen and my heart was full. He dropped to one knee, the tilled grass leaving stains on his Armani trousers. He must have come straight from a meeting in the city and didn't have time to change.

Both hands cradled my stomach, his lips pressing sweetly over my navel.

"And how are you, little one?"

My fingers tangled in his hair, pulling it free like I had done so many times.

In that moment, with the sun setting, the grazing horses in the distance, Shadow chasing butterflies, and Kaelen on his knees in front of me, I knew what true happiness was.

It wasn't the fragile, delicate thing I once believed. It was a fortress. Something forged in flames, blood, and battle. It was devotion and love. The kind of love that could move mountains and temper steel.

Kaelen was a demon, someone who couldn't afford to show weakness. Yet he did just that, giving all of himself to me.

We were two sides of the same coin, and with him, I finally felt complete.

For so long, I had been a willow, bending in the wind, a lonely tree in a forgotten field. Then I found him, a tempest tearing through the woods. In his arms, I found my roots. My alpha showed me how strong I was. What I was capable of.

I loved my demon. My alpha. My Kaelen.

And I would spend the rest of my life telling him so.

Acknowledgements

This book would not exist without the support of so many amazing people.

My husband has been my rock for over a decade now. I am so lucky to have such a supportive partner in my life. Thank you, Rog, for nodding along and smiling while I talked to you for hours about knotting, nesting, and murder.

To everyone who encouraged me to take a leap and write a mafia omegaverse, THANK YOU. I was incredibly nervous about this story (still am), but your kind words got me to this point.

To all my amazing betas and alphas, thanks for dealing with all my bullshite and crazy three am voice notes!

To my amazing street team, Lexi, Courtney, Lex, Kim, Ella, Charlie, Ashley, Ronnie, Britni, Melissa, Leslie, Julie, and Jasmine, you folks have been the greatest hype team and support I could ask for in the lead up to this release.

I LOVE YOU ALL!

About the Author

Michelle Love lives on a remote island away from civilization along with her captives, (husband, three dogs, and a kitty) and she likes it that way.

A self proclaimed nerd at heart, when not writing, Michelle loves to play video games. Some of her favorite games are Final Fantasy X, Dragon Age Origins, Horizon Zero Dawn, and Baulder's Gate 3.